Born and brought up in Ringwood, Hants, Jennie Ann Rake was a primary school teacher for many years, specialising in music. Since moving to Dorset, her passion for fair trade led her to open her own shop. When trade was slow and the thought of dusting shelves seemed tiresome, Jennie turned to writing in between serving customers. She'd heard the suggestion that there is a novel inside everyone and wanted to find out if there was one in her.

Forgetting Mr Nice-Guy is her second novel. Her first novel, *Deception, Lies and Chocolate Muffins*, was published in September 2013.

Forgetting Mr Nice-Guy

The Lamentable Love Life of Miss Bonning,
the Music Teacher

Also by Jennie Ann Rake

Deception, Lies and Chocolate Muffins

Jennie Ann Rake

Forgetting Mr Nice-Guy

The Lamentable Love Life of Miss Bonning,
the Music Teacher

Vanguard Press

VANGUARD PAPERBACK

© Copyright 2014
Jennie Ann Rake

The right of Jennie Ann Rake to be identified as author of
this work has been asserted by her in accordance with the
Copyright, Designs and Patents Act 1988.

A CIP catalogue record for this title is
available from the British Library.

ISBN: 978-184386-984-9

Vanguard Press is an imprint of
Pegasus Elliot Mackenzie Publishers Ltd.

www.pegasuspublishers.com

First Published in 2014

Vanguard Press
Sheraton House Castle Park
Cambridge England

Printed & Bound in Great Britain

For everyone who read my first attempt and asked when the next would appear. I hope they won't regret asking me!

Acknowledgements

With grateful thanks to David, Helen, Ben, Rob and Phil, who have coped with having an author in the family and who have kept my feet firmly on the ground. Thanks also to the talented team at Pegasus who have turned my scribblings into the finished product.

PART ONE

STUDENT

Chapter 1

A Significant Decision

Anyone who has known me well would have been amazed – when they eventually found out – that I, Gilly Bonning, on a dismal February day, was on the 15.50 train to Boxmouth, about to change the direction of my life completely. When I was seventeen, eagerly counting the months to when I could at last say farewell to the world of exams and course work, I was, I confess, self-willed, arrogant and stubborn. No one, neither family nor teachers had a hope of deflecting me from my goal. My mind had been made up the day I met Tim, and I'd daydreamed about a future with him ever since. However, as I sat there in the crowded carriage, my destination coming ever closer, I had to pinch myself and wonder, yet again, if another girl had taken over my brain. Then the guilt would return. It had been one of those humble pie moments, just two weeks before, when I'd admitted to the family what I'd done.

You see, I *should* have been sitting at Tim's bedside, mopping his brow, whispering sweet nothings in his ear and waiting for... No, let's be realistic. I would have been trying to wangle another early finish from Miss Gozney, then trekking across Bournemouth and battling with the tea machine outside the League of Friends – again. But no, there I was letting a bunch of strangers invade my personal space on a packed branch-line train on one of the darkest days in February, miles away from Bournemouth Hospital and the silent side-ward that I'd come to know so well. That's what happens when you allow your parents to foist their unfulfilled expectations on you, mixed in with a hefty dollop of emotional heartstring pulling. That and six long weeks of unremitting gloom and the disagreeable aspects of Pearsons' New Year Sale and some of their most disagreeable customers. Looking back, I can now imagine how Mum and Dad had worried about my state of mind in the weeks following November 21st and of the sudden disappearance of my get-up-and-go and sense of humour.

On my return home each day, one brief glance would tell them that nothing had changed and then there'd be the meaningful eye-rolling, head shaking, and sympathetic sighs. Then, every so often, they'd bring the conversation round to, 'How much longer are you intending to keep this up Gilly?' or 'You shouldn't beat yourself up over it,' type topics. If I felt in the mood for it, I'd insist, yet again, that *I* knew best and would never forgive myself if I gave up on Tim. What I didn't admit though, was that I'd already allowed the medics' remarks to sink in.

'You're wasting your talents at Pearsons, Gilly,' Mum would remark from time to time, with just enough misty-eyed regret to make her point.

'You could do better for yourself my girl,' Dad would chip in, trying to sound encouraging.

'Your school friends are half way through their degree courses already,' Mum would hint with a sigh. 'And remember what your teachers said…?'

Oh yes, thought I, and then what? A university or college degree's all very well, but what if you end up zapping price tickets on baked beans at Tescos? Even graduates aren't guaranteed a job with a pay cheque worth all that dedicated study these days. Now *that's* what I would call a waste of education.

'It would take your mind off poor Tim,' Auntie Sue had suggested. By the tone of her remark, Auntie Sue seemed to be expecting the 'poor Tim' situation to be one of the long haul variety. That certainly resonated with me, because I'd managed to convince myself of that as well, and shuddered at the prospect.

'Why not Gilly, you'd be a great teacher. You're great with kids,' said Liz, on one of her rare home visits. Liz was nicely settled in Oxford as a junior curator of a trendy gallery. With Liz adding her six pennyworth I knew it was a plot. She was hardly known for her sisterly encouragement. She was so focused on her career and bank balance that it was scary.

However, following Liz's remark, I had positive proof that the family had made a secret pact to encourage me off to a soulless study block in a dreary, concrete jungle of a campus with the drag of essay writing punctuating each joyful week. Naturally, Sean said zilch. He hadn't cultivated the art of conversation by then. Cultivating plants was more his thing, although I don't think Mick at the garden centre realised what he'd taken on. Still, it keeps Sean occupied and allows Mum to congratulate herself that her three offspring are putting their GCSE grades to good use. Correction, make that two; I'm the one who'd been frittering her life away on the Handbags and Leather Goods at Pearsons and bringing disappointment to the Bonning household – after gaining three good 'A' levels as well.

'What's wrong with retail?' I'd retaliate. 'Dad's happy enough relieving Growdon shoppers of their hard-earned cash with his trendy organic and fairtrade groceries.' I hardly dared brag about the obvious perks of snagging a bargain – but slightly imperfect – designer leather bag, every so often, and the advantage that I never had to take my work home.

'But that's different,' Mum would insist, and then remind me that Dad had never had the same chances. By the sound of it, you'd imagine she was referring to another century. Well, I suppose she was, when you think of it. Meanwhile Mum whiled away her days making tea and smiling sweetly at Allier and Co. solicitors, although her job title was actually P.A. to Martin Allier, the senior partner. It sounds important all the same. As time went by, despite trying to ignore the family's pointed remarks, circumstances seemed to conspire to encourage me and I bravely made that significant decision. When Liz added her few words on the matter, it wasn't the first time teaching had been mentioned. Some of the sixth form staff had dangled it in front of me three years before – several times.

'Music teachers are greatly sought after,' one of them had added. I ignored all of them.

In the days that followed, I felt torn, because I'd sworn I'd never give up on the daily trek to the hospital. I promised myself I'd spend every available minute waiting, watching and hoping. I'd even entertained the thought of praying. However, since making the decision, whenever there was another rush of guilt, I'd tell myself I was doing it for Tim and that he'd be proud of me. In fact, even *he'd* been known to say I was too bright to be a shop assistant.

'Not a shop assistant, Tim,' I'd insist. I hardly dared tell him about my secret daydream. I'd prattle on about my goal of becoming a buyer and working my way up in the Pearsons hierarchy.

So there I was, with my nose pressed up against the window, watching the Devon countryside flash by, on my way to Boxmouth, for an interview that could change the whole direction of my life. After all, this was the first significant decision I'd made for quite a while. A woman in a bottle-green mac had taken out her knitting as soon as she settled herself next to me at Boxminster and had managed to give me a friendly prod at least a dozen times. It was long, grey and furry, but I think she'd dropped a stitch – hence all the frantic needle jabbing. It wasn't the best place for knitting, seats being at a premium, and most of us were crammed together like the proverbial sardines. After about fifteen minutes, the train slowed, but the surroundings didn't look much like a jolly seaside town.

When we'd left the sprawl of Boxminster, the track had followed the curve of the estuary, which would have been a cheery sight on a blue-skies-and-fluffy-clouds sort of day. However, *that* day was more of the leaden-skies-and-threat-of-rain variety. Not the season for bracing boat trips either, with all that whipped up spray and biting winds. The first stop was just an unmanned halt where a single whitewashed building with boarded windows was slipping into slow decay. Bottle-Green Mac had worked up a head of steam with her needles by that time and I'd lost count of the rib jabs and the tuts of irritation every time the ball of yarn dribbled off her lap and bounced across the carriage floor. An elderly gent tried whacking it with his walking stick – that caused even more entertainment for everyone except BGM – but she managed to retrieve it and have it safely nestled between her thighs for the rest of the journey.

But just a minute, you might be wondering, what about Tim? And why all the brow mopping and hand holding? And what happened at Pearsons' New Year Sale to help nudge Gilly Bonning out of inertia? You see, although she didn't know it, Mrs Muncie-Rookes had a key part to play in all this. Anyone who'd had to serve the woman might understand, but truly, I'd not willingly wish Mrs M-R on anyone, except my worst enemy, maybe. It's time to reveal all: that something rather more significant happened three months ago.

Chapter 2

Incident in Bickerton Lane

It had been one of those November days when all the new Christmas stock was piled high but the customers were undecided about starting their shopping. They said they were 'getting ideas' and gave us encouraging grins.

'Ooh look at that! Just right for our Jan (Stan/Dan/Jen/Ben/Lin/Ron etc)!' they'd exclaim, but they wouldn't buy whatever it was. 'Be back closer to Christmas,' they'd tell us brightly. *Well, don't complain if our Jan's prezzie is out of stock by then. There's only so many miracles we can work,* we'd mutter back under our breath, or words to that effect. Tess and I had dusted every square centimetre of each shelf, and were overdue for our lunch break.

'So where's he taking you?' she asked me, in between spoonfuls of hazelnut yoghurt in the staff canteen. There wasn't a chance of Tess guessing. She's a great girl, but not on my wavelength most of the time.

'It's not that swanky new disco by the pier is it?' she asked, with a giggle. 'Swanky' is one of her new words. She must have read it in her latest magazine because it had started popping up all over the place.

'No Tess,' I told her, 'Tim's not a disco sort of chap, I've told you before. He's convinced he was born with two left feet. Not keen on the crush of sweaty bodies myself either, I tell her, or the noise, and that's just the ladies' loo.' That made her laugh.

'What about that new Indonesian restaurant by the Upper Pleasure Gardens?' she suggests, but then admits it's more in the Pearson league. Our lunch hour seconds were ticking away, so I put her out of her misery and told her Tim had tickets for a BSO concert.

'BSO? Is that a cool new boy band?' Of course, if it *was*, she'd have heard of it. What I found more surprising was that she'd never heard of the BSO – the Bournemouth Symphony Orchestra if you want the full title. How can any Bournemouth resident *not* know about their local orchestra? That just highlights the different wavelength thing I mentioned earlier. Yes, I was into the classics, not boy bands, and Tim had discovered – after quite a few heavy hints – that they were performing one of my favourite pieces on my birthday, of all days. There can't be many music fans who share their birthday with St Cecilia, the patron saint of music, can there?

I was telling Tess about the dishy clarinettist who'd be performing, just to keep her eyes from glazing over, when we both realised that we'd be in trouble if we didn't get back to the department ASAP.

'Miss G will be on the warpath,' I reminded Tess, as we dashed out to the lifts.

'Do you think she'll have us dusting the stock room?' replied Tess with a grimace, as we squeezed in just as the doors were closing.

'Not tonight she won't,' I whispered – because even lift walls have ears.

Bert the liftman gave us a cheeky wink. He's past retirement but not past caring what the Pearsons think. Bert's been a company man, man and boy, or so he says. 'I didn't mind starting at the bottom and working up,' he's told us several times. If he's ended up as a liftman – sorry, operator – where did he start? Thinking about it, it's probably his idea of a joke… lifts… up…down… hmm, yes exactly. Did that encourage us to think that if we worked really hard and minded our Ps and Qs, we'll end up as department heads like Miss G? Maybe. Tess had different ideas though. She and Jamie were planning to move in together and Tess was hoping for the patter of tiny feet, even though Jamie probably didn't know it at the time.

As for me, well on November 21st, I wasn't planning anything more than preparing the third finger of my left hand for a sparkly new piece of bling. Yes, I was convinced that as the strains of Mendelssohn's *Concert Piece in D minor* faded away, Tim would go down on one knee and propose. Well, maybe not in the concert hall *itself*, but soon afterwards. I wasn't telling Tess that bit though. The lift seemed to take an age that day, and every time the doors opened, Tess and I found something to giggle about. When old Mr Edward and young Mr Howard joined us on the second floor, we soon sobered up though. We'd learned enough by then to know you *never* giggle when the Pearsons are around. By the time we arrived back at the department, Moira Fox – deputy buyer – was glancing at her watch in a meaningful way. It was her way of saying 'late again' but not very subtly. At once, we split up and started to titivate the shelves and generally give the appearance of great activity.

That was the day of my first real encounter with Mrs Muncie-Rookes. If Moira hadn't just nipped out for a sandwich and a smoke with her mystery bus driver, she'd have grabbed the sale *and* the commission. If Miss Gozney had been around, *she'd* certainly have elbowed Moira out of the way, being senior buyer, naturally.

'Is anyone serving here?' Mrs M-R demanded in a caustic tone that would have stripped paint in an instant. Tess caught my eye and rolled hers as if to say, she's all yours. Miss Gozney was at a meeting and Debbie, our part-timer, was having root canal treatment, so I was the candidate for the poisoned apple.

'Yes madam,' said I, reminding myself that a curtsey wasn't necessary, although by the way she spoke you'd imagine it was.

'A handbag, if you please my girl,' rapped Mrs M-R, 'and no foreign rubbish!'

I may have worked on the department for a mere fifteen months, but even *I* knew that our best range was Italian. If only Moira hadn't nipped off so quickly to see lover boy, then I'd have been saved the rough side of Prudence Muncie-Rookes' tongue.

'I can show you some Frobisher and Elkins ones madam,' I said, determined to smile at the old bat. If I could sell her one from the top of our English range, the commission would be worth having.

'What's that? Do stop mumbling!' Mrs M-R snapped, then realised that her hearing aid had become dislodged. Meanwhile, I brought out bag after bag and demonstrated the pertinent features of each one. Mrs M-R proved she was an expert at finding fault with each of my sales pitches: not enough pockets, too many pockets, handle too long, handle too short, no handle, too shiny, too matt, wrong sort of closure… you get the idea? After fifteen exhausting minutes, we were almost over the finishing line, when the colour of the lining was called into question.

'I'm not sure about the green lining,' she said, with a suspicious frown. 'Far too racy!' How emerald green satin can be described as racy was beyond me, but having spent that long getting *that* far, I refused to be beaten.

'This shade of emerald is much sought after by our account customers,' I told her, with my fingers crossed behind my back and an authoritative air. 'It's far easier for locating your bits and bobs than a black lining.'

'Bits and bobs?' She shuddered and her eyes almost bulged out of their sockets. Honestly, you'd have thought I was suggesting she used it for spare condoms or a vibrator, by the look on her face.

I quickly explained the disadvantages of black linings and she eventually decided to begrudgingly part with a mere fraction of husband Ralph's huge fortune, for the very top of the range. For a few worrying moments, she debated the suitability of the clasp, until I pointed out it was the latest fashion statement in the *best* circles.

I remember how she gave me a suspicious glance as she passed over her credit card all the same. I also recall the great feeling of triumph as she swept off and the grin on Tess's face as she popped up from tidying the stationery.

'Did the old crow buy anything after all?' she whispered, but I was saved from having to reply by Miss Gozney's return.

'Miss Bonning, Miss St Clayre,' she trilled, then reminded us there was plenty to do, even on the slowest of days.

It was then that the phone rang and I'll always remember what I was doing when that awful news came. I was on my knees, counting carrier bags. It was Flora Gozney who took the call and at once, her manner changed, but at the time, I didn't realise why. Maybe it was because it was so unusual for her juniors to have personal calls during working hours. The use of mobile phones was strictly forbidden on the shop floor so a call to the department had to be serious.

'For you, Miss Bonning,' she told me, after a pause and a quiet *oh dear*. 'A Mrs Rosewell for you.'

At once Tess knew something was wrong and not just because all the colour drained from my face in seconds. She'd heard me mention Tim Rosewell by his full name with boring regularity. I reached for the phone, but my hand seemed to have forgotten what to do. Even Miss Gozney found her latent mumsy side and patted me on the shoulder before moving a discreet distance away.

'Eleanor?' I croaked. If Tim's mum was calling, it wasn't to wish me happy birthday. We got on well enough I think, but she'd never consider it necessary to phone me at work when a card in the post would do.

'It's Tim, Gilly. There's been an accident, but he's okay. He's been taken to Bournemouth Hospital,' she explained, sounding even more shaky than my right hand, and now my knees.

'In hospital!' I gasped, imagining all manner of frightening possibilities.

'What happened?' Although she said he was okay, he couldn't be *that* okay, if he was in hospital, I thought.

'There was a collision with a pensioner,' she told me. For a moment, it sounded almost comical, until I imagined a frail old man or woman stepping into the path of Tim's Corsa. If Tim was in hospital, what about the pensioner? Visions of ambulances, roadblocks, scene of accident tape and heavy police presence flashed before my eyes. I also pictured Tim turning up at court, answering charges of dangerous driving, even though he's rarely rattled at the wheel and wouldn't dream of using his phone.

'And the pensioner?' I gasped, dreading the worst, and then learnt that the old man was just a bit shaken, although his front wheel was badly bent and he'd lost half a dozen eggs and a bag of plain flour in the collision. It was still a horrifying thought though and sounded as if Tim had other things on his mind – hopefully not me. I dreaded the possibility of being the cause of three points on his licence. But then as I asked Eleanor for a few more details, the incident/accident grew more surreal by the minute. It turned out that Tim was *walking* along the High Street, crossing over at the junction with Bickerton Lane, just opposite Bagnalls the newsagents, when the elderly cyclist shot round the corner and knocked him sprawling. The pensioner was wearing a crash helmet and escaped with minor bumps and bruises, but Tim was knocked unconscious.

Then Eleanor added that the police suspected it was a case of failed brakes, but that bit wasn't clear. Compared with Tim's state, the ineffective brakes didn't really register. Next Eleanor started sobbing, due to shock, I'm sure, and it didn't take much for me to join her. I wanted to scream out how unfair it was, and how it should never have happened – especially on my birthday. But then I realised I was being selfish. I tried to pull myself together and was failing dismally when I discovered that Frank was now on the other end of the line. I said I'd come as soon as I could, and for the second time I saw a new side to Flora Gozney – a side that told me of course I could go. She may have been a hard-bitten sort of boss, but even *she* could see that counting carrier bags paled into insignificance in the light of the accident.

The journey from the centre of Bournemouth to the hospital took ages, involving several changes of bus. All the while, I convinced myself that Tim's bump on the head probably wasn't so bad and that Eleanor was over-reacting. That's what I hoped anyway. She and Frank were sat in a waiting room near A & E when I arrived, but then we had to move departments when a nurse came and told us Tim was under observation. She didn't actually utter the words 'Intensive Care', or if she did, I didn't register them, so we dutifully found another waiting room and tried to encourage each other with comments about Tim being in good hands.

The metallic tasting tea from the vending machine did little to soothe me, but it gave my hands something to hold. I'd already called Mum by then and warned her that lighting cake candles and singing 'Happy Birthday' might not be very appropriate in the circumstances.

'Of course they have to monitor patients with concussion,' Frank commented, convinced that was why it was taking so long for someone to come and update us. However, after an hour and a half, we all started to wonder what was happening.

'Perhaps they've had a rush on,' Eleanor suggested. What sort of rush I don't know, except a horrendous vehicle pile-up maybe.

At last, the door opened and a chap with a white coat and stethoscope joined us. The trouble was he'd forgotten to paste on his 'meeting the relatives' face and looked drained and ready for a lie-down in a darkened room. We all jumped to the conclusion that he was the bearer of the worst news possible.

'Mr and Mrs Rosewell?' he enquired, with a half apologetic look on his face. Then he glanced in my direction and hesitated.

'Tim's girlfriend,' Eleanor explained, all a-dither. I grabbed her hand, willing the doctor to tell us something encouraging. But then he started spouting words, which I could hardly take in… trauma…,tests… stimuli… response…

We sat there stunned, hardly moving, with our mouths agape. We'd been convincing ourselves that it was simply concussion, but amongst the flow of words, it was obvious that something more serious had happened. It was when the word *coma* featured in his spiel that shock waves zipped around the room, paralyzing us with fear: and after half-voiced questions, misunderstandings and countless reiterations that we finally came to terms with Tim's condition. At the time, it was a muddle of information, but Wikipedia helped me get a better grasp of it.

Tim sustained a head trauma (bump on the head to the rest of us) and went into a deep coma. They tried several tests, using different stimuli – sound and pain – but he hadn't responded to either because of his '*profound state of unconsciousness.*' Apparently, there are several levels of coma and Tim was on the first level. That's the level when the normal reflexes are lost and the patient doesn't react to pain and can't hear. What I learnt is that patients can move between levels. When the doctor told us Tim was in a deep coma, I think we all had the same thought – that he had only a slim chance of recovery or that if he *did* recover he might be brain-damaged for the rest of his life.

Although I can't speak for Frank and Eleanor, I guess we all had a similar sense of disbelief. You don't expect something as common as a fall to end in a coma, do you? Just think of all the times you fell over as a kid. It must have happened hundreds of times, and all you had was a bruise or some grazes. If you were really unlucky, like my best school friend Ruth, you might have broken your arm, or had stitches in your chin like Liz, when she fell off the edge of the pavement. But a coma? Then, mixed in with the shock, I felt anger. It seemed so unfair that my wonderful, kind, loving friend, with all his life before him, should be at the risk of losing everything. He was only twenty-two. After sixth form, he'd chosen to go into banking, rather than university, and was gradually working his way up through the system. By the sound of it, he'd been doing well, impressing the regional bods and would be ready for a promotion move within a few months. The only move he'd be having in the foreseeable future would be when the nurses turned him to stop bedsores.

Yes, I felt angry: angry at the pensioner, who probably shouldn't have been out on a bike with dodgy brakes in the first place, and angry with God for letting it happen. I admitted that last bit to Auntie Sue, sometime after the accident and she pointed out that it wasn't as if Tim was being punished or that God didn't care about him. I remember glaring back at her, for all her pontificating. Then it occurred to me that all over the world, innocent little kids die every day when terrorists run amok, detonating grenades and bombs, all in the name of some cause or other. It wasn't much comfort though. My anger against God still burned as bright as ever, until I came to terms with the fact that there *was* hope.

After the doctor's gloomy opening words, he assured us that many people recover well from comas and emphasised that a deep coma doesn't mean less chance of recovery. Then he warned us that some patients recover at a slow rate, but then progress to a vegetative state. How he could choose the word 'progress' when talking about that outcome, was beyond me. The words 'vegetative state' had us all shuddering and choking back sobs. When we'd recovered from that possible scenario, he had another one to offer us. Some patients emerge from a coma with physical, intellectual and psychological difficulties: in other words their movement is impaired as well as their thought processes and emotions. I seem to remember the word amnesia featured in his spiel at this point. But, he said – and this was the best bit – they had every reason to believe that there was NO brain damage in Tim's case. They'd carried out a scan and as far as they could tell, everything looked normal. He probably said this bit early on, but I was so shocked that it didn't sink in at the time. He might have even started by saying 'what do you want first, the good news or the bad news?' At that, Frank might have replied, 'we'll have the bad news first lad, and make it snappy.' No, of course he didn't, but if we'd known about the *no brain damage* bit to start with, it would have saved us from the roller coaster of emotions.

'How long, doctor?' Frank ventured, his face grey and haggard.

'Till recovery?' the doctor replied, then seeing Frank's nod, proceded to give us all sorts of statistics that made my head spin. He told us there was every chance Tim would emerge from the coma in a matter of weeks, if not days. Apparently five weeks is generally the longest time you'd expect a coma to last, although it could be longer. My first thought was that he'd be out of hospital by Christmas, and started to think what present he'd like. Then the doctor started quoting fascinating cases that we really did *not* want to hear. The one about the Polish railway worker, who woke from a coma after nineteen years only, was one such helpful example.

Oh God, I thought, *nineteen* years? Tim would be forty-one and I'd be thirty-nine by then, and our chances of settling down to family life would be trickling away, like the last few grains in an egg timer.

Then he quoted another example, a Guinness Book of Records entry I suspect, of a man who started speaking spontaneously after being in a minimally conscious state for a similar length of time. I bet that was a bit of a shock for the family. You can picture them sitting at his bedside, discussing the neighbours' dog or divorce, Mum's varicose veins or arguing over their preferences for Sunday lunch, when their relative sits up and asks for tea with milk and two sugars. Before the doctor could quote any more fascinating facts – because he was certainly warming to his subject by then – Frank cut in and asked if we might see Tim.

'Well naturally,' the doctor replied, looking almost surprised that he had asked. He then warned us not to worry about the paraphernalia we'd see in the room or clamped onto Tim. Perhaps he didn't use those precise words, but at the time my memory was more like a colander than a computer file.

So we shuffled into the room, half expecting a scene from Frankenstein's monster, to see Tim lying peacefully in his bed. There was a tube attached to his throat, keeping his airways open and his head was bandaged, hiding the place where the bike had made its impact. For some reason I was convinced that if we kept talking to him, telling him we were there, he'd wake up. We kept it up for an hour or more, hardly taking our eyes off him, willing him to amaze the medics with a spontaneous request for a cuppa, but not a flicker disturbed his deeply slumbering state.

'Apparently it could have been worse,' Eleanor told me on the way home.

To be honest, I couldn't think of a much worse outcome, apart from the obvious.

'If it hadn't been for the girl who tried to grab him and pull him out of the way, I mean.'

'Really? Which girl? Anyone we know?'

'No, I don't think so. She works in the town in Cut Above the Rest.

'Oh yes, the unisex hair salon.'

'Lena or Lorna… don't remember quite. My brain's like a sieve.' Join the club, I thought.

We must have cried bucket loads in those early days as we took turns in keeping up the bedside vigil. Of course, I made rash promises about visiting each day, proving my love and dedication and secretly hoping it would be *my* voice that would finally bring Tim back to consciousness. Sometimes I'd catch Mum and Dad giving me odd looks and sighing. It wasn't as if they'd given up on Tim's recovery, but I guess they were hoping I'd give myself some Gilly time in between all those visits.

'You'll wear yourself out, love,' Mum would murmur.

'It's bound to take time, Gilly,' said Dad, giving me a reassuring hug.

'Tim wouldn't want you moping around.' That was one of Liz's waspish remarks during a particularly fraught phone call.

'How do *you* know what Tim would want?' I snapped back. Wondering what Tim would want was impossible, to tell the truth.

Miss Gozney exceeded all expectations in the days following the accident. Even with Christmas shopping cranking up a gear, she let me work flexi-time, but I think that was because she was hoping Tim's recovery would fit in the two-five week pattern. Everyone I knew seemed to have been doing their own online research, and the amazing story of the Polish railway worker popped up several times. I expect some bright spark added it to their pub quiz questions for the festive season. Christmas was a lukewarm affair, as it turned out, and none of the Rosewells, Bonnings or close friends felt much like festive frivolity when it came to it. However, it was just as we were packing away the decs and hoovering up the last of the pine needles that the family started on about teaching. They'd been dropping hints at regular intervals, hoping I'd start to warm to the idea. Some of my teachers were quite snooty about my decision to go into retail after the slog of 'A' levels. You could see it written over their faces. So I'd spouted on about management training to show them I didn't intend wasting my life scanning barcodes at the checkout. But I could tell they weren't convinced, nor were Mum and Dad. A year on and I was still dusting shelves and minding my Ps and Qs and the only training I'd been given was first aid, just in case we had to deal with customers fainting at the expensive goods on sale. It was around that time that Mrs Muncie-Rookes added her nasty little prod.

'Sixty pounds!' she exclaimed, fingering a smart black leather clutch bag (with emerald shot silk lining and diamanté trim – NB: *not satin*). 'That's disgraceful! I paid full price for an identical one barely a month ago!'

I tried to correct her, knowing that the black clutch she'd just tossed aside like a mouldy muffin was definitely *not* the same. It was a special purchase. I know, because Tess and I had spent hours in the stock room writing price tickets only the day before for Pearsons' New Year Sale. She and property developer husband, Ralph, own half a Greek island – one of the smaller ones I believe – have a modest seven-figure apartment in Sandbanks and are on gossip-swapping terms with the Pearson clan and a few foreign dignitaries. However, despite their property portfolio and bulging bank balance, Mrs M-R liked to snap up a bargain, like the rest of us and hated to think that she'd been cheated. On this occasion, naturally *she* knew best, and flounced off – probably to complain to one of the Pearson brothers. As if being browbeaten by Mrs M-R was not enough, refereeing a tug of war over a cut-price jewellery box sent me plummeting to the depths that day. It took all my self-control not to dot both women over the head with one of our cut-price umbrellas. But *that* was the day I made up my mind.

Six weeks had passed since the unthinkable had happened and much to everyone's surprise, including mine – and most of all for Tim's sake – I sent for the application forms from Boxmouth Teacher Training College, because believe me, I wasn't applying to anywhere north of the Thames. Even so, the guilt about not spending every spare hour by Tim's bedside gave my conscience a hard time. The five-week mark had come and gone without the slightest promise of flickering eyelids, minimal consciousness or spontaneous requests for tea, and we were heading towards record book country. Applying for teacher training didn't actually mean I'd end up marking piles of books and dodging snotty noses, but if it kept the meaningful glances and comments at bay, and gave me something positive to think about, I was willing to give it a bash. After all, the college might not even want me.

When Gran heard, she was really chuffed, and pressed a fiver in my hand and told me to buy something special to wear for the interview. You can tell Gran was either out of touch with current prices or thought that Growdon market and the hospice shop offer the peak of sartorial elegance. Still, I smiled gratefully and put it towards a new lipstick from Boots. Yes, the bods at Boxmouth were willing to give me a chance. *'We are pleased to offer you an interview on 21st February at 9.30 am. Overnight accommodation is available for candidates, free of charge, but travelling expenses cannot be covered.'* Asking Miss G for the day off caused a few sticky moments.

'Exactly what sort of appointment?' she quizzed, expecting me to trot out the usual doctor/dentist/optician range. Then, 'what sort of course?' with much rolling of the eyes, as if to say 'that's how you repay me for all the sympathy and flexi-time.'

'I'll take it as holiday, naturally,' I assured her, and she brightened up considerably, but I knew my star was no longer in the ascendancy.

Auntie Sue stumped up some cash towards my train fare and Dad took a rare day off from bashing the till and checking sell-by dates, to drive me to Salisbury Station.

'Good luck, Gilly,' he said, taking care not to crack into a wide grin.

'Thanks, Dad,' I replied, sensing butterflies in my stomach 'but don't hold your breath.'

By the time the doors closed and the guard was waving his white ping-pong bat thing, I had made up my mind that if Boxmouth didn't want me, then Moira Fox had better watch out, because it'd be *her* job I'd be after.

Chapter 3

Fracas in Fore Street

Tiny specks of rain started to spatter against the train window. One of Pearsons' cut-price brollies would have come in very handy that day, but I had a horrible feeling I'd forgotten to pack a brolly of any sort. Still, I held out hope that it might have blown over by the time I reached Boxmouth High Street. Then another thought struck me. The specks could be sea spray. The train soon entered the outskirts of the town: all neat rows of redbrick semis, cul-de-sacs of smart chalet bungalows and, of course, numerous B&Bs and hotels. In between the stretches of seaside town sprawl, I caught glimpses of the wide river estuary to the west, where seagulls wheeled and swooped, hoping for a tasty fish supper. Across the water, clusters of cottages in Neapolitan ice-cream livery stared out at the water, putting on brave faces despite the harsh salt spray. Then, further south, I could just make out jagged spits of land reaching halfway across the estuary, like the crooked grasping fingers of a Macbeth crone. The view was not exactly inspiring, but I knew for a fact that Boxmouth boasted sandy beaches and dunes – just the place for Tim to relax while he was recuperating, and ideal for topless sunbathing in between lectures, I'd decided.

'Boxmouth, all change, all change,' came a voice with an unfamiliar burr, over the speaker system. Bottle-Green Mac sprinted to the end of the row, giving a few spirited pokes with her needles for good measure. She turned and gave me a toothy grin, a dewdrop twinkling becomingly from her nose.

'Very cosy,' I told her, nodding towards the grey fuzzy mass, which she hastily stuffed inside her mock Black-Watch tartan shopper. The train lurched to a halt and the scrum-down for the exits started in earnest. However, I was in no hurry. With luck, the spits and spots of rain might have had second thoughts by the time I was through the barrier.

My first taste of life in Boxmouth was not an auspicious one. In fact, if it hadn't been for meeting Fran – a fellow interviewee – I'd have marched down to the station and caught the next train home. Fran saved my temper, my sanity and probably my career. But as far as the latter, I had a few hours to wait before facing the firing squad, aka the interview panel. Just to put you in the picture, Boxmouth was chosen because of its links with Latterton Academy, that famous West Country music college. Boxmouth didn't exactly move in the same exalted spheres, but if the Latterton students want their teaching diploma, they have to grace the lecture halls of the Cinderella college for a year or two. In return, some of the Latterton professors shared their expertise at Boxmouth. The thought of clarinet and vocal tuition with a Latterton Academy professor was quite tempting. I had started to play the clarinet when I was twelve, had worked my way up through the grades over the years and left school as principal clarinettist in the orchestra, passing Grade 6 with flying colours. Since then I'd joined a small orchestra in Growdon, which had helped keep up my playing skills and had given me an extra dimension to my social life.

By the time I'd slid through the ticket barrier with my luggage, the spits and spots of rain had closed ranks and turned into a fine drizzle. It meant that the leisurely stroll I'd planned turned into a quick dash, especially with no brolly to protect my hair from becoming an unruly mess. It appeared to be half-day closing in Boxmouth, because many of the shops, and all the likely brolly sellers were closed or had sold out of their stock. One ray of hope was my plastic document wallet, containing my music certificates. Why I'd decided to take them, I've no idea, especially as I'd already listed my achievements on the application form. I suppose it was one of those belt and braces decisions, just in case anyone wanted concrete proof of my grades.

So, with the wallet shielding my sleek hairdo, I dashed up the main street – or Fore Street, as it was quaintly called – pulling my case on wheels behind me. I sprinted past dozens of unlit shop windows and was approaching the churchyard wall when something, or rather someone, came careering out at me from one of the shops that was still open.

'What the…!' yelled an angry male voice, with a few rude and unrepeatable words added for good measure. Something hard and unyielding knocked the hand that clutched my makeshift rain shelter. I had a sense of déjà vu, picturing Tim on the corner of Bickerton Lane. Whoever he was, he was a good few inches taller than me, with other dimensions to match. My knees started to buckle, but by some miracle I stayed upright, although the wallet had gone flying onto the pavement, spewing out my precious evidence.

Frantically I scrabbled around, grabbing at the flapping sheets, but not quick enough to stop the cannoning male planting a filthy trainer on my Grade 5 music theory certificate.

'Look what you've done!' I shrieked. I was furious, because it looked as if he'd done it deliberately. When I straightened up, the face that glared back at me seemed to be equally accusing.

'You should look where you're going, you clumsy cow!' he had the cheek to say, then told me my folder had almost taken out his eye. He was carrying a long black case thing, and started juggling with it, while rubbing the eye I was supposed to have attacked. Nobody calls me 'clumsy cow' and gets away with it. A red mist descended.

'How dare you!' I snapped back. I suspected he was making a mountain out of a metaphorical molehill. 'And that'll just make it worse,' I told him scornfully. 'Anyway, why didn't you look before you came charging out?' I was fairly quivering with rage by then, especially as he had mastered the art of the cynical sneer and curling bottom lip.

'Well, you don't expect people to be running headlong down the street, brandishing dangerous objects!'

Dangerous objects? What was this idiot suggesting? Oh yes, you can imagine the unlikely scenario at border control: *'Sorry madam, but you can't enter the United Kingdom with a plastic document wallet. It's classed as a dangerous weapon. Could have someone's eye out in a packed lift.'* Or maybe: *'M'lud, I apprehended this woman in possession of a sharp implement in a public place and in grave danger of causing a log-jam at Boxmouth A & E.'* Exactly. Unlikely as Growdon Town F.C. winning the F.A. Cup.

'Gross exaggeration!' I told him. He really was so full of his own self-importance, and his snooty upper crust accent did nothing to help his cause – he and the Muncie-Rookes pair were definitely from the same mould.

'I was only trying to keep my hair dry,' I told him stiffly. 'I've a very important appointment tomorrow. Now if you'd kindly remove your filthy trainer from my belongings…'

'Be my guest,' he sneered and strode off down the street. I don't usually engage in slanging matches with complete strangers, you understand. However, with a complete stranger, you *can* get away with things you wouldn't say to people you see every day; the ones who'd easily pay you back and remind you you'd overstepped the mark. I guess if you *did* know you'd see your new worst enemy again you might want to hit the backspace key and make a better stab at it. It was all down to nerves, of course. On the dash from the station, my heart had started a frantic pit-a-patting, and I was wondering how I'd coax my hair from its frazzled state back to the smooth bob that I'd perfected some hours earlier.

After Filthy Trainer had left me in peace, I sheltered in the shop doorway to give myself and my poor heart a chance to recover. Things could only get better. Unfortunately the drizzle had quickened and thickened by then, and I had to make another dash or I'd be in danger of missing out on tea and cakes at five. I had a rummage in my shoulder bag (Frobisher and Elkins seconds, in chestnut leather, with adjustable strap and magnetic closure) and found my empty plastic sandwich bag. Wiped clean and de-crumbed, it made an ideal makeshift rain hood – for only the most desperate. I sprinted past the church and then through a leafy residential area, chock-full of solid Victorian splendour, with neatly manicured lawns and smartly painted railings. Budding gardeners could make a killing here, I noted – not that I'd mention it to Sean. One of the few perks of college living would be fewer hours in Sean's delightful company. Occasionally I noticed a shabbier residence or two, with a row of buzzers beside the front door, and windows decked out in posters and other evidence of student life. Was I up to this, I wondered, this whole new world of lectures, parties – and, no doubt, illegal substances? I beetled on, hoping my sandwich bag rain hood would withstand the dreary Devon drizzle as well as the sneering glances of the locals. Another spurt of speed saw me reaching the top of a gentle slope and rounding a curve into the college entrance. The sight that met my eyes was all bland and boxy, the product of unimaginative sixties architecture.

Surreptitiously I whipped off the sandwich bag and exceeded my best time for the 100 metres sprint. As I burst into the foyer with a gasp of triumph, a girl with a rucksack sprang to one side of a chattering group. This was my first sighting of Fran.

'Whoa there, Trigger,' she chortled. 'Going for gold I see.' I liked her sense of humour, and had I been braver, would have liked her comments on makeshift raingear. She was compact and pleasantly freckle-faced, with silvery owl-rimmed specs and a tousled elfin cut, spare enough to withstand the worst of English weather.

'Sorry… a bit keen there,' I apologised. 'Gilly Bonning. I sell leather handbags and this jaunt is down to my parents' vegetarian tendencies.' Fran shot me a puzzled glance. I don't know why I was suddenly spouting such garbage.

'Hmm,' she commented thoughtfully. 'Must make purchasing footwear a tad tricky.'

'Sorry,' I giggled, 'couldn't help that… just a joke. You looked the jokey type…'

It was then that I realised it must have been the first vaguely funny comment to have passed my lips since the Bickerton Lane incident. I'd managed tears by the bucket load and long faces by the metre, but I couldn't remember chuckling. Chuckling hadn't occurred to me, because there wasn't anything worth chuckling about. I'd even ignored the mottos in the Christmas Day crackers for once. My last three months had been unremitting gloom, depression and tension. Once Tim's cheerful companionship had departed, so had my sense of humour. The set-to with Filthy Trainer down the road had unlocked my Pandora's Box of emotions, and, having given the bad-tempered ones an airing; it was now the turn of the frivolous ones. It was such a relief that they had not deserted me for good.

'Well, you have to be careful with dietary issues,' she murmured, picking up my theme and checking the possible proximity of vegetarians and vegans, 'just so you don't offend.'

I nodded, with a smirk threatening to break loose. 'Actually the folks are red-blooded carnivores,' I whispered, 'It's just the handbag department they have a problem with. Lack of career prospects.' Fran nodded sagely.

Before we could indulge in any further banter, we were whisked away by an efficient female from admin with a clipboard and not-so-efficient smudged name badge, after we'd been ticked off and welcomed. The refectory was our first stopping-off point.

'Knew I'd have to knuckle down sometime,' admitted Fran, as we munched on flapjacks and homemade bread pudding. 'You can't keep back-packing indefinitely.'

'Back-packing!' I remember exclaiming. It seemed another world, just over the border from the one of lectures, parties and teaching practices.

'Yeah, India was interesting, Bangladesh was brilliant, the Himalayas were humungous and Thailand was terrific.' Fran, it seemed, was the mistress of alliteration. When I commented, she admitted she was down to do English.

'Thailand, wow!' I sighed jealously. If I managed the Costa Blanca I'd consider I was doing well.

'Yeah, I chambermaided in Phuket to pay my way and met this gorgeous, hunky Aussie guy. Thought I'd actually cracked it at last, until his girlfriend arrived with her gleaming pearly-whites and impressive forty-inch double D's. Me, I'm two aspirins on an ironing board,' boasted Fran, pointing to her marl grey sweater. She paused to take another bite. 'God knows what'll happen to my waistline if this is their usual fare,' she sighed, 'real comfort food this.'

That should have been my cue to tell her how much I'd been relying on comfort food in the previous three months, but the moment passed when we gained a table guest.

'Here you are, Tony,' clipboard woman announced, 'room for a late arrival.' She frowned and so did Tony, his plate loaded with cake.

'Tailbacks and a jack-knifed lorry,' he muttered apologetically, quickly tucking into a custard slice.

'Never mind,' I told him, 'we've not been here long.'

At the next table, a bevy of excited sixth-formers giggled and exchanged pictures on their smart phones.

'The interview was totally freaky,' one told her neighbour, 'but I've got two more next week and I'll check out the shopping first before I make up my mind.'

'Yeah,' yawned the other, 'some of those questions were like... well it's obvious why I applied. Anyway, Boxmouth's stuck in some time warp and there's not even a Costa. Might go for Bristol, but they want two A's and a B.'

'Priorities sorted, obviously,' commented Fran, raising her eyes to heaven. 'So what made you apply?' This was aimed at Tony, who was obviously not fresh from school.

'Has to be better than wading through insurance policies. Thought I'd give maths teaching a go. Kids don't scare me. Used to be a Cub Scout leader.'

'Has to be better than coping with bolshie customers,' I added.

'And better than peeling spuds,' agreed Fran firmly.

'Peeling spuds?'

'Have had to earn the readies,' she sighed. 'Retirement home kitchen… which means spuds with everything. Better money than chambermaiding in Phuket but without the sunbathing or nightlife.'

'Ready for the off are we?' Clipboard had returned, raising her delivery by a decibel or two to cut through the sixth-form cackle. 'Theo and Esther will be here in two ticks, I hope, to show you round. Theo's one of Boxmouth's prize assets… won the Horatio Finch conducting award.'

'Sounds like they're wheeling out their geriatric music staff,' I murmured to Tony and Fran. I'd never heard of Horatio Finch, but imagined the proud holder of his award to be a benign bearded bloke with a pipe and plenty of baggy corduroy.

'Search me,' said Tony. 'Ging gang gooly is about my limit on the music front.'

'Don't think the National Curriculum stretches to that,' Fran giggled.

'Oh, I don't know,' I chipped in, 'nothing would surprise me. If it's up to me though, I'd be aiming at calypso, rap and a few good old English folk songs in my lessons.'

Fran and Tony flashed quizzical glances at me. 'I'm taking music as my main subject.'

Clipboard herded us out of the refectory like a frisky border collie, and through the common room, where the students sat, sprawled or slept. We clustered in the foyer, our luggage safely stowed in a side office, but with coats at the ready. The recent interviewees were growing fidgety by this time, some muttering about lifts or train departures.

'Well, go if you must,' Clipboard muttered peevishly, 'but this tour *was* scheduled in your letter.' The two who'd been looking for better shopping opportunities grabbed their bags and stalked out through the swing doors. 'They've already had their interviews,' Clipboard added, just in case the rest of us were contemplating doing a runner.

I started to wonder if I had any text messages, something I tended to think about most of every day. It had been a while since I'd checked, so while Clipboard was fretting about the missing tour guides, I ferreted around in my bag for my mobile. No, there was nothing except a 'hope you arrived safely' message from Mum. I pressed the 'off' key and watched the screen darken. The appearance of two pairs of denim-clad legs in front of me, drew an audible sigh from the far side of the group. Attached to one pair of denim-clad legs was a pair of trainers that registered my second déjã vu of the day. Surely it couldn't be Filthy Trainer. My heart sank. The last sight I'd had of him, was as he strode off in the opposite direction from the college. I leaned down and fiddled with the zip on my boots, wondering how I might avoid eyeballing my new worst enemy, and why he had joined our group in the first place.

The two pairs of legs moved and Clipboard was heard to trill, 'Oh, Theo, Esther... glad you could make it.'

So, no cuddly old professor in baggy corduroy, I thought in despair. And no surprise that Filthy Trainer was so arrogant, seeing as he was apparently Boxmouth's Golden Boy. Thinking about it, he was more likely to be Latterton Academy's Golden Boy if he'd won the Horatio Finch conducting award. Clipboard had been stretching the truth just a little, by the sound of it.

'You okay, Gilly? We're ready to move,' said Fran, as keen as ever.

'Just an irritating itch,' I told her, which was a mild way of describing him, although I was the only one privy to my dry humour. The chickens had certainly come home to roost.

Main hall, gym, library, lecture theatre... we trailed around behind Esther and Theo, the latter looking bored by the whole business, from what I could tell. I decided my best strategy was to skulk behind Tony, who was ideally built for concealment.

'We'll go to the music block now, if you like,' announced Esther. 'Anyone here doing music as their main subject?' Not planning to raise my hand, I feigned interest in a row of streetlights that bordered the campus on the beach side. Fran nudged me.

'Me-he!' volunteered a stick-like sixth former, with three pairs of ear-studs. 'I'm majoring in cello and viola.' Fran and I exchanged surprised glances.

'Theo, you'd better take over here,' suggested Esther. 'He's one of our top music students,' she told us in mock hushed tones.

'Give it a rest, Esther,' drawled Theo.

'Which year?' chirped the ear-studded cellist.

'Second,' supplied Esther helpfully.

'Oh great,' I remember muttering. If I ended up here I'd have to spend nine months dodging his footsteps. Correction: make that seven months, if you take off two for teaching practices.

'What's up?' whispered Fran, as we followed on behind our guides. I hadn't even realised I'd said anything.

'Him', I admitted.

'Yeah, drop-dead gorgeous,' she purred, 'but I don't think he'd give a second glance to anyone with owly specs and thighs like tree trunks.'

'You're welcome to him,' I told her acidly.

'Are you serious?'

'Hundred percent. Arrogance written all over his face. That's what winning a conducting prize does. It's obviously gone straight to his head!'

I wasn't up to confiding with Fran, but compared with my lovely Tim, this Theo was an uncouth slob. Tim would never have behaved so boorishly, and any accidental knocks would have had him offering profuse apologies. Tim was a gentleman. 'What?' Fran shot me a sidelong glance as we approached a separate block, with the words 'Music Centre' carved on the wooden beam over the double doors. 'How come you're such an expert?' We trekked down a corridor and into the main hub of the department.

'Because he knocked me flying in the street, trampled over my precious certificates and then acted as if it was *my* fault,' I hissed in her ear.

It was surprising that such a sensible girl like Fran couldn't see beneath his superficial Golden Boy veneer. A bit of female solidarity would have been helpful, but judging from her expression, she was just as mesmerized by the man as most of the girls in the group. You could tell which ones they were, as they gazed in enraptured adoration like a herd of docile Jersey cows, with open mouths, waiting to catch his next pearls of wisdom. Well, it looked as if they'd have a long time to wait. Theo of the mucky footwear was now a man of few words after his earlier outburst in Fore Street. Evidently, he'd exhausted his quota for the day.

'Oh... right. Well, accidents happen,' she remarked with a shrug. 'Just enjoy the view Gilly. You don't see handsome specimens like him every day. I love the way his hair curls above his collar, and that profile... pure Georgette Heyer hero material!'

'I'm sure I don't know,' I told her. 'Looks aren't everything.'

The group had become rather too strung-out for comfort and I had to nip up behind Tony or all my surreptitious skulking would have been in vain.

'Concert hall,' announced Theo, flinging open the door of a large auditorium with a platform, several pianos, banks of seating and a vast assortment of percussion.

'For concerts... obviously,' added Esther, unnecessarily.

We trooped in and most of the sixth-formers fell upon the percussion like a bunch of toddlers in the music corner. Keeping out of sight was becoming more difficult by the second. I nipped up to the back of the hall behind Tony, hoping he wouldn't think I was stalking him. He'd already given me a couple of odd glances.

'Great view from here,' he commented, taking the steps two at a time up to the raised seating. You'd have thought he was mounting the summit of Snowdon.

'You'll have to come and watch me play some time... if we both end up here, that is.'

'You bet.' Tony winked and grinned broadly, giving me a strong hint of something garlicky. I hadn't noticed it earlier, but then Fran had been more in the firing line, poor thing.

I took a hasty step back and did a quick twirl to admire the posters and read a plaque. By the time I turned back, my barricade had gone AWOL and there I was, in full view, with nothing to cower behind, unless I went on all fours. Fran was bopping a bass drum cheerfully and, by this time, Tony had legged it across the far side of the hall and was chatting to a short shaggy male in leathers and bike boots. I couldn't somehow imagine him calling the register or taking assembly. On the other hand, he might scrub up quite well when he put his mind to it. However, for me, the roosting chickens had tucked their heads under their wings, as I turned and found myself facing the full glare of the celebrated Theo's disdain and resentment. Although it wasn't as if he was having to wear an eye patch courtesy of my document wallet. Obviously my meagre Grade 5 theory status made me an inferior sub-species in his eyes, both of which were working perfectly well, as far as I could see. Plenty of schools would be keen enough to have someone like me who knew their crotchets from their quavers and their treble clefs from their key signatures. You hardly need a conducting award to teach primary school music.

That's when my lily-livered determination finally made an appearance and decided on a change of character. I refused to let my chance of a decent qualification be ruined by a stroppy idiot. No way. I held his gaze for a good ten seconds, my jaw clenched. At which he replied with one of those eyes to heaven huffs and crossed his arms over his chest. If I'd had more of Sean's genes I'd have given him a surly two-finger salute, but I wasn't made that way. The stick insect cellist then clamped onto his arm and coyly fluttered her lashes, which gave me a chance to nip to another part of the auditorium and try out the baby grand. I'm not a brilliant pianist as such but I manage a mean Beethoven bagatelle when I'm in the mood.

Some bright spark started 'chopsticks' – obviously nobody 'majoring' in music – so I plonked a bouncy bass part to keep them company. Next the shaggy biker slipped in a descant at the top end and a couple of sixth-formers added a triangle and cymbal accompaniment. Before we knew it, 'chopsticks' had grown to magnificent proportions and everyone except the award-winning Golden Boy was clustered around the piano. If he'd been half the man you'd expect, he'd have picked up a handy drumstick and conducted the impromptu gathering. Not him. Variations on 'chopsticks' were evidently too plebeian for the likes of him. When we finally ran out of steam and collapsed into giggles, I caught sight of him leaning on the doorframe, drumming his fingers and surveying the scene with utter distaste.

'Better get moving folks,' called Esther, who'd been impressive on the castanets, 'if you want to grab supper in half an hour.'

'Mustn't miss the fodder,' chuckled a bearded guy who'd joined the group between the gym and the library. 'It's spag bol and lamb stew with dumplings.'

We set off past a long corridor of practice rooms, hearing snatches of scales and arpeggios as we went. After that we nosed around the science labs, gasped at chicken wire sculptures in the art block and then formed an orderly queue by the refectory door.

'Coming down Kirsty's later for beer and backgammon?' This was Esther to her fellow tour guide, right behind my left shoulder, while I was trying to melt into the crush of bodies.

'After what *she's* done!' I heard him sneer. Ah well, I thought, it was nice to know I wasn't the only one in the doghouse.

Chapter 4

Introducing Lena

After the filthy trainer incident, the interview the following morning was a relative breeze. I was so fired-up with determination. The adrenalin rush around my body might easily have been going for a world record, or at least a personal best. Two weeks later, the offer of an unconditional place arrived and my parents glowed in the reflected glory, claiming it was all down to them. I beg to differ. After all, *I* was the one who braved the interview, fielded the tricky questions and won the hearts of the panel. The staff at Pearsons had version B: that I wouldn't know about an offer of a place until July or August and even *then* I wasn't sure if I'd take it. That guaranteed keeping in everyone's good books and limited sideswipes about students and the teaching profession.

'Tough interview,' I sighed to Tess and anyone eavesdropping, 'not sure if I'm up to it.' However, on August 1st I gave in my notice and left a month later, after a buffeting from the end of season sale. All the while, Tim's condition remained stable and unchanged. I'd tried reading stories to him, playing his favourite CDs and even reporting on the cricket scores. I suspect some of the staff thought I was a sandwich short of a picnic.

Arriving at Boxmouth in mid-September, I was thrilled to see Fran, who was relieved to have peeled her last spud. We plunged into a round of freshers' events and by the time we surfaced, the third years were safely despatched to their teaching practice. Once they'd returned, it was the first years' turn for a week's observation and then a preliminary visit to our teaching practice school. At first sight, the little beasts in my observation school in Boxmouth gave me second thoughts about this teaching lark, but it was too late by then. I already had a hefty student loan around my neck. Everyone else was making similar remarks about the little perishers they were observing, so I carried on, feeling a sense of solidarity with my fellow students.

By the time I was exchanging Christmas cards and promises to keep in texting contact with my new circle of friends, the term finished with just a handful of Theo sightings and two brief sneers. He was usually surrounded by a bevy of giggling groupies, who fawned and simpered and conveniently kept his attention from mere, mundane mortals such as me.

I confess that my memory of the last bit of term was a touch hazy. Foolishly, I'd underestimated the potent effects of the scrumpy cider that someone brought to one of the end of term parties. My journey home was accompanied by a sledgehammer inside my head, a fur-lined mouth and a firm determination to stick to diet cola in future. After that, I was plunged into last minute shopping in the odd moments left between helping out in Dad's shop, where customers were snapping up the remaining organic fair trade Christmas puds and other delicious delicacies.

Eventually the spring term started, with frantic lesson plans, galvanizing lectures and top tips from our education tutors, before coaches turned up to deliver us to our month long destinations. Mine was a sweet little village by the name of Netherbury-on-Teign. It was five miles the other side of Teignmouth, with no handy train station but with a bus service that was tied in with ad-hoc market days or possibly phases of the moon or something equally obscure. I was lodging with Mr and Mrs Crabtree, in a rambling, shambolic farmhouse, surrounded by a copse of silver birches and unruly bramble hedges. I found myself crammed into a tiny box room, with a few spiders and beetles for company. Fortunately, I wasn't squeamish. I suspected the room had housed livestock before I moved in. Mrs Crabtree lined up those dinky little individual cereal boxes each morning and naturally I went for all my favourites straight away. Unfortunately, the chances of more frosted flakes looked unlikely until I'd worked my way through the boring ones. I thought she might have spotted my preferences early on and invested in a whole packet, but Mrs C had frugal down to a fine art. Despite the cramped sleeping quarters and limited breakfast choices, I settled in well enough, until I caught a stray remark in the staffroom one lunchtime.

'Oh, are you lodging with the Crabtrees?' asked one of the matronly ones.

When I nodded, another one rolled her eyes and muttered something about 'Loopy Larry.'

Then the first one put my mind at rest by saying, 'Well, they wouldn't have let him out if he wasn't okay, would they?'

I didn't dare ask from where Mr C might have been released . I felt it was a case of less knowledge, less to worry about. It made sense that the college wouldn't be entrusting their students to the care of ex-convicts or mental cases. There were bound to be checks about that, even in sleepy little places like Netherbury-on-Teign. Still, I was grateful there was a lock on my bedroom door. The other member of the Crabtree household, was a yapping hound called Satan, and those Crabtrees certainly knew how to create an atmosphere of rustic calm. I'd convinced myself that Satan was paid in bones to scare away door-to-door salesmen as well as student teachers. He cowered behind the straggly hebe bush by the front gate and bared his yellow fangs at the sight of ankles. Complaining to the Crabtrees made not a scrap of difference. They simply grinned back with gappy smiles and murmurs of, Good dog, Satan.' At least I found an extra use for my lesson-plan folder. A bop on the nose and Satan had second thoughts about sinking his teeth into my pale and interesting flesh.

The class I had been assigned to – or more to the point, was lumbered with – was Year 5. There were about thirty of them, aged between nine and ten. In some cases, the girls were ten going on sixteen. I was amazed how streetwise they were. I mistakenly thought sleepy little villages produced sleepy little children. Their teacher, Mrs Frampton, appeared to be related to half the population, so I didn't dare pass the time of day with a soul or my comments would have gone the rounds and reached Mrs F's ears, embellished and Chinese-whispered out of all recognition. Topics such as the weather were about my safe limit. I took my guitar with me – three chords proving enough to strum out a passable accompaniment – and the singing was quite a hit, especially the calypso numbers. Then, if the kiddiewinks were *really* good, such as no shouting out, no rude words and no disruption, they were allowed to have a track from one of their own CDs in the last few minutes of the lesson. Being allowed to bring in their own music was unheard of, so it gave them a huge incentive to behave. Mrs F had tut-tutted a bit but as I hadn't had a riot or lost anyone on the games field – correction, the rough patch of grass between the dinner hut and the wood – then she couldn't really complain.

The news about Tim coming out of the coma was the best news I'd ever wanted, although the timing couldn't have been worse. I was in the second week of a four-week practice at the time and there was no chance of popping over to Bournemouth Hospital. Apparently, Eleanor had been trying to call me all day, but naturally you don't have your mobile on when you're teaching. The signal wasn't too good either. Netherbury-on-Teign was surrounded by hills and forests.

'He's not out of the woods yet,' Eleanor told me. That sounded rather like my situation. She sounded guarded and somewhat evasive but only added that it was bound to take a while. He'd been in a coma for almost fifteen months.

'We think Tim's suffering from post-traumatic amnesia,' said the young doctor, but not the same one we saw that first time though. I was visiting with Mum and Dad straight from my successful month's practice. The journey seemed to take ages, and we only made the last hour of visiting. The fact that the doctor was taking time to talk to us was quite amazing, seeing as we weren't related to Tim. I suppose that's what they'd decided to do when new visitors turned up, just so they were prepared for that first meeting. After the doctor's opening remark we all nodded like the three wise monkeys. I peered at his name badge. He was called Marco Fergani, although you wouldn't have guessed it from his BBC English accent.

'You're not sure then?' Dad had asked. At the time of the accident I had managed to pick up some cursory info on comas, but we were obviously moving into another area now. None of us Bonnings were known for our grasp of medical jargon. One of Mum's cousins had been a midwife, but she was now retired and living in New Zealand, not that she'd have been any use to us. Nor were we on hob-nobbing terms socially with any doctors.

'Well, not exactly,' Dr Fergani told us. 'You see it's not uncommon for accident victims to suffer from post-traumatic amnesia, when they have no memory of the moments just before the accident, due to a brief break in their short and long term memory transfer mechanism.'

The three of us exchanged puzzled glances. It was like a wall of words in a foreign language. So we asked Dr Fergani to say it again – slowly – stopping him every so often to ask questions. Afterwards I tried to write it down, trying to record his exact words, although I'm not sure I really understood it. I managed to fill the gaps with a few visits to Wikipedia again. However, that wasn't all he had to tell us. It became scarier by the moment.

'With post-traumatic amnesia,' he continued, 'the patient may have no memory of people he or she had known before the accident. They may recall names of people but not recognise them.'

'You mean he won't know us!' I gasped.

'Well… er… he may not.'

I grabbed Mum's hand and knew at once what Eleanor had meant about not being out of the woods.

'But you said you weren't sure.' Good old Dad. He pressed on, almost as if he had some sort of ghoulish fascination with the subject.

'Well, we've noticed some similarities to dissociative fugue amnesia.'

Now, as a musician I know exactly what a musical fugue is. It's when little tunes start one after the other and build up the music into a lot of mingling layers. From what I could gather, this dissociative fugue amnesia is made up of one or more episodes of amnesia, where the person forgets some or even *all* of their past. Apparently this is very rare.

'So you mean Tim might have forgotten what he was doing the day before the accident as well as the moments before the accident?' This was Dad again.

Thoughts were chasing around my brain like a whole lot of fugal subjects, but in *my* case, they weren't very melodic. In fact, the thought of what Tim might not remember was building up into the most terrifying cacophony.

'Or about his customers?' suggested Mum.

'Or about his manager?' added Dad.

'Or about his girlfriend?' I chimed in.

We watched Doctor Fergani's face for clues, but he was giving very few.

'He *will* recover, won't he?' I gasped, imagining the worst.

'Oh yes, there's every chance, but we can't really say how long it will take.'

It sounded as if Tim was lost in a huge forest, let alone a wood. All the excited hope that had been building since Eleanor's call seem to have hit a brick wall and shattered into a million tiny pieces. I asked if we could see him, although by then I was dreading that first meeting after such a long time.

'Of course.' We followed Dr Fergani with wildly palpitating hearts.

Tim was sitting up in bed reading the *Daily Mirror*. Weird, I thought, because he used to be a *Telegraph* man. He looked up quizzically, a neutral sort of expression on his face. Just imagine being asleep and out of the loop for fifteen months, missing two Christmases and all the sport and celebrity news and gossip.

'Hi, Tim,' I said, giving him one of my sunniest top-drawer smiles. I wanted to go and kiss him, but something told me to hold back – mainly the blank look on his face.

'It does my heart good to see you sitting up in bed,' Mum told him.

'That's right,' added Dad, a facts rather than feelings sort of bloke.

Tim's eyes switched rapidly from each of us as if we were lobbing balls at Wimbledon.

'I'm sorry, but I've no idea who you are,' he began. Obviously he hadn't lost his manners, although our worst fears about his memory were being confirmed as we stood open-mouthed. I could feel my bottom lip trembling. Nothing had prepared me for the shock of being a stranger to the man who had been hours away from popping the question. I'd read about this sort of thing happening to other people, but when it happens to you…

'I'm Gilly…' I tried again, thinking that my name might kick-start the memory transfer mechanism into life.

'Gilly?' he said. 'Someone mentioned that name.' He was speaking slowly, with a lot of thought lines wrinkling his brow. 'Well, pleased to meet you.' He even stuck out his right hand in my direction, intending a formal handshake.

'Your girlfriend,' prompted Mum patiently, although I could see her bottom lip was also on the point of losing its grip.

'Girlfriend?' he said, looking even more puzzled. 'I don't think so. How could you be my girlfriend when I've never seen you before?'

I must have made some sort of incoherent noises because Dad moved over and clamped a manly arm round my shoulders. My legs didn't seem to know what to do and it was November 21st all over again.

'But I was, I mean I am… we've been going out for ages…' I tried to tell him, but he just shook his head. That meant that at least three and a half years had been wiped out of his memory. We'd started going out just as I was starting my second 'A' level year. Tim's family had only moved to Growdon the year before, so we'd never known each other as schoolmates. He started at the bank fairly soon after moving to Growdon.

'Perhaps we'll get to know each other again?' I suggested.

'Oh, do you live locally?' he asked. 'They're letting me go home soon.'

This conversation was becoming more surreal by the moment. I grabbed a chair and carefully lowered myself onto it. Then Mum and Dad introduced themselves.

'I'm sure your Mum and Dad will be pleased to have you home at last,' said Dad.

'Er… yes… although they look a bit different from what I remember. Mum seems to have lost a lot of weight.'

'That'll be the worry,' chipped in Mum. 'So you remember something? That's encouraging isn't it, Gilly?' She gave me a tight smile and nodded. I hadn't answered Tim's question, but with such a huge chunk of memory missing, telling him I was teacher training in Devon seemed unimportant.

It was then that a nurse popped her head round the door.

'There's another visitor,' she told us apologetically. 'I know it's almost chucking out time, but our limit is three visitors…'

'We quite understand,' Dad told her and we gathered up our coats. But before we made it to the door, a girl rushed in, out of breath and struggling with a huge gift-wrapped box. She virtually ignored us as we flattened ourselves against the wall.

'Tim!' she exclaimed, hurling herself at the bedside chair. We all studied Tim's expression, which was predictably just as vacant as when we'd made our entrance a few minutes earlier.

'My, aren't I popular today!' he chuckled.

'Don't you remember me, Tim?' the girl gasped. It seemed to me that she'd made such a whirlwind entrance that she'd managed to miss Dr Fergani's talk.

'Lena, Lena Tuffin. I was right behind you when you had your accident. We had a whip-round at work.' She plonked the huge box on Tim's lap, looking hugely pleased with herself. Evidently, news of Tim's recovery had prompted her magnanimous gesture. Our bag of satsumas and bunch of grapes looked poor runners-up. The nurse had left us, probably checking up on other loitering visitors, so we stood frozen where we were, listening to Lena on her own steep learning curve.

'I don't remember,' Tim admitted, tearing off the wrapping. 'Although Mum and Dad said you stopped the accident being any worse,' he added, looking up and smiling.

'Post-traumatic amnesia,' hissed Dad, as quietly as he could. Lena's head snapped round in shock, her eyes like saucers.

'Really?'

'But it'll probably right itself eventually – his memory I mean,' Dad assured her.

By now Tim had revealed the biggest box of chocs I'd seen in my life.

'My, my,' he chuckled, 'there must be a lot of you at work, or you've all been very generous.'

'Just six of us actually… you know the Cut Above The Rest salon?'

'No… er… don't think I remember that either. Here, do have one.'

Tim flung back the lid and we all goggled at the sumptuous rows of caramels, clusters and goodness knows what else. Mum, Dad and Lena all dived in, but I hadn't much of an appetite for chocolate. The thought of being stuck in Devon for another two and a half years while Tim started to piece his life together was too depressing for words. Lena Tuffin was also causing me some bother. Just looking at the expression on her face told me this wasn't the first visit she'd planned. Perhaps she'd been nipping into the hospital on a regular basis…

'No thanks,' I muttered. Mum came alongside, realising that Gilly Bonning refusing chocolate was rare and therefore a situation needing careful handling.

Lena placed a predatory hand on Tim's arm and gave it a squeeze.

'Never mind about what you don't remember Tim, we'll be here for you, helping you rebuild your life.' She turned and seemed to be including the Bonnings in the remark.

'Oh most definitely,' Mum assured her. Dad and I nodded, more like wooden automatons than flesh and blood friends.

'I think we ought to be going.'

'Of course, Gilly,' agreed Mum, 'or the nurse will put us on her blacklist!'

All the while Lena was gabbling away to Tim, who was gazing at her pretty little face and sleek auburn hair that hung like a shimmering curtain down her back. I wanted to tell her that Tim and I had been going out for ages before the accident so she'd know where she stood – or rather where *I* stood. The trouble was, Tim would deny any knowledge of me, and that would hurt more than anything else.

A bell sounded in the corridor outside, so we all knew it was time to leave, Lena included.

'And here's a card from all of us,' she was telling him.

If I'd known how bad he was – memory-wise – I'd have written a full account of our friendship for him. We hadn't even brought a card with us, so there was nothing to remind him of the Bonnings, and I was desperate to help him fill in that huge blank.

'Sorry folks, we've got to get our patients settled for the night.' It was the nurse who'd returned, looking as flustered as a plate-spinner rushing up and down trying to keep everything moving – in *her* case the visitors. I stared across at Lena and indicated with a nod of my head that it meant her as well. She smiled back and had the good grace to remove her hand from Tim's arm.

'See you soon,' she told him cheerily.

'And I'll be round to see you too,' I added, making sure he was reminded of my existence.

'Great,' he said, giving us both equal shares in the smile department.

We all trooped out and Dad closed the door firmly. I'm sure he and Mum had a shrewd idea what I was going through, even before I said a word.

'What was that you said about the amnesia?' Lena asked Dad. He filled her in as best he could.

'At least three and a half years have been wiped out of his memory,' I added sadly, 'in fact all the time I'd been going out with him.'

She turned and gave me a surprised look. 'Is that so? So does that mean he doesn't remember any of it? The last three and a half years? At all?'

'Doesn't seem to.' She appeared to be showing genuine concern for me.

'Oh how awful for you. Well, you'll be able to help him remember won't you, when he's out of hospital.'

'I guess. The trouble is, I'm doing a teaching course in Devon now, so visiting's going to have to wait until the holidays.'

On my way to the hospital I'd been imagining Tim visiting me at Boxmouth. I was sharing a house with three other girls and couldn't see a problem having him over for the odd weekend. Fat chance of that now.

'Oh, what a shame,' she sighed. 'Never mind, there'll be plenty of us keeping him company and maybe, by the time you're home again, he may have remembered some of his past.'

'Hope so.' However, if he hadn't, I was worried about Tim becoming rather better acquainted with Miss Tuffin than was desirable.

'Where do you live, Lena?' I asked casually. 'In Growdon?'

'Oh no, I have to trek over from Firlea each day.'

'Ah, right,' I said, with relief. 'Quite a journey.' That would certainly limit her popping in to see him, and hairdressers are renowned for their long hours.

'Nice to meet you all,' she said, turning to go.

Mum and I exchanged anxious glances as she strode off to the car park.

'She means well, Gilly,' said Mum. 'And we've got her to thank haven't we? I mean, the pensioner might have been in a worse state if she hadn't acted so quickly, Tim too.' Up to that moment I'd hardly considered the poor pensioner, only that he was the villain of the piece.

'Tell you what, Mum,' I told her as we trundled off after Dad, 'I'm going to write Tim a very long letter when I get home, just so he knows the truth. If I leave it to Lena, who knows what he might be allowed to think.'

Mum gave me an odd sort of look, as if to say 'don't get your knickers in a twist' but I said nothing more. Being cast aside as a stranger by the man I was planning to marry was the worst shock imaginable, and I was determined to win him back.

Chapter 5

Try a little tenderness

'Great idea, Gilly,' said Eleanor as she took the letter from me. The trouble was, her eyes didn't exactly match what her lips were saying.

'Well, I had to do something, didn't I?' I protested.

'Do you want to come in?'

'No, can't stop, I'm off to catch a train back to college.'

'Ah… a shame really, we think Tim might be home in a couple of days.'

'That's why I wrote the letter… to help him remember.' Although I knew from Dr Fergani's little talk that the memory mechanism in Tim's brain had malfunctioned, so a letter wasn't likely to mend it.

'We've taken photos in, but only the ones taken more than four years ago seem to make any sense. Nothing that's happened since we've been living here is registering with him. He mentions old school friends, but that's about all and if we talk about things we're doing now, he looks blank. I think it'll be a long haul.' She shrugged in a helpless sort of way.

'Tell him I'll be back at Easter,' I told her, but she flustered a bit and said she wasn't sure what was happening then. It was just like when you ask someone if they could help with something and they start going all vague on you, needing to check their diary, etc. etc.

So I returned to Boxmouth and plunged myself into essays and lectures and anticipated warmer weather, sinking my toes in the sand and taking walks in the dunes. Mollie, one of the girls I was sharing with, suddenly started keeping very late hours. She would return when the rest of us were all tucked up in bed or in our dressing gowns at least. We discovered she'd started going out with a squaddie from the army barracks just along the coast. I was in the kitchen one evening, mixing myself a hot chocolate when Mollie came back definitely the worse for wear. She had a silly grin on her face and kept tottering around in her strappy heels giggling and telling me how fab Dan was. Dan might be fab, I thought, but pouring booze down

Mollie's throat didn't sound like a very good idea. I suspected he had an ulterior motive. I must have given her a critical look because she told me to stop moping and find myself a bloke. She went as far as to say that Dan had a friend who might suit me. I hadn't said much about Tim, but my fellow housemates had noted my less than chirpy mood when I'd returned from my weekend visit.

'I've got one thanks,' I told her, through gritted teeth, then yawned and made a quick exit. She looked slightly green and likely to spew up all over the floor. As far as I was concerned she could clear it up herself. I suspected that Fran and Amy shared Mollie's opinion about my love life, even though they didn't put it quite so bluntly. Fran had started going out with Tony – yes, he made it too – but I think they were just mates, rather than girl and boyfriend. Amy seemed to be keener on knitting than blokes. If only I could have worked up some enthusiasm for it myself we might have got on better. Somehow Aran patterns don't do it for me, although if I knew Tim was going to take up cricket again I might have contemplated knitting him a sweater.

In Edwina Beresford's music session one morning she told us about the next term's concert. Apparently, we'd have to perform some homegrown works as well as some concert favourites such as Mozart's *Magic Flute Overture* and excerpts from *West Side Story*. She told us the homegrown works were being written by the third year students and would be performed as part of their final course work. I hoped that someone would write a decent clarinet part for me that I could *actually* play. I would never deliberately sabotage someone's chance of high marks, but if they thought we were all geniuses it might be tricky.

While Edwina was giving us our next composition assignment, the door opened and who should stroll in, as if he owned the place, but your friend and mine, Golden Boy Theo. Like most females on the campus, Edwina seemed to have fallen under his spell. Predictably, there was a sharp intake of breath from the girls in the room and frisson of excitement as they gazed in rapt adoration.

'Ah, Theo,' said Edwina, all smiles, as if he had the right to disturb any old lecture he chose.

'The auditions are being held on Friday,' he told her, as if the rest of us didn't exist, 'so if you could get everyone to sign up... strings, brass and woodwind, you know. We've got the timps sorted already, okay?'

He dropped a sheet onto Edwina's lectern and then strolled out, without a 'sorry to have disturbed you.' That odious individual had *not* changed one bit.

Those who had been worshipping at the Golden Boy shrine breathed an audible sigh then started whispering excitedly at the prospect of performing for his benefit. Some of us though, needed to know exactly what sort of talent show was being planned, because that's what it sounded like. It was Barry the trombonist who was first off the mark, arm in the air as if he was still at school.

'Mrs Beresford, is this audition compulsory? Is it a bona fide part of our course and – excuse my French – what the hell is it for?'

There were times when I found Barry's bluntness very refreshing. This was one of them. Edwina had managed to flutter down from cloud nine by then and the pink in her cheeks had faded just a little.

'Ah, Barry, yes... sorry, I should have mentioned that when I was telling you about the homegrown compositions. Some of our third years have asked for auditions to help them write suitable parts. As some of you are taking singing or piano as your first study, your instrumental prowess may not be top grade, but jolly useful all the same, when it comes to teaching and so on. Nobody would want to present you with a part that was too technically challenging.' A few thunderous looks were exchanged. Edwina must have realised her choice of words was not very tactful. 'And of course, if there are any solos, they'll want to know who to approach,' she hastily added.

Edwina was working hard at an encouraging smile, but most of us had already gleaned the sub-text. In other words, the Latterton Academy lot thought the rest of us were a load of duffers – musically speaking – and wanted to have a private snigger. Although the college worked at inclusivity, you couldn't help feeling there was a certain amount of 'them and us' between the two groups of students in the music department.

'Well bring it on!' chortled Barry. 'My Grade 8's good enough for anything they want to write.'

'Good on you, Barry,' I whispered back with a smile. Unfortunately my smile might have been a bit too warm, because he took my remark as a vote of support for his dating status, gave me a fat wink and asked me out for a drink as soon as the session finished. I told him I'd check my diary! Barry (Baz when he's chilling out) had limited conversation, usually based on rugby and his town's brass band. The family seemed to run it and competitions featured in their only social life, as far as I could tell. I wasn't sure if I could cope with a whole evening hearing about that over half a pint of diet cola. In a group, Barry's not so 'in your face'. I quickly considered inviting a couple of friends along if I *did* agree.

'Mine too, Mrs Beresford!' confirmed Zoe, the stick insect cellist, clapping her hands like a pre-schooler. 'I'm game for anything… musically speaking.'

Meanwhile I was making a mental check of my favourite pieces: McDowell's *To a Wild Rose*, was my top choice, being reflective rather than showy and a piece that wouldn't need hours of preparation. After disentangling myself from Barry, I made a dash for the audition rota, only to be distracted by Tara, one of my fellow clarinettists who wanted me to join her in some duets based on Bartok piano pieces.

'It'll be *much* better than sweating through a solo,' she urged me, panic written all over her face. I didn't have the heart to tell her that Bartok was not my favourite composer and that I'd already deduced her cunning ploy was to pick a nice easy line for herself.

'Sorry, Tara,' I told her, 'maybe someone else can oblige.'

Meanwhile, the rest of the group were jostling around Edwina's rota. Eventually I made it to the front, only to see that the second years had already filled in their slots. Six forty five after a quick supper wasn't ideal, but it was better than playing second fiddle – or rather second clarinet – to Tara's Bartok selection at five thirty. Meanwhile I'd be practising my best disinterested scowl for the judging panel.

Back at the house, I reflected on my imminent exposure to the great guns of the Latterton Academy firing line. My practiced scowls might come in very handy, I decided. It was also a good thing I'd managed to press-gang a posse from my education group to join me down at the *Rat and Rabbit* later on. I didn't want Barry all to myself and I wanted something pleasant to look forward to after the audition.

There was a row of chairs lined up outside the music hall, and a girl with a clipboard on guard at the door, who was plugged in to her iPod most of the time. Incredible? No, not about the iPod; just the sitting in line, as if it was a high-powered job interview.

I'd gobbled down fish pie and peas and made it to the hall in plenty of time to hear Zoe murdering a Bach cello piece. It kept stopping abruptly, followed by her tinkling laugh. She was probably fantasising about you-know-who, hence all the wrong notes and ragged timing. Waiting for my turn I thought it would be the ideal time to text Tim, to find out how he was coming along. I tried not long after I'd returned from the weekend at home, but so far I'd not had a reply. It was odd really. He'd always been such a well-meaning, polite chap that I'd have expected a brief reply at least, even if he wasn't sure about me. We'd met, after all. He could hardly say I was a stranger, even if the memory of all our previous friendship has been wiped from his mind.

At last Zoe's Bach finished and I galvanised myself ready to go in. The girl at the door took out her earpiece and cocked her head towards the hall.

'You're the last one,' she told me. 'God, what a marathon!'

Before I reached the door another piece started, but in a much higher register. Evidently Zoe had covered all possibilities by bringing her viola as well. She was giving a spirited rendering of a folksy sort of tune – very Dvorak, by the sound of it. The doorkeeper sighed. I really don't know why she was bothering to stay there. I was perfectly able to see myself in when the time came.

'I'm writing a vocal piece with vibraphone and timps,' she told me. 'It's a safe bet and I've lined up my players already.'

'Very wise,' I told her. After another couple of minutes we heard a smattering of applause and a few hearty chuckles and the doorkeeper decided she'd had enough.

'I should go in. They'll all be ravenous by now, I should think.' It was an unfortunate turn of phrase, reminding me of Christians being thrown to the lions!

I peeped round the door, just to make sure Zoe wasn't going for an encore. But no, she was packing away her instruments and looking flushed with relief.

'Well done, Zoe,' I told her, 'real solo possibility there…'

'Can we get on please?' I knew at once who that was: male, bored, arrogant etc, yes, you've already guessed. Zoe and I exchanged glances and raised eyebrows, but she was more forgiving than me. How you can excuse rudeness just because of someone's looks is beyond me.

Half the students in the room seemed to have given up and were slouched in chairs, checking their phones.

'Do you need an accompanist?' asked a solidly built girl who sat next to Golden Boy Theo at a long table. Her name, I learned, was Tatiana. By the look of her, she was taking it all very seriously. Theo, however, was deep in conversation with another girl who was regularly draped around him.

'Not bothered,' I told her casually, 'but there's a piano part if anyone wants to play it.'

I set up my music and waited for the chatter to stop.

'Your turn, Theo,' said Tatiana, with a smile.

'Oh… you,' he said, looking up and giving me a scornful look. I could do scornful, so I gave him one of my best. Tatiana's eyes zapped towards Theo in surprise.

'Some history here, I detect,' she muttered, just loud enough to reach my ears.

'Go on, you lazy sod,' giggled his other companion, shoving him playfully, 'might have a budding soloist here. Then it's back to mine for a few treats.'

I could tell from the general sniggering that the few treats might not all be of the edible kind.

He eventually made it to the piano, but not before snatching the music from me. Even Tatiana and the girl offering the treats (well, that's only my guess of course) were heard to gasp at his arrogance.

'What's this then?' he sneered, reading the title that was clearly visible.

'One of the classics,' I told him.

'I think Beethoven's more in that line,' he commented snidely.

'Of the *clarinet* repertoire,' I hissed.

'Actually, it was written for the piano – one of the pieces in the *Woodland Sketches Suite, dearie,*' he huffed, condescendingly.

'But adapted for the clarinet,' I snapped back, 'and the name's Gilly Bonning, by the way. I don't answer to 'dearie' as it happens.'

Catching sight of the rest of his team, they resembled a row of cod, with open mouths and mad, staring eyes. Possibly they hadn't seen the darker side of the Golden Boy's character, although I'd be surprised if I was the only student in the whole college to be treated like that. Without a 'by your leave' he set off at a punishing pace, not even waiting for me to set the beat, and ignoring the speed and style marking. So much for his know-it-all attitude.

'Excuse me,' I said, wondering if he'd noticed that he was alone, 'it's marked *"with simple tenderness"*.' To my amazement, he actually stopped and I swear I glimpsed a brief flush cross his features.

'Tenderness,' I repeated, more to myself than anyone else, 'a quality sadly lacking these days.'

The whole group was silent now and for at least five seconds, if not more, you could have heard the proverbial pin drop.

'I'll count you in,' I told him firmly, but I could tell he wasn't used to being directed. So I did and, despite my racing heart, knocking knees and swirling stomach, I managed a passable performance, without a single embarrassing squeak from my clarinet.

'Thank you, Gilly,' Tatiana gushed, 'very expressive.'

I nodded in her direction and was out of that place as fast as I could decently manage. That's why an evening down the *Rat and Rabbit* with Baz and the gang was a welcome relief. Do you know, I even considered risking a small cider considering the way I stood up to that bully with an attitude problem. It deserved some sort of celebration. I really couldn't care less what sort of part any of them decided to give me. I'd made my point, and that's what mattered.

The following morning I took ages to surface and it wasn't another hangover either. Something so utterly horrendous happened at the *Rat and Rabbit*... that it makes me shudder just to think of it – which is obviously what I *don't* want to do. Well, it all started really well, as most things do. There were eight of us sat in an alcove, and Barry didn't mind in the slightest that I'd invited some friends along, because he'd invited Phil and Sam as well – both brass band buddies, naturally.

Phil – cornet and euphonium – had brought along a book of music jokes, and we were passing it round and reading out snippets. We were lucky to bag our alcove, because within half an hour, the place was heaving with squaddies, locals and students. When I managed to grab the book from Fran, I dived straight to the trombone section, and we cracked up at Barry's expense.

'Right, what do four trombones at the bottom of the sea sound like?'

'No idea!' shouted most of the group.

'Well, almost right, the answer's *a good idea!*' Groans all round, naturally.

'Hey, here's a good one: what do you call a beautiful woman on a trombonist's arm?'

'A bloody miracle?' suggested Phil.

'So close,' I teased, 'you're getting the idea... it's *a tattoo!*'

Barry groaned, but couldn't help chuckling. He snatched the book off me, determined to get his own back.

'Right, Miss Bonning,' he said, struggling to keep a straight face, 'how do you get two clarinettists to play in time together? *Shoot one of them!*'

I told him that was unfair, but none of the musicians in the group really minded. It showed we had a sense of humour.

We all chipped into the kitty and Phil and Sam went off to buy the next round. By then I'd had enough of diet colas, so I was onto cider – but not that cloudy scrumpy stuff that did the damage last time.

'Hey, looks like your friend's turned up,' whispered Fran, conspiratorially.

'Which particular friend?' I asked her.

'Oh, you'll soon find out.' The book had done the circuit and I was ready with another gem once the lads were back at the table.

'Hey Phil, did you see this one? Two women were having a chat. The first one asks the second: What instrument does your nephew play? The aunt replies: Euphonium.'

The first says: 'Okay, I'll call him, I just thought you'd know!'

'The old ones are the best,' chuckled Phil.

'And Baz, last trombone joke,' said I, knowing it might be a bit risky, considering his size, 'How many trombonists does it take to pave a drive?'

Barry raised his eyebrows and shrugged.

'One, if you spread him very thinly!'

'Watch it Bonning!' he chuckled, taking a lunge at me.

It was just horseplay, but I swapped seats with Isobel. I just needed to keep on the safe side. The last thing I wanted was Barry thinking that the teasing was a sign of true affection. Perish the thought! Isobel wasn't one of the music students, but she was more Barry's type. They were both from the

Midlands, to start with. I remembered looking up then, after swigging half a glass of cider and seeing the jolly audition panel at the bar, knocking back pints and J2Os. I snatched up the book again and found the perfect piece of revenge. After all *he'd* almost ruined my audition.

'Right, folks,' I started, but they were all busy chatting except Barry, who obliged in his usual very unsubtle way. 'Pray silence for Gilly Bonning!' he bellowed, loud enough for Golden Boy at the bar to turn round.

'What's the difference between the alto clef and Greek?' The non-musicians gazed at me boggle-eyed.

'Some *conductors* actually read Greek!' I was feeling quite relaxed by then.

'Why did they bury the conductor twenty feet down?' By then even the Latterton students were waiting for the answer.

'Because deep down he was a nice guy!'

I didn't get any further, because Tony said it was his turn. One brief glance told me my quarry wasn't terribly amused by Phil's collection of humour. The girl who'd offered treats was conspicuous by her absence, I noted.

After another round of drinks and jokes I was bursting for the loo and it was on the way back that the unthinkable happened. It was quite a low-lit bar, but if Fran had been with me I'm sure it wouldn't have happened.

'Hey, you!' the humourless conductor hissed, grabbing my arm and glaring at me venomously. 'Any chance of shutting that mouth of yours?'

'You're hurting my arm,' I protested. He was too, even through the layers of my chunky sweater. His mates thought it highly amusing, although none of mine had spotted me through the crush of bodies.

'I said,' he repeated, almost shaking with fury, 'any chance of shutting that blabbermouth of yours?'

'Can't you take a joke?' I snapped. 'Where's your sense of humour? Gone the same way as your manners?'

'Go on, snog her!' shouted one of his mates. 'That'll stop her blabbermouth!' And he did! It was the most unlikely, vile and shocking thing I could imagine. He still had hold of me and pulled me so roughly that I stumbled right into him. Then down he swooped, like a sink plunger and for several seconds I couldn't breathe. His mates were cheering and whooping and all I know was his mouth and teeth were pummelling mine, while I struggled to free myself. 'Filthy beast,' I screeched, aiming a swipe at his face.

'Can't you take a joke?' he mimicked, and then pushed back through the crowd to much cheering and chuckling from his posse of mates and hangers-on.

I stumbled back to Fran and co, my poor lips bruised and throbbing, and had a good sob on her shoulder.

I don't know what else happened after that. I think the Latterton lot must have made a quick exit. God, that man gets worse. I woke in the night and found myself sitting up in bed sweating. It was the scariest nightmare ever, with Theo the beast cornering me down by the beach path and pinning me to the fence until I told him twenty rude jokes about woodwind players. After that he tried to rip my blouse open, which is when I woke up in a right lather. I couldn't wait until the end of the summer term, when he and his snooty lot were due to leave the place for ever.

Chapter 6

Ulterior motives

After that horrifying business at the *Rat and Rabbit*, and then my usual frantic effort trying to catch up with essays, most of the last part of the spring term flashed by in a haze. Fran told me I was the envy of half the college, being snogged by he who shall be referred to as The Beast. The titles of Golden Boy or even Filthy Trainer were much too good for someone like him. The thought of half the college knowing was embarrassing but unlikely. I tried to convince her how awful it was; a vicious attack, an abuse, a violation of what kissing is supposed to be. Following that evening I went in for sunglasses and headscarves in a big way and used circuitous and lesser-frequented routes just to avoid goggling girls, if there *were* any. Meal times were a bit tricky, but leaving mine until the last half hour usually guaranteed the company of bookworms, and therefore those least likely to be interested in the latest gossip. I think I may have over-reacted. I'd been guilty of that before. When Zoe heard about it, she speculated that The Beast's behaviour was his way of having his revenge on one of the Latterton girls, rather than as a reaction to my innocent little jokes. She'd heard unconfirmed rumours that he and Kirsty had had another bust-up, hence not at the *R and R* on the night in question. So why take it out on me... the humourless creep! I wasn't sure about Zoe's theory, considering what he'd said about my blabbermouth.

Back at home for the Easter break I was hoping to see Tim, although he hadn't replied to my text. The reason could have been that he'd changed his number or more likely his phone. His old one had probably been in its own coma for fifteen months. Then I tried phoning the Rosewell landline at least half a dozen times and left messages, but still no word from him. Of course they could have all gone away, hence Eleanor's odd manner when we last met. I don't know why she didn't come straight out with it and tell me they were planning a holiday, rather than go in for all that shifty body language.

Anyway, plan B was to go to Cut Above the Rest, book myself a trim and cross-examine Lena. It wasn't as if I didn't trust her, I just didn't want to be shrugged at, as in Eleanor's case. I couldn't imagine Tim being back at work for a while yet. What if he'd forgotten all his bank training? Mind you, he was a bright chap, so it wouldn't take him long to learn it all again. Meeting old customers might be slightly more tricky. Imagine the scenario: '*Ah hello, Mr Rosewell, good to see you back again...*' and the poor customer being met by a blank stare. There was bound to be a lot of that to start with. I made a mental note to try the bank as well.

By the end of the day, Plan B had been successfully carried out, although I needed several cups of hot chocolate and slices of toast and honey to calm down after all my investigations. Comfort food was my only way of coping. I managed to speak with Lena who was doing a bleach job for a wrinkly little lady, who looked seventy, at least. She was juggling squares of silver foil and a brush of gunk, trying to transform the woman's wispy grey hair back to its former glory, a few years too late. We agreed on a trim an hour later if I was prepared to wait until then. I would have waited much longer than that, but didn't tell her as much, just in case she was in the mood for wasting my precious time. There were the usual queues at the bank, so I tried the enquiry desk, ringing the bell at least twice before someone deigned to appear.

'Tim who?' asked the young woman, evidently one of their newer recruits. You'd have thought that the news of a member of staff waking from a fifteen month coma would have been the subject of plenty of coffee break chats. Steve the manager wasn't much more help, but at least I established that he expected Tim to return to work at some point. On the matter of dates, he was somewhat vague. The Eleanor Rosewell shrug certainly was becoming infectious.

Back at the salon Lena breezed through the usual hairdresser repertoire – they must train them in this at college – somewhat limiting my chances of interrogation. Perhaps she'd suspected my ulterior motive?

'So when did you last visit Tim?' I asked her. Unfortunately that coincided with a ding of the doorbell and Lena calling to Tash to shampoo the latest arrival. Then she ummed and aahed and finally told me a date some two weeks before.

'The poor love's still not much better,' she reflected. 'Probably needs a good rest, you know, to give his brain a chance to put itself right.'

I didn't think it was just a matter of rest; after all he'd been conscious for almost six weeks.

'Is he having flashbacks?' I asked her. She snipped away and hesitated long enough for me to add, 'like remembering things that happened before the accident.'

'What, you mean just before the bloke with the bike appeared?'

'Yes, and things he was doing around that time, and people he'd met since moving to Growdon.'

'Don't think so.' Lena appeared to have lost her interest in the subject.

So the Gilly Bonning episode in his life was still a closed book.

'Do you happen to know if there were plans to go away, only there's no answer at home?'

'A bit more off the length?' she asked, completely ignoring my question.

'No, that's fine,' I told her, studying her distracted expression in the mirror. 'Are the Rosewells away?' I asked her pointedly.

'Mm? Oh... er... there *was* talk of one of those lastminute.com deals. Sounds as if they managed to find one,' she told me airily.

And they didn't tell me! I was none too pleased, but I did my best at plastering on a non-committal face and commenting about the break being a good thing for all of them as a family.

She was just tidying up round the back of my neck when I spotted a postcard propped up on a shelf of over-priced conditioner. At a guess, the view was a typical Costa beach, with artificially blue sky and bronzed beach babes cavorting on the sands in front of a high-rise hotel.

'Do customers often send you cards?' I asked. Just then I was envying anyone able to jet off to the blissful heat of a Mediterranean resort while we were in the grip of a typically cool and depressing English spring.

'Some do, the regulars mostly.'

Now, I don't usually have unreasonable suspicions about people, but a little niggle suddenly lodged in my mind. Maybe it was because the subject of the Rosewell family absence and lastminute.com deals had just been mentioned that I was desperate to find out who'd sent the card. Lena was about to flash the mirror at the back of my neck when the receptionist called her over. That's when I reached for the card. Well talk about gob-smacked! I couldn't believe my eyes when I turned it over and saw the message: '*Thanks a lot, cheers Tim*' It was addressed to '*Lena and her lovely girls*'.

I must have sat there in frozen disbelief for at least half a minute, hardly breathing and yet thinking of a few colourful phrases for Lena Tuffin.

Before I could get rid of the card though, she was back, catching me red-handed and open-mouthed in disbelief. There was I in suspended animation while she did a pretty good copy herself, realising that I'd uncovered her convenient lies.

'You knew!' was all I could manage, but my eyes must have hinted at the rest of what was swilling round in my mind.

'Er... well... I didn't want to upset you,' she flustered, 'seeing as you didn't know he was away.'

'Didn't want to upset me? How do you think I'm feeling now? All hunky-dory? (That's one of my gran's sayings.) Thrilled to bits?' I was barely whispering because my voice had just about given up, or perhaps it was because a salon full of customers and stylists were goggling at us.

'I'm sorry, Gilly, I really am. I realise now it would have been better to tell you, but I assumed you'd know, seeing how you and Tim had been so close.'

'Had been?' Hearing that word stung me more than anything else.

'I expect there'll be a card on the way for you,' she told me as she flicked hair from my neck and removed the floral cape.

'I hope so.' I must have somehow got myself to the cash desk and paid, but I don't recall much, except that someone had turned on Radio 2 to cover any embarrassment. I seem to remember Lena mumbling something about how sorry she was, but I just nodded and left the place as quickly as I could. I hadn't even asked her why Tim should have written '*Thanks a lot*' on the card until I remembered the giant box of chocs, so I suppose it wasn't any more than a thank you. Still, she could have been more straightforward. And, by the way, there wasn't any postcard of beach babes, palm trees or bronzed sun worshippers sipping iced cocktails by a blue pool waiting for me when I got home.

Two days after the start of the misleadingly named 'Summer' term, Mollie made two announcements at breakfast: there was no marmalade left and she was convinced she was pregnant. I really don't know why she bothered to mention the marmalade. Perhaps she was trying to soften the effect of her own personal situation.

With hardly a pause, Amy waded in with a vote for the life enhancing properties of honey and said she could start on a pair of bootees. Fran asked her if she'd done a test. Fran's a very practical sort.

'Well no, but I can tell,' Mollie told us smugly. As a matter of fact, she *did* look a bit off colour, but not in the newly pregnant glowing sort of way. I asked her if Dan knew yet, but no, he was still in ignorance of impending fatherhood.

Later I advised Amy to put away her knitting patterns, being a tad on the early side. It's a good thing I did. A week later Mollie told us she wasn't pregnant after all and could she borrow some of our child development notes because she was two essays behind. Only two essays? With her fun-packed, boozy nights out I was amazed she'd managed to do *any* essays.

'It was probably just something you ate,' Fran observed, putting down Mollie's state of health to a tummy bug. That didn't go down well with Mollie, who convinced herself that it was a lost baby. She wouldn't reveal Dan's feelings on the subject, which I thought was interesting.

Yes, essays were my current concern, on top of a huge, five thousand word, child development assignment. In the Easter break we all had to ask a family we knew well if we could observe one of their children – with parents present of course. The college was ultra-careful on child protection issues. We had to observe the child's language development and gross and fine motor skills – no, nothing to do with driving daddy's car! Gross motor skills are large movements that are performed with most of the body, like rolling, crawling, walking running and jumping. Fine motor skills are about how we use our fingers, hands and arms. After that we had to present our observations after reading several chapters of the course handbook, making references to it, to prove that we'd read it and not just used it as a doorstop.

My little cherub was three-and-a-half-year-old Daisy, the youngest of the Templeton tribe who live at the other end of our road. We'd known the Templetons for years and I'd often babysat the older three. Steph, her mum, suggested I took Daisy to the swings and slides, which sounded easy. The trouble was, I decided to do without the pushchair and spent most of the time saving Daisy from dog poo, stinging nettles and the contents of rubbish bins, all of which she found fascinating. She had an eyebrow-raising line in conversation that included interesting revelations on Mr and Mrs T's 'rude bits'. After half an hour in Daisy's company I'd gleaned quite a detailed description of after-hours entertainment at number thirty-seven, none of which would be finding its way into my study, but would be eternally logged in my memory. In fact, if I met Mr T in the pub, I'd have to work out how to stop blushing into my J2O or he'd work out that Daisy's observational skills and vocab were well ahead of her years.

If that wasn't interesting enough, something even more eyebrow-raising happened around that time when I was beavering away in the college library. I was sitting right by the window, making even more notes and finding a few impressive quotes to scatter amongst my pearls of wisdom, when Desmond Morsby sauntered past, puffing away at his pipe as usual. Desmond was my education tutor who fancied himself something rotten. I admit, 'God's gift to women' might be an overstatement, although *he was* a brilliant lecturer. It would be difficult to put an age on him, but I'd hazard a guess at late forties. So, there was I chewing my biro and generally admiring the burgeoning leaf buds on the shrubs on the other side of the glass, when Desmond stopped and half turned towards the window. I gave him a bright smile, as if to say, '*look at me slaving away and not wasting my time down on the prom*', when he beckoned me and nodded in the direction of his office. Could my last essay be *that* bad that I needed a one-to-one?

When I entered his office he was engaged in his favourite occupation of cleaning out his pipe and still not giving any hint of how bad my essay had fared.

'Sit down, Gilly,' he told me, between a lot of scraping and odd pipe maintenance noises. How some women find pipe smokers sexy is beyond me.

'Well, how's life treating you?' he asked, putting his pipe aside and leaning back nonchalantly, hands behind his head and displaying unsightly damp patches under his arms like maps of Australia.

'Not so bad thanks,' I replied guardedly, wondering what trap he might be setting.

'And how's the love life?' he asked after a bit of tuneless humming and much concentration on a cobweb that looped across one corner of the room.

'Love life?' I squeaked. Clearly this was a pastoral chat and not a lecture on my essay writing progress.

'None to speak of really,' I told him candidly, although later I regretted not concocting an imaginary boyfriend. Telling him the Tim saga was the last thing on my mind.

'Well, you surprise me, Gilly,' he said, with an odd glint in his eye. 'Perhaps you need to find yourself a mature lover. You don't seem to be the sort of girl who's attracted to mere lads.'

How he came to that conclusion, I couldn't imagine. If I'd been wearing socks they'd have shot onto the carpet tiles in a flash. Naturally I didn't want to show old Desmond that I was surprised or even shocked by his advice, so I foolishly smiled what I thought was a sultry smile and nodded wistfully.

'Maybe,' I added, trying to show how cool and self-assured I was. After all Tim *was* a few years older than a lot of my fellow first years, so Desmond wasn't far out.

'And if anyone my age invited you to bed I'd imagine you wouldn't have a problem about saying yes,' he continued smoothly, his eyelids flickering like an adder closing in on a shrew. It was then that the nursery rhyme about a spider and a fly came to mind, as there wasn't an adder and shrew version as far as I knew.

I must have gulped a few times, while still clutching onto the super cool persona I'd been exhibiting up to then. Was he implying what I thought he was implying or was it just bluster from an old Romeo who was worried about losing his touch? We all knew there was a Mrs Morsby and some little Morsbys.

'Well, that's an interesting thought,' I gulped and then managed to remember I had a piano lesson. Grabbing my bag of notes, I was out of that study quicker than Mrs Muncie-Rookes snapping up bargains in the Pearsons' New Year sale. I beetled down the corridor, feeling a burning flush on my cheeks from the shock. I didn't stop running until I reached the music block, which seemed as good a place as any in the circumstances.

I crashed through the double doors and down towards the pigeon holes and lockers, relieved that no one was hanging around ready to quiz me on my scarlet woman potential. My heart was in overdrive. How would I cope with my next education lecture, let alone the next two years? There was nothing for me in the 'B' pigeon hole, so I just stood there reading all the notices, although all the letters seemed to be jumbled – or maybe it was just my scrambled brain.

'Hi, Gilly! Oh I was hoping to catch you!' came a female voice.

I must have jumped several inches because the next words were, 'Sorry, didn't mean to scare you.'

It was Tatiana, with her fresh-faced jolly grin and barely constrained matronly bosom. My capacity for speech seemed to have taken temporary leave of absence, because although I tried a simple 'hello', nothing came out. I could manage nodding though.

'Goodness, you're very pale. Are you okay?'

Still no words came, but I just about managed shaking as well as nodding.

'Oh, Gilly!' she gushed, and clasped me to her soft, squashy chest and patted my back as if I was a frightened puppy. Nobody had been that kind to me for ages and the floodgates of misery burst open. I sobbed in her arms and let all the Tim and Lena upset come pouring out.

It must have sounded complete gibberish, but she carried on patting and making sympathetic noises. Next came a handful of tissues, so I could mop up the rivers of tears and drool. I must have looked gross.

'So Tim was in a *coma*?' she asked, in suitably hushed tones. 'For over a *year*?'

Good old Tatiana, she must have had incredible hearing to pick out the salient points from my torrent of random ramblings. I was back to head nodding again, while I tried to finish mopping and wiping.

'And he doesn't know you?' she exclaimed. 'How awful, how tragic!' Now she had joined in with the head shaking. 'You poor, poor girl.'

What with all the snuffling, blowing and throat clearing I'd no idea that Tatiana and I were no longer alone, until I heard three unwelcome words drop from her lips.

'Oh, hello, Theo.' However, compared with being almost propositioned by a lecherous lecturer, being in the company of The Beast seemed marginally safer. The fact that he was sober probably had something to do with that.

'Poor Gilly's been telling me something really sad.'

'I heard.' Surprisingly, the voice sounded a lot less arrogant than on previous encounters, but I wasn't ready to risk any unnecessary eye contact with him. Three ghastly encounters were quite enough, thank you very much.

I carried on in head down position, still dabbing away with soggy tissues and listening for the sounds of retreating footsteps, which came eventually. After that, Tatiana thrust a folder of music in my arms and told me that one of the third years had selected me to perform a solo in their composition.

'Your playing was *so* sensitive and expressive,' she told me, with an encouraging grin.

'Eventually,' I replied meaningfully, remembering the false start that could have wrecked the whole piece.

'There'll be a couple of practices of course, and we'll get the details pinned up here in the next week, I hope,' she said, indicating the notice board. 'Now, time for tea and cake, I think. Shall we walk over together?'

Tatiana, I'd decided, would make the perfect chaperone. By the look of her impressive arms, she'd probably knock flying any predatory males without breaking stride. I nodded gratefully, and let her guide me to the door.

'Spot on!' she agreed. 'Hope it's bread pudding!'

Chapter 7

Mayhem in the music hall

I wasn't sure if I was particularly keen on Fran's 'brilliant' idea for the summer. Stripping bed sheets and cleaning hair out of plugholes, even in the most exclusive of Torquay's hotels, didn't exactly have me panting with excitement. Money or not, we all have the same bodily functions and mishaps. I told her this in my usual blunt way and watched her face deflate like a balloon on barbed wire. She clearly hadn't thought about anything more than the pay packet when she saw the chambermaiding ad in one of the county broadsheets.

'But it could be *fun*,' she tried again, then emphasised the sunbathing and nightlife benefits. "And we get *free* accommodation."

'Probably in some damp cellar or stuffy attic garret, with a minuscule bathroom on another floor that we share with half a dozen illegal immigrants.'

Fran couldn't live in cloud cuckoo land a moment longer. She was usually such a practical no-nonsense type. I couldn't think when the rose-tinted specs had mysteriously landed on her nose – until I happened to overhear Tony telling one of his mates that he'd got himself a bar job in the very same swinging resort. You'll probably pick up the hint of sarcasm in my use of the word 'swinging' if you appreciate that not much swings in Torquay except the emergency alarms that hang round the necks of the geriatric residents and day trippers. Now at this stage I have to admit that there are some genuinely really trendy parts of Torquay, safe from a take-over from the blue rinse brigade. I knew that because of a day trip Tim and I took once. It was organised by the Growdon W.I. and, being short of a few bums on the coach seats, we were invited along by Tim's Auntie June. Perhaps the Growdon W.I. had chosen the wrong day, but the Zimmer frame snarl-up on the prom when half a dozen coaches disgorged their passengers was like the scrum-down on pension day in Boxmouth post office. The queues at the ice cream vans were even worse, as the senior citizens dithered over which variety was less likely to play havoc with their dentures. Why didn't they all go for vanilla and have done with it, I don't know. That's what I'd do. Those ice cream tycoons have a lot to answer for. Now all the false teeth wearers need at least an extra two minutes choosing time to speculate on the pip content of 'choc-a-berry surprise' and 'summer fruit extravaganza'. Especially if you're running in a new set of dentures.

The thought of chambermaiding for that demographic group did not exactly fill me with enthusiasm.

'Are you sure I won't be a gooseberry?' I asked Fran, not imagining that she and Tony would welcome my presence when they were wandering hand in hand along the prom, gazing at the sunset.

'Fat chance of that,' she told me. 'Tony will be shaking cocktails most evenings. We might manage a swim or a picnic on the beach though, and of course you won't be a gooseberry. There'll be plenty of others around, I expect.'

Fran's powers of persuasion cranked up a gear and I reluctantly agreed to fill in the forms. I also decided to use my worse possible handwriting and scrawl illegible answers in the hope that I'd be rejected.

The thing is, I'd just heard that Tim had started back at work, but was having to repeat his training, which must have been quite weird for his co-workers, some of whom were several grades his junior. I heard that from Mum, who had been keeping me up with the latest happenings in the Rosewell household. She realised I'd up be up to my neck in coursework, which meant a fair sprinkling of music assignments on top of the major education one. Now, I had a dilemma. I needed cash, that was obvious, but I also needed to keep in touch with Tim. From what I'd seen of Lena Tuffin, I sensed that she saw herself as some sort of Florence Nightingale reincarnation, all eager for hand-holding and anything else she thought was important in Tim's recovery process. The sensible decision would be to get a summer job in Growdon, although some aspects of working in Torquay – swinging or not – were quite appealing. The trouble was, there weren't many opportunities for holiday work in Growdon, unless it was doing something boringly mindless in one of the few little factories or warehouses on the industrial estate. In the end Torquay won, with the intention of planning an extra visit home before I whizzed off to sample the delights of south Devon's nightlife.

Fran and I had to give the name of a referee on our forms, so I put Edwina Beresford as mine. She was a much safer bet than Desmond Morsby. The only way I'd been able to cope in his lectures was to keep eye contact to the very minimum. If he had to vouch for my good character, he might just remember how I flew red-faced out of his study. Having thought about that conversation several times I'd come to the conclusion that maybe it was just one big leg-pull at my expense. Old Morsby had probably chuckled his way home that night, amazed how I'd reacted to his remarks. That comes of trying to act cool and sophisticated. Next on my to-do list was to plan a weekend home, if by chance anyone was crazy enough to offer me a summer job, or could manage to decipher the scrawl on the application form. I was longing to speak to Tim, show him some photos – in the hope of jogging his memory – and make sure it was *my* hand he was holding.

It looked like the weekend between the Boxmouth carnival and our end of year concert was the only suitable one. There was usually a dance or a party most weekends, and I didn't want to end up as Gilly-no-mates. Sitting alone in my room listening to Radio 3, while everyone else was out over-indulging, getting seduced and generally having a wild time was not very appealing. There'd be plenty of time for being sober and sensible once I'd qualified. Hopefully, by then Tim would have remembered he was about to propose to me when the biking pensioner careered into him, would pop the question, and I'd be dazzling all my friends with a solitaire diamond set in white gold. We might even have a wedding date and… well, I knew I shouldn't get carried away. Just having him with his memory back would be enough for me. So I logged on and found one of those train ticket websites where you can get incredible bargains just by being super organised and forward thinking. I could hardly wait to see him again.

On the subject of end of year concerts, I'd been dutifully tooting away at the clarinet solo that Tatiana had passed on to me, written by someone called Rob. It seemed to move through several different keys at random and change time signature every couple of bars or so. In other words you had to struggle to hear any obvious tune, but it certainly made the most of the clarinet's range – from deep fruity bottom notes to shrill top ones. In fact Rob's piece was quite interesting and adventurous, but to be perfectly candid, I prefer more lyrical music myself. I was just emerging from a heavy session in one of the practice rooms one morning when Tatiana came bustling past.

'Oh, Gilly, bit of a panic with Laurel's ensemble piece!' I must have given her one of those *'who's Laurel?'* looks, because she did a mental re-wind before plunging on.

'Gothic, with plaits and no boobs,' she told me, lowering her voice. Gothic, plaits, no boobs, I thought, hmm, couldn't quite imagine her in a classroom. Not that boobs have anything to do with it, of course.

'Her first violin's only gone and gashed her middle left hand finger on some barbed wire and it's turned septic!'

'Ooh nasty!'

'I know it's very last minute, but I suggested you. I know she'd intended a violin to take the lead but I told her about your playing and she thought you sounded perfect! You see, Laurel's already playing viola in the piece and getting someone to conduct has been a nightmare. I think Alec's having his arm twisted. I'm already page turning for the pianist,' Tatiana gabbled, all flushed and wide-eyed in a beseeching sort of way. I couldn't think why Laurel wasn't doing her own dirty work in trying to fix up a replacement.

Did I *really* want another dollop of practice time on my plate, especially as the weather was on the turn again and I was dying to jump into my bikini for a tanning blitz in the sand dunes or even on the back lawn. So… more tooting away in the practice rooms? Well, not really my activity of choice, but Laurel wasn't one of the Beast's groupies, so I reluctantly agreed, remembering Tatiana's matronly bosom and puppy dog patting.

'She'll sort out the clarinet part then?'

'Absolutely. I'll text her now. She'll be *so* relieved!' gushed Tatiana.

'And I'll have the music when…?'

'In your pigeon hole by tomorrow at the latest,' promised Tatiana, 'and we'll have to have a run through on Thursday after Rob's piece, okay?'

Why did I agree to do it? I've asked myself that a dozen times at least.

I turned up at the music hall at the appointed hour and it was only then that Gothic Laurel thrust the music in my hand, telling me I was a life saver and that Maddie was now on antibiotics and hoping to be back on form in time for her Grade 8 exam. I was none too pleased, especially when I noted the four sharps in the key signature and all the fiddly little runs and great swathes of semi-quavers cavorting all over the place. However, I nodded matter-of-factly and took up my position for Rob's piece. Rob was conducting and although he referred to Brendan and myself as 'clarts' which sounded vaguely rude, the run-through wasn't too bad at all. My solo was only sixteen bars long, while the piano was virtually the only accompaniment plus some gravelly bowing on the double bass, but it sounded quite effective, even I had to admit that.

'Brill, guys!' He gave us the thumbs-up and reminded us of the last run-through in a week's time, which would fit in neatly before my weekend back home.

'Fancy a beer later?' Brendan asked me as he was putting his clarinet back in its case.

'Maybe,' I told him, 'but I've got Laurel's piece now, so I'll have to see.' His invitation sounded fun and the perfect way of unwinding after the day I'd had – education essay to finish, science study to titivate and desperate search for the right pair of sandals to go with my new (charity shop new!) linen mix trousers and jacket.

'Half eight down the *Rat* if you're free. There's a gang of us going.'

However, I never made it to the *Rat*, thanks to Laurel's lack of brain cells, sketchy memory or both. We were re-grouping and Laurel was transforming into the frantic, but giggly prima donna by the second, as she scurried around making sure everyone was ready. So far, Alec hadn't turned up, so I was wondering if Laurel was going to have to conduct with a nod, wink and the odd flick of her bow on top of holding down her own part. Tatiana, perched beside Will the pianist – a bespectacled bloke with rampant acne and a wispy beard – was taking up more than her fair share on the double piano stool, owing to her generously proportioned hips, but was holding firm with a look of grim determination on her face. I heard Will mutter something about arm room, but Tatiana seemed to be oblivious.

'Where's Alec?' I hissed to Laurel, as she squeezed past, nearly knocking my stand and music flying.

'Oh, he couldn't make it in the end… something about an interview I think,' she replied, 'so in the end I had to go down on my bended knee. Oh, at last!'

The door crashed open and God's gift to women and the music world in general hurtled in, lip curling with distaste as he surveyed Laurel's motley line-up. I groaned quietly and ground my teeth, remembering the ghastly business at the *Rat and Rabbit*. It was the first time I'd been face to face with him since then. That was *all* I needed, especially as I had to sight-read Laurel's scrawl, that looked more like the effort of a spider with a bad case of cramp.

'Right, let's get this show on the road.' The Beast tapped the stand in front of him pompously – his default setting I should guess – and the lower strings and the piano struck up bravely. My part wasn't until at least half a page later, so I counted the bars carefully, to make absolutely sure I'd come in on time.

Now, at this point it's important to reveal that I don't have that mystical gift of 'perfect pitch'. That's when a random note is played and the clever clogs with perfect pitch might say, *'That's g below middle c'* or whatever it happens to be. Everyone then gasps in amazement. Another slightly technical detail, important to bear in mind with what happened next, is that the clarinet is a transposing instrument, just like trumpets, bassoons, cornets and French horns. Our music has to be written out in a different key that makes allowances for our different pitch and fits in with the rest of the ensemble.

With a bar to go before my entry, I took a deep breath, fixed my attention on Laurel's wild semi-quavers and then launched into my part, hoping my fingers would rise to the challenge. They did, but after only two bars, I knew something was horribly wrong, and it wasn't my playing. In fact anyone who wasn't tone-deaf, would have known there was definitely something odd going on, unless Laurel was really pushing out the boundaries and having us play in different keys. I caught her eye and the same thought had evidently occurred to her.

'Oh God! What a racket!' Our exalted conductor flung down his baton and lobbed a filthy look in my direction. 'What key do you think you're playing in?' he demanded, as if addressing a half-wit.

'The key of the music I was given,' I snapped back, 'which, if my memory serves me well… um, let's see, ah yes, four sharps mean the key of E major.' To be honest, the sarcasm mixed with an air of innocence wasn't fair on Laurel, I realised later.

I glanced in her direction, saw her turn an interesting shade of grey and knew that she'd at last worked out her mistake. 'But as my clarinet, like most, is in B flat, my music should have been transposed a tone higher than the rest of the group!' I declared triumphantly, directing my remarks to the Beast. 'That's if I'm supposed to play in the same key as the rest of the group.'

'Then transpose it!' he snapped back, glowering at me evilly.

'What? At sight? Into six sharps? At *that* speed?'

'Oh, Gilly, I'm *so* sorry,' muttered Laurel. 'Somehow I thought you played flute. I completely forgot you played clarinet and that I needed to transpose it.'

'It's in a pig of a key too!' I grunted sullenly.

'Shouldn't bother anyone as opinionated as you!' brayed the Beast, with a smirk. I heard a groan from the direction of the piano stool and guessed it was Tatiana.

'Takes one to know one!' I snapped back, fixing him with one of my best classroom frowns.

Anyone in the group who might have been having a private chat or a quick texting session in the unscheduled break suddenly fell silent, except for a stray mention of 'snogging' and a snigger in the back row of the strings.

'Sorry, guys,' sighed Laurel, with a shake of her head, 'my fault entirely.'

Glancing across at her music for the first time since we'd ground to an undignified halt, I could see exactly what was wrong. A quick check on the rest of the group confirmed this too. I hoped for her sake, that she really *had* had a memory lapse, because a third year music student shouldn't be making that sort of mistake – especially a Latterton student.

'Er... right... we'll need to reschedule...' she flustered awkwardly, 'how about next Tuesday? I should have Gilly's part ready by then.'

There were a few mms and yeahs.

'In Paris most of next week,' came the disdainful voice I knew well.

'All right for some,' I heard someone mutter sarcastically.

'Right,' sighed Laurel, 'when are you back? Friday?' He nodded.

A few of the more organised ones quickly flicked through their diaries and muttered in general agreement.

'Sorry, Laurel, second year trip on Friday,' someone volunteered, 'but we can slot in a practice when we get back, as long as we're free for Sasha's 'do' later on.'

'Okay,' sighed Laurel again. 'How does seven sound?' There were a few 'yeps' and 'sures', but I knew I'd be on a train home by then.

'Sorry, Laurel,' I admitted, 'I'm going home that weekend.' This was greeted by a wave of huffs and groans. 'Perhaps you can get someone else to take the part. Perhaps Maddie's finger will have recovered by then.'

'Or perhaps you can forget about running home to Mummy and Daddy,' sneered the Beast.

'Or perhaps you can postpone your trip to Paris!' I retorted. There was another awkward silence and an embarrassed cough or two. Could it be, I wondered, that I was the *only* one to stand up to him? Were they all so much in awe of him and his precious conducting award that they'd morphed into terrified zombies who'd fall in with everything he said?

'No can do,' he snarled, 'it's been arranged for ages!'

'So's mine!' I snapped.

For all her Gothic bravado, Laurel looked ready to crumple. Her bottom lip started to quiver, making me feel guilty. But really, if she'd engaged a few more brain cells, especially in the comparative instrumental keys department, we wouldn't have been embroiled in a slanging match.

'Okay, how about this?' It was Tatiana to the rescue once more. She'd relinquished her share of the piano stool and had gone to give Laurel some of the bosomy hug treatment. 'We'll have a run-through now – minus the clarinet part – then meet up Tuesday – minus Theo – then have a complete run-through just before the concert, as long as everyone makes sure they're note perfect. Does that sound possible?' she suggested brightly, willing us all to agree.

So that's what happened. I had to sit there another WHOLE HOUR, enduring the Beast's baton waving, grunting and snide comments, and everyone else's missed cues and requests for yet another go through a *'particularly tricky passage please!'*

It was mind numbing, but at least I got an idea of how the piece was supposed to go. By the end, Laurel's lip was holding firm, and not just because of the presence of assorted ironmongery, but my temper had found the end of its short fuse. I was in 'lying down in a darkened room' territory, not quaffing halves of cider or J2Os in the *Rat and Rabbit*. It was when I put my head round the kitchen door and Fran – in sprightly mood because of some silly texting – asked me if I'd had a good practice, that I finally blew my top.

'Oh, Gilly, just chill, hey? It's just a mere trifle in the big scheme of things!' she told me breezily. 'If you saw the street beggars in the less desirable parts of Phuket and the slum areas…'

'Okay, okay,' I sighed. I was in no mood for her tales from Thailand and her preachy stuff about poverty just at that moment. I was still smarting from being humiliated about my playing. If I had been able to do all that transposing at sight and at speed and in the worst key imaginable, I'd be setting my sights on a solo career, not training as a primary school teacher. I also wondered what or who some of that group would end up teaching. Clearly not beginner recorders.

Chapter 8

Photographic evidence

By the time I was sitting snug on the Salisbury train, the countdown to the end of term was into single figures. Boxmouth carnival had been a scream, one way or another. Someone in my education group had suggested dressing up in tin foil dresses over our bikinis, and inviting punters to tear off a *tiny* piece in return for a donation in our collecting boxes. It was a good cause after all – starving children in the Horn of Africa this time. Fran was particularly keen on that. Between us, we must have cleaned out the Co-op and all the independent retailers of their cooking foil. By the end of the day we ended up with a collar of foil round our necks and our cossies on full view – on one of the hottest days of the year too. Comments of 'I'm roasting!' caused many a titter that day. Naturally, some of the local blokes had grabbed more than a tiny piece of foil for their fifty pence and others had jokingly offered a tenner for a full strip – cheeky so-and-sos! Some of the group ended up displaying their wobbly bits for longer than they'd have liked. In fact, there may have been a few locals who'd have willingly paid one or two of the girls to cover up some of their more unsightly flesh. That's the trouble when there's bread pudding on the canteen menu. It does nothing for the figure. Fran, however, played safe with a one-piece, complete with little skirt effect. She and bikinis are not compatible, she told us. Understandable, I guess, considering her lack of bust and tree-trunk thighs.

Before I set off, I was determined to leave nothing to chance on my trip home. A quick phone call to Eleanor helped me manage to wangle an invitation to tea on Saturday afternoon, emphasising – of course – that I wanted time alone with Tim. I turned up armed with stacks of photos, ready to jog his memory yet again. Wearing the same clothes as in one of the pictures was, I thought, a particularly clever touch. He was sat reading in their conservatory when I arrived, looking as scrummy as usual, except for his hair, or rather lack of it. He'd never favoured the closely cropped look before. It had been more of a Hugh Grant flopping-over-the-forehead-type-of-style, the sort my fingers could never resist. I wondered why he'd decided on such a drastic change... new image maybe? I tried not to show too much shock or disappointment. If *I'd* been out of circulation for so long I'd probably want a makeover of some sort to re-establish my identity.

'Oh hi Gilly,' he said, smiling. That was progress I thought, until he got up from his chair and tried to shake my hand. What was he thinking? I'd been hoping for something much more intimate.

'No need for formalities,' I giggled, trying to sound casual. 'Okay if I sit down here next to you?' I certainly wasn't going to be palmed off with the armchair with the rising foot rest. For a second or two he looked worried. Maybe he thought I was going to arm wrestle him to the ground and have my wicked way with him?

'So, how's it going at... er... Plymouth... no... um Torquay?'

His recent memory obviously wasn't too hot either.

'No, Boxmouth actually. But you remember Torquay, do you?' This sounded promising. Perhaps there was a glimmer of hope. My thoughts went straight to my stash of pictures, but it seemed too soon to bombard him with them. After all, our last meeting had been at the hospital, with Tim newly hatched from his chrysalis. Although I'd written to him I'd never had a reply. I hoped he'd taken time with the letter, and not tossed it aside with the hundreds of other good wishes messages that must have been sent. Apparently he'd even made the local headlines, with a radio crew descending on him, once he was home, I'd found out recently. He was quite the celebrity.

'Er, not really; Pete Willoughby's nephew has just signed for Torquay United, that's all.'

Despite the unpromising start, I steamed on, giving him edited highlights of my first year. When I say 'edited', what I *really* mean was 'sanitised.' References to Theo Rescorla – yes, that was his full name – were strictly off limits.

'So your main subject's music then? What instrument do you play?' My fragile hopes of a breakthrough plummeted, but I did my best to disguise my feelings. We evidently had a lot of ground to cover. Two years before, the sofa and some items of clothing would have been a little rumpled by now, but there we were, all prim and proper, light years away from any fumbling and rumpling. I started to wonder if he didn't find me attractive any more. The spark that had been so evident between us in the early days seemed to have died, along with his memory, although my love for him was just as strong as ever. I had to face it, I was still a relative stranger to him.

'Ready for a cuppa?' said Eleanor, bustling in rattling her tray of mugs and a plate of fairy cakes. 'And guess who's dropped by?' she added brightly. 'Such a nice surprise!' I'd been digging in my bag for the photos when there was a shrill 'Coo-ee!' and in bounced Lena, flashing a smile at Eleanor as she bustled out for more rations. This was the second time I'd met Lena Tuffin and she reminded me, as before, of an over-exuberant puppy.

'Oh hi, Gilly, fancy seeing you again!' Yes, *fancy*, I thought dismally, just as I was about to take Tim on an illustrated trip down memory lane.

'Like Tim's new hair style? Makes him look... ooh... really hot!' she simpered. 'Did it as a 'welcome back to work' prezzie, didn't I Tim?' He nodded genially.

Lena cocked her head to one side, as if expecting some applause. When it didn't happen, she pursed her lips and stared at us, noting the narrowing gap between our shoulders. I'd been engaged in a little furtive shuffling along the sofa since I'd sat down.

'Any room for a little one?' Without waiting for an invitation, she squeezed in on Tim's other side, kicking off her pumps and tucking her legs under, a grin lighting up her face. 'Ooh, piccies!' she squealed. 'Mind if I have a peep?' She grabbed the wallet eagerly before I could say a word and flicked through them, keeping the stack close to her chest. Every so often she'd pause and study one with much furrowing of the brow and then carry on flicking. I realised I was staring at her and when Tim caught my eye, I felt just a bit embarrassed about it and turned away. There was something about Lena's avid interest that disturbed me.

'Gilly, could you lend a hand?' It looked like I'd been assigned skivvy duty for the day instead of being a guest. Eleanor had reappeared with sliced Battenberg, an enormous teapot and a hot and bothered expression. I wanted to suggest she might remove her tights and her cardi, but decided against it. The veins in one of her legs bulged in an unsightly way. It can't have been pleasant for her on such a warm day. Meanwhile Tim watched us all, with a gentle smile playing on his lips. He seemed to be enjoying all the attention, although it wasn't as if he was an invalid. In fact I found myself wondering why he hadn't jumped up and said something like, '*That's okay Mum, I'll give you a hand.*' Thinking about it, I couldn't recall that sort of thing happening in the past. Eleanor liked to wait on her men hand and foot, then complain about it afterwards.

'Just finished work have you Lena?' I asked, as pleasantly as I could as we tucked into a pile of salmon and cress sandwiches. The geographical implications of Lena 'dropping by' made no sense unless she'd come straight from work.

'Yeah, that's right. Had a wedding party to do earlier on. What a nightmare! Some brides expect the impossible! I had to fix on a false bit in the end. There was no way she was getting ringlets with all those layers.'

'But you worked your usual magic, did you love?' chuckled Eleanor fondly. I was picking up a chummy-almost-part-of-the-family vibe that worried me. It was as if she was the baby cuckoo pushing the baby sparrow out of the nest, and I was the baby sparrow.

Lena just giggled and polished off another sandwich. Goodness knows where she managed to stash all the food she was shovelling away. She was like a bean stick. And just how long was this 'popping by' going to last, I wondered. Frank had come to join us by then, peppering his conversation with in-jokes and leg-pulls at Lena's expense, that showed how well she had wormed her way into his affection. He'd been like that with me once, but now he seemed more distant and reserved. I felt like an outsider and it upset me, although I tried to stay bright and cheerful as they joked together. I even managed a chuckle or two of my own, just to feel part of the gathering, but my heart wasn't in it.

'Go on, Tim, you can manage that last slice of Battenberg, can't you?' urged Eleanor, some twenty minutes later, after we'd covered the weather, brother Ian, and his latest girlfriend crisis – and rumours of the next-door neighbours' plans to emigrate to Australia.

'Emigrating are they?' asked Lena with a notable amount of interest for a bunch of relative strangers. '*My* mum and dad have been talking about a change of scene, as it happens. They're getting a bit bored with Firlea.' I was surprised it had taken them so long. Firlea was just a boring string development of dormer bungalows with no heart and nothing at all to recommend it.

'Not Australia, I hope,' put in Tim, pouting. Oh yes, I thought, why not Australia, and take your precious daughter with you, while you're about it.

At last she left, with much hugging and kissing all round – me included, although I think it was only for show – and then I grabbed the photos, which she'd left in a messy heap on the floor. She hadn't even bothered to tidy them away in the wallet.

'Remember Torquay?' I began, once we were alone.

'Well, not really.' Tim shook his head. 'Can't remember ever going there.'

'We went on your Auntie June's W.I. trip two years ago. There's a photo in here somewhere.' I flicked through the wallet, ready to amaze him, but couldn't find it. 'It must have slipped down the side of the sofa when Lena was having a shuftie,' I muttered. We pulled out the cushions and reached down the side and even looked underneath, pulling the sofa away from the wall.

'Perhaps it's in your bag,' Tim suggested. So I tipped out all my disgusting and embarrassing rubbish and checked every single zipped compartment, although the chances of a stray photo ending up in any of them was unlikely.

'Did you have them out on the train?'

'I think so.'

'Perhaps you dropped it and didn't notice.'

'Oh no, I hope not! It was the one of us on the prom, eating 99s and I was wearing this T shirt and jeans. You were in a striped top and chinos.' I thought this detail would add credence to my missing evidence.

'What about the rest of your snaps?' said Tim. It was quite endearing when he came out with such quaint, old-fashioned words as that. He picked up the pile, but for some strange reason there wasn't a single one of the pair of us amongst them. There were ones of Tim sitting on the beach, throwing chunks of pasty to seagulls, making stupid faces and arm in arm with Auntie June, and ones of me hopping around in the sea with my jeans hoisted up and posing by a statue in some gardens.

'There must be more here,' I gabbled, feeling very hot under the collar – in a manner of speaking. But there were just views of Torquay and assorted family groups – taken by one or other of us. It was very odd. 'And I was hoping one of them would jog your memory,' I moaned, dismally. Then I had a horrible sick and sinking feeling in my stomach, and it wasn't anything to do with the salmon sandwiches. Could it be, I wondered, that Lena had put them somewhere, such as in her handbag? Surely not. She wouldn't stoop to that would she? But after the business of the postcard, I wasn't too sure I could trust her any more.

'Are they on the sideboard?' Tim suggested, wandering over and peering hopefully under the embroidered runner Eleanor and Frank has brought back from Ibiza, and then behind the letter rack. 'Nope.'

Eleanor poked her head round the door while we were pulling out the furniture and generally ransacking the place like a couple of criminals.

'Whatever's up?' She stood there goggling at us, probably working out how long it would take to put the room to rights.

'Some of my photos are missing.' I told her. 'Lena was looking at them earlier, but I'm sure a few are missing now.' I tried not to sound as if I was accusing her of blatant theft, but that's obviously how it came over.

'Are you suggesting Lena took them?' Eleanor gasped, her eyes like saucers.

'Well, no, I didn't mean that,' I mumbled, although that's exactly what I was thinking.

'It's just that I know there were a few of Tim and me in the pile and now I can't find them. I... I thought maybe... er... Lena might have dropped some accidentally on the floor when she was looking at them... or...'

'Or you dropped them on the train,' Tim suggested again.

'Yes,' I sighed, 'probably under a seat on the train.' Accusing Lena wouldn't go down too well in the Rosewell household I realised, and Tim might be right.

'Or in Lost Property at Waterloo,' he suggested cheerfully, as if lost property offices were full of kind chaps only too ready to reunite dozy passengers with their belongings. Or in a rubbish bag, I thought dismally, that's already been dumped in a skip. Losing Tim's affection was bad enough, losing the photographic evidence made it all ten times worse. However, there was one thing for sure, Lena Tuffin was not going to get her mitts on my boyfriend, even though she might have got them on my precious pictures. From now on it was going to be war between us, subtly disguised of course.

Chapter 9

Endings and beginnings

After that disappointing trip home there were just a few days left of term. On top of the hours of practice with Laurel's three sheets of cavorting semi-quavers, I had two main orchestra rehearsals and, of course, the final run-through two days before the concert.

'Black and white would be a good idea,' Edwina casually mentioned after we'd puffed and scraped our way through Mozart's *Magic Flute Overture*, and one of the cellists had asked what we should wear.

'Telling us earlier would have been even better,' Brendan was heard to mutter, 'unless you include black boxers and a white vest.'

'What, and drive the women in the audience wild?' I joked, 'as well as most of the hot-blooded females in the orchestra.' I think Edwina might have picked up Brendan's mutinous muttering because she then qualified her instruction with the word *'sensible'* and *'as long as you keep your boobs and thighs covered.'*

'So that's a no-no for my lap dancing costume then,' I giggled quietly, causing a ripple of guffaws from the trombones and other assorted brass in the row behind.

So there was then a mass exodus to pillage Boxmouth's charity shops – of which there was an abundance – snapping up anything vaguely decent in the designated colours. To my great delight I found a jaunty little black silk bolero and puff-ball skirt in Cancer Research, and gleefully snaffled them from under the nose of one of Latterton's violinists. She gave me a dirty look, which I chose to ignore. With the strategic use of safety pins, my boobs were safely contained out of harm's way, and in no danger of distracting our exalted conductor or anyone else for that matter. Edwina, in her wisdom, had decreed that I should sit separately at the front of the ensemble for Rob's number, even though my solo was relatively short.

'You might as well stay put,' she told me when we were working out the seating for Laurel's extravaganza, 'and then we can re-group for the main orchestral pieces.'

Given a choice, I'd have preferred to have tucked myself away at the back. Prominent solo spots didn't sit too comfortably with me, but Edwina and the rest of the music tutors had worked it all out between them, having to accommodate the choir as well, so I stayed shtum.

On the night of the concert, the hall filled up with students, tutors, local dignitaries and a sprinkling of parents who were combining the musical entertainment with carting their offspring back home. Mum and Dad had dutifully booked into a local B & B and sat grinning at me from the fourth row. I hadn't realised it at the time, but the adjudication had taken place at our final rehearsal, so that the third year students would have their final mark before term finished. Three of the tutors had trooped in and sat at the back of the music hall with clipboards and inscrutable smiles. No wonder Rob and Laurel had been several degrees cooler than usual. In two years' time I'd be going through the same trial by semi-quavers. Although I'd decided already that I'd conduct my own piece when the time came, rather than ruin my composition with too many impromptu nervous squeaks. Some of my fellow musicians scrubbed up rather well when we were all assembled and not an unrestrained boob could be seen, although it was a close thing with some of the more daring females, who opted for necklines a few centimetres south of decent, much to the delight of some of the blokes. Desmond Morsby certainly had an eyeful when he sauntered past as we were tuning up.

The concert itself was a triumph, especially as all the third year compositions seemed to come off quite well. There were plenty of nerves and jitters between us, but because the marks were all in, nobody needed to worry too much about the performance, except for the sake of giving the college something good to celebrate. My strategy of keeping cool and limiting eye contact with The Beast paid off. I could hardly ignore him after all, especially as he was conducting one of the orchestral pieces as well as Laurel's and his own. Now that was weird – his piece I mean – *really* weird. He had scored it for high sopranos who had to gabble in a made-up language, after the style of Karl Jenkins, but even more way-out. And as for the instruments... there was even a bagpiper brought in specially and a whole percussion section of gamelan instruments, such as gongs and xylophones. The whole thing was very OTT. Was I surprised? Not in the slightest. To tell the truth, I was relieved he hadn't written incomprehensible parts for the woodwind section. Goodness knows what sort of horrors he might have included.

What kept me in a positive frame of mind was a snippet of overheard conversation between two of his groupies, who bewailed the news that he'd accepted a position in a top French music academy – hence the Paris trip. Whoopee! Soon those few miles of water were going to separate us for good. You see, if it really *was* a top French music academy, he'd hardly be bothering to leave it for an English one would he – unless it was one of the prestigious London ones. The likelihood of our paths crossing was about a million to one. The after-concert party was sheer joy in the light of that revelation. The college caterers had excelled themselves and the domestic team had transformed the main refectory into a relatively elegant partying venue. Several of the college rock bands took turns providing music you could actually dance to, and with the lights turned down, it was relaxing enough to enjoy without having to make small talk with people you'd rather avoid.

Mum and Dad opted out of the party, staying only for a glass of wine and then heading off to their B & B to wind down with tea and biscuits. Everything would have been fine except for… ah yes, there had to be something threatening to spoil what could have been a perfect evening. Brendan had been getting rather keen in the last few weeks of term. I guess I'd been sharing more than the usual amount of giggles with him at practices – just to keep my sanity – and he'd picked up the wrong vibes and thought I was available. We were just standing by the buffet table reflecting on the evening's experience and chuckling over some of the third years' offerings, when he clamped a predatory hand on my shoulder. Whoops, I thought. I tried to shrug it off – literally – but Brendan had put away three lagers by then and was too loosened up to detect my mood – or chose to ignore it.

'Shall we dance?' I suggested, hoping a jog around the floor would keep him from any more pawing.

'Great,' he agreed, but the band changed gear and we ended up in an awkward clinch, shuffling round in a circle, Brendan breathing heavily on my neck.

'Time for a cool drink,' I announced as the last chord sounded, and then shook myself free. Back at the bar he downed another swift half and his arm went back into clamping mode.

'Er, Brendan,' I said brightly, 'I think I need to head off now. Lots of packing to finish and all that.'

'Oh come on, babe.' Babe? Now I knew for sure, the drink was talking.

'Really, Brendan, I mean it,' I tried again, keeping pleasant. He was a nice guy, but I wasn't in the market for relationships.

'Babe, babe,' he murmured again, aiming for my mouth, but I wasn't keen on a face full of beery breath.

'You heard her,' growled a voice very close behind us. I all but leapt out of my bolero and puffball skirt. The owner of the voice must have been only a few inches away, possibly goggling at my cleavage from his superior vantage point. 'She wants to go, so how about unclamping your sweaty palm right now?'

The voice was a familiar one that I loathed with a red-hot passion. Yes, it was high and mighty Theo Rescorla. However, on this occasion I was grateful for his snooty intervention. For one scary moment I thought he and Brendan were about to enter into a drunken brawl, but Brendan was of moderate height and no match for Mr-High-and-Mighty. Amazingly Brendan unclamped his hand and shrugged off in the direction of some third year girls who looked as if they were hoping for some male attention.

'Thanks,' I mumbled, a word I thought would never cross my lips, given the company I was in.

'Hmm,' he murmured, avoiding any eye contact. 'You weren't bad for a Boxmouth student.' With that he strode off. High and mighty described him perfectly. He couldn't even be pleasant when paying a compliment, if that's what it was supposed to be. But did I care? Not a jot. He'd be off to France before long and out of my hair for good.

So the term ended and I had barely two days for a quick turnaround and then headed off to Torquay for eight weeks of dealing with plughole hair and mopping up the occasional unscheduled bodily function mishap. You wouldn't believe how little time there was for strolling on the prom, paddling in the sea and grabbing a bite to eat, when you're chambermaiding in a mid-price three star hotel. Correction: it was more like pushing your way past day trippers, steering clear of screaming kids and queuing for ages for soggy chips. Viv the manager persuaded us to take on laundry duties, with the appropriate pay rise – and even lend a hand in the kitchen when the Slovakian cook threw a wobbly one week and took to her bed with a bottle of vodka and an itinerant street musician. Viv didn't know about the vodka and the bloke, naturally. She thought Marta had been overdoing it a bit and needed a complete rest. Fran and I knew different. Our room was next door and the partition wall didn't leave much to the imagination. Still, the extra cash was handy. Whenever Fran and I were in danger of telling Viv where she could stick her job, we remembered the advantages of liquid cash flow and saved our comments for when she was well out of earshot. Sun, sea and sangria it was not, but it was surprising how much pleasure I had from reading my bank account print-outs and working out what I could buy with my savings before term started.

While blitzing the Bournemouth stores and boutiques at the beginning of September, I couldn't resist dropping in on Handbags and Leather Goods at Pearsons, to say 'hi' and catch up with old friends and enemies. Both Tess and Moira were flashing engagement rings, and Moira and her bus driver bloke were in the final stages of wedding plans whereas Tess and Jamie were still saving up for the ceremony of the century by the sound of it.

'Five thousand on a *dress*!' I gasped. 'You can't be serious!' I'd want to wear mine all through my honeymoon if it cost that much. Tess nodded smugly after divulging how much the swanky sparkler on her left hand had cost. In my opinion, a ring is a symbol of love and there's no point spending four figure sums on something that you could leave by the washbasins in a public loo or that might slip off while you were weeding the borders. I gazed at Tess's dazzling diamonds with more than a touch of jealousy. If Tim hadn't been mown down by a wayward cyclist, I would have been putting the finishing touches to the table favours by now and ticking off the acceptances on the guest list. Naturally they all wanted to know about Tim, and made sympathetic noises when I reached the amnesia bit.

'Bop him on the head and he'll soon come round,' Moira told me, as if she was an expert in the field.

'That's just a myth,' I replied calmly and tried to fill the gaps in her knowledge, but it was like casting pearls before swine. She simply wasn't interested.

Just as important as sorting out my winter wardrobe was a visit or two to Tim, to remind him that I once featured significantly in his life. Why he was still living with his mum and dad was somewhat puzzling. The trouble was, he was one of those people who'd prefer to save up for a good deposit so they can take a step onto the property ladder straight from living at home. With the way prices were rising in our area, it could take him ages, so every visit would mean Eleanor and Frank were in close attendance. It certainly used to limit our options in the romance department in the winter months when we were seeing each other, when al fresco canoodling was out of the question.

'I think he's going out later,' Eleanor told me when I phoned to find out if I could drop in on them. 'Cricket friends, I think,' she added vaguely.

When I arrived, he was togged up in smart designer gear – quite different from the styles in the pre-coma days – and looked good enough to eat. I wondered then if it was the cricket club award night. I'd been to a couple of them with him in the past and had sat bursting with pride when he'd won 'Best all-rounder of the season' award on one occasion.

'Nice shirt Tim,' I told him, then thrust a Torquay rock gift pack in his hands, adding a lingering kiss on his cheek for good measure. He took the ribbon-tied box a bit awkwardly and seemed to be struggling for the right response. A brief *'thanks Gilly'* would have done, but a few 'mms' and 'aahs' had me wondering if he'd lost his sweet tooth along with his memory.

'Very thoughtful,' he managed eventually, then asked me when I was going back to college. I managed to stop myself saying something clichéd such as, *'I've only just arrived and here you are trying to get rid of me.'* 'And did you manage to get your snaps back from Lost Property?' He asked, obviously convinced that I'd dropped them and the fact they were mysteriously missing was nothing whatsoever to do with a certain *Thieving Magpie.* (Opera by Rossini – my little joke! But you know to whom I'm referring.)

'No,' I told him, and shook my head. However, I'd never phoned Lost Property at Waterloo. I was so sure I hadn't carelessly dropped any, but that they'd been smuggled out by the other guest that afternoon.

'That's a shame,' he commented, but didn't sound very convincing. I think he was just being polite. All the while, however, he seemed on edge. Perhaps it *was* the annual cricket club bash and he was getting nervous about his chances of winning some cup or other. I'd heard that he was back in the second eleven, which was progress indeed.

I cornered him on the sofa and entertained him with episodes from my chambermaiding experience, making sure that I sprinkled them with my flirtiest smiles and the odd hand on his arm stuff, when I wanted to emphasise some little gem.

'I think I remembered something the other day,' he said, after a pause in my spiel.

'Really? What?' My pulse started racing. Could this be the breakthrough I'd been longing for?

'Something to do with buying tickets, not sure what for, but the number twenty-one came into it somewhere.' He shook his head and then checked his watch.

I licked my lips in anticipation. This was most certainly a sign that the mists were clearing.

'Tickets?' I gasped. 'Tim, they may have been concert tickets.'

'You think so?' He checked his watch again.

'What, a pop concert you mean?'

'No...'

The door opened and Eleanor stuck a frazzled face round, her eyebrows executing an interesting trampolining movement.

'Have you seen the time Tim?' she asked, obviously concerned about his timetable for the evening.

'Er... yeah... um...' he muttered, his eyes flicking around the floor region. 'Sorry, Gilly, but I'll have to say 'bye' for now... gotta be going...'

'Soon, *quite* soon,' Eleanor added, with more eyebrow gymnastics. Her heavy hints were clearly meant for lingering, unwelcome callers as well as for her busy son.

'Have a nice evening,' I told him, smiling warmly. 'I'll call you before I leave on Wednesday.'

'Yeah, great.'

'Bye, Gilly,' Eleanor said, hustling me to the door as if there was a fire drill.

As I was strapping myself into Mum's Metro and turning on the radio, I noticed the traffic in the close was getting busy. It seemed that nearly everyone was hitting the clubs and pubs except me. The next door neighbours had evidently stopped their dithering about pastures new and now had a spanking new 'For Sale' board along their drive. As I set off, the memory breakthrough perked me up considerably. Perhaps remembering the concert tickets would soon connect in Tim's mind with me and our wonderful relationship. I was *so* excited! In a few days, memories of the lost three or more years could come flooding back like a mighty torrent crashing through a leaky dam wall. If so, then he'd surely call me and tell me of his undying love.

'Yes, yes, yes,' I whispered, imagining the scene playing out in my imagination.

At the end of the road I paused long enough for a blue Mazda to turn in, and caught a glimpse of sleek auburn hair and a smug grin. It was Lena Tuffin, who didn't appear to have seen me. No wonder Eleanor and Tim were like a pair of cats on the proverbial hot bricks. So, he was taking *her* to the cricket club knees-up. I imagined a scene where Tim might have another flash-back while he was quaffing a pint or two and then realise he was with the wrong girl. I imagined it like the church scene in that old movie *The Graduate*, where the guy discovers his true love is about to tie the knot with a bloke she doesn't really love. That scene wasn't exactly like the Tim-Lena-Gilly triangle, but claiming back a lost love was certainly at the heart of it. In between bouts of packing, I had to nip into Growdon for last minute essentials such as jotter pads, filing wallets, a lip pencil and one or two of my favourite mags. Rosemary and Ray, old friends of the family, have the newsagents on the corner where Tim had his collision. They'd picked up a lot of extra trade at the time, with nosey parkers going in asking them for all the gruesome details. As it happened, they'd been dealing with a queue of customers buying lottery tickets at the time, so they hadn't witnessed anything worth talking about. The subject of a seven million pound rollover seemed to have been more newsworthy for some. I knew this because Ray and Dad exchange gossip and bemoan the state of retailing at Chamber of Trade meetings on a regular basis. I'd also learned that their daughter Penny was apparently the only one of the family who had seen what happened. She has quite severe learning difficulties, so questioning by the local constabulary turned out to be tricky.

Penny would sit near the shop window, watching the world go by while crocheting incredible doilies and suchlike. For all her learning difficulties, she has an amazing aptitude for creating things with her hands.

Rather than visit the national chain stores, I always buy my mags at Bagnalls and support the small independent traders. Being the daughter of a retailer, I know the importance of using local shops and keeping a vibrant and interesting high street. It's been the subject of dinner table chat all my life, so much so that I feel guilty shopping online or hitting the retail parks with their tempting megastores. So, before heading back to Boxmouth, I nipped into Rosemary and Ray's and stocked up on *OK* and *Hello* and a few tubes of my favourite mints.

'How's tricks?' asked Ray, as he keyed through my purchases. I gave him an update, which naturally included Tim's flashbacks.

'Bad business that,' Ray sympathised. 'Young man knocked for six like that! You'd never credit it, would you?'

'It's affected Penny too,' chipped in Rosemary, in a whisper, as she opened up a box of fruit pastille tubes to replenish the display.

'In what way?' I wanted to know.

'Well, she's taken to chanting the name of one of those famous Russian writers.'

'What?' I sputtered. I couldn't think of anything less likely, and wondered if Rosemary was joking, although if she *was,* she was disguising it very well. HoweverI knew she wouldn't joke about her daughter's disability. As we were talking, Penny was just a few feet away with an iPod plugged in, her head gently nodding to the rhythm, as she crocheted her way through a ball of silky peach yarn.

'A Russian writer? Why should she do that? Was there someone in the shop at the time chatting about Russian writers?' Rosemary and Ray's clientele was very mixed, so it seemed quite feasible that a couple of intellectual types might have been embroiled in discussing *War and Peace* while queuing for their Euro Millions Jackpot tickets, or whatever was the flavour of the month.

'We think there must have been,' remarked Ray, with a shrug. 'I know there were a few strangers in here at the time, as well as our regulars.'

The way he said that suggested that the usual bunch were more into chick-lit, sci-fi, horror or whodunits.

'So what does she say?' Tim's accident was surreal enough, let alone Penny's unusual manifestation. 'Tolstoy? Chekov?'

'No, Pushkin,' Ray told me, matter-of-factly.

'Pushkin?' I trawled the deep recesses of my brain and failed to retrieve a single enlightening fact about the writer.

'I looked him up,' continued Ray, nodding. 'Alexander Pushkin, 1799 to 1837, born into Russian nobility and best known for *Eugene Onegin*.' It sounded as if Ray had learned this by heart, which might come in handy one day in a pub quiz trivia round.

'Ah yes, the story that Tchaikovsky turned into an opera!' I said, surprised that I'd forgotten the music connection. 'Well, how weird. I suppose the two things happened at the same time – hearing the name mentioned and Tim's accident – and Penny remembered what she'd heard. It must have sort of locked it in her mind.'

I turned round and glimpsed her through a display of New Forest fudge, briar pipes and postcards and watched as she sat gazing out of the window. I wanted to go and say 'hello', but as I went closer I realised she was nodding off. As I watched her gradually drifting off, her lips moved and the sound I thought I heard was 'Pushkin'.

'You're right, she said "Pushkin",' I gasped and turned to meet Ray and Rosemary's gaze. 'How weird!'

Chapter 10

A scheming little vixen
and other developments

The night of the annual cricket club bash didn't mark the return of Tim's memory, because I heard nothing after that evening. Still, knowing that some memory *had* begun to trickle back kept me going. Back at college, being a second year had a completely different feel about it too. Of course there was a new intake from Latterton, and I was pleased to discover there was no one amongst the great and gifted who was anywhere near as rude and arrogant as Theo Rescorla. In fact, compared with him, they seemed quite normal. Some were highly skilled musicians, but they didn't parade it round in a showy way. Brendan had also cooled off considerably, much to my relief. As soon as he noticed a well-upholstered bubbly blonde lugging a double bass and rushed over offering to help her carry it, I knew my days of sharing a joke with him had more or less ended. Fran and Tony apparently had had a few rocky moments, but seemed set fair for a blossoming romance as the term wore on. Mollie seemed to be happy enough with Dan and was still as slim as a stick of Boxmouth rock, so it looked as if they were taking all the necessary precautions.

As the nights drew in Amy started knitting a nativity, complete with a heavenly host in several shades of white and cream. She'd never been one for parties and had a very outspoken opinion on the demon drink, as she called it. Could it be that she'd slip from young woman to little old lady and completely miss out her mid-life years? It was a depressing thought.

'Why don't you stay in and help me sew on sequins?' she asked one evening, waving a pair of angel's wings in my direction. I was fluffing blusher over my cheeks at the time. 'Can't think why you want to hang around in someone's smelly room with drunken yobbos and vomiting girls.' Can't think where she got all her information, but I decided against making some smart-alec remark.

'That's the future teaching profession you're talking about,' I wanted to say, but buttoned my lip instead. In fact, it would have been a great term if it hadn't been for one significant call I had from Mum. She would keep me updated on Growdon happenings, usually by letter. Although Mum was the proud owner of a Nokia, she found the necessary thumb exercise just a tad too taxing for regular text messaging. Most of her updates were the usual family stuff. I hardly ever heard from Liz who was too wrapped up with work, boyfriend and the swinging art scene in Oxford to keep in regular touch, and Sean... well, he's a closed book as far as his big sister is concerned. So the phone call? It was a somewhat worrying update on the Rosewell household, or rather something affecting them.

'We heard on the grapevine that Frank and Eleanor's neighbours have sold their house,' Mum told me, but not in her usual chatty tone. I was puzzled. It wasn't earth shattering news that warranted a special phone call.

'Oh yes,' I replied, 'that's nice for them.' As far as I knew, the Rosewells never had much to do with either of their neighbours, so a new set might have been quite welcome, if they were the right social background and so on. Eleanor could sometimes be a little snooty about those details.

'Hmm,' murmured Mum doubtfully, 'well, you might not agree when you hear who's buying.'

'Who?' I demanded, picking up Mum's negative vibes.

'Of course it could be sheer chance.' she rambled on, starting another circuit of the mulberry bush.

'Mum!'

'It's the Tuffins.'

'The Tuffins? Lena's family? Lena can't-keep-her-hands-off-my-boyfriend Tuffin, you mean?'

My heart clicked into overdrive and I swear there was sweat forming on my forehead, despite the central heating deficiencies of my digs.

'Yes, *those* Tuffins. Old Lily Glover told me in the doctor's waiting room this morning.'

'In the doctor's waiting room? Why, what's wrong Mum?'

'Oh nothing much. I just needed some more HRT pills,' she replied casually.

There was a moment or two of chilly silence while I digested the Tuffin house move bombshell. No wonder Lena's attention snapped into third gear when the subject came up in July.

'Oh Crumpets!'

'Exactly. Thought you'd say something like that,' she agreed grimly. 'Or worse.'

'She'll be popping in all the time borrowing a cup of sugar or—'

'I doubt it, people don't do that these days,' countered Mum.

'Oh, I wouldn't put it past her,' I snapped, 'to revise that quaint old tradition. I'm sure she'd make an art form of it.'

'What *are* you on about, Gilly?' she retorted in an exasperated tone. However, *I'd* seen the way that young woman had been working on a crafty scheme to plant herself in number one position for Tim's affections.

'Or leaning over the fence and chatting to Tim while she pegs out her lacy thongs and bras.'

The pictures my mind was creating contained X certificate material and sent a shudder right down to the toes of my fleecy mules.

'Possibly,' agreed Mum, 'but they won't be moving this side of Christmas, according to Mrs G. Goodness knows how she knows the details. I think she must be an old friend of Eleanor and Frank.'

'Ah, straight from the horse's mouth.'

'In a manner of speaking, yes. As a matter of fact Eleanor's mouth has struck me as having some equine properties, on more than one occasion.' We giggled.

'Well, thanks, Mum. I'd better get out my prayer mat and ask the celestial powers-that-be to lob down a spanner -'

'A what?'

'In the works, Mum.'

'Oh yes. Absolutely. Quite understand, love. Tim and Lena might get a bit too cosy.'

'Unless he has a memory breakthrough. I really thought it was a whisker away.'

'Hope it is, love.'

Mum didn't sound terribly convinced, but it's not difficult to find yourself feeling like giving up on something when you've been living with it for so long.

'The cunning little vixen!'

'Ooh, that's a bit harsh,' said Mum.

'An opera by Janacek!' I added. 'But it's a good name for Miss Tuffin.'

'Good to hear you haven't lost your sense of humour.'

'Don't bank on it, Mum,' I told her grimly. 'I think it's barely holding on by its fingernails.'

'Oh and your Auntie Sue is going on one of those booze cruises with her new fancy man, Terry Ridgeway.'

'Fancy!' I chuckled, 'I mean, well I never! So does that mean they're an item?'

'Hope so. Mind you, agreeing to go on a booze cruise together isn't necessarily a sign of undying love. Still I hope so. It's been a while now – being by herself.'

'Booze *cruise* did you say? Sounds a bit grand.'

'Ah maybe not a *cruise* as such. It's more of a daytrip to France – Calais I think. I've given her some cash so she can pick up a few bottles for us.'

Great, I thought, dismally. Still, passing the Christmas break in an alcoholic haze could possibly take the edge off disappointments in my love life.

Mum's main news was just what I didn't need to get me through the craziest part of term. Sewing sequins on angel's wings didn't quite take my mind off the house buying machinations in Growdon either. In fact, sitting quietly listening to Amy drone on about knitting patterns sent my mind racing back homewards even quicker. She wasn't the most scintillating in the conversation department. As Christmas rushed at us like a high-speed train, ideas for seasonal jollity popped up all over the place. A group of us decided that some upmarket carol singing would be a good excuse to knock up the local tutors and cadge some of their festive cheer – the liquid variety, naturally. We were collecting for lifeboats this time, a cause that resonated well in a coastal community. After trudging round the most affluent parts of the town, finding deserted homes or nervous au pairs – and therefore limited donations and certainly no liquid cheer – Beth decided we should abandon the tutors' homes and just look for signs of life in the next few available houses.

'Doesn't old man Morsby live round the corner?' piped up one of the lads in my education group, who also played the oboe. So we all trooped off after him and delivered a hearty rendering of 'While Shepherds Watched' in four part harmony with impromptu descant in the last verse from a few brave sopranos. I was rather hoping it would be another nervous au pair offering fifty pences, so we'd be able to scoot off quickly, but no such luck. With an extravagant flourish, the man himself whipped the door open while we were launching into 'All glory be to God on high' and stood at his threshold beaming.

'Come on in,' he said, rubbing his hands eagerly. 'Oh Trixie, could you rustle up some mulled wine?' he called to someone inside and then, after instructing us to remove our boots and shoes, herded us into a vast sitting room where a log fire blazed and a half emptied brandy glass stood abandoned on a little side table. Whether Trixie was their au pair or Mrs M herself, I did not know. I'd wondered what Desmond's other half might be like, after that business in his study. Perhaps she'd been a beauty in her youth, but had deteriorated drastically once she'd hit forty and was tending towards shrivelled prune qualities. Or maybe she was going through a mid-life crisis and had called a halt, or had severely rationed Desmond's conjugal rights. We were jostling for position in front of the crackling logs, when in breezed the most attractive forty-something woman I'd seen in ages.

'Here you are boys and girls!' she announced, carrying a huge tray of steaming glasses and a plate of mince pies. Our eyes were out on stalks – especially those of the lads. She had mid-brown hair that curled below her shoulders, a flawless skin, made up to enhance rather than overpower her features, and stylish jersey separates that emphasised her well-proportioned figure. Why, in heaven's name, was Morsby ogling students when he had all that beauty on tap?

We tucked into the steaming offerings and munched on home-made pies, which were followed by slices of stollen and bowls of crispy snacks. It was the best fodder we'd been offered that evening, by a mile. It certainly beat the bag of cheesy hoops and packet of humbugs that we'd snagged earlier.

'And all in aid of the lifeboats!' he exclaimed, thrusting a folded twenty pound note into our collecting box. 'Jolly good show!'

Trixie floated round with a jug to top up our glasses, while Desmond reappeared with a plate of feather-light sausage rolls.

'Fancy a roll?' he asked, suddenly looming up on my blind side. His tone sounded heavy with innuendo, but I ignored it and grabbed the nearest one and managed to spray crumbs on their beautiful carpet.

'Thanks,' I muttered, once I'd gained some control over my mouth.

His snaky eyes flickered lazily at me in a disconcerting way while I munched.

'Any progress with boyfriends?' he drawled in my ear.

'Oh yes,' I improvised, 'got a new guy back at home and we're in a rock steady relationship thanks.'

His eyes narrowed and then flickered again.

'That's good,' he acknowledged, with a sly grin. 'A pretty girl like you deserves to enjoy a slice of the action.'

'Oh definitely plenty of action,' I confirmed, nodding enthusiastically. 'I nip home every two or three weeks to keep the flame burning brightly – romance-wise.'

His eyebrows shot up to where his hairline should have been, had he still had any there. Desmond was well on the way to the Friar Tuck look.

'Well done, Gilly!' he chuckled, then winked and carried on with his plate. I hoped that would have put a stop to any further remarks.

After plenty of quaffing and scoffing, Beth reminded us we should be on our way, so we gathered in the hallway to collect our footwear. There were some childlike giggles coming from the top of the stairs and two blonde-haired cherubs were spotted watching us through the bars of the landing.

'Eloise! Giselle!' called Mrs M severely. 'To bed, you naughty girls!'

It was then that I noticed her accent. There had been rather too much of a hub-bub before.

'Swiss? Belgian? French?' I whispered to one of the other altos as we left.

'French I'd guess,' she whispered back, 'if the names are anything to go by.'

We carried on with our carols for another half dozen houses then called in at the *Rat and Rabbit* for our final performance and collected a fistful of fivers and so much loose change that our box felt like a lead weight.

'Well done, guys!' Beth called as we were about to go our separate ways. It occurred to me then that she'd taken on Tatiana's mantle most effectively.

I wasn't sure when Sue and Terry were planning to set sail and fill their boot with festive booze, but I had an interesting reminder about their trip when I went to my pigeon hole down in the music department just before term ended. I had an essay about symbolism in Mozart's *Magic Flute* to collect – all that freemasonry type stuff and initiation rites and so on, absolutely fascinating. Sure enough, the essay was awaiting collection, complete with an encouraging B+. There was also a pile of Christmas cards, one of which had a colourful sticker where the stamp normally goes. I'd assumed it was one of those charity parcel stickers that you get sent in the post, and that some public-spirited individual was doing their bit to spread the word and some festive cheer. Having scooped up the pile, I headed off back to the house to pack and finish the washing up I'd abandoned earlier. I was crouched close to the coal-effect gas fire, sipping a hot chocolate and opening my post, when I realised the colourful sticker was in fact a French stamp. Auntie Sue, I thought, although it didn't look like her handwriting on the envelope. More than likely it was Terry's. What a sweet thought! However, in her usual scatty way, she'd forgotten to sign it. It was an authentic French card, with Joyeux Noel printed inside. I made a mental note to thank her when I sent her my card. I'd decided to make my own for once, with one of those stamp and ink pad sets.

Christmas! What can I say? It was quite a rollercoaster of a time – emotionally – especially just before the day itself. The Growdon grapevine had been working overtime and the latest news was that the Tuffin purchase was going ahead without a hitch, with a neat little chain of four all lined up and everyone behaving themselves. I thought it was so unfair, considering how many broken chains you hear about with buyers pulling out and vendors changing their minds and so on. For once I managed to avoid check-out duty in Dad's shop, my bank balance still boosted by my summer in Torquay. I spent the time shopping and then gift-wrapping everything in brown parcel paper and red raffia bows. Sean has always kicked up a rumpus if there were no chocolate shapes dangling from the tree, so I hit the Growdon high street hoping to scoop up the last few for his secret Santa present. We'd all drawn a name and it was the third year in a row that I'd pulled out Sean's.

I was walking by Tim's bank just before lunchtime, the day before Christmas Eve and, on the spur of the moment, thought I'd put my head round the door and see if I could catch him on his way out, maybe to grab a quick sandwich together. One peep told me it was just a bit busy in there, with a queue snaking round and almost out of the door. The clerks were sporting Santa hats and flashing reindeer antlers, some looking somewhat embarrassed by their seasonal headgear. There was no sign of Tim, but interesting to note, Lena was one turn away from the front of the queue, cradling a huge cash bag and a paying-in book in her arms. I decided to head on up to Bagnalls in a desperate search for choccy stars and trees. The queue there was almost as bad, with several customers waving fivers for their Euro Million scratch cards. Penny was in her usual place, with mistletoe earrings and something red and glittery growing from her crochet hook. There was no iPod in place because Ray and Rosemary had 2CR on their radio, which was blasting out carols to keep up the spirits of the weary shoppers. I chatted to Penny, keeping the subject matter to her current project and the weather, while she smiled and nodded.

'Looks a bit like snow,' I observed, studying the sky and noting some leaden-grey clouds assembling in the east. I pointed at them and then watched the steady flow of pedestrians crossing over Bickerton Lane towards us.

All at once, Penny dropped her crochet hook and started trembling, tears filling the corners of her eyes.

'What's up, Penny?' No answer. She pointed at the stream of pedestrians, her finger shaking and pointing towards something that was clearly upsetting her.

'Pushkin, Pushkin,' she seemed to be repeating, although the only clear part of the word was the 'sh' sound.

'Pushkin?' I repeated over the blare of the radio. She nodded and her lower lip trembled. Maybe she was having a flashback. I looked out at the pavement and lane and stared at the people passing by. Lena was one of them, her money bag now flapping in the breeze.

'Pushkin, Pushkin,' Penny continued, her finger moving in line with Lena as she crossed over the lane and then passed out of sight. Penny shook her head and tears rolled down her cheeks. I patted her shoulder and then alerted Rosemary, who came to take her daughter for a cup of tea and a toffee fudge bar.

'She saw Lena Tuffin,' I whispered to Rosemary, before she disappeared, 'the girl who prevented the pensioner on the bike from—'

'Oh yes, I remember,' cut in Rosemary, 'seeing her obviously brought it all back.' She shook her head sadly. It occurred to me then that Lena must make that trip every day to bank the salon money. Poor Penny, with her vantage point she must have had dozens of reminders of that November 21st.

The Christmas festivities, when they came, followed the usual pattern. Of course we ate too much and I even managed to invite Tim round to have a meal with the Bonning household. It wasn't quite the same as in the pre-coma days because he treated us as acquaintances rather than friends.

'I've remembered something else,' he told us, after Mum had dished out seconds of roast veg. 'It was something to do with a speech. I was in a hall and there was a lot of applause.'

That sounded like the annual cricket club bash. But why had he only just remembered it? Going there in September should have jogged his memory – if that was where he was going that evening.

'Do you remember who was with you?' I asked him, knowing it was me.

He shook his head. 'I don't think there was anyone with me, as such,' he said, 'although there seemed to be a lot of people there… but I'm not sure.'

'Ah.' There wasn't much I could say.

'But that's progress, Tim,' commented Dad with an encouraging smile.

'Yes, definitely progress,' agreed Mum. 'Sounds like it's just a matter of time.' She caught my eye and nodded brightly. He excused himself after we'd had coffee and a few chocs each from the huge box Mum had been given by the partners at work. After that Auntie Sue arrived with Terry and we settled down to 'Give us a clue' and several glasses of their haul from the Calais shopping trip. In a lull in the evening, however, we had a very odd conversation.

'Lovely Christmas card, Gilly,' remarked Auntie Sue, 'you really needn't have gone to such trouble.'

'Oh well, I enjoyed making it,' I told her, 'and it was so sweet of you to think of sending one from France when you were only there a short time.'

'Er… um… I thought that 'thank you' bit in your card a bit odd actually,' she said, looking puzzled. 'You see, I didn't send you a card. We only just had enough time to choose the booze, pay for it and load it, didn't we, Terry?'

'Yep,' confirmed Terry, rolling his eyes as if remembering the experience with some discomfort. 'We were cutting it *very* fine.'

'I see. Well, I only guessed it was from you, because I knew you were going to France, although it wasn't signed.'

'Maybe you've got a secret admirer, Gilly,' suggested Auntie Sue.

'Hmm,' I muttered, hoping it wasn't a certain Desmond Morsby.

The French connection certainly made sense. That family probably popped across the Channel regularly to visit Trixie's relations and buy all sorts of pretty French things, cheap booze and maybe the odd pack of Christmas cards. The thought of him deliberately sending me an anonymous card was rather unnerving, but I thought it best to say nothing. It was pure guesswork after all.

'You don't sound very convinced, Gilly,' remarked Terry. 'A pretty girl like you should have a whole string of admirers.' Then he gave me a sly wink.

Later on, when I was getting ready for bed, I plucked the French card down from the shelf. The fact that it wasn't signed was so frustrating. It had a picture of wooden puppets on strings, each with a drum or trumpet, some music notes in a pattern round the edge and a sprig of holly in each corner. The artwork was really very good and I wondered if the artist's name was on the back. Cecile Du Blanc was all I could see. The sender either had something to hide or was in too much of a rush.

Could it really have been Terry Ridgeway, I wondered, putting two and two together and wondering if that sly wink he gave me was his way of telling me he'd been responsible. But would he have known my college address? Would he have had the time? I hoped it wasn't Terry. Life was complicated enough without having my Auntie Sue's new bloke becoming side-tracked with a girl half his age. Then another unwelcome thought came into my mind. Of course there was someone else with a French connection, but he wouldn't, would he? Not with *our* history… Theo Rescorla? Surely not. Definitely not. I lay in bed awake for ages that night, turning round in my mind the possible identity of the anonymous sender, feeling unhappy and doubtful about any candidate. Then, just as I was dropping off, I remembered dear Tatiana, but she wasn't the shrinking violet sort who'd be too disorganised to sign a card. Tatiana had always been a full-on, in your face character who'd surely have added a little comment with a good wish. Whether or not she was in France, was another matter. Still, I clung to the thought that she'd been the sender and that was reassuring enough to send me into a deep and peaceful sleep.

Chapter 11

Bazooka Billy

Nothing could have prepared me for the sight that greeted me when I arrived back at the start of term. Fran had arrived half an hour ahead of me and flung the door open before I'd barely turned the key in the lock. She faced me with mad, staring eyes and a quivering lip, as if in a state of shock.

'What's up, Fran? You look awful!' I gasped, wondering if she and Tony had started the New Year with a bust-up. I dumped my bags.

'It must have happened a while ago. It's a mess!' she gabbled.

'*What* must have happened?' I demanded, taking her by the shoulders.

'That!' she shrieked, standing to one side and pointing to a smelly pool of water along the hallway. 'The pipes have burst! There's water *everywhere!*'

It was indeed a mess. Most of the damage was on the landing, but because none of the doors fitted – it was an old Victorian terraced house – water had seeped into all the bedrooms and trickled down the walls to the ground floor.

'Have you reported it?'

'Yes, phoned college straightaway.' Of course Fran would have thought of that, whereas I would have gone into headless chicken mode. 'They'll sort out somewhere temporary for us. I think someone's coming down to inspect the damage later.'

Of course it was our fault for turning off the central heating on the day we left. It had been a fairly sunny and dry December and we thought we were being frugal at the time, however, over Christmas the temperatures had plummeted and forecasters were telling us it was the second coldest December since 1659 in central England. It never occurred to us that coastal towns would be as badly affected. We thought it would be relatively mild. How wrong we were. Still, there was nothing any of us could have done about it.

Amy and Mollie arrived within minutes, both shocked by the devastation that faced them. Unlocking my door, I was horrified to see patches of mould starting to appear on the carpet and water stains on the floor cushions and rag rug that I'd bought to liven up the room. Worst of all though, was the discovery that my shoebox of photos was past saving. I'd left it on the floor next to my bed and the evil tide must have swept straight at it, fusing all my precious pictures together in a sticky mess. What Lena Tuffin had started, the sub-zero temperatures had finished off in dramatic style. I picked up the soggy pile and tried to peel it apart, but the slightest pressure lifted the print clean away. The shock of the discovery hit me like a thump in the solar plexus and tears spurted down my cheeks.

'Who's wailing like a banshee?' came Mollie's voice outside in the corridor.

'Gilly?' She rushed in holding an armful of dripping towels. I hadn't realised I'd been making so much noise. 'Oh bad luck,' she said, seeing my ruined keepsakes. 'Amy's wool pile's a washout,' she sighed and then she wandered back to finish her own salvaging.

Within an hour or so we'd been allocated temporary digs, but had to split into pairs. Fran and I found ourselves sharing a room chez Doreen and Eric Guy, a good twenty minutes' walk from the campus. They offered seasonal B & B, with a single rose on their sign, but it was a better prospect than rising and falling damp and galloping mould.

'Come in, dearies,' welcomed Doreen, trying to fling an arm round us as we struggled in and giving us a blast of nicotine mixed with lavender scent on the way through. Apart from her fuchsia lace-ups, orange lipstick and parrot earrings, everything else about her was monotone beige. Husband Eric, a wiry man with trim moustache, stood to attention at the end of the hall, snappily turned out in Viyella check and well-pressed slacks. I ducked away from Doreen's motherly arm and managed to collide with a brass umbrella stand, then narrowly missed a collection of corn dollies lined up along the wall.

'Whoops!' I exclaimed. Fran caught my eye and winked at me once she'd managed to stop Eric launching into his life history with a tactful, 'perhaps later.'

After two weeks we were well settled into the term and our new digs. Our tiny room was a triumph of shabby chic meets charity shop, with a touch of kitsch. Doreen and Eric were keen collectors, and their impressive displays were generously shared around every room of the house. Sitting down in the loo was particularly challenging, with so many knitted loo roll covers jostling for position. Doreen was also a keen crochet aficionado and had fashioned numerous cushion covers in cheery shades, some of which called for the use of sunglasses to appreciate their bold colour schemes. Still, the house was warm, clean and dry and we were welcomed as surrogate daughters to make up for Doreen's all-male production line – Adam, Alan, Andrew and Antony – all of whom are now living independently. Evidently Doreen had been so transfixed with the first page of a book of baby names that she'd never bothered to look any further.

Whenever we popped our heads outside our door, Doreen or Eric would often appear and offer us a cup of tea, coffee or cocoa, depending on the time of day. According to Eric, his wife's brew 'puts hairs on your chest', forgetting that was the last quality we wanted from our beverages! When he handed me a cup of the dark brown liquid and I foolishly wrinkled my nose at it, he shamed me by declaring, 'You'll not want that gnat's pee rubbish that some people call tea, will you?' Rather than incur Eric's sarcasm, I learned to accept their generous offers and keep my mouth shut and my nose-wrinkling under strict control.

If we wanted to watch TV in between our lectures and scintillating social life, we had to sit with Eric and Doreen in their chintzy sitting room, complete with cabinet of dinky toys and animal themed teapots. We soon learned that Doreen and Eric were quiz show addicts who shouted out answers in their own private point-scoring battle of the brains. The addition of two trainee teachers in their household turned out to be a welcome bonus. Enlisting us and our brain cells, not only increased the competition but also gave our stay an interesting extra dimension

'Hey, Gilly, be in my team for the music round lass and I'll slip you a Jaffa cake,' wheedled Eric, one day.

'Eric Guy, you are shameless!' snorted his wife. 'Don't listen to *him*, Gilly,' she whispered, 'be in *my* team and I'll make it *two* Jaffa cakes and a strawberry cornetto!' Fran received the same overtures when it came to the literature round and our cake consumption rocketed.

Eric was also keen on the 'gee-gees' as he called them, and every Saturday afternoon you could hear him shouting 'Come on, my son!' as he cheered on the runners from Market Rasen or Newbury. If you dared to ask him a question, he'd interpret that as an invitation to give a full run-down on the history of the sport. Eric was an expert on life histories, full stop. After the first few times I decided I wouldn't make that mistake again. We were allowed to use the dining table for our written work, but to be truthful, I preferred to stay in college and hide away in the library – well away from the windows, naturally – to limit eye contact from passing tutors. Amy and Mollie managed to land themselves a prize catch in accommodation – each with their own room and telly. Some people have all the luck! They even had their own entrance and I'd bet fifty to one, that Dan had also been sampling the delights of the upmarket lodgings.

Valentine's Day came and went without anything vaguely heart-themed in the post for me. Mum had sent me one of her newsy updates, which confirmed my worst fears about the Rosewells' neighbours' sale – it had gone through without a single hitch. The only delay had been due to emigration red tape for the vendors. This was all gleaned from Lena, by way of a sneaky ruse on my part. I'd persuaded Mum to book herself a trim, although she'd taken a lot of convincing, and it wasn't because Lena had made a hash of my cut either.

'But Angie's been my hairdresser for years,' Mum protested, during one of my phone calls. 'She'd be really upset if she knew someone else had been getting their hands on my hair. You know she comes round regular as clockwork every six weeks. It wouldn't be fair on her.'

'I know, Mum,' I sighed, 'but Lena Tuffin has been trying to get *her* hands on Tim and I need to know what's going on. Surely you can sacrifice just *one* trim or colour rinse for me. Tell Angie you had an emergency cut on a three-day break at a Warner Leisure Complex. It's for a good cause, after all.'

'People don't have emergency hair appointments, Gilly,' she pointed out, unconvinced by my plan, 'emergency dental treatment yes, but having your roots retouched or an inch off your fringe hardly counts as an emergency.'

In the end, she agreed to do it and reported back every detail she'd managed to pump from Lena, after telling her she'd been highly recommended by several friends.

'Start with flattery,' I'd advised, 'she's a sucker for it.'

So, in the second half of February, around a year since Lena Tuffin had first burst into my life, she and her family took up residence on the outskirts of Growdon and within sugar sharing and undies flapping distance of the Rosewells. It was yet another nail in the coffin of my hopes to become Tim's wife. Little by little he seemed to be drifting out of reach, as Lena seemed to be closing in for the kill. Yet, one lightning flash of memory could scupper her devious plan and re-establish me as No.1 in his life. Much as I'd have loved a quick visit home, the term – like many of the races Eric watched – was full of hurdles that I had to clear. In the summer term all my year were due to be shipped off over the border into Cornwall for our second teaching practice. That was preceded by a short fact-finding visit before Easter, to meet our classes and get an idea of what we'd be expected to teach. Lesson planning would then begin in earnest.

When the list of our schools went up in the education department, I was struck by the places, many named after obscure saints or bristling with zeds. We were about to enter a different world, one of vast open spaces with bleak lunar landscapes, treacherous rocky coves, disused tin mines and precious few shops. We had to pack for an overnight stay and, for some of us, the journey to our school took the best part of a day. Fran pitched up in a village near Bodmin Moor, but I was further north, in a quiet resort with sand dunes that put Boxmouth's to shame. But would *OK* magazine find its way to this last outpost of the British Isles? I wasn't sure and made a diary note to stock up at Bagnalls in the holidays.

I was allocated to the Penmorgan household – a family of seven, the five children having to squeeze into two bedrooms because of me. And there was sand EVERYWHERE in the slightly shabby three-bed bungalow: in the butter and marmalade dishes on the breakfast table and covering every floor and flat surface in the entire building. I know toast is supposed to be crunchy, but toast in the Penmorgan household crunched in a more sinister way. The youngest toddler wobbled around with drooping nappies and a constant layer of grime stuck to its face. At the other extreme, two skinny teenage girls slept top to tail in a single-bedded box room. The school where I'd be teaching was a short walk up the road. It was a class of thirty 9-10-year-olds and the class teacher was a mountain of a woman, with a laid-back disposition towards life and a positive attitude towards students. Who'd blame her? She'd have a month to catch up with her paperwork and fill in the odd report on my progress. I thought I'd get on well with her after our meeting. How I'd cope with sand in the sandwiches, on the soap and in my bed I was not so sure.

After that short visit we were back at college for a couple of weeks before the Easter break. In that time, something I saw on Doreen and Eric's TV gave me my own flashbacks and sent me reeling. Yes, we were still there. The refurbishment at our house was taking *much* longer than we'd hoped: new plumbing system, new carpets and redecoration etc. On the day in question, it was just an ordinary boring Saturday afternoon and I was down in the sitting room working on my teaching practice plans when Eric came in, brandishing his latest copy of *Sporting Life.*

'Mind if I watch the gee-gees?' he'd asked, with a twinkle, but turned the set on before I'd opened my mouth. He zapped through the channels and settled himself in his favourite armchair.

'Fine by me,' I told him. I'd been on his quiz team the previous evening and was the proud owner of a virgin packet of custard creams, just because I knew Mussorgsky composed *Pictures at an exhibition.*

It's odd how you can sometimes block things out on the TV, even with the volume turned up. It's also interesting how some remarks can cut right into your subconsciousness.

'Now into the parade ring we have number seven 'Bazooka Billy' trained by Joe Rescorla...' A homing device in my brain picked up the name instantly and I couldn't help but follow the action on the screen.

'Rescorla?' I repeated, aware of a butterfly fluttering starting in my chest.

'He's the trainer,' Eric commented knowledgably, 'one of the best.' He consulted his paper, then added. 'Owns that little beauty as well.' I watched the scene at the racecourse, as a horse was being led by a young stable lad.

'Really?' Of course, there could have been no connection whatsoever, but an odd sort of compulsion made me drop my pen and curl up next to a pile of Doreen's cushions on the sofa.

Eric reached for his mobile and I heard him putting a fiver on Bazooka Billy.

'Sixteen to one!' he told me, with a twinkle in his eye. 'Crazy price!' He tapped his nose in a knowing way. By now the camera was picking out little clusters of owners and other hangers-on who appeared to be giving their jockey last minute instructions, while he prepared to mount. Eric sensed that I was in the market for some of his wisdom.

'It's the Lincoln Handicap, and that's the parade ring,' he told me. 'It's the first race of the flat season.'

'Handicap? Why a handicap?' Although I'd picked up some of the jargon, most of it was still foreign to me.

'Ah, well you see, the horses have to carry weights in their saddles, to make sure they're all starting on equal terms. It mainly depends on the horse's form.'

He noted my blank look, although I was only half looking at him as I scanned the screen for horse number seven.

'They *should* all cross the line at the same time, but I've never seen that happen!' he chuckled.

'Oh. And *flat* season?'

'No jumps, no hurdles, they run it over a straight mile, which means no bends,' he said. 'There's my boy,' he added, pointing excitedly, 'Bazooka Billy, beautiful beast, just look at him!'

The horse *did* look handsome, but I was avidly studying the cluster of men and women, all taking turns to pat him. Because of the headgear it was difficult to make out the features of some of the group.

'Which one's the trainer? The owner?' I asked casually. Eric pointed out a middle-aged man in country tweeds who was giving his jockey a friendly earful. The jockey nodded and smiled, but Joe's face was only side on. Even so, I fancied I could see a family resemblance – the same strong profile with pronounced brows.

'Is he married? Only there was someone with that name at college last year,' I asked Eric.

'Bit old for you, Gilly!' Eric chuckled.

'No, I don't mean that,' I protested. 'I was just wondering if the chap at college might be his son, that's all.'

'Ah, I see. Well Joe *was* married once, to Julia Faversham, as she was – an absolute stunner. But they divorced after only a few years. He's a bit of a ladies' man, by reputation.'

'Any family?'

'That I don't know,' replied Eric. 'I haven't heard of any.' The camera panned round and homed in on some others. That's when I saw him, all togged up in flashy morning suit, with an older couple.

'That's him!' I exclaimed.

'What? The Rescorla chap? Old flame is he, Gilly?' Eric chuckled.

'You've gone all pink in the cheeks, lass!'

The door opened and Fran slid in, in time to catch Eric's last remark.

'Wondered where you were, Gilly,' she said, picking up the atmosphere in the room, 'and no, Eric, he's not an old flame. Gilly and Theo Rescorla were old sparring partners last year.' She turned her attention to the TV when she realised no one was paying her any attention. 'I say! There he is!'

She sat down and there were now two of us gawping at the set with our mouths open.

'Not Joe's son then?' I couldn't help being just a little curious.

'Nephew, more like,' observed Eric, studying the group clustered around number seven. 'I'd say that the other bloke is Joe's brother, and the younger one his son.'

'Well, well, not just dishy and talented,' giggled Fran, 'but well-connected too!'

'No manners, arrogant and self-opinionated,' I reminded her, 'rude... snooty...'

'And miles away, so calm down lass and let's watch the race, shall we?' I could tell Eric was wishing he had his own telly upstairs.

'Yes, but Lincoln's not far enough, as it happens,' I muttered, remembering the French connection.

'Doncaster,' snapped Eric, sounding rather edgy, 'the Lincoln is run at Doncaster. Now lass... button your lip and I'll slip you a couple of Jammie Dodgers later, or a whole packet if Bazooka Billy wins!'

Fran and I exchanged glances. 'Fancy him yourself, do you?' I goaded. 'Tony wouldn't like to know he's got a rival!' Fran made a face, roughly translated, 'so what!'

Eric swivelled his eyes round and put a finger to his lips. By then the runners were all lined up ready for the off. Some bloke in the crowd was then picked out by the cameras. He was wearing a long shaggy coat and a hat with earflaps and was waving his arms around as if he was sending a message by semaphore. The commentator then told us that the odds had shortened on two of the runners, including Bazooka Billy. On hearing this, Eric rubbed his hands and grinned.

'He's come in to ten to one, from sixteen to one!' he told us smugly. 'I told you it was a good price!'

The crack of a pistol sounded and the horses set off in a flurry of tossing manes and tails.

'Look out for peach and purple, with black stripes across the chest and round the cap,' Eric told us, but it was virtually impossible to pick out number seven from the knot of horses, until they started to string out.

'Mr Melody is coming up on the rails,' the commentator told us, 'and boxing in Bazooka Billy.' Eric muttered a few expletives under his breath and balanced on the edge of his chair. 'Now Mr Melody is a length clear.'

In spite of myself and my aversion to the name Rescorla, I was willing the jockey in peach and purple to find his way out of the pack, until the one in front of him moved to the outside and started steaming ahead.

'Come on, my son!' urged Eric, jumping up from his seat and waving his arms around.

'Come on, Bazooka Billy!' I screamed.

'He's heard you,' joked Fran. 'Look, he's moving up on the inside!'

Sure enough, Bazooka Billy's jockey had given his mount a quick flick on the flank and the horse had responded, his ears pricked.

'And now Bazooka Billy's closing in on Mr Melody, with Daffy Duck and Solomoto leading the chasing pack.'

'Come on, my son!' yelled Eric, thinking of his sixteen to one bet, no doubt.

'Yes, yes it's neck and neck!' The commentator's jabber went from mildly unintelligible to virtually incomprehensible and we were all on our feet jumping up and down, waving our arms in the air, with the crowds in the stands yelling fit to burst. The two leading horses were straining for all they were worth as they approached the line and anyone like Eric, who'd placed a bet earlier in the afternoon, was probably just as red in the face as he was.

Doreen came rushing in with a cloth and a squeegee and joined in the general hysteria, managing to spray water all over the place, although none of us cared or dared to take our eyes off the screen for an instant. It was totally gripping.

'He's got his nose ahead!' I shrieked. 'Come on, Bazooka Billy!'

The jockey flicked his whip, all scrunched up over the horse's neck as the commentator's verbal diarrhoea shot up an octave and the crowd went wild.

'And Bazooka Billy crosses the line, by a short head!' We all leapt up and down hugging each other as if we'd personally scored a winning goal for England or a century to win the Ashes. Even Fran was yelling her head off, which – for a non-sporty type – was pretty amazing.

'Sixteen to one! Sixteen to one!' crowed Eric in jubilation, punching his fist in triumph. 'Eighty quid! Eighty quid clear – I always pay my tax up front! Eighty smackeroonies!'

'Drinks are on you tonight then,' giggled Doreen, 'and make mine a double gin and tonic, ooh and a bag of pork scratchings!'

We all collapsed back in our seats and watched the jockey as he made his way to the unsaddling enclosure, met by a jubilant Joe, who patted the horse and walked alongside chatting as he went. By this time, the commentator was reeling off a whole lot of facts and figures that went right over my head, but by the look of Rescorla senior, this was quite an achievement. Then the rest of the family waded in, all backslapping the little jockey and bursting with second-hand pride at his efforts.

'Ooh, Mr Dishy!' squealed Fran, knowing she was winding me up on purpose, 'bet he'll be sinking a few glasses of champers tonight!'

'And then nip back on Eurostar, out of harm's way.'

Doreen had left us quivering with excitement for a minute or two, but then reappeared with a bottle of amontillado, four teeny glasses and a sharing size pack of smoky bacon crisps.

'Better not say 'no',' I whispered to Fran, as we grabbed a handful each and watched as Doreen did the honours with the bottle. 'Who knows, we might even develop a liking for sherry!'

'To absent friends,' she announced a few moments later, raising the chunky little gold-rimmed glass.

'And enemies,' I added, 'and to Eurostar and their dedicated staff, to a swift departure and safe arrival on the other side of the Channel.

'And to Bazooka Billy!' added Eric, after raising a questioning eyebrow in our direction. 'God bless him! And may he enjoy his oats tonight. I certainly will!'

Doreen threw him a saucy look and sniggered, so Fran and I left them to it. After all, there was plenty of time to claim my Jammie Dodgers.

Chapter 12

Supping Tetley and eating Vera's fancies

Two days later, I had some amazing news… Dad had been nominated for a business award. And even better, the gala night was to be in my Easter break. Mum phoned me up to tell me the news, obviously bursting with pride. I was quite excited myself and started speculated on the chance of splashing out on a new outfit for the occasion. Dad would want his fan club to turn up looking the business, naturally. I tried telling Mum about the horse race, but it – like horse racing jargon – went over her head. I don't blame her. Dad's news was far more important.

It was great to be back at home at last with only a week to the big day. I learned that there were several categories in the awards and that Dad had been nominated because of the ethical nature of his shop and recognition of his effort and determination in championing fair trade. We all agreed that he certainly deserved a public pat on the back, even if it only came in the form of a certificate to put in the shop window. I'd never heard about this award event happening in Growdon before and said as much to Mum.

'Ah, but it's a new thing,' she told me. 'I think the town council, social services and the chamber of trade are responsible for it. I saw something in the Growdon Gazette back along.' So we quickly rummaged through our wardrobes and came to the same conclusion, that a shopping spree was definitely in order.

We decided to give the Growdon shops our trade and headed off for the designer outlets in Forest Court. Mum quickly found a lovely inky-blue cross-cut skirt that flattered her figure. There was a pretty matching top, with tiny beads around the neck and cuffs. She looked stunning and every inch the winning shopkeeper's trophy wife. However, I was more difficult to please. We carried on browsing in the other shops and at last, I found exactly the right below-the-knee shift in deep teal – one of my favourite colours. So I took it to the changing rooms and guess who was just emerging from one of the cubicles with a glittering black number over her arm…? Her name begins with an L and it wasn't Lily Glover. Lily's more in the Cancer Research and AgeUK range. Oh yes, it was my confirmed enemy Lena, looking smug and self-satisfied.

'Oh hi, Gilly,' she chirruped, 'nice colour!'

'So's yours,' I told her, although I find black quite depressing as a rule, probably because it doesn't suit me. Wearing black as an orchestral player, however, goes with the territory, as the cliché goes. 'Very elegant,' I added.

She glanced at it and smiled. 'And worth every one of the ninety pounds,' she crowed, 'seeing as it's such a special occasion.'

'Hmm, always worth spending that little bit extra, isn't it!' I agreed with her, although my teal shift was more in the fifty pound bracket, and much more than I'd usually spend. Lena stood with her head on the side, as I'd noticed before when she's waiting for a gasp of astonishment or a round of applause.

'Special occasion?' I hardly dared ask her, but knew she'd tell me sooner or later.

'I've been nominated for an award,' she boasted.

'You too?' At least I could match her for once.

Her simpering smile crumpled for a second as she digested my reply.

'Yes, my Dad's been nominated for a business award.' Perhaps Cut Above The Rest was in the same category, I wondered.

'How nice.' The tone of her voice somehow didn't match her words. Eleanor Rosewell sometimes shared this shortcoming. 'I've been nominated for a community service award – local hero or heroine category. Honestly, I can't imagine why. I mean, I only did what anyone would have done. It wasn't any big deal.' She was obviously referring to the Bickerton Lane incident.

No big deal? However that was exactly how Lena was treating it.

'That was ages ago though, wasn't it?' I remarked.

'I know,' she giggled, 'people have long memories.'

'Not everyone though.' She knew exactly what I meant and how tactless that remark might have been if it hadn't just slipped out as it had, all gushy and innocent.

'Yeah, course… sorry… not so good for Tim of course.'

I told her I'd better get a move on or Mum would wonder where I was, so she went off to part with her ninety hard-earned pounds while I went to try on my fifty pound bargain. It was perfect and fitted beautifully over the hips, with a gentle scooped neckline that hung in soft folds and three-quarter length sleeves: smart and sexy at the same time. Unlike Mum's and Lena's there was no bling, so in a year's time it would make the ideal interview outfit. Yes, in a year's time I'd be filling in forms and going for interviews! Ideally, I'd be hoping for a convenient vacancy in Growdon, but anywhere within a ten mile radius would be fine. Dad had already promised me I could have his old VW when he was ready to upgrade to a newer model. I was hoping Tim didn't have the same intentions for his love life because my suspicions were that Lena surely had her claws into him. I went to pay for my smart teal number and there was Mum, valiantly wearing a patient smile on her face while Lena prattled excitedly.

'Oh there you are Gilly, Lena and I have been swapping nomination news!' she told me with the slight raise of an eyebrow.

'Oh, so do you know who nominated you?' I asked. Then Lena became uncharacteristically coy and dipped her eyes to the floor.

'Well… er… it's a closely-guarded secret…' she whispered.

'Same with Gordon's,' Mum told her. 'He *thinks* it's someone from the Chamber of Trade…'

'Oh, what you mean one of his mates?'

'No idea. If it is, they haven't let on.'

'But wouldn't they want to be nominated themselves?' I pointed out. 'Especially if they're shopkeepers as well. Why nominate someone who'd be competing against you?'

'Well, there's nothing to stop people nominating each other, is there?' replied Lena, wide-eyed and innocent.

'What? You mean, *I'll scratch your back if you scratch mine*?' gasped Mum. By the look on her face she found this suggestion highly insulting, but Lena just shrugged and managed a pale imitation of her earlier grin.

'Oh well, we'll soon find out won't we?' She checked her watch and flicked her hair back. 'Must be off, there's a cut and blow dry waiting for me in ten minutes. See you on the night!'

We waited until she'd scooted out of the door before we dared to open our mouths. There seemed to be a head of steam building up inside my head, like a pressure cooker about to blow. However, Mum's must have been worse.

'The cheek,' she hissed, trying to keep her voice down, 'suggesting it's all a set-up!'

I grabbed Mum's arm and dragged her out of the door. An assistant who was rearranging one of the displays had already aimed a few disapproving frowns in our direction.

'Par for the course Mum, and typical of Lena. I don't believe she has an iota of tact.' So I took Mum to Lucy's Patisserie and we indulged in cappuccinos and an apple Danish each, by which time, both of us had simmered down considerably.

After that, I left Mum to go to the library and thought I'd go to Tim's bank, knowing Lena was safely back at the salon. For once, he was due for his break and agreed to spend it with me, although I was so full of coffee and pastry, I wasn't in need of sustenance myself. We settled on a bench in the little park by the war memorial and it was like old times, catching up with news and sharing the odd joke.

'That Eric sounds quite a character,' he chuckled, when I told him about Eric's fascination with horses and TV quiz shows.

'Yes, I've learned a lot about gee-gees over the past term.' However, I didn't mention the name Rescorla during our chat. Tim would probably tell me I was harbouring resentment against the guy, which I know is true – and tell me I should just let it go. Thing is, I'm not ready for that yet, or ever. After chuckling over my stories of Eric and Doreen, Tim then revealed that he'd had another flashback. Hopes of Gilly Bonning establishing herself in his life briefly woke from their deep slumber. He had, after all, been smiling in a particularly heart-warming way during our chat. It was as if we were connecting again, just as in the early days of our friendship.

'I remember being on a stage, with a crowd of faces smiling at me. The cricket club chairman was presenting me with a cup.'

'Then?'

'I remember a few camera flashes and that's about it. The doctors have told me that memory usually comes back gradually, with the events further back in the past being remembered first.'

'Well that fits.'

'Yes, but then I've also remembered the concert tickets...'

'Which was connected with the day of the accident. So nothing else?'

He shook his head. 'My mind seems to be pulling all sorts of odd bits out of the bag. It's very confusing. One of the doctors said you can have islands of amnesia.'

It sounded to me as if Gilly Bonning was a castaway on one of those islands.

'Tim, we were going to a concert in Bournemouth on the day of the accident. Remember that letter I wrote to you shortly after you awoke from the coma? The accident happened on my birthday.'

'Oh the letter, yes. I'm afraid it didn't make much sense to me. It was like reading about someone else's life.' He held my gaze and must have realised how gut-wrenching that must have been for me.

'On your birthday too,' he sighed. 'What an awful birthday present!' For a moment I thought he meant the concert was an awful present and my face must have shown it.

'No, not the concert, er, obviously not the concert, I mean the accident.'

'It was the worst birthday ever,' I admitted, but never dreamed of hinting that I'd had a few unrealised hopes for that evening beyond holding hands with him in the concert hall. A couple of mums with buggies strolled past, their little ones enjoying a quiet snooze. For all my hopes of a career in education, I felt an ache inside, wishing I could be like them, happily married to Tim and proudly pushing our own baby. No sense daydreaming, I told myself. With fifteen months of my training to go I couldn't afford to be broody. There was the small matter of a student loan hanging around my neck.

My mind zapped back to the accident and then to Lena's news.

'Do you see much of the old bloke who knocked you over?' Tim swallowed a mouthful of sandwich and nodded.

'Bill Kerridge? Once or twice, but he's stopped using his bike. His wife's banned him.'

'Probably wise,' I agreed, nodding.

'Anyway, I'll be seeing him soon, at the awards night.' He frowned and started folding his empty crisp packet into small squares. I wondered if it was me being overly suspicious, but Tim seemed just a tad awkward about the event. It was time to tell him about Dad's nomination.

'Wow that's great,' he said with a grin. 'So you'll be there as well?'

'Naturally. Look, I've just bought this gorgeous dress.'

He peered in the bag and made some vague blokey remark.

'You could sit with the Bonnings if you like.' Even as I said it, I knew his seat for the evening was probably already reserved by a local heroine nominee.

'Well... um...' There was more than a hint of embarrassment, so I didn't prolong the agony. I loved him too much for that, even though I suspected that someone else was making decisions for him.

'Or on the next table, or well, we'll catch up then,' I gabbled, feeling rather hot under the collar, in a manner of speaking. That's it Gilly, slap on a bright smile, keep cheerful, don't turn into a jealous cow. He visibly relaxed. 'Yeah, we'll certainly do that.' Ah well, I thought; two steps forward, one step back.

The Growdon Awards Gala Evening arrived with mounting excitement and an air of general celebration in the town. We turned up in all our finery – Mum and I with our hair and nails done – because we knew the local press would be out in force; hopefully the Bournemouth Echo included. Sadly Liz couldn't make it because of the launch of a new exhibition at her gallery. And Sean? Well, he kept muttering on about hell freezing over (or words to that effect) before he wore a penguin suit, despite telling him that penguin suits were not expected. He went out with his mates instead, following the usual pattern of beer, chips, general over-indulgence and then staggering home at an unearthly hour. Auntie Sue even persuaded Terry that his rugby sweatshirt and jeans would *not* be suitable, so it was sharp suits all round. Dad's staff were there to cheer him on, and we made up a table of eight, so fitting Tim in would have been a bit of a squeeze. Not that I'd have minded.

As Mum and I had predicted, the Rosewells and Tuffins were together – probably joined at the hip most days – although brother Ian and his girlfriend were conspicuous by their absence. Instead – and this was the first surprise – Bill Kerridge and his wife were with them, supping pints and port and lemons and looking very cosy. The three course meal was followed by long speeches, plenty of laughs and the nail-biting nominations bit, just like the Oscars and Grammy awards on TV. As the M.C. went through the different categories we cheered and clapped each nomination, showing our support, because we knew it could be a Bonning name in the frame, before long.

'In the Green Community Award category…'

I gave Dad a sharp nudge in the ribs to remind him to put his beer down and stop his asides to Terry. We must have held our breath for every one of the four nominations, learning that customer (and town clerk) Wendy Wicks-Porter had been responsible for Dad's, with Jonty Allbright from Round Table seconding.

'And the winner is… Gordon Bonning of Growdon Fair! A great cheer erupted, showing Dad's popularity within the community. He'd been proactive in pushing for Growdon to achieve Fair Trade Town status, which was due to happen by the end of the year.

'My, my!' he exclaimed, fanning himself with the menu card, 'would you believe it!' In the end, Sue and Mum had to push him out of his chair to go and receive his plaque and certificate. Flash bulbs popped – well, not exactly true with digital cameras – Dad beamed and the Bonning clan were on their feet. It was the best moment of the evening and the most noise I'd made since cheering Bazooka Billy in the Lincoln Handicap.

'Well done,' mouthed Lena, turning round in her seat and waving.

Next came some local industry awards, then it was the turn of food producers. Eventually – as the climax of the evening, according to the M.C. – it was the local Hero or Heroine Award, and a frisson of excitement hovered over the Rosewell and Tuffin table, while they exchanged excited glances. By now I'd told myself to put aside my prejudices and be ready to applaud Lena's quick thinking and selfless action at the time of the accident. If I'd have been with Tim at the time, I'd certainly have wanted to stop him from disappearing under the wheels of a bike.

'And the final nomination is Miss Lena Tuffin,' announced the M.C., who then summarised Lena's valiant action, 'nominated by Tim Rosewell and seconded by William Kerridge.'

Mum and I gasped in unison and exchanged amused glances. That was very neat, but very unlike Tim. He'd always been a 'let's not make a fuss about it' sort of chap. I craned my neck to catch a glimpse of his expression, but his head was down – probably out of embarrassment.

'And the winner is… Miss Lena Tuffin!' Up she shot, beaming, twirling round and waving at the applauding masses, as if she was some aspiring 'A' list celebrity. Then she went tripping up to the stage, the beads and sequins on her ninety pound purchase all glinting in the light as the press closed in for shots. After they'd had their fill, all the winners were called up for a group photo or three, then we made a stampede for the bar. It was time to mingle and a chance for me to chat to Tim and the others at his table.

As I was waiting to get a word in – he was locked in a cheerful verbal exchange with a reporter – I went to introduce myself to Bill and his wife, who sat somewhat dazed at the general noise and excitement. We exchanged pleasantries and I brought them up to speed on my connection with Tim.

'Such a nice lad,' said Bill, a trifle sadly. 'If I could have that day over again I'd have stayed at home and cleaned out the pigeon loft.'

Vera his wife stroked his hand and sighed. I didn't know what to say except something about having a few days in my own personal history when I'd wished I'd stayed in bed, out of harm's way.

'But I feel I've made up for it now, by agreeing to support the nomination, like.'

Vera nodded. 'It's been good for Bill… something positive to do, you know.'

My ears pricked up at the words 'agreeing to support'.

'Who suggested you as seconder, Bill? Was it Tim?'

'Oh no, haven't seen Tim to speak to for a while now. Don't get into Growdon much these days. No, it was the lass – Lena.'

'Lena asked you?' Another gasp escaped from my unguarded mouth.

'Yes, she phoned up and asked if she could come round and see how Bill was getting on,' Vera replied. 'She liked my baking, didn't she Bill?'

'And while we were supping Tetley and eating Vera's fancies, she told us young Tim was nominating her for this award and needed a seconder,' said Bill, nodding and smiling.

'She said Tim *had agreed* to nominate her, I seem to remember,' put in Vera, 'not sure whose idea it was in the first place, but we both thought she deserved it, didn't we Bill? Could have been a lot worse if it hadn't been for her.'

The disclosure that Lena actively sought her nomination, had approached Bill and – I'd wager my next year's student loan – had approached Tim as well, came as eyebrow raising, to put it mildly. She'd probably worked out her strategy, down to what she'd wear and how to corner her prey. Both men were quiet, mild sorts of blokes and very likely the proverbial putty in her hands. The bitch! She'd told us the nominations were a closely guarded secret! Now I know who was guarding it – Lena Tuffin and the two men she'd persuaded to do her bidding.

'And she offered to give me a quick trim while she was there,' said Bill, 'and a really neat job of it she did too.' Now my suspicious antennae were really crackling. The words, bribery and corruption hurtled around my befuddled brain. Was that her little scheme? You scratch my back and I'll scratch yours, as Mum had pointed out. Tim seemed to be on her list of clients already, now here was Bill. Oh yes, I can imagine it: *'Fancy a trim? Free of charge actually, but there's a little favour…'* The scheming so-and-so!

'Mm, very neat,' I agreed, nodding, and thinking that wasn't the only thing that was neat. I was wondering what devious methods of persuasion had been employed on Tim. My mind then started boggling in an alarming way, with all sorts of pictures flashing through, some with X certificate warnings this time.

A quick glance told me that Tim and the reporter were finishing their chat, judging by the body language, so I wished Bill and Vera well and grabbed an empty chair – probably Lena's. She, however, was still holding court with the local paparazzi up by the stage. You could almost see *OK magazine, here I come,* written on her face.

'Oh hi, Gilly! Great evening eh? Bet your Dad's proud,' said Tim cheerfully.

I'd never seen him in a D.J. before. He carried it off very well and looked gorgeous, especially with the red spotty bowtie and matching hanky peeping out of his breast pocket.

'Amazed actually. He's not used to public acclaim. He just gets on and does his thing because he's passionate about it, always has been. It's the rest of the family who are proud, because we know how hard he works and know he deserves recognition.'

Quite a good speech, Gilly, I thought, and wondered if I might have a chance to repeat it to one of the hacks who was looking for a story.

Meanwhile I needed to find out if Miss Lena Tuffin, our local heroine, had really engineered the whole nomination thing. If Tim could change from the *Telegraph* to the *Mirror*, maybe his natural reticence had been given a knock on the head as well.

'So when did you decide to nominate Lena?' I thought I'd start with the assumption that it *was* Tim's idea and that Vera had been mistaken about the conversation. She might be a game old bird, but that didn't mean her memory was faultless.

Tim's relaxed smile briefly hid behind the cloud that seemed to flit across his face. His eye contact swivelled away and he appeared to be studying his place setting card with unusual concentration.

'Oh... now let's see... Well, it came up quite recently, actually.'

'You read about it in the *Gazette*, you mean?'

'Oh no, I think Lena may have spotted it. You know me, Gilly, I usually go straight to the sports pages.'

I nodded. It was interesting he was ready to admit that we *did* have a history.

'And she told you?'

'Well yes, otherwise I might not have known.'

'So you decided to nominate her? To give her a surprise?' I paused, knowing that my use of words was deliberate. I was really hoping my suggestion was closer to the truth than Vera's. Tim's attention switched back to the table setting card and I noted that his flickering eyes refused to flicker in my direction. Was that one of the tell-tale signs of someone telling lies or about to tell lies? If it was, he must have been putting up quite a fight. His mouth was set in a straight line, as if refusing to let the lie pop out. He was the same old Tim I knew and loved, not one given to bold impetuous action, and unlikely to have beaten a path to the *Gazette's* offices demanding a nomination form. The pause lengthened into an awkward silence until, mercifully, Frank turned round and clapped a hand on our shoulders.

'Where's the funeral?' he quipped, chuckling. When all we could manage was an embarrassed shrug, he steamed on. 'Right, who's ready for a re-fill? Tim, another pint of Ferkin? Gilly, what's your poison ? J2O?'

For the sake of the occasion I nodded and smiled. 'Thanks Frank, that'll be lovely.' He went to elbow his way through the scrummage at the bar, and Eleanor came to join us, glowing with excitement after her own moment of glory when she'd been pinned down for a comment for the *New Forest Journal*. A jazz trio struck up in the corner of the room and I wondered what were the chances of a whiz round the floor with Tim, until Frank reappeared with a tray of drinks, sweat pouring off him.

'Here, get these down you.'

Then Lena came bounding back, like Bambi prancing around a flower-filled meadow. She started gabbling about the interview she'd just given.

'One of them asked if I'd ever thought about a modelling career!' she squealed. 'Just imagine!'

'Better keep a look out in my *OK* and *Hello* mags, then,' I remarked, working hard at a relaxed and amenable expression, despite a growing collection of unworthy thoughts swirling round inside.

'No, no,' she demurred, fluttering her lashes. 'I'm not *that* newsworthy or glam.' She made it sound like a throwaway line but it was just like a carrot, dangling in front of Tim's, Frank's and her Dad's noses.

'Of course you are,' they chorused in unison. I could visualise the tiny spark on my short fuse bursting into flame, so, for the sake of appearances, I murmured some excuse about catching up with an old school friend and made a hasty retreat, clutching my glass. There was only so much of Lena Tuffin I could take – about ten seconds' worth at a time was probably my limit and I was well past that.

Chapter 13

Of missionaries and Morsby

Before long I was back in Boxmouth and Mum posted on to me the latest edition of the *Growdon Gazette*, because when I'd called in Bagnalls just before the end of the Easter break, Ray had just sold his last copy. In fact, I soon realised I'd left it rather late, because there were no more copies left in any of the newsagents and stores in the whole of the town, which goes to show how community minded we are. Mum promised to ask around at work to see if someone had a copy surplus to requirement, because it was the edition with reports and pictures of the awards evening. Despite Lena's triumph that night and my suspicions about how she'd wangled it, I wanted to see the pictures and reports because of Dad's own slice of fame. I'd timed my last bit of shopping to fit in with another lunch time rendezvous with Tim. I was feeling just a bit guilty about my probing questions on that night and needed to smooth things over, so that he wouldn't get the wrong idea about me.

Tim readily agreed when I phoned him at work and we met in the war memorial park. I'd found an old pre-coma diary and picked out a few key events in it, hoping that one of them might penetrate the fog in his mind. But no, there weren't any flashbacks as such, but I felt our relationship was making headway until reality hit home. It would be quite a time before I'd see him again, what with the teaching practice looming and a pile of time-consuming assignments demanding my attention. Meanwhile Lena would be making the most of it, leaning over the fence on long summer evenings and enticing Tim with glimpses of her frilly undergarments wafting in the breeze. 'I'll send you a postcard,' I promised him, and gave him a lingering kiss on the cheek before we parted company outside the bank. Then I dashed along to see Ray and Rosemary, with my list of life-savers for the month in the wilds of Cornwall. Penny wasn't there on that occasion, so I browsed through the magazines while Ray was busy at the counter with two other customers. The background easy listening CD must have finished by then, because I became aware of their conversation. It wasn't that I was deliberately eavesdropping, but it's a small shop and you'd often hear all sorts of interesting gossip and juicy snippets when queuing at the till.

'What did you say your auntie's name was?' asked Ray.

'Beryl Aston,' the one with the pony-tail told him.

By this time I was homing in on the racks of boiled sweets. It was a tricky choice.

The other chap, with crew cut and round-rimmed specs, turned round and reached for some sherbet lemons.

'Always used to be my favourite,' I told him, 'until I discovered rhubarb and custard.'

'But not in a handy wrapper!' he chuckled, showing an interesting pair of gold fillings.

'Ah, but they *are*,' I replied, whipping a bag off the rack to show him the pink and yellow striped sweets in cellophane twists.

'What *will* they think of next?' he chuckled.

'Oh, they've been around quite a while. You can probably buy them almost everywhere. And these rosy apples are great too,' I gushed, pointing to a bag of little green and red balls.

'Ah but Rich and I aren't here very often. It's just a flying visit.'

'What, to see your auntie? Sorry, I couldn't help overhearing.'

'That's okay.' When he smiled, there were lots of little creases round his eyes as well as a flash of gold in his mouth. 'Yep, she's the closest relative we have now. We've just spent a couple of weeks with her before flying back.'

'Ah, flying in and then flying off!' I joked, warming to his chumminess.

'Story of our lives these days,' he said with a shrug.

He smiled and adjusted the rucksack on his back and took a bag of each variety of sweets.

'Better make sure these go in the hold luggage. It'd be a shame to have these confiscated at security.'

He went to pay and I made my selection, thinking what a nice bloke he was. His friend with the pony-tail – although of course it must have been his brother Rich – was still chatting with Ray.

'Hey, Gilly,' said Ray, breaking off from his customer, 'these two were in the shop when Tim had his accident.'

'Really?' Rich, the one with the pony-tail, turned round. You could tell at once they were brothers.

'Yeah, Jim and I were stocking up on good old-fashioned sweets before flying out to Thailand,' he told me. 'Do you know him then?'

'You could say that,' I sighed. 'We were going out at the time.' Rich and Jim exchanged glances.

'Not anymore?' asked Jim. Then I told him what had happened and how things were now. 'So he's all right then? He's getting there?' he asked, showing concern.

'Slowly.' I sighed and shrugged.

'But you weren't with him when it happened then?' That was Rich this time. He glanced at his brother as he said it and raised his brows.

'No, it wasn't *this* girl...' faltered Jim.

'Gilly,' I supplied. 'No, I can tell you exactly where I was and what I was doing when I heard what had happened. You know how it is when some big disaster happens – such as 9/11 – people can tell you what they were doing at the time they heard the news. Well, I was on my knees sorting out carrier bags at Pearsons department store in Bournemouth.'

Jim nodded. 'But he's on the mend, you say? That's good.'

He turned back to Ray and pulled a note from his pocket.

'Did you see much? I mean did you hang around for the police?' I asked them.

'No, we were just off to the airport,' said Rich, 'and there was a whole bunch of people milling around, so we guessed there were enough witnesses to give statements and who would have seen what we saw.'

'Yeah, Lena had the best view,' I told them both. Jim was tucking the sweets away by then and looked ready to leave.

'So where are you flying?' They almost felt like old friends by then.

'Back to Thailand,' said Jim, 'back to work.'

'In the tourist industry?' I asked. 'My friend was out in Phuket before college. She had a brilliant time. Said the night life was amazing!'

'No, we're missionaries. We work in refugee camps on the north-west border with Burma,' said Jim, quite serious now. I took a step back and did a sort of double-take. I'd never met a missionary before and admit it was rather unnerving. Jim chuckled.

'Don't worry, we're quite normal. We haven't got horns!'

Ray chuckled as well. 'In fact the exact opposite, eh lads?'

'But you're not wearing sandals and beards! You don't *look* like missionaries!' I gasped, then I realised how stupid I must have sounded.

'No, we're not the stereotypical Jesus freaks,' Rich assured me, breaking into a huge grin. 'But we've got to fly – literally!'

Even though I wasn't sure about missionaries, I was warming to these two – what a shame they were just leaving, I thought.

'Drop by when you're back, won't you,' called Ray. 'You can tell me what you've been reading. Pushkin was it last time?' Rich and Jim exchanged puzzled glances.

'Pushkin? Never read him. Prefer thrillers, don't we Rich.'

'Ah, right,' said Ray, 'must have been someone else then.' I knew what he meant, but it was too long a story to explain to two chaps rushing for their plane.

'Back in two years,' added Jim, making for the door. 'Nice to meet you, Gilly.'

'I'll be teaching then,' I told him, 'all the best.' And off they went, rucksacks joggling, chatting away, leaving the shop strangely quiet.

'It's not every day you meet missionaries, is it?' remarked Ray wistfully.

'And they looked sort of... ordinary... like us!' I sighed, realising how I'd enjoyed that brief exchange with Jim.

'Show's how you can grow up with the wrong idea doesn't it,' reflected Ray. 'And bang goes my theory about the likely suspects for the Russian classics.'

'Oh yes, the Pushkin connection. So, no one else you can think of?'

'Gilly, I know my regulars, after twenty-five years of running this place and – not wanting to be rude – the most highbrow stuff the majority of them are likely to read are the microwaving instructions on a frozen ready meal.' We had a guilty chuckle.

'Now, Gilly, can I help you, love? I see you're stocking up again and not letting the big boys get their grubby hands on your hard-earned cash.'

He reached for my shopping and started ringing it up.

'And a *Growdon Gazette* please.' Ray reached round to grab one off the piles he kept behind the counter.

'Sorry love, our missionary friends bought the last copy,' he told me apologetically.

So that's when I rushed off to Smiths and the rest and found I'd missed out.

Significantly, before I returned to college, Mum and I had a few heart-to-hearts on the subject of the Tim/Lena/Gilly triangle, as I started to call it. She even suggested I stop expecting a breakthrough, because she could see what it was doing to me.

'What if he *never* remembers?' she ventured. That was Mum's way of saying, *give up Gilly*. Really, it surprised me that Mum was being so negative.

'Of course he'll remember,' I insisted. 'He's having flashbacks. It's just a matter of time.'

'And you'll just put your life on hold until then? You'll stop looking at other boys, not go out on dates, tell them you're already promised? Because if you do, you'll be just like those girls who devote themselves to ageing parents and end up as old maids.'

'You're blowing things out of proportion!' I'd yelped.

'I'm just trying to make you see what could happen,' she insisted. 'Are you going to ignore every nice boy who smiles at you or asks you out?' This was quite something for Mum, who had always been very fond of Tim. The question hovered in the air unanswered and that's how we left it.

I had to get my summer wardrobe sorted out and my cases packed, yet Mum's attitude rankled with me and caused me several sleepless nights. On one night in particular, as I lay tossing and turning, a shocking possibility presented itself to my troubled mind. What if Tim *had* remembered that we used to be very close, but decided he preferred the Lena option to the Gilly one? I imagined him looking at the two possibilities in his life and deciding to make a new start. After all, how did *we* know how much he remembered? How did we know anything about his state of mind? We took it all on trust. We all believed him because basically he was a nice guy. Then I dismissed the rogue thoughts in my dozy mind, reminded myself that Tim didn't have a deceitful bone in his body, turned over and went to sleep.

Before long it was May, which meant that the battle with the Penmorgan sand was in full flow as well as the battle with the kiddiewinks at the local primary school. No, it was not so much a battle, more a game.

'Miss doesn't do it like that!' some bright spark piped up on my first day when I was getting them ready for outdoor P.E. Can't remember what they thought I was doing wrong at the time, but it caused a few sniggers and kick-started my determination to bluff, bluster and generally outwit the little darlings. The school had a real family feel and they had a dedicated band of dinner ladies who turned up each morning and churned out *real* Cornish pasties as large as a dinner plate, and other good old-fashioned fare. It made up for my diet of sand at the Penmorgans.

At the weekends, in between marking books and writing out lesson plans, I went out for walks with the family. Mrs P. obviously felt it was part of her hostess duty to show me all the local landmarks. So we'd set off with a picnic and rugs and find secluded coves or dips in the sand dunes to keep us away from the icy blast coming off the Atlantic Ocean. One advantage of that time of year was that it wasn't quite the holiday season, so there was no jostling for beach space amongst teeming hordes of day-trippers and holiday makers. When the tide was out the beach seemed to stretch endlessly, with a scattering of limpets and razor shells and glistening fronds of seaweed. Every so often the local windsurfing fraternity would turn up and zip to and fro on the waves that frothed up alarmingly in the more open waters beyond the natural harbour. I liked it best when I could explore the caves that are magically revealed once the tide has retreated. The younger Penmorgans loved that too and morphed into little ghouls, shrieking and bellowing into the void to try out the echoes.

Up on the cliff top, while trying to find the best picnic spot, we came upon an adder basking in the sun, nestled in a hollow, minding its own business. Of course this was quite a common experience for my hosts, but the sight of its coils sent me into a panic, my toes curling up inside my shoes. It woke and slid away swiftly while we stood frozen, like players in a game of musical statues.

'Can't do you any harm,' one of the teens told me dismissively. 'They're more frightened of you.' Still, I wasn't ready to cosy up beside it and offer it a nibble of my ham sandwich.

'I thought they were venomous,' I told her nervously.

'Yeah, but you don't hear of anyone dying of an adder bite, do you?'

'Well, that's very comforting,' I told her bravely, hoping my toes would hurry up and uncurl.

Then my brain reminded me of something or rather some*one* equally scary with a snake connection. As Mrs P. handed round bags of crisps and lobbed a few cereal bars at us, I speculated on the expected arrival of an education tutor to observe my teaching. I'd already had a visit from one of the music staff in the first week and that had gone well. Please God, let it not be Desmond Morsby, I prayed silently. Just because he was my education tutor, it didn't mean he was the only one who could do the appraisal. I had cute and cuddly Lionel Potter last time – safe and reliable as a dish of rice pudding. Desmond Morsby, on the other hand, was more like a chicken vindaloo – best kept at a distance or there could be explosive results! Sylvia Meakin – a new tutor since September – would be even better. She was quite a fashionista and I could imagine us having a girly chat together, after the necessary formalities, and getting the low-down on where she bought her shoes.

To my dismay, it wasn't Sylvia or Lionel who appeared in the P.E.-cum-dinner hall a few days later, but the dreaded Desmond. He slid slimily round the door with his snake-eyed smile and settled on a wobbly bench, with a benign nod of the head. I'd warned the kids that I had a visitor due who wanted to see them on their very best behaviour. Of course, that wasn't strictly true but I wasn't averse to trying every trick in the book. I was hardly going to hint that it was *me* who was under scrutiny. By the time we'd reached the end of the lesson, Desmond taking a cursory glance at my planning sheets, it was almost lunch time.

'Well done, Gilly,' he murmured, sidling up to me as the kids were changing out of their kit and casting sniggery glances in our direction.

'Is that Miss's boyfriend?' one girl whispered to her friend, behind cupped hands but loud enough to cause a smirk on Desmond's face. It was just the sort of remark to convince him that he was still a young buck and in with a chance with someone half his age. I practised one of my sternest frowns, which put an end to any more cheek.

'How about a spot of lunch at the *Crab and Lobster*?' he murmured, inclining his head a little too close for comfort, but at least keeping quiet enough to avoid flapping ears. My eyes snapped open with shock. I wasn't sure about taking lunch off-piste, as it were, but thought it should be safe enough, being in a public place. Lionel had always brought his plastic box of sandwiches and sat in the staffroom for the debrief.

'Um… er… I'm not sure… um.' Memories of that scary study meeting came flashing back and I couldn't swear to it, but I may have shuddered.

'I'll clear it with the head and promise you'll only be having an orange juice, if that's what's worrying you. I'm sure you could do with adult company.'

For some reason he'd forgotten that there was plenty of that in the staffroom. Oh yes, I thought, there's poor Gilly cast adrift in a foreign land, with no handy train link to speed her back to her lover boy each weekend. I started working on a plausible story just in case Desmond's debrief strayed from teaching skills.

As we left the school, the light drizzle that had kept the kids inside all morning, turned into a heavier version. Sitting safely in the school grounds for the debrief was then firmly knocked on the head. The *Crab and Lobster*, perched on the edge of a steep hill that led down to the beach, was just gearing itself up for the dinner rush. I use that last term in a purely understated way, you understand. There was a sprinkling of affluent greys in the village, taking advantage of term time cheap breaks, and a handful of these were already sipping their sherries and halves of best bitter as they perused the menu. Now here was my dilemma. As Desmond waited at the bar, should I make a quick recce to find the least hidden of seats – to ensure an audience for any unprofessional behaviour, and therefore nip it in the bud – or should I join him at the bar and pay my way, so as not to be beholden to him? There must be some code of conduct about tutors treating their students to pub lunches, such as no, not likely or never. Or maybe he was just going to add it to his travelling expenses or hotel bill?

A couple were just vacating a handily placed table, so I threw my jacket over a chair to bag it, and then scooted up to order a cheese and pickle sandwich and orange juice.

'My treat,' insisted Desmond, on seeing me brandish my wallet. 'I'm sure you deserve one, being stuck in this godforsaken hole,' he murmured under his breath. What could I say? *Thanks all the same but I'm not that skint and this isn't a godforsaken hole.* No, my sense of self-preservation triumphed and I managed a bright but brief smile with the minimum of eye contact. Sandwiches arrived, plonked down by a woman who could have been the mum of one of my pupils. Or was I becoming hypersensitive about being seen in a pub in the middle of a working day? Note: for hypersensitive read guilty. I started imagining whispers at the school gate, pursed lips, knowing looks and rumours of a student teacher disporting herself in public with a married man.

'Excellent lesson, Gilly,' said Desmond eventually, after downing half his drink and munching his way through a ham roll. 'Good communication; decisive and focussed.' I sat up and felt myself light up with pride.

'Thank you,' I murmured, wishing he'd keep his volume control turned a little lower. Now most of the bar would know who I was and where I should be. I looked round, hoping there weren't many locals among the clientele. I sensed paranoia setting in.

'The head's pleased with you too,' he confirmed, 'so you can take it from me that you've passed with flying colours!'

The flourish that he added at the end of his comment made me wish I *could* disappear through a convenient crack in the floorboards, but none appeared. I quickly chomped on my sandwich, aware that I'd be due back in the classroom in half an hour, ready to register the children and deliver a science lesson.

'So, how's lover boy then?' he enquired, with a gleam in his eye. 'Must be missing his regular Gilly fix!' he added, with much eyebrow raising. That's when I regretted boasting about my fictitious weekly visits and was horribly aware of a few suspended conversations around us. Even the barman had paused in polishing a beer mug and had a lascivious grin plastered over his designer stubble. Desmond chuckled and swallowed a large mouthful of something that was hopefully low in alcohol. He probably had another student to embarrass that afternoon. I didn't imagine a tipsy tutor tottering into school to be very well received.

'Ah well, you know what they say about absence and the heart,' I countered confidently, 'and anyway, our daily chat on Skype certainly makes up for the real thing.'

'Skype eh? Surprised they've heard of it down here.' I couldn't believe how dismissive and arrogant he was. If he'd had plans to hang around, I don't think he'd be very welcome at the *Crab and Lobster*.

On the subject of Skype, the Penmorgans probably hadn't heard of it. They weren't heavily into technology and their pc looked like a vintage model.

'Oh yes,' I improvised, 'our evening chats certainly keep us going.' I added a little meaningful glance, hoping Desmond didn't think I was in the market for anything *he* might have on offer.

'Jolly good!' He rubbed his hands enthusiastically, and I hoped he wasn't warming them up before placing them on my knees. I shifted in my chair to keep out of reach. 'Can't have a lovely girl like you pining away for want of some male attention.'

'Oh I'm getting plenty of that,' I assured him, glancing at my watch. 'In fact, there's twelve of them waiting for me back at the school any minute now.'

'Really? Is that the time? Well, mustn't keep the little Romeos waiting must we?'

I was up out of my seat and half way to the door before he realised he was alone.

'Hold on now, Gilly, I'll give you a lift to the school gate,' he offered.

Anyone who'd missed out on Desmond's pronouncements certainly would then have had no doubt where I spent my days. Buckled and belted in position he selected first gear and just managed to brush my thigh in the process. Keeping my eyes locked on the windscreen, I contained my irritation to a brief flick of my hand in his direction and a comment about an annoying little gnat in the car.

'Is there?' he asked, with an air of innocence.

'Hmm,' I replied, 'but I don't think it'll cause me any more bother. It's amazing how one little nip could cause a whole lot of trouble, which wouldn't be very nice, would it?'

'Indeed,' he agreed nodding and changing gear without any unnecessary deflection. He seemed to understand my veiled threat and I was certain that Desmond Morsby would hardly dare make any more passes, use any more innuendos or be slack in his gear changing, especially in my company.

Chapter 14

Reach for the doughnuts and the Victoria sponge

Fresh back from teaching practice, I was more than ready to relax at home for a few days over a short mid-term break – they call it study leave, although I don't think much study gets done. A chance to catch up with Tim was part of the appeal, so I phoned him at work, guessing my timing was about right for his lunch time. I'd arrived home late the night before, far too late to phone him, and told Mum and Dad not to bother waking me in the morning, so of course I overslept. He was busy with a client I was told by some young thing, who was shaping up to be a promising jobsworth type in a few years' time, after keeping me on hold for several minutes.

'I'll see if it's possible for Mr Rosewell to return your call,' she added, in a very business-like manner.

'Tell him it's Gilly. I'm a friend… a very *good* friend,' I emphasised, with a slight giggle, hoping she'd understand.

'Well, you'd better give me your number all the same, just to be sure. Mr Rosewell's very busy with clients today.' It was annoying, but I decided to do as she suggested. She was probably a trainee who was keen to make a good impression at her end, if not at mine.

Half an hour passed while I flicked through Mum's copy of *Good Housekeeping*, but my phone sat beside me, fully charged, recently fed but horribly silent. I started to suspect the girl had forgotten to pass on my message, but then chided myself for my impatience. After all, Tim might be at the point of setting up a very lucrative new investment account. Like the mums waiting at the classroom door for the teacher to finish the lesson, I'd have to wait my turn as well. So I fixed some cheese on toast and a cup of tea and checked my emails yet again, just in case Tim had thought to send me one. He wasn't too hot on emailing actually, and always used to say it was too much like being at work. There were no new emails worth reading and the ones in the spam folder looked frankly disgusting. An hour passed and then I decided to try texting him, although he wasn't too hot on texting either – too fiddly for someone with large thumbs, he'd often joked.

By then it was well after two o'clock and quite late for a lunch break, unless he'd managed a quick mouthful of sandwich and a slurp of coffee in between clients. It was just the same for me on my teaching practice when it had been my turn for playground duty. I'd had to make the quickest dash to the loo and head outside straightaway, hoping the child on teacher's coffee duty wouldn't spill half of it on the way out. As a matter of fact, I was surprised some schools still let the kids risk scalds and burns in these days of health-and-safety-gone-barmy. Back to Tim's hectic day. Tempting though it was to make another call, I set myself the task of finishing my teaching practice assignment. If he hadn't phoned by then, I'd definitely make that call and see if I could pop round his house later. I didn't have much more to do, but once finished, I re-read it, ran a spell check, added a bibliography at the end, making sure I'd attributed the quotes to the correct sources and then printed it.

There had still been no call, so I convinced myself that maybe Tim or the girl had forgotten. I tapped in the number and held my breath. Annoyingly it was a different voice that time, so I had to explain, very patiently, who I was and what I wanted all over again.

'I'll see if he's free,' said a mature female voice. 'Who shall I say is calling?'

Vivaldi's *Four Seasons*, entertained me for at least two minutes before the same voice piped up, telling me Mr Rosewell was in a meeting and could I phone him on his home number later.

'Tell him I'll phone at seven. That'll give him a chance to have his supper in peace,' I told her casually. 'Could you pass on the message when he's free?'

Yes, it was frustrating, but at least he wanted me to call. It was just a busy day.

I'd agreed with Mum that I'd have a bash at spag bol for tea, so I carried on with that and thought about the evening ahead. If Tim wasn't free, I had the following day – the afternoon and evening at least to meet up with him, because his branch was one that opened on Saturday mornings. Soon the spag bol was bubbling away nicely, so I laid the table and picked a few flowers for a little centrepiece. Mum didn't usually work all day on Fridays, but the partners were having an office reorganisation and had offered her overtime to get it finished. She was exhausted when she arrived home and so I played the doting daughter ready with a cuppa and strict instructions that she should relax and put her feet up. Dad was never home till six, so we had plenty of time for a catch up chat first.

'Poor you, working all day,' I sympathised, once I had her sat down on the sofa.

'I know,' she sighed, 'but the extra money will come in very handy. How about your day love?'

'Well, the good news is that I finished my teaching practice assignment and it's all printed out and ready to hand in.'

'Sounds like you've had a hard working day too. Have you got plans for tonight?' she asked.

Then I told her about my frustration over trying to meet up with Tim at lunch time and how he must have been too busy to call back. As I was telling her, her smile vanished and she sat open-mouthed with an odd look on her face. I knew something wasn't right.

'What time was that?' she asked, in a tentative sort of way.

'Around one I guess, then again between half three and four. The poor chap was tied up with clients the whole time, by the sound of it.'

'Well, that's very interesting, or strange, or maybe it wasn't... He may have just popped out and—'

'What was strange, Mum?' I asked her. She was clearly holding back on something I should know about. However she wriggled in her seat and frowned. 'It could have been a look-alike...' she murmured, but she didn't look entirely convinced.

'Mum!' I demanded. 'For goodness sake spit it out!' She shrugged but carried on all the same. 'I went down to the deli next to Bagnalls and bought some lunch as a treat for all my hard work, and I thought I saw Tim going into that new coffee shop opposite his bank. It must have been around one, and—'

'And what? So he popped across to buy himself some 'proper' coffee for a change,' I said, making quote signs with my fingers. 'What's so odd about that? That's probably the only break he had all afternoon.'

She paused and seemed to be thinking about it some more.

'Well, I had to go along to the curtain shop while I was on my break. I've ordered a new blind for the landing window and needed to fix a time for the fitting. So I went past the coffee shop and I'm sure I saw him in there.'

'I know the place, it opened back in April didn't it? They always seem to have long queues though, sometimes almost out the door. So I suppose the poor chap was having to wait for his lunch.'

'No, he was sitting down and he wasn't alone,' she said almost regretfully. Her face had that *'you're not going to like what I'm about to say,'* quality about it.

'Lena Tuffin?' I whispered. Mum nodded apologetically. I thought about it for about half a second before exploding. 'That girl on the phone was lying through her teeth!' I seethed. 'She could have said he was out!' I couldn't decide if I was more niggled by the fact that he was spending his precious lunch hour with Lena or by the dippy girl who couldn't get her facts right.

'Probably rushed off their feet,' Mum observed. 'Too busy or couldn't be bothered to find out.'

'Hmm, you're probably right,' I agreed, but regretted not phoning him the night before. If I had, *I* might have been the one sharing a table and a lunchtime coffee instead. 'Still, he knows I'm phoning around seven, so perhaps we can fix up something then.'

Then I noticed the look on Mum's face. It was just like the one when we had that heart-to-heart back in the Easter break, but I chose to ignore it. As far as I was concerned, Mum was looking on the gloomy side when it came to me and Tim and our chances of getting back together again. Just before seven I had Mum and Dad sat down with mugs of coffee, with *The One Show* about to start, while I went to call Tim on the kitchen phone. It rang for quite a while and I wondered if I could possibly have misdialled a number I knew by heart. So I tried again and this time it was answered by a breathless male voice, but not Tim's.

'Ian?'

'Yep, who's that?'

'Gilly.'

'Oh… er… yeah. You want Tim?'

'Yes, he asked me to call him this evening, so I'm doing just that!' I replied brightly. Ian told me he'd go and see if Tim was in, which I thought a bit odd, because it's not as if they live in a mansion. Ian isn't exactly the sharpest pencil in the box and sometimes he has seemed to be in his own dream world.

After a short while I was treated to some more heavy breathing. It was Frank this time, who'd not been told by his youngest son that I was waiting patiently on the line.

'Ah… Gilly, how are you? Working hard eh?' he asked. As I hadn't phoned for a casual update on my course I had to hurry him along and get to the reason for my call.

'I'll go and see if I can find him,' he said.

Perhaps I'm old-fashioned in my thinking, but didn't these Rosewells still sit down to a meal together? They used to, or perhaps it was just for my benefit when I was a regular guest at their supper table. Or, maybe, I had picked one of those evenings when everyone was doing their own thing, passing like the proverbial ships in the night, flinging packets in and out of the microwave and eating on the move. Thinking about it, we're like that sometimes. So I waited patiently, preparing myself for the chat I'd been longing to have since the Easter hols.

After another minute or so there was more heavy breathing – Eleanor this time. Were they stood around drawing lots for who was going to speak to me next?

'Sorry, Gilly,' she gasped, a trifle on the irritated side, 'have to be quick… just off to *Weightwatchers*. Sorry you've just missed Tim. He went out about five minutes ago. He's got net practice. Anything urgent?'

'Net practice?' Oh yes, cricket practice, I remembered, wondering if I might wander on down and manage a quick conflab in between the bowling.

'Yes, they've all gone off to Buckhurst for a change.' Why was she sounding so jolly? She must have realised how I'd be receiving that news. Buckhurst was *miles* away!

'But he *knew* I was phoning at seven,' I protested, trying to keep the edge out of my voice. 'He gave a message to the girl who spoke to me earlier that I should phone this evening. I told her to tell him I would phone at seven. He *knew!*

'Did he? Well, you must have missed him by a minute. He went with

Darren Weatherhead. Darren was early for a change.' Bully for Darren, I thought mutinously. What did she expect me to do? Give the speedy Darren a round of applause?

'I'll catch up with him tomorrow then,' I told her, trying to sound positive. 'Tell him I called.' There was a sound rather like a grunt from the other end of the phone and then I heard Eleanor calling to someone, but she must have put her hand over the receiver as she did it.

The following day, just as I was towelling my hair dry from the shower and deciding which outfit would be sure to wow Tim, the letter box clattered and a letter plopped onto the doormat. Clutching a towel around me, I nipped downstairs to see what the postman had delivered. It was addressed to me, but the handwriting wasn't familiar, and there was no stamp. As I torn it open I could hear a car drawing away outside and by the time I'd reached the sitting room window, it had vanished from sight. The letter was from Eleanor, telling me – in no uncertain terms – that Tim was now going out with Lena and that all my pestering phone calls were becoming irritating. I went ballistic.

'How dare she!' I yelled, standing in the hall in my towel. Mum came rushing downstairs to find me shaking with fury.

'What does she mean by 'all the pestering phone calls?' I seethed. 'I only phoned twice at the bank and at *exactly* the agreed time last night! The girl told me he'd said to phone in the evening, for goodness sake! I was *doing* what *he'd* suggested!'

I really blew my top. Mount Vesuvius had nothing on me. Meanwhile Mum stood there, probably wishing she'd picked up the letter first and steamed the envelope open and had a quick shufti for vetting purposes.

'And he's going out with Lena, is he? When did this start, I wonder?'

Mum went into the kitchen and I heard the clink of kettle on taps as she filled it for the default solution to disasters big and small – a cup of tea. But still I fumed, even after a second cup. What right had Eleanor to warn me off? Couldn't Tim and I still be friends? I'll give Mum her due. She didn't utter a syllable of '*I told you so*', or '*I could see this coming*', or any other meaningless and unhelpful comments. She dug out a bag of doughnuts from the freezer and let me pig out on them and bury myself in soaps and sitcoms on the TV and *While You Were Sleeping*, which made me cry buckets. I couldn't wait to get back to college. There were so many unanswered questions whizzing around in my mind. Did Tim know his mother had been poking her nose in where it wasn't wanted – wasn't wanted by me anyway. Did he ask her to write the letter because he was too embarrassed? Surely not. Did Lena suggest to Mrs R that she should write the letter out of motherly concern for her poor confused/harassed son who was being pursued by a girl who was suffering from delusions? Hmm, I wouldn't find that hard to believe. I spent a while wondering about texting Tim, but knowing his large thumb problem I couldn't be sure if he'd reply, especially if he was the puppet being manipulated by the two scheming puppet mistresses. But I texted him anyway, telling him I'd received a letter from his mother and found it very upsetting. He didn't reply.

Sometime later, it occurred to me that the reason for no return texts might have been a more practical reason than I'd imagined, after all you can use those little prodding sticks on mobiles if you can't manage with your fingers and thumbs. The reason must have been that he had a new phone and new number. Realising that I might have lost my last lifeline to him, made me more depressed than ever. Perhaps Mum was right, perhaps he'd never remember the times we had together. It was ironic that in my bag was a photo that Tim's Auntie June had sent me – one she'd taken in Torquay of Tim and me cuddling up together and looking obviously besotted with each other, proof that we'd once been an item. I had written to her, explaining that I'd somehow mislaid a photo that had great sentimental value, and asked if she had a spare one I could have. June Coopman was Frank's sister, so I thought she might be a safe bet to approach. If she had been Eleanor's sister I'd have thought twice about doing that.

It was a relief to return to Boxmouth after that episode. Earlier in the term Doreen had asked Fran and me for our mobile numbers when we finally lugged our last loads from her house and we could at last move back into our refurbished digs.

'Might be nice to invite you round for tea and some of my home baking one afternoon,' she had suggested in her mumsy sort of way. We had nodded and given our numbers thinking – like passing acquaintances on package holidays – the intentions were good but, in reality, she'd never get round to making that call or fixing that get-together. However Doreen was true to her word. It was not long before the end of term, with frantic music practices in progress and a pile of assignments awaiting their finishing touches when my mobile vibrated into life with an unrecognised number. It was Doreen chirping at me excitedly, asking if Fran and I were free on Wednesday afternoon for tea and cake.

'Just a slice or two of my Victoria sponge,' she promised, 'and maybe a cream tea, if you're up for it?' Fran and I were definitely 'up for it'!

We turned up with a bunch of flowers and box of chocs as a 'thank you' and were told we were naughty and shouldn't have, but I know they both appreciated the gesture.

'Got a special treat for you, Gilly,' announced Eric, after we'd each polished off a scone and we were onto our second cup of tea. Fran gave me a puzzled glance, as if to say *what have you done to deserve a treat?* I shrugged. There was enigmatic grin on Eric's face and Doreen let slip an excited giggle. Something was afoot. He reached for the TV zapper and the screen filled with noisy crowds, horses and the man with the odd earflap hat making semaphore signals. Fran and I exchanged more puzzled glances.

'Bazooka Billy's running in a handicap,' he told me, winking. 'Thought you might like to see how the fella's coming along!'

'You mean the horse? Well, er not especially. Is it important, the race I mean?'

For a moment Eric's grin faded and I felt guilty about being so off-hand.

'Well, they've had the big race already, but I noticed the name in the *Racing Post*...'

Fran let out a giggle. 'Ah-ha, the Rescorla connection!' She rolled her eyes and then reached for another slice of cake.

I ignored her. 'Another handicap?' I commented casually, noting that the horses were being led round the parade ring, just like last time. The only difference I noticed, was posh frocks and huge fancy hats on the female followers, who were flapping their race cards in the midsummer heat.

'Wow!' breathed Fran, surprisingly. She wasn't heavily into fashion, but the camera was picking up an amazing selection of well-heeled young fillies wearing outfits that would have gobbled up a whole year's tuition fees.

'Another scone, Gilly? You look like you're wasting away over there.' This was Doreen who had indeed spotted that I wasn't presenting my former youthful bloom and comely curves. Since Eleanor's evil letter I'd lost half a stone at least, but I wasn't prepared to let her know the reason.

'Oh you know, Doreen, teaching practice certainly keeps you on your toes, doesn't it, Fran?' She nodded, her mouth still busy with Doreen's excellent sponge.

'Important race meeting then?' I asked, making sure the subject of my weight loss didn't become the focus of Doreen's concern.

'Royal Ascot,' cut in Eric, who was following the action on the screen avidly. 'And there's the fella,' he announced, 'number four, see, Gilly, and it's the same jockey as last time.'

The camera had picked out Bazooka Billy and the commentator was listing his recent achievements (or form, as Eric said) which didn't sound as good as his appearance at Doncaster.

'Only offered at twenty to one today,' he observed reflectively. 'Might be worth an each way bet though.' I asked him what that meant and he explained that you'd get winnings even if your horse came in second or third, but not as much as if it came first. So he grabbed his mobile and placed a modest bet. 'This is the Royal Hunt Cup,' he told us.

Meanwhile Doreen was oohing and aahing over some of the outfits and saying she'd love to go to Royal Ascot one day.

'Not without a hat old girl, and I'd need to win the lottery to buy you one of them beauties!'

'Oh no, Eric, I'd have one of those macerators!' she declared, beaming.

Fran and I convulsed into our teacups and Eric chortled quietly to himself.

'What's funny?' Doreen asked us blankly. 'I've seen some very nice macerators in the charity shops in town.'

'Have you love?' chuckled Eric. 'Would you troll off to Ascot with a bog on your head?'

'Fascinator, Doreen,' gasped Fran, when she'd recovered enough to speak.

The penny dropped. 'Oh dearie me,' Doreen giggled, blushing crimson, 'whatever next!'

What with all the hilarity, we almost missed some close-up shots of Bazooka Billy with his jockey and the Rescorla clan.

'Shush, woman!' Eric warned her. I don't know why, but I couldn't stop myself staring at the screen, wondering if my old sparring partner was there again. Surely he didn't have the sort of job that allowed him to flit to and fro between England and France whenever he wanted. Mind you, with *his* attitude nothing would surprise me. Then a familiar profile appeared and the camera picked out two women on either side of him.

'Ooh, looks as if he's got a girlfriend,' observed Fran. The younger of the two was about twenty, stick thin and scantily clad in something short and diaphanous.

'Perhaps she's a French girl he's managed to pick up; someone who hasn't seen the *real* Theo Rescorla,' I retorted.

The young thing looked confident enough in his company and the rest of the party seemed in high spirits. They'd probably been knocking back Pimms or Bucks's Fizz all afternoon.

'Well, *I* wouldn't mind being there,' put in Doreen staunchly, 'never mind what you say about him, those Rescorlas seem to be having a fine old time.'

After that, Eric ordered us to eat up the rest of the scones and let him concentrate on the race. The horses were all at the start by then and Eric observed that Bazooka Billy was sweating and seemed quite skittish. He was pulling on his reins and the jockey seemed to be having trouble calming him down.

'Can't wait to be off, I expect.'

'You may be right, Gilly.' I'd never been *that* good at sport in the past, but the very worst time at sports days was being 'on your marks' and waiting for the starting pistol – or was it the whistle? The horses were still somewhat frisky but the starter fellow probably decided they were as ready as they'd ever be and got them going. He had my sympathy. Some of the kids on my teaching practice were like that when we were doing playground warm-up races.

The 'gee-gees' thundered down the track like a cavalry charge and morsels of scone and teacups froze in mid-air. I began to understand how some people become hooked on this racing lark. We couldn't see Bazooka Billy for a while because he seemed to be in the middle of a group, all trying to catch the front runner who had shot ahead very quickly. Had he put on a spurt too soon? Would anyone have a chance to catch him? The jockey seemed to be making heavy weather of it, or maybe he was biding his time? Soon they were in the last two or three furlongs and we were out of our seats as we saw Bazooka Billy finding his way through the following pack. Eric was calling out his *'come on my son'* stuff again, but the leading horse was lengthening the gap ahead of the rest.

'Come on, you can do it!' someone in the room called. It might have been me. He certainly was doing his best and the jockey was hunched over his neck, flicking the whip like crazy. As the finishing line came into view Bazooka Billy gained on the leader, but he was never going to catch him.

'Second place!' cheered Eric. 'Well done Billy Boy!' We all jumped around as if we'd been responsible, although it wasn't quite the same as before. To my shame I envied the girl in the floaty diaphanous dress, laughing and joking with the Rescorla clan as they welcomed Bazooka Billy back to the unsaddling enclosure.

Chapter 15

Puzzling over Pushkin and Valentines

When I returned to Boxmouth for my final year, I was surprised to learn that the college hierarchy, in its wisdom, had switched the third year teaching practice to the first part of the spring term. That meant one very long autumn term with little more than unrelenting lectures after the excitement of hosting Freshers' Week for the new wide-eyed intake of first year students. On the love life front things were dire, until Brendan had a brief rift with his busty blonde bass player and I was next in line for his attention. Yes, I'd grudgingly decided I wouldn't cut myself off from male attention like a dusty old maid, just as long as it didn't become serious. I was realistic enough to accept that I didn't have quite the same appeal and pulling power as the busty bass player and that I was purely a matey stop-gap, and that's the way I wanted it. Brendan and I shared a couple of pints and chats at the *Rat and Rabbit*, while he burbled on about why they'd broken up. Clearly he was smitten and it was only a matter of time before one of them would go crawling back to the other. I guessed correctly that Brendan would be the one doing the crawling.

The news from Growdon did little to cheer me. Mum had spotted Lena and Tim together more than once and had been completely blanked by Lena. Tim, on the other hand, had pretended to look in a shop window as Mum approached – probably too embarrassed to look her in the eye. I suspect he'd had more flashbacks. Why else would he be embarrassed? Ray and Rosemary also had some news – quite distressing, as a matter of fact, particularly for Penny. Although Rosemary knew Penny would sometimes go into her Pushkin mantra, she hadn't quite worked out what it was *really* about, especially as the two missionary blokes had been struck off the list of possible Russian literature enthusiasts. She and Ray knew it was linked with the day of the accident and that the sight of Lena crossing the street had triggered something, but it still didn't make any sense. Lena, after all, had been hailed as the local heroine. Of course, the wisest move would have been to suggest Penny sat in a different room, but for most of the time she seemed to love looking out at the town, with all the bustle of shoppers, dogs and traffic to entertain her. So they let her keep her routine, but worked out the best time to take her back to the sitting room and put on a video; the time when Lena made her daily bank visit. But best laid plans, as they say…

One lunchtime, Ray was serving a queue of customers as usual while Rosemary was restocking the postcard rack, when Penny started shrieking and going into the loudest Pushkin rant ever. That set off a dog that had been tied up outside the door and a toddler in a pushchair joined in too. One poor old dear almost had a heart attack and in the mêlée two girls managed to steal four large boxes of Milk Tray and a card of cigarette lighters. All Rosemary could see, so she told Mum, was Tim walking along the street and then Lena running along behind, trying to catch him up, but definitely *no* bikes or cars coming up the lane set on a collision course. They had to call for an ambulance because the old dear went deathly white – the police as well, because of the shoplifters. In the middle of it all, Penny was inconsolable. Mum said that Ray and Rosemary were seriously considering asking Rosemary's sister to help with some new arrangement – and not before time.

Christmas was a welcome refuge of home comforts, with the family keeping all the same traditions ever since I can remember. However with Liz and Sean busy with their own social lives and Sue and Terry announcing their engagement I felt as if part of my life was missing. To be honest, we were all thrilled about Sue and Terry and I didn't begrudge her flashing her pretty opal ring under our noses. She deserved something lovely happening in her life. It was Liz's situation, however, that made me jealous. It sounded as if she had met the man of her dreams, although she only teasingly fed us small snippets of information about the mysterious Lenz, who was an art historian and was obviously taking up much of her spare time. She drove back to Oxford the day after Boxing Day, telling us that she was flying over to Berlin to meet Lenz's family and visit a few art galleries. Sounded like a busman's holiday to me, or was that just sour grapes on my part?

My final teaching practice started just a week after the start of the absurdly named 'spring term' – in other words, the time of year which is bitter cold and we are all reaching for our thermal underwear and fur-lined boots. It was in a suburb of Plymouth, where virtually everyone I met spoke in the broadest of accents and supported Argyle. It took me at least a week to understand what the children were saying. They told me I sounded 'posh' and sniggered at frequent intervals until I fixed them with my well-honed evil eye. The school was half way up a very steep hill, which made playground duty interesting or even treacherous on icy days. My worst moment was not due to skidding on the ice, but due to out of control skipping ropes and flapping hemlines. After that I stuck to trousers: much warmer and less chance of underwear mishaps. It was real bandit country, according to the couple who fed and fussed over me. They were relative newcomers to the area and it sounded as if they had regretted the choice of location. However I survived the bottom pinching (the caretaker), the wolf whistles (the year 6 Lotharios) and the age eleven-going-on-nineteen girls who were streetwise beyond their years. I emerged from the four weeks of practice with high praise from Sylvia Meakin and a pile of home-made thank you cards from my class. I was on the home straight at last, as Eric would have said.

When we arrived back at college, most of the student population was in the grip of Valentine fever, with a disco planned for the weekend. To be perfectly frank I had no interest in going, and was even planning a quiet night in with Amy and a few knitting patterns for company. She had moved on to knitting Noah and his animals by then and had lined up giraffes, polar bears and alligators along one of the windowsills in the sitting room. However, my plans for knitting took a nosedive when Amy announced that she was going away for the weekend. A significant gleam in her eye and a slightly enigmatic air alerted the rest of us to the unlikely possibility that Amy had at last found herself a bloke, but we didn't go as far as asking her. There were plenty of signs though, when we stood still long enough to notice them. She had taken to wearing eye shadow, which was definitely a first, although she hadn't quite got the hang of applying it. She was also spending much longer fiddling with her phone and chuckling quietly to herself. It reminded me of Liz at Christmas. I don't think any of us could imagine what sort of bloke would go for Amy, or vice versa. Maybe someone with a penchant for Fair Isle sweaters? Maybe someone cuddly with the same taste in documentaries and bracing country walks? Maybe someone she'd met down near Newton Abbot, where she'd been teaching?

On the morning of the disco I decided to wander over to the music block with a book of Bach's *French Suites* for company while the rest of my friends were scouring the charity shops for outfits to wear later on. On the notice board there were various lists of lectures and significant dates for the rest of term. We were due to study nineteenth and twentieth century composers in preparation for our final composition assignment. Before bagging one of the practice rooms, I wandered over to the pigeon holes, just to check on any stray messages, although I didn't expect to see anything there. After all, I'd been out of circulation for over a month and hardly expected any of the music tutors to have planned anything which needed my immediate attention. There was, however, a solitary envelope in the 'B' section, with my name typed on it and addressed to 'The Music Department, Boxmouth College, Boxmouth, Devon.' There was a stamp on it, but because the postmark was very faint and slightly smudged, I couldn't work out where it had been posted, although I could just make out the date, which was the day before.

I turned the envelope over in my hands and wondered if it could possibly be from Tim. After all, although he knew I was at college at Boxmouth, he certainly wouldn't know my precise address. The sender clearly didn't know exactly where I lived. But why type the address? Why not write it by hand? Perhaps it *was* from Tim, and he wanted it to be a surprise when I opened it. I'd recognise his handwriting straightaway. My heart started hammering excitedly. The envelope was creamy white and not a cheap type of paper either. There *had* to be a card inside. It felt like a card. Had the memory breakthrough happened at last? I gulped a few times, just staring in amazement at what I was about to open. Carefully, with trembling fingers, I slipped a finger under the corner of the flap and gently eased it open. It seemed sacrilege to ruin such beautiful paper. And yes, there *was* a card inside. A Valentine's card.

A hot flush that started in my cheeks, spread down my neck and around my ears all at the same time. I savoured the moment, gazing at a simple sketched heart on the front, outlined in silver. It was not the usual style of card I'd expect from Tim. He often chose slightly jokey, cartoon type cards. It might be a pair of cats smooching up together or a couple of lovebirds cooing on a branch. Maybe his new persona had acquired a superior taste in cards? After all he had changed his reading habits and his hairstyle, what was to stop him changing his shopping habits?

'Oh wow!' I gasped in wonder, feeling intoxicated with a heady rush of desire. If only I had decided to go back to Growdon for the weekend. But surely it wasn't too late, I thought, wondering how soon I could make my escape.

Then I opened it up and felt a different sort of rush, a rush of disappointment. It was not signed. There wasn't even a kiss or an enigmatic remark or question mark. It was completely blank. For a moment, I remembered the unsigned Christmas card. Was it the same sender? Still, someone had thought to send it. It *could* have been Tim, it *might* have been Tim, but after the disappointing time I'd had in his company since he'd regained consciousness, I wasn't holding out much hope, especially after Mum's sightings before Christmas. I tucked the card inside the back cover of Bach's *French Suites* and ambled down to the practice rooms, pondering on the reason for sending an anonymous card. It could have been a cruel joke, sent by someone who knew about my sad love life, or lack of it. But why choose so beautiful a card if that was the case? I spent half an hour working away at one of the suites, but my heart wasn't really in it. It was miles away. After that I tried a few scales and arpeggios, but my fingers skidded and slipped all over the keys and I couldn't co-ordinate my hands. After another few minutes I gave up and decided I needed to do something that would take my mind off Tim. I'd go to the second hand bookshops and trawl through the shelves for some escapist fiction to wallow in. Then, on my way back to the house, I made a brave decision. I would phone Tim's bank. It wasn't yet midday, and his branch closed at twelve thirty on a Saturday.

Digging out my phone, I scrolled through and found the number and then pressed 'Okay'. A male voice answered and my poor heart skipped a few beats to start with, until I realised it wasn't Tim's.

'Is Mr Rosewell in this morning?' I ventured, not sure if I was up to speaking to him.

'No sorry, he's not in today. He's still on holiday.'

'On holiday?'

'Yes, he's been away these past two weeks. Can I help you?'

'Er no, I'm a friend, it wasn't actually bank business,' I said, apologetically. 'Where has he been?'

'On a skiing holiday, Austria I think, lucky bloke!'

'A skiing trip? That's a first!'

'Yeah, he's gone with a friend.'

'Oh, right.' I didn't prolong the conversation after that. I'd heard enough and I really didn't want to know which friend he was with. I knew then that it hadn't been Tim who had posted the card the day before, with its British stamp.

For the disco that evening I tarted myself up, drowned my sorrows and frustrations in rather too much cider and danced with as many blokes as I could lay my hands on. Fran and Tony were making up for lost time over the past four weeks and were wrapped up in each other's arms all evening, I noticed. All right for some, I thought, enviously. Mollie and Dan were all loved up as well, almost glued together on the dance floor. Most of the best blokes seemed to be spoken for and I wondered if any of the spare ones had been responsible for the anonymous card.

Someone called Tom tried snogging me as we shuffled round the dance floor, his tongue making most of the action, but I gave him the slip when I told him I needed the loo and dashed back to the safety of the house by myself. I think he was one of the locals who'd found his way in. Not my type at all. I may have been Gilly-no-mates but I wasn't *that* desperate. As I staggered down the road, reflecting on my sorry state, and the state my head would be in the morning, a tight feeling closed around my throat and there was a stinging in my eyes. The wretched sob that I'd managed to keep at bay earlier in the day, at last escaped and I found myself blubbing noisily. It was all so *unfair,* I thought angrily, as tears coursed down my cheeks and sobs grew increasingly louder. All the while vivid pictures of Tim and Lena swooshing down ski slopes flashed in my mind's eye and I fervently hoped one of them had broken a limb or two – preferably Lena, of course.

Chapter 16

Churlbury

Before long, it was time for me and the rest of my year at Boxmouth to enter the real world. Mum and Dad had been sending me copies of the *Growdon Gazette* and I'd been firing off applications to all the local schools. In reality, there hadn't been many vacancies. Fran had been having the same problem, so we'd both chipped in to spend some of our precious cash on copies of the *Times Educational Supplement*, to spread our net wider. Fran was looking in the Yeovil area, although she was adamant that nothing would tempt her to live at home again. After three years of relative independence, we were all ready to cut the umbilical cord for good. When I asked her about Tony and did they have any plans, she went all coy on me and smiled an enigmatic smile.

I'd never heard of Churlbury until I saw an ad for a Year 5 class teacher at Churlbury C. of E. school, near Shealton-on-Stour. I'd not heard of Shealton-on-Stour either. They're in Dorset and if you don't have your own transport, the only way you can reach Churlbury is by bus from Shealton-on-Stour, or taxi if you can afford the fare. Dad and I clearly needed to sort out the car situation before long, which would help if I ended up teaching in an out-of-the-way place. The thought of using buses drove me potty. On the day of my interview, I had to set my alarm for a shockingly early start. How I managed to find my way onto the right train was a miracle. My eyelids still felt gummed together by the time I'd reached Boxminster. At least there was a trolley service on the mainline train so I could indulge in a hefty dose of caffeine to prod my brain into action.

What sort of questions would they ask? What sort of questions would *I* ask? That was the awkward bit. I could imagine reaching the end of the interview, breath a great sigh of relief and then find that the panel wanted to know what *I'd* like to know. Then I'd sit there like an oversized goldfish, with my mouth opening and closing and nothing coming out, feeling like a prize fool. That's what had happened when I went for the Pearsons interview. Never again. Amy went off to an interview the week before me but she was much too smart to be caught out like that. It was a little village school near Swindon, and being one of those highly organised individuals, she had a notebook full of impressive questions that she fired off at the interviewing panel, she told us smugly. She probably had them quaking in their shoes. I wouldn't want Amy as my teacher, I can tell you. I'd probably be in detention every week. However, they were obviously so impressed that they offered her the job on the spot *and* a two-bed apartment in half of a barn conversion for an incredibly low rent. Amazing!

I told Fran that there must be some catch there, such as the head's horrendous reputation or the school being at the very bottom of the league tables, or there was an Ofsted due the following term. Fran remarked that it sounded like sour grapes (again) but admitted she couldn't help feeling envious. Mollie had been looking peaky again – mostly in the morning – and couldn't even manage half a cup of coffee at a time, which made us think that maybe she really *was* pregnant this time. She and Dan had had a huge bust-up at Christmas and she'd told us all that he was nothing but a beer-guzzling tosser who was barely literate. Then a month later it was all back on again. None of us dared mention the words 'Afghanistan' or 'desert' or 'tour of duty'. It was bound to happen sooner or later though. It doesn't take much to work out that every regiment is bound to take a turn. We didn't notice any feverish filling in of application forms by Mollie when the rest of us had several on the go. That was significant. When I arrived at Shealton-on-Stour station on the day of the interview, it was virtually deserted except for a bloke with an earring and ponytail in the ticket office. He directed me to a bus stop just a few yards along the road, so I didn't have much chance to check out the shopping opportunities. It looked quite promising though, especially when I spotted a Cath Kidston bag winking at me from the window of a very tempting little boutique. I didn't realise that sleepy little Dorset towns that were hardly more than overgrown villages would have even heard of Cath Kidston. I'd imagined the height of extravagance to be hand-embroidered tea cosies on the W. I. market stall. The place was bound to have weekly markets.

I didn't have long to wait and in a few minutes the little single deck bus was trundling along through winding back lanes, overtaking the occasional tractor, stopping every now and then to pick up yet another pensioner who flashed a bus pass and greeted the driver like a member of the family. They'd exchange the latest news about Mrs So-and-So who was still waiting for her new hip or little Caleb who'd just cut his second tooth or old Mr Jethstone who wasn't likely to last the day. At times, it felt like a journey in a bygone era. At least no one tried to climb on board with a cage of chickens or a crate of cabbages, or am I being too clichéd? I mean, I was still in the UK after all and not in some tiny corner of an eastern European country or Baltic state, although one passenger *did* sell the driver – Reg, so I learned – half a dozen eggs, but not as barter for a ticket. Fortunately, my interview was not till two, after which I'd have to catch another bus back in time for the five twenty train, unless I could play the poor stressed-out candidate and wangle a lift with someone at the school. There was bound to be at least someone on the board of governors or one of the staff who lived in Shealton.

Reg dropped me right outside the school, which was still in session at the time. It meant I could cross the playground without having to duck footballs or dodge skipping ropes that might have flicked up the skirt of my dress and flashed a glimpse of black bikini brief. I speak from bitter experience of my final teaching practice. Enough said about that. I found the front entrance easily enough, but trying to get inside was virtually impossible. Schools are more impregnable than prisons these days. At the rate we're going they'll soon be installing retina image recognition at the door I shouldn't wonder. There was a keypad for the cognoscenti who tap in their number each morning, but I had to resort to speaking to a grill and hoping someone would hear me. Fortunately, I was expected, and a jolly lady appeared, beaming over her half-moon specs, and pinned a visitor's badge on my jacket.

'I'm Pru,' she told me brightly. 'Welcome, Gilly. Mrs Karthew's interviewing another candidate at present, so I expect a cup of tea in the staffroom would be a good idea.'

'Music to my ears,' I agreed, and managed a nervous giggle. Why I should have been nervous speaking to a school secretary I really don't know. I suppose I'd seen enough of the village – its sweet little pond, edged in well-tended grass, a half-timbered pub and bow-windowed general stores – to tug on the heart strings and suggest that this was *exactly* where I wanted to begin my teaching career. Of course, there may have been a sprinkling of wife swappers, drunkards and wastrels among the population, or was I slipping into that bygone Thomas Hardy era again? Nevertheless, I didn't care that the nearest Cath Kidston stockist was half an hour's bus ride away. What's half an hour when you're surrounded by such quaint, rustic charm? On second thoughts, I should be completely mobile and independent by the time the new term starts – once Dad's decided which make and model he wants for his new motor so that I can take possession of his old one.

As Pru escorted me along a corridor, there was a faint purposeful buzz simmering in each room, and not a single bellow or shriek. This was in stark contrast to the Plymouth school.

'Rich tea or digestive?' offered Pru, who reminded me of a robin hopping on a twig.

'Ooh, spoilt for choice!' I giggled, but a little less nervously.

'The other candidate will be finishing very soon,' predicted Pru, 'then Mrs Karthew will give you a quick guided tour once the children are at lunch.' That was generally translated as: *Mrs Karthew will do her best to give you a good impression of the school without some little perisher ruining her efforts.* Quiet it may have been on our trip along the corridor, but they were probably all playing 'heads down, thumbs up' as a special treat, or tidying their work trays.

After five minutes – while Pru had left me to soak up the general atmosphere of the school by scanning the notice board, noting the absence of clutter and assessing the interior décor of the ladies' loo – the other candidate made her entrance, accompanied by the head. When I'd seen the name Olive Karthew in the advert, I'd imagined a buxom, rosy-cheeked country matron, close to retirement, with a sagging bosom and sagging cardi to match. Instead she was about ten years younger, sharp-suited and immaculately made up. Her only concession to practical work wear was her smart leather gilt-trimmed loafers. Her greying hair was swept up in a near chignon and tiny gold and diamante studs twinkled in her earlobes.

'Olive Karthew,' she said, introducing herself, 'and you must be Gilly Bonning.'

The other candidate, whose name I later discovered, was Kate Maxted, had by now melted into the background, but not before I'd taken in her dark auburn curls and gorgeous chocolate leather coat. Of course it *could* just have been a charity shop bargain. 'Ready for a quick tour?' asked Olive, inviting me to follow her.

On the way we passed a group of smartly dressed individuals, including at least two dog collars and a mayoral chain. This was the interviewing panel of local worthies, all ready for their lunch.

'Year 5,' Olive announced, whipping open the door of a bright room with huge windows on one side which overlooked a neat line of rose bushes and the front driveway. They would have all seen me arrive, I realised with horror. There was a piano in one corner, with a trolley of percussion instruments beside it. I nodded and murmured something about how bright and airy it was, just like the house hunters on *Escape to the Country*. Having peeped inside the other six rooms, Olive strode ahead of me, out into the back yard and along a path to a swimming pool (evidence of a keen fund-raising PTA) and then a large field, surrounded on all sides by a high hedge. I was trying hard to find something about the place that I disliked, but there was nothing. At the back of my mind I considered Kate, who looked so self-assured as she'd sashayed into the staffroom, to be the only obstacle. She was bound to be offered the post, with all that confidence oozing from every pore, I told myself.

By the time we reached the staffroom, it had filled up almost to bursting point. The kitchen staff had wheeled in a trolley with plated dinners and the interview panel were already seated round the table, tucking in ravenously. The hospitality at Churlbury C. of E. amounted to a child-size portion of shepherd's pie covered in congealed gravy. At least I didn't have to squeeze myself into a child-size chair and shoehorn my knees under a child-size table in the hall with the chattering masses. Instead, I had to balance a tray on my knees and hope I didn't tip it on the floor. An advantage of having congealed gravy however, meant no chance of spattering it all over my lovely teal dress. I'll admit I was surprised the school hadn't laid on the usual quiche and salad buffet – obviously a sign of the times. The rest of the staff were opening up plastic lunch boxes and making tea. I looked up and noticed Kate was chatting to a young bloke who had committed a major sartorial error of wearing brown shoes with a blue suit.

'Ah, you must be Jeremy Jeeves,' Olive gushed, approaching him with an outstretched hand. It took my brain precisely two seconds to work out I had another rival for the post. There was something about Jeremy's demeanour that shouted 'candidate' rather than 'educational book rep on the scrounge'. The three of us balanced trays and exchanged potted life histories, while each was probably silently speculating on the strength of the competition. Jeremy was now in top contender position in my mind. Equal opportunities aside, another male member of staff was bound to be considered advantageous by some, and by the way Jeremy was holding court, he seemed convinced of that himself.

While we were wolfing down our shepherd's pie, the door opened and a woman with a worried expression poked her head round, yoo-hooed in Olive Karthew's direction and beckoned for good measure.

'Mrs K, sorry to bother you, *Zebedee trouble*,' she hissed, rolling her eyes and making sympathetic grimaces. Something – or more to the point – someone, had just tarnished the Churlbury rustic idyll. Some of the staff nodded knowingly and a track-suited balding chap in his middle years quickly abandoned his lunch box and assured Mrs K he'd deal with it.

'Thanks, Morris.'

'He's the deputy head,' Kate informed us, in a whisper. 'Teaches Year 6.'

It struck me that Kate was surprisingly well acquainted with the set-up. With her aura of confident self-assurance, she'd probably been introducing herself to the entire staff while I'd been goggling at the swimming pool, admiring the tambourines and checking out the castanets.

We stacked our plates, and then collected bowls of syrup sponge and custard and managed to overhear Mrs K murmuring – not quietly enough – to one of the dog collars, about some 'older brothers', 'bad influence' and words to that effect. I tried to feel matter-of-fact about my eavesdropping, convincing myself that *every* school in the country had its share of 'bad influences', yet fervently hoping that Churlbury wasn't being too greedy in that department. To cheer my two rivals, I added some spice to our conversation by breezily informing them of my final teaching practice experiences.

'*And* there were rumours of the head having a fling with one of the dinner ladies!' I told them, in dramatic hushed tones.

'Golly gosh!' gasped Jeremy, right out of the Bertie Wooster mould. Kate and I exchanged surprised glances and possibly came to the same conclusion: that he'd be better placed in a private fee-paying establishment.

'So why did you apply here?' Kate asked me, managing to quell the giggle that had threatened to erupt a moment before.

'Oh, I decided I'd had enough of bandit country and anyway I'm a Growdon girl by birth, so I wanted to be reasonably near home territory.

'If this one doesn't work out, I'm applying to Bransfield,' commented Jeremy casually.

'Oh yes, Bransfield – strictly for the offspring of the rich and famous,' said Kate nodding.

'That's the one,' confirmed Jeremy. 'But I only want to teach the junior forms of course. They're advertising for head of music in the lower school.'

There wasn't any more time for chit-chat because it was then the bell sounded. Like a well-drilled platoon the interviewing panel disbanded, and the staff rushed off to their classrooms, Morris quickly ramming the rest of his sandwich into his mouth after a brief but frazzled reappearance. Kate flung a silk scarf around her neck, touched up her lipstick and wished us luck. It was then that my knees started knocking louder than a pair of castanets. I was shown into Olive Karthew's office, where the panel were arranged in a cosy semi-circle.

One of the dog collars was in the chair – the Reverend Woodfine or something like that. He was definitely the more senior of the two, but not by more than five years. The other one was introduced as the curate – the Reverend Simeon Veltman – very smiley and keen on taking notes, but not at all my idea of a curate. For one thing he seemed much too old. I thought curates were *young*. Come to think of it, he may have been writing a sermon. There was also the lady mayor of Shealton-on-Stour, who was there because Churlbury feeds into the secondary school there. I think the shepherd's pie and syrup sponge had taken its toll, because after a brief smile when the Chief Rev was introducing the panel, she went very quiet and seemed to be sleeping in the corner, and had to be nudged when the interview was being wrapped up. There was also a parent governor, a foundation governor – whatever that meant – and at least one titled old gent. The names passed in one ear and out the other and all I could do was smile brightly at each one and hope I didn't make an awful gaffe.

'So what made you choose teaching?' asked the Chief Rev earnestly, leaning forward with clasped hands. It seemed an odd sort of question to ask someone who'd just about finished their training. For a moment an icy sensation swirled around my stomach as I struggled to recall how I'd replied to a similar opening gambit at Boxmouth over three years ago.

'Well… other people seemed to have recognised my potential before I'd realised it myself,' I began, trying not to sound too tentative. 'So I thought, why not? Maybe I *do have* a natural aptitude for it?'

'And?' Chief Rev prompted, still in earnest mode, although his sidekick, the curate, was beaming broadly.

'On the first day of my first teaching practice I knew I'd made the right decision.'

'Really?' queried Mrs K, raising surprised eyebrows. The icy swirl in my stomach turned into a solid block. Surely that wasn't the wrong answer. As far as I was concerned, it was true for me.

'Well,' I continued, desperately trying to salvage my chances, 'I'd really enjoyed the first term, the child development and the theory of learning, but I couldn't wait to put it all into practice. It was even better than I'd anticipated; hard work, naturally, but I never had a moment's doubt that I had found my vocation.'

Even *I* was surprised by my eloquence. If I'd been on the panel, my mind would have been made up immediately. There were a few nods round the table and murmured 'mms' and 'aahs', except for the mayor, whose murmur may have been a gentle snore. Mrs K looked suitably impressed.

'Well, it took me until my final teaching practice to reach that point,' she chuckled.

The icy block inside me started to melt.

Junior Rev was still scribbling avidly, but when he surfaced at last, he gave me a surreptitious thumbs-up that nearly made me giggle. After my shaky start, the rest of the interview seemed to go quite well and there were plenty of pleasant agreeing noises, which boosted my confidence. The youngest member of the panel was a parent governor who was keen to find out my ideas for developing the extra-curricular music. I was ready for this one and gave her my prepared spiel.

'And how would you see the school playing its part in the annual Churlbury Midsummer Music and Arts Festival?' she asked, giving no clue as to whether it was a hot potato type issue. The trouble was, my preparation hadn't unearthed a single clue that Churlbury even *had* an Arts and Music Festival. Maybe it was still in its infancy? It certainly wasn't featuring on the village website, unless the webmaster wasn't quite up with the diary of events.

I gulped and then gazed at the woman, trying to gauge the sort of reply she was expecting or hoping for. It felt as if I was paddling a flimsy canoe through shark-infested waters. If the school's participation in the festival was a contentious issue, my reply might easily alienate me from half the panel. There was no way I was going to know if the young parent governor was at loggerheads with the head over the subject. Olive's expression gave me no clue.

Junior Rev had paused in his note-taking and was giving me half a smile and a pair of cheekily raised eyebrows. I took this as a hint that a positive answer would meet *his* approval at least. I took a deep breath and told them that school involvement in community life was, in my opinion, very important. I added a few noble-sounding phrases such as 'contribution to village life', 'sense of pride' and 'encouraging high standards of performance' and made sure I smiled a lot as I said it.

'Puts bums on seats as well,' commented one of the men who hadn't said much up till then. Mrs K flashed an acid glance in his direction.

'Quite,' commented the Chief Rev awkwardly, and quickly moved on to the part where I could turn questioner.

I didn't want to sound mercenary but I needed to determine the chances of affordable accommodation in the area. After all, Amy had managed to land herself a prize catch by being bold enough to ask. So I took a deep breath and asked. It *was* a practical concern after all and although Growdon was about forty minutes away, I didn't relish *that* journey each morning.

'Over to you, Freddie, I think,' said Mrs K, catching the attention of the oldest member of the panel, whose full name, I discovered later, was Sir Freddie Lanary.

'Ah yes,' he croaked, with a twinkle, 'Bramble Cottage is currently available. I'd thought about giving the successful candidate first refusal on it. Er, it might need a little work on it though.'

There was another chorus of 'mms' and 'aahs' and another discrete thumbs up from Junior Rev.

'That... er... sounds wonderful,' I replied, wondering if Bramble Cottage was little more than a rotting hovel and that the tenancy being available was a way of hiding the truth that no one wanted to risk living there in the first place.

'The Frintley Estate has some of the prettiest parkland and woods in the area,' added Chief Rev, as if that was reason alone to live there.

I asked a few more general questions about PTA involvement and inter-school events in the area, just to sound as if I wasn't just interested in my own wellbeing. They thanked me for coming and then I was free to go. After a quick dash to the loo, I went to wait for the Shealton bus, my knees under control and my insides nicely settled at last. As I sat in a carriage of the five twenty from Shealton-on-Stour, hurtling through the dusk on the way to Devon and waiting for the trolley dolly – as Dad refers to them – to lurch and clink her way along to my seat, the images of Churlbury became imprinted in my mind. Within a few days, I would know my fate, although it would be agony waiting. At least Junior Rev seemed to be on my side. If Jeremy Jeeves had used too many 'golly gosh' type phrases in his interview, I wondered what sort of impression he'd have made. I hoped it was an unfavourable one.

Chapter 17

The Zebedee factor

'Coffee, black no sugar,' murmured Simeon Veltman, handing me a mug and managing to brush my hand into the bargain. 'Nice to have you on board, Gilly.' A smile creased his face in a way that added to his wrinkles but somehow didn't take away his boyish charm. Simeon Veltman must have been about fifty, with a roundish face and greying hair and eyebrows that waggled independently when he spoke. He would have been quite a dish in his younger days.

'Nice to be here,' I replied, trying to stop staring at his remarkable eyebrows. 'Do you live in the village as well as your... er...'

'Wife? Cat? Mother-in-law?' he asked, with a grin.

'Boss, I was going to say.' I meant the vicar, but wasn't sure how to refer to him.

'Ah boss,' he chortled, 'well he's all-seeing and all-knowing and everywhere!'

Simeon waved a spare hand around and almost knocked my coffee flying.

'Oops, sorry my dear, I was referring to *God*,' he whispered, leaning close enough for me to see the greenish flecks in his eyes, 'but you meant Harry I suppose, who tries to keep me in order.'

'Yes,' I giggled, 'but I was surprised that two clerical gentleman could be living in such a small village. I mean there can't be *that* much work to do in a place this size, can there?'

'Clerical gentleman?' mused Simeon, 'That sounds very grand, but actually my dear, Harry and I have *eight* churches to look after: Lesser Brimble, Greater Brimble, Brimble-by-Stour, Gussage Maidbury, Little Maidbury, Stour Maidbury, Marbeck and Churlbury of course! The fact that we both live here is co-incidental.'

'Goodness, eight churches!' I exclaimed, 'Sunday mornings must be frantic!'

'Hmm, it's quite busy, but some of them have to take their turns, such as Matins once a month or Evensong once a quarter. It's the funerals that take up a lot of our time, ageing population you see.'

'Yes, I can imagine,' I commented, 'but it must be difficult keeping up with everything.'

'Ah, well we have a website too, just another little job to keep me occupied. You can log on and find out which church is having which service, just so you don't turn up and find an empty church.

I hoped he wasn't meaning me when he used the word 'you' in connection with turning up for services. I wouldn't admit it to him, being so new to the scene, but my idea of a Sunday morning involved a long, lazy lay-in reading magazines, eating breakfast around eleven followed by a long soak in the bath, and then plenty of TV soaps. It didn't feature shivering in a dusty pew trying to work out what the archaic language in the prayer book meant and then emptying my purse in the collection plate for the privilege.

'Well, I'll bear that in mind. Of course I don't know if I'll have broadband access where I'll be staying,' I told him, knowing that to be a good guess.

'Ah but you'll be able to use the school computers. I think most of the staff use their laptops here.' Trust Simeon Veltman to know that.

Yes, there I was in the staffroom of Churlbury C. of E. Primary School on the opening day of the Churlbury Midsummer Music and Arts Festival and ready to meet my class for the first time. That afternoon, the new rising five intake would be coming into the reception class for a couple of hours and the rest of the classes would move up to their prospective room and teacher for the autumn term. The Year 6s had already been bussed off to Shealton-on-Stour Upper School for the day, getting the feel of being small fish in a very large pond for a change. I was feeling a bit like a minnow in a brook, being swept along by a gentle current, hoping I wouldn't be gobbled up by fierce carp. The possibility of making a wrong move or accidentally ignoring one of the village benefactors was filling me with terror. There was bound to be a highly tuned bush telegraph which had already spread the word about the new recruit at Churlbury C. of E. , down to the colour of my lipstick and my approximate shoe size.

After the interview, it had taken two days for the job offer to arrive and then I had to have the medical clearance which also took much longer than you'd imagine. Eventually I was pronounced fit enough to withstand the rigours of the teaching profession, and my contract was duly sent, signed and returned.

For a few days, it felt as if I was walking on air, amazed that I'd risen above Kate and Jeremy to secure my dream job.

'Jammy Beggar,' sighed Fran. She was filling in her third application form at the time – for Marbeck Primary, which wasn't far from Churlbury, as it happened. She'd been disappointed to have narrowly missed securing (according to the interview feedback) the Leigh job, which would have suited her better. Tony had already been snapped up by an Ilminster school. While I was starting to feel at home in Churlbury C. of E., Fran was getting her nerves in trim for her interview at Marbeck that afternoon.

'Just think Fran,' I had gushed excitedly, when she told me about the interview, we could be still seeing each other on a regular basis!' I'd also learned that the eminent Walter Flemington lived over at Marbeck andhad his finger in most of the local musical pies.

I'd been invited to stay overnight, with agreement from the college, and would be spending it with Pru Stebbings who, I discovered, ran a small B & B business as well as being school secretary and church organist. Mrs K had suggested that attending the festival would help me plan for the following year as well as introduce me to many of the prominent locals. That sounded useful, but what concerned me more was the state of Bramble Cottage, and the chances of seeing it before signing an agreement and committing to paying rent.

'Walter Flemington's really looking forward to meeting you, Gilly,' Olive had told me. 'He does most of the conducting and I'm sure he'd be only too happy to give help and advice.' He sounded a hundred times more agreeable than Maestro Rescorla.

Mum and Dad were thrilled when I phoned with the news that I'd landed the post.

'Sounds like it's time to sort out the motors,' promised Dad. When I phoned two weeks later to tell them about my school visit, no motor had yet materialised, but Mum was keen to pass on that Eleanor and Frank knew one or two people in the Churlbury area.

'I bumped into Eleanor and Frank in Sainsbury's at the weekend,' she told me. 'Frank's cousin Geoff sometimes plays trumpet in a band over that way.'

I trawled back through my mind for anything Tim might have mentioned about his trumpet playing first or second cousin Geoff, but didn't recall any passing reference to him being musical or where he lived. After all, *'over that way'* might be anywhere in a twenty mile radius, so I dismissed that little snippet as fairly irrelevant. He probably played in a brass band, and there were plenty of those around. The chances of exchanging pleasantries over sherry at an after-concert reception with the Rosewells seemed unlikely. It was interesting, however, that Mum had made time to chat with Tim's parents, especially as she'd been feeling quite embarrassed and awkward about the whole business. I mean, what do you say to the woman who was within a whisker of becoming your daughter's mother-in-law, but then writes the sort of letter that *she* wrote?

On the Tim front, there was no more news, other than he was scoring plenty of runs for Growdon 1ˢᵗ eleven. As long as he wasn't scoring with Lena Tuffin, I thought dismally, but he probably was. The news about the skiing trip had rather cemented Tim and Lena's relationship in our minds and was a subject that we barely touched on. Of course, we didn't know that Lena was the friend who'd gone with him. It could have been another bloke, such as someone from the cricket team.

From time to time I'd wondered if he'd regained any more memory, but even if he had, Mum – my spy on the ground – wasn't likely to find out. I imagined Eleanor and Lena making a binding pact that information about Tim's flashbacks would be kept even more classified than state secrets.

'Perhaps you'll meet the man of your dreams in Churlbury,' Mum remarked, during one of our regular catch-up chats.

'*Mum*, the average age in Churlbury is over fifty and I thought I'd already met the man of my dreams!' For me Churlbury meant gainful employment, not romance. Being offered the post confirmed, without a doubt, that the significant decision I'd made three years before was the right one.

They'd advertised that *'music would be advantageous'* and so I reckoned I stood a better chance than Kate, who'd divulged that her main subject was art. The biggest surprise though, on the day of my midsummer visit, greeted me when I went to hang up my jacket in the staff cloakroom, and Kate

Maxted breezed out of the ladies' loo.

'Kate, what are *you* doing here?' I exclaimed. She was the last person on earth I'd expected to see. Correction; Jeremy Jeeves was the last person.

'Same here!' she gasped. We soon discovered what wonderful move of fate had been at work.

'My Year 4 teacher had the all-clear at her twelve-week scan the day after the interview, but handed in her notice anyway,' Mrs K told us, confidentially. 'She and Patrick have been trying for ages. She was all set to take maternity leave, but they're talking of moving closer to Patrick's work and her parents in Portsmouth, so we had two vacancies to fill!' Kate and I exchanged delighted grins.

'Such a relief, I can tell you,' confided Mrs K, 'with two such strong candidates.' Our delighted grins melted into smirks.

Kate and I sat in on the assembly led by Reverend Veltman, straight after morning break. He was wearing his long black cassock, and a hideously large wooden cross on a leather thong dangled round his neck. To illustrate his talk he used two dog hand puppets – Mr Woofer and Mr Sniffer – whose antics had the little ones shrieking with laughter. It struck me that he had missed his vocation as a children's entertainer, or maybe he did that as a side-line. I couldn't imagine a curate's stipend was very generous. Unfortunately, his ventriloquist skills were not very well practised, and every so often there was a discernible groan from the staff who sat along both sides of the hall on crowd control duty. I thought the groans were a bit harsh, so I decided to give him plenty of encouraging smiles. He seemed to like that, judging from the smiles returned in my direction. I hoped he realised I was showing him support and not admiration. There was something about Simeon Veltman that reminded me of a bouncy puppy, a characteristic shared by a certain Lena Tuffin. After we'd mumbled our way through the Lord's Prayer – which seems to appear in a different version depending on the school, the vicar or the head – Mrs K quickly took over. She introduced Kate and I as new teachers and invited the children to give us a welcoming clap. After that, the classes trooped off to their rooms and we had time to familiarise ourselves with the curriculum plans for our own year groups.

'Let me show you the planning cupboard,' said Mrs K, inviting us to follow her. I wondered if it was her whimsical way of describing a tiny room used for planning meetings as opposed to the room for relaxing and refuelling. She flung the door open and clearly there was no whimsy about her description. This was indeed a cupboard chock-full of lever arch folders, all neatly labelled for every subject according to the long and medium term curriculum plans for each key stage. It was impressive with a capital <u>I</u>, emboldened and underlined. A 'wow' escaped our lips, which seemed to go down well with Mrs K.

'I think you'll find everything you need here,' she commented, 'although I think the music could do with revamping Gilly. We've been struggling on without a music co-ordinator for quite a while. I'm sure *both of you* are ready to bring some fresh new ideas to your subject areas.' We smiled obligingly, although I wasn't feeling overwhelmingly innovative and bursting with fresh new ideas. Having the whole caboodle handed to me on a plate was more to my liking at that moment.

'I'll leave you to it, but do come and knock on my door if you've any questions.'

She beamed encouragingly and swept off. 'Ah well, better pitch in,' sighed Kate. 'This place beats my last teaching practice school into a cocked hat – whatever that means.' I knew exactly what she meant.

That was the relatively easy part of the day; the prospect of meeting my new class released butterflies in my stomach, especially when I saw the list of names. There was one in particular that jumped out at me – Saul Zebedee. I recalled with some foreboding the incident on interview day and the muttered exchange between Mrs K and the dinner lady. Still, I'd had plenty of colourful characters to deal with on my three teaching practices. This Saul Zebedee couldn't be worse, surely? The children filed in, good as gold. A few nervous giggles broke out, but otherwise there was no sign of a major disturbance to threaten those first crucial minutes when I would stamp my authority on that little lot. Gilly Bonning was no easy pushover; in fact she was no pushover at all and no nine-year-old upstart was going to get away with twanging a ruler, let alone murder. Twenty-eight pairs of eyes regarded me with a mixture of excitement, suspicion, apprehension and nervous anticipation. They may have been sweet little Year 4s, still biddable and keen to learn, but I knew enough to be on my guard. My eyes needed to be swivelling in all directions, ready to pounce on the slightest toe out of line.

'I'm Miss Bonning,' I told them brightly, 'and I'm to be your new teacher next term. This afternoon we have a chance to get to know each other.' Yes, stating the obvious I know, but it gave me a chance to assess the general atmosphere and – more to the point – the trouble quotient.

'First of all, I want you all to make a name card for me,' I told them. 'Here's one I made earlier.' I held up mine as an example, which was decorated with music notes and cats. 'Now you can decorate yours with patterns or pictures of things you like.' It was my way of learning a few names as quickly as I could and to pinpoint young Saul. Most of the class beamed at me and whispered excitedly to the rest of their table as I passed around the rectangles of card. 'Make your letters big and bold,' I instructed them, 'and then I'll know who you are. You can then put your finished name card in front of you.' A boy in the furthest corner screwed up his face in a grotesque grimace and shoved the boy next to him, making his pencil skid across the card and then drop onto the floor. The rest of the group gave him the evil eye and I strode over giving him mine for good measure. Was this the infamous Saul Zebedee? He stared at me peevishly, jutting out his bottom lip and snarling defiance. A ripple of whispers spread across the room and the name Saul featured widely. If I'd guessed correctly, this was the thorn in my flesh.

'Stand up, Master Zebedee!' I ordered, hoping I'd come to the right conclusion, otherwise there'd be serious egg on the face of the new Year 5 teacher. A look of surprise abruptly replaced the peevish pout and he shot out of his seat, while several of the girls tittered nervously.

'How did you know my name Miss?' he asked suspiciously, and a little too confidently for my liking. He may have only been nine years old but he had already perfected the art of surliness.

'Oh, you'd be surprised, Saul,' I told him, with my best and most sinister glimmer. 'Teachers may not have eyes in the back of their heads, but their hearing is pretty sharp.'

'But it was Rufus Kale's fault,' he complained, 'he took my rubber.'

'No he didn't, Saul!' sneered a girl sitting opposite.

'Okay, enough! Now down to work all of you.' Rather than go in with all guns blazing and issuing threats that I might not have time to follow through to conclusion, I decided to give him a challenge. Boys like him, I'd learned, thrived on outdoing their peers. Judging by the bulging pencil case, he had every conceivable colour at his fingertips. I was banking on him being a budding artist and hoped my challenge would appeal to a competitive nature.

'Now sit down, keep your hands to yourself and see if you can make the best name card in the whole class.'

After that, they all settled quickly to writing a short piece about themselves, their family and pets, also illustrated with more artwork. There was a pair of sweet little twins called Phoebe and Flavia who drew very well-developed treble clefs and wrote about their flute (Flavia) and oboe (Phoebe). I made a diary note of their names ready for my school orchestra in the autumn, delighted to learn that it wouldn't just be a collection of violins and recorders. To keep everyone busy, and limit the chances of insubordination in the ranks, I had some word searches and puzzles ready to give out when they were finished. Despite the slightly shaky start, the class beavered away happily and were rewarded with a story before they went home. *The Elephant's Child* from the *Just So Stories* usually went down well, and I had them chuckling away with the silly voices I used for the different characters.

As they trooped out to the playground, where the mums, dads, grans and carers were having their daily gossip, I congratulated myself that young master Zebedee had met his match. I stood at the window and watched them pair up. Saul slouched over to a tall skinny young woman, with tight jeans and a lot of lipstick. He tugged at her arm to prise her attention away from her friend who was jiggling a pushchair with a bawling infant. There followed a lot of discussion and pointing towards the classroom, at which I retreated and cleaned the board. After a minute or so, I edged along the wall and peeped past the vertical blinds that were partly drawn to keep out the sun. The Zebedees and friends were ambling down the drive, Saul dragging his lunchbox and sweatshirt after him. What his older brothers were like and what sort of bad influence was rubbing off on their younger sibling was 'need to know' information that could wait for another day. I just hoped that they weren't into poking disgusting offerings through letterboxes or setting fire to washing or any other anti-social behaviour to relieve the boredom of country life.

Chapter 18

Bramble Cottage

'Of course you must see Bramble Cottage,' Mrs K agreed – or Olive as I should call her, as we're now on first-name terms. She phoned Sir Freddie and it was arranged that she'd drop me off, as there was plenty of time before the start of the festival that evening. Pru Stebbings lived nearby, so it wouldn't take me long to nip back, rest, eat, change, and still be at the church in time for seven.

'I don't know what kind of state it's in,' admitted Olive wryly, as she pulled out of the school car park in her gleaming Toyota, 'but if any repairs are needed, I'm sure Freddie would be only too happy to oblige. By the way, Freddie's gamekeeper-cum-estate manager Stan Murless will be meeting you at the cottage.' Then seeing my reaction to the word 'gamekeeper' she chuckled and assured me he wasn't anything so nifty or amorously inclined as Mellors of Lady Chatterley fame, and must be pushing seventy at least.

Olive dropped me off outside a pair of impressive gates which had been helpfully left open. A notice on one side advised passers-by that this was Frintley Estate, that there was no through-road and that trespassers would be prosecuted. In other words, the woods might look pretty, but don't expect to roll up and find picnic tables and a car park. I set off down a long winding drive, having tiptoed gingerly over the cattle grid, and admired a vast meadow on my left which was home to a flock of sheep, many of whom lay panting in the late afternoon sun. To my right was a wood of mainly deciduous trees – oaks, beeches and silver birches – where birdsong echoed and the occasional rasping chirrup of a grasshopper could be heard.

After a couple of hundred metres, the drive veered to the right and down a gentle slope. On the left, another field, bordered by clumps of trees, containing a few bullocks. Beyond that I could see a further wooded area and a brief glimpse of deer grazing contentedly beneath wide spreading boughs. It was the perfect pastoral view for any aspiring landscape artist, keen photographer or jigsaw manufacturer, and it was wonderful to think that I was being offered the chance to drink in all that dreamy Dorset countryside each day. I sighed with pleasure and fervently hoped that Bramble Cottage hadn't been ironically named on account of needing a twenty-first century prince on horseback to attack the surrounding vegetation with a sword, scythe or regulation county council hedge trimmer.

So far, there was no sign of a cottage, although of brambles, nettles, ferns and rampant grasses there was an abundance. As I continued along the drive and rounded the gentle bend, Frintley Grange gradually came into sight, peeping through a long avenue of trees that flanked the final approach. It resembled the four-square dwelling with central door and matching windows on either side that I'd often drawn as a child. Frintley Grange, however, had much grander proportions, many more windows on the first and second floor and a flight of steps leading up to the front entrance, all in matching grey stone. If a pumpkin carriage drawn by a team of mice had drawn up outside, it wouldn't have looked out of place. By then I was wishing I'd asked Olive to take me to the door. My feet were hot and sweaty from a whole day in school, in the wrong footwear for mid-summer temperatures and my arms ached from hauling my overnight case plus a carrier bag of work folders that I'd been encouraged to take away with me.

At last the wood on my right thinned out enough for me to catch a glimpse of brickwork, a washing line and a couple of outhouses in a clearing a short distance from the drive. Sure enough, I soon reached an open grassy area dotted with bushes and evidence of an overgrown path which led up to an unruly honeysuckle hedge and rickety garden gate, bearing the name 'Bramble Cottage'. If Frintley Grange had been Prince Charming's palace, this little dwelling was surely Hansel and Gretel's gingerbread cottage. The gate creaked rustily on its hinges, announcing to any slumbering wildlife that it was time to take cover. What I'd thought at first was a pile of logs covered in an old blanket, to one side of the front door, twitched into life, sprouted arms and legs and gradually took on the appearance of a gnarled old man. He scratched at various parts of his anatomy and grinned amiably as I scampered down the path that led to the dark green painted door, now peeling and showing signs of neglect.

'Ow do young, Miss?' he called. 'You'm Miss Bonning is you?'

We made our introductions and then he produced a large key and opened up the door after a brief struggle, and proudly flung it open.

'Lily and I used to live here,' he told me with a sigh, 'but we moved into the servants wing at the big 'ouse when Lily took over as 'ousekeeper back along. It's not quite the same, but at our time of life it's nice to have the comfort of central heating and proper plumbing.'

Hmm, I thought, as opposed to *this* place that has neither. In due respect to Stan and Lily's former home, I managed to smile and made appreciative noises as he showed me through the living room to the lean-to kitchen which lead to a tiny bathroom and toilet. Even on a warm summer evening, the rooms at the back of the cottage felt cool, the dusty lino floor was covered in flies' corpses and spectacular cobwebs were strung across the walls and ceiling.

Upstairs was hardly any better. There were two rooms, and one was scarcely bigger than a cupboard, although most of the doors and windows seemed to fit well enough and might just keep the place snug and warm if I could persuade Sir Freddie Lanary to drag the cottage into the twenty-first century.

'Very quaint and homely,' I told Stan, who flashed his toothy grin. The more I looked, the more I decided that Sir Freddie would need to stump up a thousand or two on plumbing, electrics, insulation and central heating before I agreed to risk my health in there. After all, there was bound to be plenty of decent little flats for rent in Shealton-on-Stour if I was prepared to drive over each day. But the more I considered the setting, which was idyllic and a better prospect than any characterless purpose-built box, the more I hoped Sir Freddie would be prepared to throw enough cash at this little gem, rather than let it sink further into decay. I made a mental list – taking out pen and notepad wouldn't have been diplomatic – thanked Stan profusely and scuttled back up the drive to Pru's, for toad-in-the-hole, cups of builder's brew and Victoria sponge.

By ten to seven, we emerged in our best frocks, freshly showered and made-up and were whizzing along to St Cuthbert's in Pru's old rust-bucket of a motor. 'Whizzing' wasn't a true description, as it happens, but it was much better than an unseemly sprint. Her 'old man' as she called him was in the *Dog and Ferret*'s dart team, with a crucial match that evening, so he wouldn't be sat in a pew applauding his wife's nimble performance of Widor's *Toccata*.

'Would you turn pages for me, Gilly?' she asked, as we arrived.

'What? Me?' I'd been hoping to skulk at the back and spy on the locals.

'Why not? I usually have one of the Girl Guides, but the last one I asked panicked and very nearly pulled the music onto my lap. I don't think anyone noticed but there were a few frantic bars of wild improvisation while we managed to push the pages back on the stand between us.'

'Oh, goodness.' Actually there was quite a heavy Girl Guide presence I noticed. Two were on guard outside the porch, armed with a pile of programmes and a collecting dish for the pound coins that concert goers were dropping in.

'Okay, Pru,' I agreed, 'but will anyone see me? What if *I* pull the music on your lap? It wouldn't make a very good impression!'

We slunk in and eased our way through clusters of DJ-clad chaps and ladies in black ensembles with red rose corsages, towards the narrow organist's seat which was squeezed in between the choir stalls and the organ console itself.

'If you're prepared to perch on the far end, you can sneak round through the vicar's vestry,' Pru whispered. 'I'll show you.'

We slid into the vestry and then battled our way past brooms and buckets along a gloomy little passage that led to the far end of the organ, by way of a curtained alcove.

'You can share my seat, but you won't be in the public eye,' she chuckled. 'My bulk will hide you quite effectively I think. There's nothing of you. We can sneak up just before the choir pieces, so no one will notice us. I'm not playing for the choir – they're doing unaccompanied madrigals.'

'Right, you're on,' I promised, 'but only because you make such good toad-in-the-hole!' I'd always loved Widor's *Toccata* and being up at the business end of the piece would be a thrill-a-minute experience. I hadn't told a soul before, but *that* was the piece I'd planned to have at my wedding to Tim.

Back in the body of the church – which had filled up quickly in the moments since I'd been familiarising myself with the page-turning seat - we assessed our best position in the few remaining spaces.

'Oh, Gilly, I've been looking for you everywhere,' gasped Olive, who descended upon us in a fluster, draped in burgundy silk. 'Walter's keen to say hello, but we're running out of time.'

A dapper gentleman with a white goatee beard, scarlet cummerbund and twinkling eyes appeared behind her shoulder.

'Charmed,' he said smoothly, reaching for my hand and kissing it reverently. 'We'll catch up later, Gilly. Olive has been telling me *all* about you.'

Olive raised an eyebrow in surprise. 'In the interval?' I asked, melting slightly in his suave presence.

'Well… er… it *may* be a little fraught then, but there's a reception afterwards in the rectory, so perhaps we can leave our little tête-à-tête till then?'

I nodded enthusiastically. A tête-à-tête with the festival director with a glass of bubbly in my hand sounded the perfect way to end an evening.

Pru and I persuaded a family of four to shuffle along their row so we could be well placed for a quick exit at the crucial moment. Walter was now on his rostrum and a hush descended in eager anticipation of the evening's entertainment. We were treated to string quartets, a guitar duo, a Joyce Grenfell monologue, some Shakespeare sonnets and then the Marbeck Singers arranged themselves on the chancel steps for some madrigals. Pru tapped my arm and we quickly made our exit as the singers were still rustling their music. We hovered in the wings as the fa-la-las echoed round the vaulted ceiling and basses droned while sopranos warbled. To rapturous applause, Walter and his choir took their bow and Pru and I shunted along the organ seat ready for the curtain closer on the first half of the evening. She gave me a wink, arranged her fingers and feet over the keys and pedals and launched into a gloriously uplifting rendition of one of the best-loved organ solos. With a heightened sense of responsibility I carefully took hold of the turned-back corner of the right hand page and flicked it over as Pru nodded. The pages behaved impeccably. I settled back on the seat as Pru worked her way through the next two pages, my eyes glued to the notes, not daring to look away for a moment. The rich and fruity sounds reverberated around the building, and shivers of excitement coursed up and down my spine. I imagine I wasn't alone.

Pru brought her performance to a hair-raising climax and we both sighed with relief.

'Better than a Girl Guide,' she chuckled, the sweat pouring off her brow. She gave my hand a pat. 'I could kill a glass of Pinot Grigio!'

'Me too,' I agreed, but not before I reminded her that she should take a bow. Someone at the back, obviously not versed in refined concert-going customs, was cat-calling loudly, whooping and clapping furiously. A few starchy-faced concert buffs turned and frowned but the rest of the audience stamped their feet enthusiastically until Pru had emerged to curtsey, glowing with pride.

'You were brilliant,' I told her, when at last I joined her in the drinks queue.

'And so were you, Gilly,' she said graciously, 'I might have known the piece more or less by heart, but I still feel safer if I have the dots in front of me.'

We grabbed a glass each and sucked in our breath to ease our way along the aisle and to find enough space to lift our elbows without causing a mishap or two.

'Cheers!' I gulped down a mouthful and gazed round at the chattering masses. A face came into view and my heart sank. A loud gasp must have escaped from my mouth because Pru was staring at me full of concern and asked me what was wrong. It was Eleanor Rosewell. My wonderful evening had turned to ashes. If she latched onto the crowd who were planning on hob-nobbing with Walter, Sir Freddie and some of the village elite at the reception, then it would be my worst nightmare, and trumpet-playing Geoff's fault. He was bound to be one of the ones in tight-fitting DJs and tired-looking dicky bows.

'You look as if you've seen a ghost!' Pru leaned towards me and put her hand on my shoulder. Had she thought I was about to keel over?

'You could say that.'

'Shall I fetch you a glass of water?'

'Er, no, I'll be fine. It's just the heat in here.' She nodded and sipped her wine, agreeing that she was feeling a little warm as well.

'Magnificent!' came a voice. Walter Flemington had wormed his way through the crowd and was plonking a celebratory kiss on Pru's flaming cheeks. 'I hope you've another popular piece up your sleeve for us tomorrow night Pru? I must admit I've been so caught up with choir and orchestra rehearsals that I hadn't taken much notice of the solo pieces in the programme.'

'You'll have to wait and see, Walter,' she teased, grinning.

The tide of concert-goers pushed past us and for a few moments I assumed that Eleanor had found a far corner to bless with her presence.

'And of course you'll be coming up with lots of ideas yourself, won't you, Gilly?'

I jumped guiltily, realising that Walter had probably been addressing me for the past few moments and I hadn't even been listening.

'Oh... er... um... yes, naturally,' I stammered, hoping I wasn't appearing as a complete ninny.

'Ah, there's Geoff. I need to have a word with him about his solo. Geoff, could you spare a minute?' He beckoned over a stout man with moustache and bushy eyebrows who was holding a glass of orange juice and stuffing crisps in his mouth. Meeting Tim's distant cousin, Geoff, was low on my list of priorities, especially if Eleanor and Frank were following on close behind.

Pru, by this time was chatting with a couple of friends and blocking off my escape route on one side. Walter had been joined by Simeon and a mousey-looking woman as well as Geoff. I was hemmed-in on every side, with only my half-empty glass of Pinot Grigio for comfort. Walter and Geoff started discussing technicalities about semi-quavers in the allegretto section and the change of tempo just before the piece went into the rondo. Geoff nodded and then gulped some juice, wiping his moustache on his hand. I studied the tile pattern on the floor, hoping that Walter's little pep talk would quickly draw to a close, until I realised that Simeon and the mousey woman were still hovering nearby, possibly thinking I was being either rude or stand-offish.

'Hello Reverend Veltman, hello... er... um?'

'Oh, this is my wife, Alison – Alison, this is Gilly Bonning, one of the new teachers I was telling you about.' He beamed proudly, as if my appointment was due to *his* excellent judgement. Alison Veltman smiled shyly and mumbled a quiet hello.

When people say that some couples grow like each other over the years, they might well have met Alison and Simeon. They had the same roundish faces and greying hair, although Alison was altogether more reserved. I couldn't imagine her winking cheekily or being as chummy as her other half. In appearance, however, they were like a pair of comfy slippers.

'Pleased to meet you, er, Alison.' She was well buttoned-up in navy blazer and pleated skirt, which seemed a bit 1960s for someone who would have only been a baby then.

Beside her, I felt very daring in my figure-hugging teal number, dressed up with a little black shrug.

'You look lovely this evening, Gilly,' Simeon remarked. He wouldn't have recognised the dress from the interview, although he'd already given my scooping neckline plenty of attention . Alison blinked at him and frowned. Perhaps she'd noticed where his eyes had been as well.

'Alison works part-time at the library,' Simeon added, as his wife seemed lost for words or was mentally composing a verbal lambasting about keeping his eyes away from Gilly Bonning's cleavage.

'Oh that's useful, having a library I mean,' I replied awkwardly, giving Alison an encouraging smile. She certainly looked as if she needed one.

'Ah, Simeon, Alison, good to see you both,' said Walter, turning back in our direction and putting an end to an embarrassed silence. There was another moment of panic for me as Eleanor hove into view once more, and this time our eyes locked – hers in surprise and mine in horror. Maybe she'd had a suspicion that I might be there after her Sainsbury's meeting with Mum. If that was the case, perhaps she'd come to crow about Lena Tuffin and rub my face in the mud as far as my old relationship with Tim was concerned. Perhaps she'd surprised Frank by insisting how keen she was on music festivals and how she was dying to hear Geoff's band. Well, if she did, I didn't want to know. She was almost upon me, and with Walter and the Veltmans now engrossed in an earnest conversation about woodworm in the belfry and Pru still giggling away with her chums, I had no other course of action but to smile sweetly and greet Eleanor as if she wasn't the writer of poison pen letters.

'Hello, Eleanor, fancy seeing you here,' I said brightly. 'Lovely concert isn't it, and Geoff's ready for his spot, is he?' Eleanor's eyes blinked wide in surprise. Hmm, I thought, she hadn't bargained on that. Geoff had by now puffed his way back to the rest of his mates and Frank had filled the gap. His face, always friendly in the past, was stuck in an awkward grimace.

'Oh, er… yes, I'm sure he is,' agreed Eleanor, who was unlikely to know the first thing about Geoff's solo. 'We're keen on hearing him, aren't we, Frank?' Frank nodded and then peered at the dregs of his fruit juice. He was evidently on driver's duty, whereas Eleanor was knocking back her wine with obvious relish. 'Oh yes, we're huge music fans,' she declared. 'I love the classics, especially after seeing that Amadeus film.' Frank nodded benignly. 'Amadeus Wolfgang wrote some smashing tunes,' she continued.

'Mozart you mean?'

'Oh yes and him too.'

'It's Wolfgang Amadeus Mozart, as a matter of fact,' I told her, trying not to smirk.

'There's no need to be all hoity-toity with *me* Gilly Bonning,' she snapped.

'We hear you've got a job here,' Frank remarked in an effort to change the subject, 'but it's a bit off the beaten track, isn't it?' The way he said it made it sound as if Churlbury was cut off from the rest of civilisation with no transport, broadband or running water.

'Yes it's a bit short on amenities – shopping wise,' remarked Eleanor with a sniff.

'Surprisingly, the retail opportunities – or lack of them – didn't feature highly when I applied for the post,' I replied. 'And it's only about forty minutes from Growdon, isn't it?' I continued brightly. 'I'm sure I'll be nipping over quite often once I've got my car, to keep in touch with old friends.'

'Some of them will be planning weddings in the next year, I shouldn't wonder,' she said smugly.

'Come on, Eleanor,' murmured Frank. He grabbed her elbow and steered her back through the crowd. The thoughts that passed through my mind were too X-rated to record, although a gag and handcuffs featured quite prominently.

Just then a bell sounded, signalling the end of the interval. I'll bet I wasn't the only one to breathe a sigh of relief. After the delights of the Churlbury handbell team, the festival orchestra spot, a recorder consort and renowned local wordsmith reciting Gerard Manley Hopkins poems, the Rosewells did *not* turn up for the post-concert reception to my great relief. It was – and I secretly hugged myself with delight when I heard – for performers and *specially invited* guests. Well, I guess I qualified twice over, after my dazzling display of exemplary page turning. There was a pregnant pause while the audience trooped out, after much hugging and kissing and cries of 'super' and 'wonderful evening!' Then, via the back entrance – the north door – the specially invited guests and worthy musicians sneaked across the churchyard and through a gate into the rectory garden.

I thought it was amazingly generous of Rev. Woodfine to be hosting the concert receptions – all three of them – as the festival was from Friday through to Sunday evening, with time off for Matins, naturally. Then Pru told me that he and his wife Veronica were simply doing just that – hosting – and that the catering was being shared between various village organisations. Friday was the turn of the W.I. Unfortunately my dream of sipping champagne on the rectory lawn took a quick nosedive, when we arrived to find that sandwiches and coffee was the only refreshment on offer.

'It's the Mothers' Union tomorrow,' Pru added, 'and the cricket club wives on Sunday, which means I'll be making a plateful myself.'

'Oh, are *you* a cricket widow too?' I gasped, then realised how stupid I was. It wasn't as if I was married to Tim. Pru gave me a quizzical glance.

'Anything you're not telling me *Miss* Bonning?' she giggled.

'Er, no… my boyfriend's a keen cricketer…' What was I saying? I couldn't possibly refer to him as my boyfriend any longer and quickly tried to change the subject. 'So no booze then,' I sighed, taking a sip from my cup.

'Oh, I don't know,' replied Pru, with a mischievous look. 'I wouldn't be surprised if Sir Freddie turned up with a bottle or two from his cellar. It *has* been known!'

Fairy lights twinkled from the apple trees and along a pergola that stretched across the back terrace. Flickering candles in lanterns winked through the shrubs and tall grasses and the heady scent of rambling roses perfumed the late evening air. All that was missing was a dishy bloke to take me in his arms and smother me hungrily with kisses. Fat chance of that, I thought sadly. The French doors had been flung open to reveal a vast table bearing platters of delicious fare, with not a boring doorstep in sight. We sampled salmon and beetroot, brie and grapes (very adventurous for a W.I. I thought), cheese and chives and ham and mustard. There were oodles more. Those W.I. ladies certainly knew a thing or two about sandwich making. They had also made jugs of rich, filter coffee and circulated at regular intervals with trays of a delicious aromatic brew.

'No sign of anything stronger,' I murmured to Pru.

'No, but Sir Freddie has been a bit tied up so far,' she observed, nodding towards a cluster of handbell ladies who were indulging in a spot of hero worship. 'Looks like he needs rescuing. Those ladies seem to be very persistent. If only they knew!' she added with a giggle.

'Ah, Gilly, my dear, and how did you like Bramble Cottage? Olive told me you went and had a recce this afternoon.' It was Chief Rev Harry who'd loomed out of the shadows to appear at my shoulder, steaming mug in hand. I enthused over the best bits, such as the beautiful view and the peaceful setting, but he could see I was skirting around a great big but.

'Freddie's not short of a bob or two,' he chuckled. 'I think he should be able to spare a few to improve the place. I've driven past it dozens of times and hardly ever seen signs of life, so I don't think it's been kept up to scratch. Heating? Plumbing? Electrics?'

'Dire,' I admitted, 'or non-existent.' He nodded gravely and grunted.

The earlier resolve about my repair wish list had withered somewhat by then. The prospect of giving Sir Freddie my list of requirements was now quite daunting. After all, the rent he'd mentioned following the interview seemed very reasonable. Well, perhaps now I knew why. It didn't seem fair. There was Amy landing herself a snazzy new barn conversion and here was I faced with a damp shack still in its pre-World War I state.

'Come on, Gilly, let's do the deed,' encouraged Harry conspiratorially, 'we can't have you freezing to death in there.' He strode across the lawn, scattering the handbell ladies with a purposeful glint in his eye and we were soon engaged in listing Bramble Cottage's shortcomings, liberally peppered with positive praise about its situation and value for money. 'Now what it needs is heating,' Harry suggested firmly.

'Heating?' Sir Freddie queried, as if the idea that the place should have any was as unusual as requesting a swimming pool or a hot tub in the garden.

'Yes, Freddie, you have central heating at the Grange, I presume?'

'Hmm, I believe so.'

'Right, so you couldn't possibly deny Gilly the same home comforts, could you?

Sir Freddie glanced at me and I assumed my best 'damsel in distress' demeanour.

'Plagued by chilblains,' I whimpered, nodding.

'Oh poor girl,' breathed Simeon, sympathetically, who had emerged from the shadows. He added a few arm pats for good measure.

'And you'd be wise to have the electrics checked and the plumbing too, while you're about it,' continued Harry determinedly.

'Really?' croaked Sir Freddie, his eyebrows shooting up in surprise.

'Hmm,' Harry murmured with concern, 'it's probably a disaster waiting to happen. Better safe than sorry, as they say.' I wondered how many more clichés would be trotted out.

'Round pin plugs, loose wires,' I sighed. In fact, for the second time that day I wondered exactly how long it had been since Stan and Lily had lived there, and whether Sir Freddie had been stretching the truth somewhat when he'd told me that the cottage was becoming available.

'Oh well, we can't have that, can we?' Harry added, pursing his lips.

'No, no… dear me,' agreed Sir Freddie. 'I'll get Gosling, Potts and Sawbridge – my agents – to deal with all that and you must give me your number, Gilly, dear, then we'll sort out the contract.'

He winked and patted my arm, until I wondered if I was no longer a student teacher, but had turned into a tabby cat, considering the amount of pats I was attracting.

'Well, we'll all drink to that, eh, Freddie?' prompted Harry, with a nudge.

'Oh… er… yes indeed, and I have just the stuff for that.' He looked round the garden, squinting at the knots of musicians and guests. 'Now where is Simpkins? He's got half a dozen rather nice bottles in a case for me somewhere.'

Simeon rubbed his hands eagerly at this.

'Simpkins is his manservant,' Harry told me discreetly, tapping the side of his nose and winking meaningfully, 'worth his weight in horse manure, and a jolly good chap. Ah, think he's been spotted!' With that he grabbed me by the hand and before the church clock struck half past ten, we were standing round toasting my new home and career.

'Welcome to the village, Gilly,' gushed Veronica, who had managed to produce a tray of glasses. 'I'm sure you'll be happy here, but I'd get an alarm fitted, if I were you. Living in that wood does have its drawbacks!' I wanted to ask her what she meant. Was there a dangerous gang of drug addicts or criminals living there that no one had mentioned? Was there a witches coven majoring in sacrificial dances and nude orgies? Her remark was hardly reassuring

'Oh, I expect I'll be all right,' I replied confidently, hoping she was over-reacting. 'Cheers!' Perhaps I'll get a dog, or a cat, I thought, although a husband would be even better, but the chances of that seemed to be very slim indeed. The only attention I seemed to be attracting was from middle-aged married men or a pensioner with a penchant for male company if I interpreted Harry's meaningful glance correctly.

PART TWO

TEACHER

Chapter 19

You could have heard a spider cough

Rain lashed down relentlessly, in typical British summer style, sliding off the bald and shaven heads of the two deliverymen, before hanging precariously on their noses and then plopping onto their overalls. It was late August, yet it felt like November. Earlier in the week, it was still unquestionably summer, with combine harvesters frantically tearing up and down the surrounding wheat fields trying to strip them while the weather briefly relented. The end of term had coincided with a long stretch of dreary dampness, when nothing moved except banks of threatening clouds and bucket loads of rain onto the Dorset landscape below. My plans for relaxing on Mum and Dad's back lawn while I revamped the school music scheme were dashed to pieces. I took up temporary residence in the conservatory and listened to the constant drumming on the roof instead. Being at home, however, meant that I could nudge Dad towards that car business he'd been putting off for too long. Leaving the shop in the capable hands of one of his most experienced assistants, we trawled through most of the car forecourts in Boscombe, Christchurch and New Milton and he eventually splashed out on a three-year-old Citroen in sunshine yellow. We joked that he'd easily find it in any car park compared with the metallic grey one I was inheriting from him. Metallic grey, however, suited me very well. It would be easier to conceal in my isolated location, amongst the dark undergrowth.

In between my schoolwork, I searched the Growdon shops for kitchen equipment – most of Bramble Cottage's range were museum pieces – and occasionally poked my head round the door of Tim's bank. Inevitably he was tied up with a customer.

'Twine, string or rope?' I joked on one occasion, fed up with yet another lame response. The girl gazed back at me blankly. My dry humour was evidently lost on her. After that, I considered phoning him. Nobody could possibly accuse me of pestering him – it had been a whole *year*, for goodness sake. When I did, I was treated to the same pat answer, but resisted the temptation to make jokes about bondage. For a few mad moments one day, I even entertained the ruse of pretending to be Lena Tuffin, just to see if he'd deign to take my call, but at the last minute I lost my nerve. I suppose I didn't want to be faced with knowing that *she* was more of an attraction in his life than Gilly Bonning. Yes, even after the news of his skiing trip and Eleanor's smug prediction, I still held out hope that I could be more than a passing acquaintance to him.

'Which room?' grunted the shaven-headed bloke, as he sweated, dripped and struggled with one end of the polythene wrapped bedframe. Which room? Did he seriously think I might be considering bedding down in the lean-to kitchen or the living room, as if my poor knees were past climbing stairs?

'Um… well the bedroom actually,' I told him apologetically, trying not to sound sarcastic. 'The larger of the two rooms,' I added helpfully. Mum had insisted on treating me to a brand new bed and cooker, and had even arranged for the old ones to go to the local tip.

'You don't know how many beetles are gnawing their way through the frame or what horrible livestock there might be breeding in the mattress,' she said, shuddering.

'Or how many previous residents have snuffed it while lying on it,' added Dad, gloomily. The delivery men heaved and groaned their way up the dog leg stairs, knocking lumps out of the wall on their way. It looked as if I'd have to get busy with filler and paint, judging by some of the holes in the plaster.

Since my last visit, Bramble Cottage had been dragged kicking and screaming into the twenty-first century. The electrics had been overhauled, the water now flowed in a clear crystal stream rather than spluttered and gasped in a filthy rusty trickle, and shiny new radiators stood proudly in each room. Painters and decorators had been hired and spiders had been made homeless in the freshly spruced-up interior.

'Which way for this then?' the small bald one croaked, after mopping his brow with a well-used rag. Their cargo had the words 'Electric Cooker' printed on all sides, but I still smiled sweetly and directed them through to the lean-to. With only three ground floor rooms, there really wasn't much choice.

'Will you unwrap and connect it?' I asked nervously, surveying the wrappings bound by tough nylon tape.

'Lummy no, Mrs,' exclaimed the small bald one in surprise, 'we just deliver 'em. You need a sparky to do the rest, or ask your hubby.'

'I don't have either of those, as it happens,' I replied haughtily. The crisp five pound note, that I'd put by as a tip, stayed safely in my pocket. Those two might just have dumped their load in the front garden if I hadn't whipped the door open the second they'd drawn up outside.

'Cup of tea?' I offered brightly, but they shook their heads and muttered something about dropping off a three piece suite in Swanage. Before their van had rumbled over the cattle grid I had punched Pru's number in my mobile, poured out my tale of woe and she was recommending someone called Matthew who lived round the corner, but was in great demand.

'There's usually a long waiting list for his services.' Put that way, he sounded like a high-flying surgeon.

'That's a shame,' I replied mournfully.

My euphoria at being an independent working girl at last was hitting the hard reality of having to cope with my limited skills set. Admittedly, Sir Freddie – or his agents – had sent the boys round to decorate, run the mower over the waist high grass on the lawn and even top up the gravel at the front, that did the business as a parking area... BUT... my life seemed to be full of buts. My dream of rustling up a tasty home-cooked meal died a speedy death. It would have to be pot noodles and salad, but as I'd only just moved in and the second-hand fridge was behaving itself, that would be no hardship.

'Sorry not to be very helpful,' sighed Pru apologetically. 'Our Phil's living much too far away to help out now, or else I'd have pressed him into service.'

Phil was the younger of her two sons, who'd qualified as an electrician and had now set up his own business. The trouble was, he lived in Manchester.

'Alan's due home from work in an hour's time. He could help with the bed, but the electrical know-how hasn't rubbed off on him yet. I once asked him if he could change a plug and he went off to the hardware shop and came back with the sort you put in a sink!'

'Well, I'm not sure if *I* could change a plug,' I admitted.

'Nothing to it,' breezed Pru. 'I asked Phil to show me, so I'll teach you. But that doesn't help with the cooker does it?'

I told her not to worry, that perhaps I might have a ramble over the estate, search out Stan and sweet-talk him into helping.

'Tell you what, Gilly, you *could* ask Simeon.' I remembered the arm patting, the long clerical garb and found something didn't quite fit with expecting him to connect a cooker. Actually, the arm patting had nothing to do with it, but it was part of the reason why I found myself objecting to him coming to the cottage. She sensed my hesitation, or disbelief, or both.

'He used to be something high up in electricity before he trained for the church.'

'What, you mean he was C.E.O. of Southwest Power or scaled up those wooden poles... you know... hard helmets, harnesses and high voltage stuff?'

'No, not quite,' she giggled. 'But he knows his electrics. Why not call him, otherwise try Yellow Pages.' So, taking my courage in both hands I did just that – calling Rev. Veltman, I mean – and he was almost out of the door before I'd finished explaining my predicament.

'You and Alison could come over for a meal, by way of a thank you,' I told him, but he was so eager to help that I don't think he heard my offer. Ten minutes later, he was standing in my kitchen with a bulging tool bag and a winning smile.

'Beats writing sermons,' he told me cheerfully. Yes, well I guess quite a lot of activities are better than writing sermons, unless you really enjoy lashing out at your congregation with all that fire and brimstone stuff. However, Simeon didn't strike me as a fire and brimstone sort of chap, nor as an electrician, come to that.

I left him to it and went upstairs to finish removing the plastic wrapping from my lovely new bed. Two minutes into the job I realised that there was the challenge of fixing parts of the frame together, with a note in the instructions that they recommended the job being done by two people. I wondered if I had all the tools I needed, but the instructions weren't too clear to my inexperienced eye.

'You probably need an Allen key,' Simeon told me, matter-of-factly after I'd popped my head round the kitchen door. 'Have a look in the bag of screws and so forth. They should have provided everything you need. It's an

'L' shaped piece of metal with a hexagonal end,' he added, noting my blank expression. I wouldn't have known an Allen key from a skeleton key.

'Don't worry, Gilly. When I've finished here I'll come up and take a look. Probably have it fixed in a jiffy!' Simeon was certainly showing plenty of promise. If the preaching didn't work out he could make a fortune as a children's entertainer as well as a side-line in electrical work. He'd be in great demand, and the money would probably be better too. Still, the church was his vocation, and I'd learnt a thing or two about following *my* vocation in the past three years, so who was *I* to criticise what he was doing?

Half an hour later, we were both standing in my bedroom, which felt ever so slightly awkward. It could have been worse; there could have been underwear strewn around the place.

'No, definitely no Allen key,' he confirmed. 'Poor Gilly, what a welcome.' He patted me on the back in a show of sympathy and then – to my relief – removed his hand and rummaged in his bag for an impressive set of Allen keys, all jingling on a wire strap.

'I'll go and make tea and leave you to it for a while, shall I?' I said, choosing to ignore the instruction about two assemblers. I nipped down the stairs, started the brew and even wiped down a couple of kitchen shelves for my mugs and wine glasses. There were still a few boxes stacked up round the living room, but I wasn't planning on sorting them out straightaway. Eventually, after quite a lot of 'you catch hold of that end' and general heave-ho and shunting round the tiny room, the bed was assembled and Simeon flopped down on it in a perspiring heap.

'Jolly comfy,' he gasped, testing the springs and inviting me to try. I wasn't quite sure about the wisdom of joining him for a bounce, but squatted on a corner, just to show willing. He was a man of the cloth after all, and a married one at that. If he wanted to move up to vicar and have his own parish he'd hardly be trying any hanky-panky. After swigging down our tea, I showed him the even tinier second bedroom where I had an inflatable camping mattress and a sleeping bag. If my bed hadn't materialised I'd have used those as a temporary measure.

'All ready for visitors, I see,' he observed brightly, 'and boyfriends?'

'Um… well…' should I tell the truth, I wondered.

'Oh surely you've got one or two of those, a pretty girl like you.' There was a certain twinkle in his eye that I'd seen before. The scary time in

Desmond's study also came flooding back.

'Yes of course... a boyfriend. Well, he's been working very hard, yes very hard so... um... always tied up with customers. And he's been quite unwell... er...'

'I'm not surprised, that's what happens when people work too hard. They wear themselves out.'

'Well, he had an accident, and... Well it's been a bit of a long haul.'

'I'm sure you've been a great support to him,' Simeon chimed in, 'and he's a lucky chap. I look forward to meeting him.'

Oh great, Gilly, I thought, now you'll be expected to produce the invalid boyfriend. The chances of that were so remote that I knew keeping up the pretence would be almost impossible. Being quizzed by Simeon on a regular basis and having to come up with yet another excuse why I hadn't produced him for general approval was bound to wear me down.

'Er... he's not well enough to travel...'

'But you said he's always tied up with customers. So I take it he's well enough to work?' Ah, trust me to get myself in a pickle, I thought.

'Yes, he works, but that's about it.' I wasn't sure how convincing that would be.

'Not much of a life for the poor chap, all work and no play and all that!'

Was there steam building up inside me? Simeon was like a terrier with a rabbit cornered in a woodpile. He just wouldn't give up. I shook my head sadly, hoping he'd finally get the message that the subject was too painful to discuss any more. Yes, Gilly Bonning was going for the sympathy response and... oh no... there was that consoling arm round the shoulder yet again, with a chummy squeeze of reassurance thrown in for good measure.

I made a quick escape, on the pretence of checking my mobile, which I'd conveniently left downstairs.

'Want me to give you a hand with your unpacking?' he offered, having followed me downstairs and now stood gazing round at my tottering piles of bags and boxes.

'Oh no, I'll be fine, honestly... and there's that unfinished sermon of course...'

By then he was picking things up, as if he was at a bric-a-brac stall or car boot sale and I started to wonder how to get rid of him.

'Nice photo,' he mused, gazing at a pile that had spilled out of a wallet.

It was one from the Growdon Awards Gala, but not very flattering because I'd been caught with a silly grin on my face. It was just a head and shoulders one, taken before my chat with Bill, the cyclist.

'Oh that one… mm, I wasn't going to keep it, it's not a good one. I look like a Cheshire cat.'

'Oh, I disagree. I think it's charming.' He stood gazing at it while the steam in my head increased. 'Actually we're thinking of having a rogues' gallery of pictures in church… or at school. Could I take this one for it?'

'Be my guest. And thank you for your help, but I'm sure your sermon needs some of your attention now,' I said firmly, turning aside and gathering up the rest of the photos.

I think the penny must have dropped at last. I heard him sigh while I pretended to busy myself with my jumble of belongings.

'Too right,' he agreed smiling, as I went ahead of him to the door, just to make sure he got the message. 'Harry says pastoral care is my gift, but I need to brush up on my sermons. All part of the territory!' he chuckled, then ducked down under the straggling foliage in the porch and set off down the path, whistling as he went. I closed the door, turning the key for safety, and leaned against it, my heart thumping away like a pair of bongos. What he didn't realise was that I'd caught sight of him out of the corner of my eye. Just remembering it made me shudder. Before stuffing the stupid photo in his pocket, I'd seen him furtively put it to his lips and close his eyes in a soppy, dreamy way. I re-ran through my fevered brain all the patting, sympathetic comments and over-friendly smiles. He might have thought that was part of his armoury of pastoral care, but it had put me into a proper tizzy, especially the photo business. *That* was definitely beyond the bounds of pastoral behaviour as far as I was concerned.

All at once, I felt very vulnerable and in need of the support of the sisterhood; other like-minded females onto whom I could unload my worries – and preferably those who didn't have any connection with Churlbury or the local church set-up. I needed dear old Fran, and Kate might be a good ally if I could trust her to be discrete. Fran had landed the Marbeck job on the day I was getting to grips with the troublesome element of my new class, turning pages for Pru and hob-nobbing with other favoured guests on the vicarage lawn. When I told her about Walter Flemington and his orchestra being leading lights at the village festival she reminded me that she'd been told to leave recorder group at the age of eight for hitting other children over the head with her instrument and refusing to say sorry.

'It was my mum's fault,' Fran had told me, with a shrug. 'I don't think parents should foist their unresolved dreams onto their poor kids.' Of course I knew all about parents' expectations. I was a prime example of one that had at last come up to scratch after several years of hand wringing and offering of prayers to the Almighty.

'But you could always join the Marbeck Singers,' I had suggested. Fran still wasn't convinced, saying she couldn't read music and she wasn't going to risk being pelted with rotten eggs for singing all the wrong notes at the festival or having me sit in the audience making faces at her.

'You're thinking about Thomas Hardy peasants,' I told her. 'The Churlbury Festival is much more highbrow.'

'Well that counts me out!' There was no answer to that.

That was two months earlier, and since then Fran and Tony had dived off to Torquay again to wait on the blue rinse brigade and top up their bank balances, while I'd been slumming it in Growdon. Now Fran was in her own tiny one-bed flat somewhere over the border in Somerset, but within easy commute of Marbeck.

I punched her number into my mobile. Churlbury might have its drawbacks, such as one village shop and a frisky curate, but the mobile signal for my network was always as tanked up as a stag in the rutting season.

'Hello my old friend,' gasped a croaky voice on the other end. 'How's it down in Dorset?' she asked, putting on a phoney accent.

'All the better for hearing your dulcet tones,' I giggled. 'Fancy a trip over here? I can offer you afternoon tea in my cottage garden.'

'Ooh, posh!' she gasped, but not so croaky this time. We pencilled in two possible dates and left it for me to find out if I could tempt Kate away from the family estate down near Dorchester.

Oh yes, Kate's folks had cash – oodles of it, by the sound of it. That leather coat of hers wouldn't have been a charity shop bargain after all. The Maxteds' money came from their vast farming estate – mainly dairy – which fed into a thriving organic yoghurt and ice cream business. They also had several spare fields for caravan rallies and the odd pop festival. Although my time spent with Kate had been fairly brief, she'd been only too ready to boast about the family empire. My dad's little grocer's shop sounded very plebeian by comparison. There was also a Maxted heir to the estate, namely Ewan, who was a few years older than Kate and nicely settled in a general practice near Bridport. Kate had mentioned more than once in the short time we'd chatted, that Ewan was unattached. I wondered if she was sizing me up as sister-in-law material, so I dropped vague hints about a boyfriend in Growdon. I managed to catch Kate in between shopping in Bath and a yachting trip to Cowes in her dad's sixteen-footer.

'Ooh yes, I'd love to come over!' she squealed excitedly. Yes, a trip to Bramble Cottage was probably just the timely reminder she needed about how the other half live. She'd be able to breathe in the aroma of the working classes and remind herself that not every house has a Jacuzzi in the bathroom and that many people can only afford lastminute.com bargain breaks, or self-catering cottages rather than jet or sail off on their hols to Bermuda or the Seychelles. No, I do her disservice. Kate had seen enough of the other half as a student.

The days before the start of term dwindled to single figures and I was able to introduce Kate and Fran at long last. They were so different that I felt nervous about the meeting until the moment they exchanged glances, grinned and started chatting as if they were old friends. I was delighted. I'd emptied every one of my tottering pile of boxes and made the place quite homely – but not in a crocheted tea cosy and chintzy curtain sort of way. The garden was still holding its own, but there was plenty of time for work outside while the weather stayed reasonably dry.

'So what's the local talent like?' asked Fran, as we scoffed Jaffa cakes and chocolate fancies. 'Anyone likely to fit the Tim vacancy?' Like Mum, Fran had given up on Tim's chances as No.1 man in my life ever again.

Kate lifted a quizzical eyebrow. 'Thought you were spoken for, Gilly.'

'Hmm, well I *have* been,' I admitted, 'but it's sort of complicated.' Fran rolled her eyes.

'The trouble is, I seem to be attracting the wrong sort of attention,' I sighed. 'It seems to be the story of my life.'

'She thought one of the college tutors made a pass at her,' Fran murmured. Yes, I'd told her about that unfortunate incident in the end, but toned it down a fraction, just in case she felt in the mood for whistle blowing. 'And she had the wrong sort of attention from one of the other music students. He was dishy but rude.'

'Not just rude, Fran, he was vile, and he kept picking on me. In fact, he seemed to get a perverted pleasure from doing it.'

'Oh poor you,' sympathised Kate.

'And now it's happened again… which is why I needed propping up.' Kate and Fran exchanged interested glances. 'And advice.'

'So who was it?' Kate asked, obviously intrigued. 'Anyone *I* know?' I was in a quandary. Should I tell her and risk something filtering back to the Veltman household? I started pulling at the hem of my T shirt, wishing I hadn't started in the subject.

'Come on, Gilly,' insisted Fran. 'You can't leave us dangling like this!'

'Well, it's the curate.'

'Simeon Veltman!' gasped Kate. 'Surely not!'

'What's he like?' quizzed Fran. 'Tall, dark and gorgeous?'

'Not so you'd notice,' replied Kate, 'more medium, losing it – his hair I mean – and almost past it, actually, but still quite a sweetie.'

They looked at me with disbelieving eyes.

'It's true!' I insisted. 'He's been giving me odd little smiles, keeps patting me as if I'm his pet dog, arm round the shoulder treatment and even gave me a thumbs up in my interview.' They exchanged more glances and shook their heads.

'Well, a thumbs-up in an interview *is* a bit odd,' agreed Fran, 'but it doesn't sound as if there's anything to be worried about.' Then I told them about the photo and this time Fran agreed it was not the usual or desirable behaviour for a clergyman. Kate, however, had an inkling that shed some new light.

'Ah, I think I might know why he did that,' she murmured enigmatically. 'There's something sad in the Veltmans' life. Their only child died, aged six months.'

'I can't see how that's got anything to do with the photo business.' I shook my head. 'And how do you know about his past?' I demanded. Alison and Simeon were well into their middle years, so the death of a baby must have been quite a few years ago. I just couldn't see the connection.

'Simeon and Alison used to live between Dorchester and Weymouth,' Kate began. 'They ran a very successful electrical business and Dad used to call him in to fix things on the farm. They were late starters as far as marriage was concerned. Alison was into her late thirties when she became pregnant. I remember Mum saying how wonderful it was that they were going to have a family at last.'

'Ah,' Fran and I both sighed, preparing ourselves for the rest of her tale.

'She apparently had problems while she was carrying the baby, but went into labour quite naturally and everything seemed fine, until the little girl was born.'

Kate looked at us both, pausing. 'There were severe problems and the baby was only given a short time to live. The fact that she lived six months was a miracle, according to Mum.'

'Oh, that's so sad. Poor Simeon, poor Alison,' I sighed.

'They called her Gillian.' You could have heard a spider cough.

'It was after that, that Simeon decided to train for the ministry and they moved away. I didn't know they lived in Churlbury until I saw him at the interview. In fact, I'd forgotten about his family tragedy until I told Mum I'd seen him and she reminded me about it.'

'He was remembering the dead baby,' sighed Fran, wiping away a tear.

'Ah, well if that was what it was about,' I murmured, 'I'll forgive him, poor chap, although I'd have thought a picture of a baby would have been more likely to make him behave like that.' You see, I wasn't convinced.

Chapter 20

Hobnobbing with the Maxteds

He was gazing in the jeweller's window when I saw him, the same window that I'd sighed over dozens of times, trying to choose my ideal ring. It had been so long, I'd almost come to terms that, short of some lightning flash/thunderbolt type miracle, the chances of meeting him were as likely as Bazooka Billy winning the Lincoln Handicap three years in a row, or Auntie Sue winning the lottery. She wouldn't have bought a ticket at gunpoint, which only emphasises the unlikelihood of such an outcome. I was well into my first term, and thought I'd give myself a short break from endless marking, record keeping and – more to the point – taming the wilderness outside Bramble Cottage, and enjoy Saturday like the rest of the population. That forlorn plot could possibly become a garden once more if only I was prepared to spend every available second out there with the assortment of rusty hoes and spades that were mouldering in one of the old outhouses. However, I wasn't so desperate to spend my precious time gardening and there'd be plenty of time in the spring, I decided.

Yes, I thought I'd drive over to Growdon, have a mooch round town and then spend the evening with Mum and Dad and catch up with *Strictly Come Dancing*.

'Hi, Tim,' I said, probably sounding more surprised than anything else. Now that the cricket season had finished he would have had his Saturday afternoons free once more. The fact that he didn't have Lena hanging on his arm was a miracle. Maybe they'd broken up, I wondered? Maybe I had a chance to win his affection again? I remembered the old days when I wasn't on Saturday duty at Pearsons. We'd go for walks into the country; throw pebbles in brooks, wobble across cattle grids and explore different parts of the New Forest, enjoying the beautiful colours of autumn. Ah... happy days. I'd tip-toed along the pavement, hardly daring to breath, for fear of alerting him to my presence and possibly scaring him off.

'Oh... hi, Gilly.' His eyebrows shot up, his face turned from pale putty, through pale pink to puce in two seconds flat and his eyes started flickering nervously. Was I that scary? Had I smudged my mascara into panda eyes or forgotten to brush away the toast crumbs from my lips?

'Fancy seeing you in Growdon,' he continued, still a tad awkwardly. 'I thought you were at Boxmouth.'

'Not any longer,' I told him, and then gave him a quick update, all the while aware that he kept furtively flicking his eyes towards the shop window. Yes, he'd been gazing at a row of real sparklers, nestled cosily on deep blue velvet pads. They were engagement rings, and I feared that Lena Tuffin still had him in her grasp. Why else would he be so engrossed in precious metals with hefty price tags? Eleanor Rosewell's smug prediction reared its ugly head again

'And how are things with you Tim?' I asked brightly. 'How's your amnesia?' I refused to avoid the subject now that I had him standing in front of me, with no customers queuing up for the benefit of his financial expertise.

'Well,' he started, nervously licking his lips and executing a quick head turn to check he wasn't being watched or overheard, 'I remembered the trip to Torquay.'

'With Auntie June?' Some butterflies started a rumba in my stomach and my daydreams shook the dust off their fairy wings. He nodded.

'And ice creams on the prom?' He nodded again and smiled just a trifle smugly as if it was some great achievement, which it was, in a way. 'Well, that's brilliant. Any more?' I asked him eagerly. After all, the trip to Torquay wasn't too long before the accident.

'We used to go for walks, I think,' he said tentatively.

'Yes, yes... we did!' I agreed, my heart beginning a steady gallop.

This was *such* good news, although why he was acting so nervously I couldn't understand. Perhaps he'd parked in a thirty-minute bay and was on the lookout for an over-zealous traffic warden. Setting that aside, it sounded as if several jigsaw pieces of memory had slotted into place.

'And there was something about a concert.' He faltered and shook his head. I wanted to take his hand and give it a squeeze, but having him in front of me, chatting like that was enough for the time being.

'Yes, we spoke about that before, about going to a concert on my

birthday. Remember that time we met just before the night of the awards?'
Tim grimaced and then nodded. 'We were going out for ages before that
Tim.' He nodded again and smiled warmly, with those lovely little crinkles
around his eyes. 'We were *very* close.'

I wasn't being pushy, I wasn't badgering him; I was being as gentle as
possible, as if I was standing in front of a striking red admiral, with my net
poised. I didn't dare mention his mum's evil letter. It might have broken the
magic of the moment. However, someone else had that privilege.

'Tim?' A strident female voice cut through the traffic and pedestrian
noises and jolted him back into nervous eye flicking mode. He turned and
greeted Growdon's scissor-wielding heroine with a brief peck on the cheek.

'Oh you,' Lena observed scornfully, eyeing me with suspicion, 'I thought
you were over Churlbury way.' Ah, I thought, so *she* knew where I was
working, even if she hadn't told Tim. It proved there was a conspiracy of
silence going on.

'*You* knew?' Tim turned and goggled at her, frowning. 'But why didn't
you mention it?'

'Oh… er… only just…' Lena shrugged as if to suggest that news of my
whereabouts wasn't exciting enough to share with an old and dear friend.
'Anyway Tim,' she smirked, grabbing him by the arm, 'we've got some
shopping to do, haven't we *darling*?' A horrible, but inevitable, thought shot
through my brain. They were about to buy an engagement ring. That would
account for all the guilty eye flicking and nervous over-the-shoulder glances.
More significantly, it meant that he'd probably remembered much more
about his relationship with Gilly Bonning than he was admitting. Lena
smiled triumphantly. It seemed that she had won the battle for Tim
Rosewell's affections and, ironically, I was standing there to witness it. My
heart couldn't have sunk lower if it tried. Metaphorically speaking, it was
probably floating in the pipes beneath the pavement, set on course for the
sewage works.

'Ah well, must be off,' I snapped coldly, and turned back in the direction
of the car park, imagining two pairs of eyes boring into my back.

Tears were dripping down my cheeks by the time I reached my car, and
if I hadn't been sporting panda eyes before, I was now. On that short walk,
I'd imagined all sorts of painful things I'd like to have done to Miss Tuffin,
involving matches, hot liquids, super glue and sharp implements. My

imagination had certainly been working overtime – at Sunday rate with a bonus incentive. How I managed to arrive at Mum and Dad's without colliding with stationary vehicles or clipping any innocent kerbs and bollards I'll never know. The amount of salty spray swooshing round my eyeballs made it difficult to see through the windscreens. Inadvertently, I switched the wipers on and wondered why it wasn't making any difference before I remembered it wasn't actually raining. No wonder I had attracted odd stares from the few motorists I could make out through my infernal waterworks.

'Whatever's up?' gasped Mum, grabbing me by the shoulders and shooting a worried glance at my heap of metallic grey machinery that was parked at an odd angle outside the chain-link fence.

'It's Tim... and Lena,' I moaned, sniffing noisily, 'they're getting engaged... I just saw them about to choose the ring!' Why I went so far as to say that, I really don't know. After all, I hadn't been standing beside them in the shop while Lena tried one for size.

'How on earth...?' Mum must have realised that the chances of me standing calmly in a jewellers watching this happen were pretty remote. She shook her head in disbelief, took me by the hand and headed off to fill the kettle, dragging me after her, still snivelling like a five-year-old.

Two custard creams and a cup of tea later, Mum had cross-examined me to draw out the salient points of my encounter.

'Now you don't know that they were about to choose a ring,' she told me firmly.

'But he was gazing at a row of diamond solitaires in the window,' I wailed.

'And is that all there was in the window?' she probed, raising her brows inquisitively.

'Well no, but I know he was staring at them!'

'But that doesn't mean he was about to buy one,' she reasoned. 'I might drool over a Stella McCartney cocktail dress in one of the hairdressers' magazines, but that doesn't mean I'm going to rush off to the nearest stockist to buy one!'

'That's not the same, Mum,' I protested. 'Tim was standing right outside the shop and Lena said, *'we've got some shopping to do, darling!'* So it proves they were about to go in there.' She still wasn't convinced.

'But not necessarily about to buy an engagement ring. She may have deliberately said that to suggest that's what they were about to do.'

'To wind me up, you mean?'

After that we changed the subject and started weighing up the chances of the contenders on *Strictly*, or maybe we were both in denial. I know Mum had tried, more than once, to persuade me to lay it all down, as if Tim was a lost cause, so it was a surprise that she seemed hard to convince on the engagement scenario. I wondered if it was Mum's way of saying 'it's none of our business.' Watching the romantic waltzes and sexy Argentine tangos on *Strictly* wasn't the ideal TV viewing for a girl who had witnessed the final tolling of the death knell on her marriage hopes. The dancers on the screen seemed to take on the appearance of Tim and Lena for some strange reason. My imagination was certainly working overtime again, and it was pretty depressing.

Back at school Kate told me about a spare free ticket to a swish do her mum was organising in aid of the lifeboats. Anthea Maxted is the local co-ordinator in the Dorchester area. I'd been persuaded to own up about my now non-existent love life and Kate seemed to have taken it upon herself to find Tim's replacement, as if it was a personal crusade.

'Mum's cousin Fiona was going to come, but she managed to get a cancellation for her hip replacement and isn't exactly ready to bop the night away or even struggle out of her cottage.'

I was mentally reviewing my modest wardrobe, mostly gleaned from the impressive range of Boxmouth's charity shops and doubted whether any would be glitzy enough. The teal shift certainly couldn't be dragged out again.

'Say you'll come,' urged Kate. We were in the staffroom, drinking coffee and bracing ourselves for yet another wet Friday morning. The children had been like little beasts, rattling the bars of their cages during the first lesson, and both of us were exhausted already.

'Okay,' I agreed, 'as long as you don't tell all your friends that most of my wardrobe comes from Oxfam and Cancer Research.'

'Not a word… promise,' Kate agreed. 'I'd better give you the address.' She scribbled it on the back of an old staff meeting agenda and pushed it across the coffee table.

'And you'd better pack a bag and stay the night. These shindigs go on till midnight at least.'

I studied Kate's scrawl and wondered if I'd ever find the place. 'It's at your home?'

'No, we've hired a mini-bus. Just as long as you arrive by seven, you can leave your car in the yard and come with us. Daddy's usually very generous with the champers!'

Delia Chalcroft, the Year 2 teacher cocked an eyebrow in our direction and muttered something about 'how the other half live.' Fortunately, the bell signalling the end of break sounded at that precise moment, which stopped Kate making any cutting remark that she might later regret. We'd learned quite quickly that Delia had an over-sized chip on her shoulder about the moneyed classes. I made a mental note to pop into the library at the end of school to study an Ordnance Survey map. It would be altogether quicker and cheaper than going online and downloading and printing a map – Olive was stickler for keeping to the rules on the use of school resources. *Every* single photocopy and print-out had to be accounted for, which was a bit of a blow, because dear little Bramble Cottage still had no phone line and the chances of broadband looked as likely as Delia Chalcroft booking a weekend break at *The Savoy*.

I waited until the playground had cleared of mums and minders before poking my nose out of the school door. Mrs Pudwell – the very pushy and opinionated mother of little Sorrell – had taken to quizzing me about her daughter's progress on a regular basis.

'She's doing fine,' I'd told her several times, but had the distinct impression that being fresh out of college made my opinion less trustworthy than the previous Year 5 teacher.

'Mrs Bateson used to do spelling tests *every* day,' she'd remarked at the parents evening, back at the end of September. 'Tarquin could spell 'lieutenant' and 'rhythm' when he was in Year 5.' Bully for Tarquin, I'd thought at the time, but instead I'd smiled and suggested Mrs Pudwell invested in some spelling lists of her own. I don't think that went down very well and she'd been lying in wait for me ever since.

By the time I made it to the library door, I'd passed the time of day with Cheryl Clynes from the general stores, who was topping up the basket of kindling and the Halloween pumpkins outside the shop, and then closely escaped bumping into Hayley Zebedee when she came charging out of the back of the *Dog and Ferret* with a bag of washing and a scowl that would curdle custard. Meanwhile, dear Saul had been terrorising the ducks on the village pond with his best mate/worst enemy Rufus Kale. I never knew from one moment to the next about the status between them. Earlier in the term they'd been caught with thorns, trying to become blood brothers, then declaring World War III between the two families. Now, it seemed they'd agreed to combine forces in the lead up to Halloween and Guy Fawkes.

I'd been hoping it might be Imogen's turn at the library. She'd promised to set aside for me a couple of books by my favourite romantic fiction authors if she happened to spot them. It was the chatty and gregarious Alison instead. Somehow admitting to Alison that my favourite reading matter wasn't the latest Booker prize winner, Dickens or Tolstoy gave me an unreasonably guilty conscience. She looked a likely candidate for heavyweight intellectual stuff – probably polished off huge chunks of the bible before breakfast and then ploughed through volumes of sermons for recreational wind-down after supper. She briefly looked up as I slid inside on tiptoe, but smiles were obviously on short rations or she'd already used up her day's quota. Where did she hide her O.S. maps, I wondered, glancing round at the compact but well-ordered shelves. A couple of Year 6 girls were trying to smother giggles in one corner – possibly browsing through one of the magazines under the pretence of doing some homework research. Alison turned her head sharply in their direction and shot an irritated glance. So far the maps were proving hard to track down and I was swiftly running out of time. I had a huge stack of marking to wade through if I was going to give myself a free Saturday for buying a new outfit. I also had to factor in two hours to make myself presentable, pack an overnight bag and reach Kate's in time. I decided to brave Alison's irritation and ask for help.

'Er, Alison, I was looking for the Ordnance Survey maps,' I began tentatively. She was shuffling lists, ticking off titles methodically and adding a few weary sighs along the way. It was the first time I'd been face to face with her since the Midsummer Festival. Imogen had been on duty on my previous visits. Alison looked up and unfurled a reluctant smile, which took fright and vanished promptly.

'Over there, past the encyclopaedias,' she hissed, 'but you can't take them out.' I couldn't understand why she was whispering. The only two customers in the corner were too wrapped up in *OK* or *Hello* to care.

'I know, I just want to check something.' I scuttled over in the general direction of her pointing arm and soon found the map in question. After a struggle, I managed to unfold the section I needed, and noted the crucial roads, turnings and approximate distances.

Job done, I tiptoed over to the desk to whisper a brief 'thank you', but Alison was too quick for me.

'I see this has been reserved for you,' she announced, holding one of my favourite author's offerings between her finger and thumb, as if it was a soiled pair of pants.

'Oh yes,' I admitted coolly, 'just getting it for a friend who's lost her ticket. I'm into weightier tomes myself.'

'We can replace tickets, you know,' Alison replied, giving me a challenging stare, 'for a small charge, of course.'

'Of course,' I agreed. 'I'll tell her.'

'And you may find this interesting,' she added, reaching for a pristine over-sized volume awaiting attention on the trolley beside her. *Theory and Practice of Experiential Learning in Key Stage 1.*

I eyed the book nervously, assessing its suitability as a handy doorstop and tried to think of an excuse to decline her kind offer.

'Oh but I specialise in Key Stage 2,' I remarked airily, 'so it's not particularly relevant.' Apart from ensuring that I nod off into a deep sleep after half a page, I thought. I slid my library card across the counter and grabbed the preferred page-turner with a chocolate muffin on its cover.

'Each to their own,' murmured Alison, raising an eyebrow in obvious distaste.

Next morning I hit the Shealton-on-Stour charity shops with a vengeance. The town was much bigger than I'd first imagined. I scooped up a bright scarlet shoestring strap number for under a tenner and some chunky black beads for 50p. I was ready to dazzle the young consultants, aspiring company directors and hedge fund managers who I imagined would be on the lookout for a suitable young filly to provide heirs to their family estates. Oh yes, if a slice of the Rosewell estate wasn't shimmying in my direction, I was ready to try my luck amongst the well-heeled lifeboat supporters. Half of them were bound to be yacht owners who'd think nothing of casting off for Sark or the Scillies on the odd weekend.

At a little before six thirty, I was turning in through a pair of crumbling stone gateposts, my overnight case beside me and my pulse already performing a neat canter. As I rounded a curve in the drive where two ancient oaks formed an arch of gnarled branches, the sight of a handsome old manor house fairly took my breath away. Admittedly it didn't have the splendour and proportions of Frintley, but as the last rays of the setting sun cast a honey glow over the weathered stonework, it took on an impressive charm and character that came a close second. A couple of Range Rovers, a sporty soft top and a gleaming Merc were already lined up outside.

'Gilly!' Kate came rushing out, cutting a dash in emerald silk and eighteen carat accessories. She grabbed my case and rushed me inside, giggling enough to suggest that daddy had already cracked open the champagne. 'Ewan's dying to meet you!'

Oh yes, I thought, Ewan Maxted, heir to the Maxted millions and doing very nicely as the most recent addition to a general practice near Bridport. We virtually skipped up the wide staircase, where ancient forebears stared imperiously from their gilded frames, and then along an oak panelled corridor to my guest room.

'I'll leave you to get sorted, then come down and join us in the sitting-room. It's just off the hall. You'll know where we are by the sound of Uncle Douglas's laugh – can't miss it – and the sound of popping champagne corks, of course!'

I gazed round at the draped four-poster, chaise longue and antique dressing table. Delia was right. This was definitely how the other half lived. Apart from the antique furniture, the room was a shrine to Farrow and Ball and The White Company, judging by some of the labels. Lucky old Kate Maxted I thought enviously, marking her spelling tests and maths books surrounded by all that opulence, while I had to tape the living room window frames of Bramble Cottage to stop vicious night breezes whipping round my neck. So far my new central heating had been a long way short of effective. I sighed with pleasure at my new surroundings, popped my nightie under the pillow and slithered into my glad rags.

Perfumed and glossed up, I retraced my steps and headed for the clinking of champagne flutes and Uncle Douglas's braying laughs.

'Here's Gilly, everyone!' Kate squealed, tripping forward to steer me into the family circle. 'Dad, Mum, let me introduce you.'

'Charmed,' said Jeremy, squeezing my hand and then pumping it vigorously.

'Heard so much about you,' added Anthea. 'Come on now, Ewan, a drinky for Gilly here.'

I blinked at the gathering that was fairly bristling with DJs, white bow ties, heirloom jewellery and the intoxicating aroma of expensive perfume. Kate gushed over my outfit and gave me a knowing wink.

'Gorgeous frock,' she sighed, fingering the fabric and nodding in approval.

'Gilly, at last!' boomed a male voice. 'Grab hold of this, you scarlet woman!' It was Ewan, who greeted me as if I was an old friend. He chuckled and leaned forward to kiss both cheeks in turn. I sipped my drink and appraised him shyly from behind the bubbles. He was Oxbridge rowing eight material, broad-shouldered, broad-chested, clean-shaven and strong-jawed with deep auburn hair, rather like his sister's. Not quite my favourite colouring in a man, but he was undoubtedly a good-looking specimen.

'Kate's been whetting my appetite,' he told me enthusiastically, 'and I'm not disappointed!' He planted a huge palm on my spare arm and guided me over to the inglenook where half a tree was blazing in the grate. We did a quick speed-date style introduction before Anthea steamed over to remind us that wagons were about to roll.

'Time for a quickie, I reckon,' said Ewan. Then, noting my shudder, added, 'Not keen on champers?'

'Oh yes, love it,' I agreed, hoping he hadn't suspected that his 'quickie' had been mistaken for something more carnal. He certainly gave every impression of being a prize stallion flying out of the stalls.

The party was eventually chivvied out of the drawing room into a mini-bus and off we roared down the drive to an even bigger estate with sprawling manor house and gilded ballroom.

'Enjoying yourself?' asked Kate, after the first hour had whizzed by. We had sneaked off to the ladies' powder room on the first floor, which was a suitably converted suite of rooms.

'You bet,' I gasped chuckling, 'although it would be nice to dance with someone other than your dear brother for once. He's very attentive and determined.'

'Hmm, I *had* noticed,' Kate said wryly. 'Don't worry, we'll nip down the back stairs and head for the far entrance. I'll see if I can find cousin Nick and introduce you. He's in the Territorials, just back from a six-month tour of duty in some sandy place and gagging for a spot of civilised female company who doesn't hang around in desert fatigues most of the time.'

Giving Ewan the slip, we found Nick loitering by the buffet table with two heavyweight horsy females who were chortling at his witty one-liners. Nick had missed out on the Maxted auburn genes, but what he *did* have on top was receding rapidly. Still, he was nimble-footed and scooped me off for a Gay Gordons, which ended in uproar as couples collided, ducked and tripped in time to the music.

'Time for a breather?' he suggested as the final chord sounded. We grabbed fresh glasses from a passing waiter and wandered through the French doors. Out on the terrace we leaned on the stone parapet and gazed at distant lights twinkling in the bay about a mile away.

'A world away from Afghanistan,' Nick sighed with feeling.

What could I possibly say? I hadn't been further than the Costa del Sol on a family holiday. Instead I murmured in agreement.

'Land mines, sniper fire, choking heat... God, I'm relieved to get back unscathed.'

'Yes, I'm sure.' My fund of pithy remarks was at an all-time low.

'And great to be back in such sparkling company,' he said, turning to grin at me.

'Well, it's a change for me too,' I began, but got no further. He suddenly lunged at me and gave my lips the most vigorous massaging since I'd had to fend off Brendan in one of his desperate moments at the *Rat and Rabbit*.

'Ooh... Nick!' I gasped, surreptitiously wiping my lips. 'Time for a spot of supper? I think all the champers is going to my head!' And yours, as well, I wanted to add.

'Jolly good,' he chuckled and led me back to the buffet table, where the teeming hordes were filling their plates. I wasn't sure about his comment about my sparkling company and wondered if he was busy making plans to take advantage of my woozy head. Alarm bells started clanging loudly.

'Ah-ha, Nick, you crafty sod. See it didn't take you long to get your hands on the new crumpet!' It was Ewan, balancing a pile of sausage rolls on a plate, with a determined gleam in his eyes.

'Excuse my brother's subtle language, Gilly,' giggled Kate, who popped up on my other side, with Louie, her latest admirer in close attendance. 'Just bop him with your handbag and tell him to remember his manners.'

'You heard your sister,' I told Ewan, trying to keep a straight face, but secretly revelling in all the attention. Having two eligible bachelors vying for my attention certainly made a change from being propositioned or sighed over by middle-aged tutors or curates. Of course, it wasn't quite the same as being with Tim. These two were much more frisky and I had to admit that their shenanigans were rather entertaining. Ewan chuckled in between mouthfuls of pastry and then looked suitably contrite.

'Beg pardon, ma'am,' he croaked, pulling an imaginary forelock. 'M'be you'd allow me the next dance?'

'Hmm, seeing as you asked so politely.'

Kate grinned and nodded in approval. 'That's more like it big brother!'

We gorged on smoked salmon, pancetta and asparagus tips, devils-on-horsebacks, cheeses, pâtés and more prawn canapés than I'm prepared to reveal. In fact if my fancy scarlet frock hadn't been gathered to hang loosely under my boobs, I'd have started to look more like a pot-bellied pig.

'Now tell me Miss Bonning,' murmured Ewan as we swayed around the dance floor to a slower number after the usual pop and rock favourites – oh yes, we had music for bright young things as well as for those of more mature years – 'How come a gorgeous girl like you hasn't got a steady boyfriend in tow or a posse of them lining up to take turns for your favours?' His question sounded so casual, but I suspected Kate had already disclosed my sorry past.

'Could say the same about you,' I retorted, giggling.

'Steady boyfriend?' he chuckled in mock camp style. 'Ooh, not my scene dearie!'

'You know what I mean!'

'Ah well, this could be fate,' he intoned, wide-eyed and laying on the drama. 'Two lonely travellers, cast adrift on life's oceans, looking for a soul mate or -'

'Or a rubber ring?' I spluttered, finding his humour irresistible, although I couldn't honestly admit to being particularly smitten in an amorous way.

He steered me expertly round the floor and I reflected on my good fortune. Yes, Gilly, I told myself, you *could* do a lot worse. Ewan was well set up in general practice, heir to the Maxted – well if not *millions*, then quite a decent amount – and great company. He'd be a very handy escort around the Dorset scene until someone more likely to light my fire turned up – or until Tim's memory had all the missing bits filled in and he'd tell Miss Tuffin to take a running jump. Yes, Ewan Maxted was quite a find and might be my entry to hunt balls, yachting weekends, house parties, race meetings… it was quite a yummy line-up and would add a touch of spice to my quiet schoolteacherish life.

At midnight, we all streamed out into the garden for fireworks, then were reluctantly decanted into buses and four-by-fours. My eyes should have been in need of matchsticks by then, but the adrenalin was still whizzing round my body and I didn't want the night to end.

'Cocoa, hot chocolate, hot toddy anyone?' asked Anthea, once our party had shrugged off their coats and had clustered round the inglenook where someone had dutifully kept the fire blazing.

'And a bedtime story?' whispered Ewan wickedly in my ear. 'I'm said to have quite a good bedside manner.'

'Keep it for your patients then,' I giggled and frowned as if to say, *I'm not an easy pushover.*

'Getting on like a house on fire I see,' commented Jeremy, as he passed by on the way to his favourite armchair. 'And I hope the lad's been behaving himself, Gilly.' There was an engaging twinkle in his eye.

'Well eight out of ten so far,' I replied, feeling very much at home with the jolly Maxteds.

A little later, at my bedroom door, Ewan was keen to cement our newly-fledged friendship.

'A good night kiss at least, hmm?' he whispered smoothly, taking me gently by the shoulders and looking down at me – was it fondly or was it more to do with champagne and hot toddies? At least he was asking permission, and not like the smash and grab sink plunger style of the beastly Theo Rescorla, Brendan on a bad night and Territorial Nick.

'Thank you for a lovely evening Ewan,' I sighed, and went up on tiptoe to plant a delicate kiss on his cheek.

'The pleasure's all mine, ma'am.' He replied and swooped down like greedy gull snaffling a seaside sarnie. Oh dear, I thought, as he crushed me in his bear-like grip, there was the sink plunger action again, and Ewan was going for a record attempt.

Chapter 21

Fireworks at Frintley

When I arrived back at the cottage the following day, I was not alone. There was a new resident asleep upstairs, recovering from an exhausting day and becoming acquainted with the new surroundings. Ah-ha, you may think, that Gilly Bonning's a quick worker. Poor old Tim is old news, cast aside like last week's *Hello* magazine, and replaced by a new, red-hot, romantic interest – all because money speaks the right language to a poverty-stricken young teacher.

As I woke up in the beautiful guest bedroom that morning, there was a pixie with a sledgehammer digging for victory inside my skull. My tongue felt like sandpaper and the folds of skin under my eyes looked like a pair of soggy teabags. I felt terrible. I sat up in bed and tried to open my eyes, but they seemed to have been glued together while I was asleep. My mind rewound to Ewan's record breaking snog and the question, *was I alone* rattled through my befuddled brain. I blindly patted the rest of the bed and was relieved to discover that there was definitely no evidence of human flesh nestled under the duvet. I flung back the covers and staggered to the en-suite to empty my straining bladder and then dowse myself in the shower. The sight that greeted me in the mirror was truly alarming. One glance at me over the breakfast table would certainly cool Ewan's ardour.

Half an hour later I managed to drag myself downstairs and found I was not the only one with a sledgehammer and sandpaper problem. Every clink and clatter of the cutlery sent ripples of pain throbbing through my head. It was the grandmother of all hangovers and as I drained cup after cup of strong black coffee I found the power of speech gradually returning and the pixie in my head lobbing ping pong balls for a change. Peering round the side of a conveniently placed box of bran flakes I noted that Ewan was an interesting shade of greenish grey, that contrasted horribly with his bloodshot eyes and his dark auburn hair that stood up in distressed peaks.

I'd assumed he was the kind of bloke who'd been weaned on champagne, but all he could manage was grunts and coughs which made a change from last night's gutsy guffaws and slapstick humour. I breathed yet another sigh of relief. Ewan looked as much like a frisky stallion as Stan Murless after a hard day hacking the hedgerows on the Frintley Estate.

'Right, on your feet! Time for some fresh air!' Jeremy Maxted announced breezily as he folded his napkin and pushed back his chair. 'I think Anthea and I have had enough of the Moaning Chorus by now, and by the way, where's Nick?'

'Last seen with someone called Arabella,' muttered Kate wearily, 'but I can't swear where it was.'

'Oh well, if they appear now they'll go hungry,' put in Anthea stiffly.

Ewan managed a half-hearted smile as we trooped out into the hall.

'Great evening,' he murmured croakily. 'We must do it again sometime.'

'Hmm,' I agreed politely.

I first glimpsed Minnie as she skittered out of a stable at the back of the Maxted estate, closely followed by numerous brothers and sisters.

'Oh how sweet!' I trilled, admiring her long white whiskers, white bib and paws and glossy, black back and tail. 'Do they live out here?'

'Yep, and work hard for their living, feasting on the local vermin,' Kate told me. 'Their mum is half wild, but Fergus – our gardener – has wormed his way into the affection of the kittens and they're all hand tame now.'

'And ready to fly the nest,' added Jeremy, 'in a manner of speaking. Help yourself, do.'

I reached for a pretty, black and white bundle of fluff and fell in love with my new little whiskery friend, who purred like my Gran's old Singer sewing machine as soon as I scooped her into my arms. I named her Minnie. So my drive home included a quick supermarket splurge for my new companion's dietary and toilet requirements, while trying to keep her contained in an old cardboard box on the passenger seat beside me. The indignant yowls that accompanied our journey, were impressive for such a tiny creature. Once in the cottage, she angrily exploded from the box, took the stairs in three or four huge leaps, disappeared under my bed and curled up to sleep off the rigours of the car journey and the shock of losing her playmates. Would I ever live up to them? Still, Bramble Cottage probably could provide her with plenty of vermin to bat around and toss in the air.

I had just whipped out the teabag from my mug, after ploughing through the remnants of my marking, when there was a knock at the front door. I froze. Knocks at the door were so unusual, especially when not preceded by the sound of a motor and the crunch of tyres on gravel. Whoever it was had crept up on the grass. Peeping round the edge of the curtain was out of the question and peering through the letter-box was too obvious.

'Ah, Simeon!' I exclaimed after I'd plucked up courage to open the door. He stood on the doorstep beaming, with the words 'a cup of tea would do nicely' written across his forehead in invisible ink. Could this be one of his famous pastoral visits? Perhaps, I thought with a gulp, he was checking up on me? So far my only church attendance had been for the school's harvest festival. It hadn't been a particularly auspicious occasion either. I'd spent most of the time making sure Messrs Zebedee and Kale kept well clear of the cooking apples and swedes after one of the rascals had tried out his football skills on a stray one. One minute we'd been bellowing out 'We plough the fields and scatter' and the next minute a swede had rumbled down the aisle and clipped Harry Woodfine on the ankle. Deputy head Morris Uridge went puce and swiftly moved in to separate Rufus from Saul, which was safer than separating the two of them from their breath, although I'd be surprised if his fingers weren't itching to do something like that. Meanwhile Pru carried on pumping away on her instrument, Simeon retrieved the swede, a few eyebrows were raised and the moment passed. Rufus and Saul's comeuppance was just around the corner, and on that occasion Morris took it upon himself to mete out suitable punishment – the games cupboard had never looked so clean and tidy the following day.

On my way out of the church there had been no sign of Simeon's Rogues' Gallery and there certainly had not been any mention of one at school. I'd started to wonder where my photograph was languishing. It would be interesting to hear what he had to say on the subject.

'Cup of tea?' I asked brightly. With less than two hours before evensong, I calculated his visit would be a brief one.

'Super.' He rubbed his hands and grinned.

'I was just making one anyway, before seeing to my guest.' His eyes swivelled round and his grin faded.

'Guest?' The unspoken – so you've got a man here – was fairly obvious, judging from his expression.

'Asleep upstairs, getting used to the surroundings.'

'Ah.' I grinned secretly to myself, already planning how I could give him a big clue as to the identity of my guest, although 'guest' was a misleading word.

He sat down a tad nervously while I went to re-boil the kettle and grab another mug. 'Well, not a *guest* as such, more a new resident,' I said, popping my head round the door.

'Oh?' Having already inspected my sleeping arrangements back in August he was now putting two and two together and making more than the usual total.

'From the Maxted estate,' I continued airily, as I stirred the tea.

'Oh the Maxteds, hmm yes, I know the family – as well as Kate of course.'

'We bonded straightaway.'

'You and Kate?'

'Me and my new resident,' I sighed. 'Sugar?'

'No, just milk,' he answered awkwardly. 'Well, I'll be quick, seeing as you're obviously busy with erm…'

'So this isn't a pastoral visit?'

'No, it's about the church Carol Service. I was hoping to enlist your help; school choir, orchestra and all that.'

'Ah, yes I expect I'll be able to rustle up something. Two or three items? Nativity play?'

'Nativity play already organised, thanks. I believe Olive's got that in hand.'

He slurped his tea nervously and eyed the stairs. 'Don't worry, fast asleep last time I checked. It's been quite a demanding last few hours I can tell you.' Simeon's eyes almost popped out of their sockets and he gulped down half a mugful.

'Are you sure you're doing the right thing?' he asked, once he'd recovered his equilibrium. 'I mean, it's not always wise to rush into things.'

'No, I'm sure we'll be fine together, as soon as we've sorted out the diet and toilet arrangements. It feels like a match made in heaven!' I assured him grinning.

'Really? Aren't there some other issues you should be considering?' His eyes were still swivelling round. In fact, he reminded me of Tim.

'Oh no, I think those are the main considerations,' I told him, glancing down at the floor. 'If I get those right, the rest will be a breeze.' I thought by now, the identity of my new resident must have percolated his befuddled brain. After all, there was a huge bag of cat litter propped up by the kitchen door and two trays of kitten food beside it. Bramble Cottage was not exactly well equipped with storage.

'Well, I'm pleased you'll be able to contribute to the Carol Service. It's on the last Sunday of term, at six o'clock. Can't have the kiddies up too late, you know.'

He handed me his mug and got to his feet.

'I'll start working on the orchestral piece this week,' I promised him. 'I wrote a song called 'Star Bright' when I was at college. It shouldn't be too difficult to arrange.'

Simeon stuffed his hat well down past his ears and donned his cycle clips.

'Take care, Gilly.' The look on his face was one of his deep and meaningful ones.

'Will do.' I made a move towards the kitchen and then remembered that I meant to ask him about the Rogues' Gallery.

'Time to wake sleeping beauty I think. Perhaps I'll give the pilchards a whirl.' I picked up a tin and studied the label with interest.

'On toast?' he asked, his hand on the door handle.

'No, in jelly of course!' I giggled, brandishing the tin. By the time I had stopped laughing I realised Simeon had gone. 'Drat!' I muttered, flinging the door wide open and seeing his back view disappearing down the path.

'Simeon! What news about the Rogues' Gallery?' I called. He hesitated for a moment and glanced over his shoulder.

'Er, dropped off the AOB at the last PCC meeting when Mrs Digby the secretary had a funny turn,' he called. It sounded gibberish to me, being unversed in the mysterious machinations of church affairs. I shrugged and went back inside hoping he'd picked up all the obvious kitten clues. If he hadn't, the man was either blind, slow on the uptake or both. I concluded that he'd nipped off quickly to hide his embarrassment.

The following day I was plunged into feverish activity. The photocopier in the staffroom was well past simmering point as it spewed out dozens of carol sheets for the lunchtime choir practice. Every seat was taken and almost as many squatted on the floor of my classroom, giggling and fizzing with excitement. However, I knew their little game. There was a bitter snap in the air and some reckoned it was better to be snuggled up in Miss Bonning's classroom than freeze in the playground.

'You're in here to sing,' I reminded them firmly. 'We're preparing for the Carol Service at the end of term and anyone messing around will be out on their ear.' They may not have understood what that expression meant, but my tone of voice conveyed enough to warn them what was expected. 'So let's have everyone up on their feet ready for some deep breathing and warming up exercises before we start.'

With much scraping of chairs, they did as I said and we set off on our preparations.

'Star Bright' went down very well, especially when I dangled the possibility of a little solo group taking a verse or two by themselves. Some of the more precocious and competitive ones giggled and postured to each other as they speculated on their chances with that. 'Now the orchestra will be joining you in this piece, so some of the instrumentalists here will not be able to sing. We need you playing your instruments.'

There were a few quiet moans and pursed lips, but I ignored them.

'Miss, will there be any solos for the orchestra? I love playing solos,' piped up one of the McArdell twins. I still couldn't tell them apart unless they were brandishing their flute or oboe or wearing their matching bobble hats with their initials knitted into the brim.

'I'll think about that... er...'

'Flavia, Miss.' She turned and grimaced at her sister and we dipped into the second verse.

At the end of the day, I was releasing my weary group to their parents and minders when I noticed a knot of mums shooting me odd looks, with much head shaking and furrowed brows. There was usually something to get their tongues wagging – generally homework projects or money for school trips that one or two had complained as being *extortionate, and what do we pay our taxes for?* Phoebe and Flavia went tripping out full of excitement and started tugging on their mother's arm. Mrs McArdell had

216

high-level involvement in the Dorset music scene and was one of the leading lights in a local opera group. I tried not to let it bother me, but I imagined her at my first school concert ready to give me marks out of ten. Then I spotted Mrs Westropp. I needed a word about her son Merlin's missing homework. Naming him Merlin was clearly asking for trouble. Before I could catch her though, Mrs McArdell strode over, followed by the gleeful twins.

'Ah, Miss Bonning,' she began with a purposeful expression. 'I trust the twins will be given their usual solo spot at the Carol Concert.'

'Service actually.'

'What?' she asked briskly, evidently annoyed at being corrected by a mere stripling of a music teacher.

'It's a Carol *Service*, in the church, an act of *worship*.' You'll remember I'm not too hot on church attendance, but the woman needed to understand this wasn't being organised just for her daughters to parade like little prima donnas. She looked at me quizzically as if I was speaking some foreign tongue, then seemed to curl her lip irritably.

'Same thing, surely.'

'Well not exactly,' I countered brightly, 'but I'm sure your girls will be given every opportunity to play their part in the school's contribution.'

'We're doing a song called 'Star Bright',' squeaked Flavia, excitedly.

'Star Bright? Who is the composer?'

'Gilly Bonning actually,' I told her crisply. Now she'd be ready to score me on my composition as well as my organisational skills.

'Oh, I see,' she replied, pursing her lips. The girls squealed and sniggered together, having learnt their teacher's name.

'Mrs McArdell's been bending your ear I see,' murmured Olive, as I escaped back into the warmth of the building, ready for coffee and a chance to defrost my toes by the staffroom radiator. I nodded and decided that a straight face was the best option. I hadn't yet worked out which parents were safe to criticise. 'Does it every year,' Olive continued, raising her eyes to heaven. 'Those two were apparently given recorders for their first birthday. I ask you! Anyway, we'll talk about the Carol Service at the staff meeting tomorrow. And, by the way, Sir Freddie's invited us all up to Frintley for his bonfire birthday party. He'll be eighty.'

'What, kids and all?'

'No, just the staff plus other halves and… er… boyfriends of course… and a few of the Churlbury bigwigs and well-connected high flyers naturally. His last bash – for his seventy-fifth – was quite an extravagant do; not the usual boring hamburger sort of affair. Bring your doggy bag.' She winked wickedly as she made the last comment.

Predictably, Ewan had texted back promptly when I invited him to come over. It wasn't his first text either. If I say he'd bombarded me with them since the lifeboats evening I wouldn't be exaggerating. How a G.P. had as much time for texting as he had was beyond me; in between patients and home visits, I suppose. Despite his best attempts we hadn't seen each other since then. Fran and I had a weekend together, exploring the delights of Marbeck and then Ewan was busy with a weekend conference after that. I was fairly cool about that. He wasn't exactly my idea of the perfect partner – not that I'd tell anyone, except for Fran. When I did, her reaction was predictable.

'So, you've got this young G.P. drooling over you and you're still holding out for Tim to come to his senses?'

'It's not that, Fran. We just don't bond. He's nice enough, but there's not that special spark.' She'd given me a cynical sort of glance and pushed a packet of Jammie Dodgers in my direction.

'Gilly, would you let me be perfectly frank with you?' It sounded ominous and I recognised that certain look in her eyes and the way she was building up to something. 'Again?' she added, with emphasis. Oh yes, there were some subjects that had well-worn tracks leading up to them. I groaned. We'd had these little chats before.

'Some relationships are slow burners, Gilly. Sometimes it's not a grand passion from the very first glance.'

'I know it's not. Tim and I started out as friends of mutual friends.'

'There, you've admitted it! Sometimes it takes time, like Tony and me. We started as casual friends, mates you know, having a laugh together, going out for a drink. Well, you know because you were there as well.' I nodded, predicting exactly where this was leading. She'd chastised me for my blinkered view on available specimens of the male species when we were chambermaiding in Torquay. 'But it's different now.'

The comment hung in the air, waiting for a reaction.

'Well, I guessed it must be when you were desperately applying for posts and working out the mileage to Tony's school. Even *I* had worked out it wasn't because of the shopping over at Ilminster. So, has he asked you? You know?'

'Well, it's sort of come up in conversation and he admits he's not even put off by the size of my thighs so -'

'Was that the acid test then?' She giggled. Fran had often joked about her tree-trunk thighs, although they weren't anything like tree trunks, unless she meant a moderate silver birch.

'That and my cooking of course. Haven't perfected gravy yet, but I'm getting there.'

'Oh, so it's down to gravy!' I exclaimed incredulously. 'Perfect the art of gravy making and he'll pop a ring on your finger. Where's the romance?'

'Don't change the subject, Miss Bonning,' she said sternly, and then I noticed a twitch at the corner of her mouth and a badly stifled smirk. We collapsed in giggles.

'And you believed me!' she chortled. 'Ahem, now setting that aside, give poor Ewan a chance to ignite the spark. Who knows, he may turn out to be the perfect match.'

'Oh very witty, Fran – match... spark!'

'Okay, okay' she giggled, 'but when am I going to meet Mr Hunky-let-me-hold-your-hand-and-wipe-your-fevered-brow-Maxted? Or are you planning on keeping him hidden away?'

'Play your cards right Miss Quinlan and I'll fix it for you to come to Sir Freddie's bonfire party – his eightieth birthday – posh nosh and landed gentry included!'

Kate agreed to bring Ewan as her guest and Fran came as mine, although I don't suppose anyone was counting how many of us turned up that night in the dark.

'Welcome, Gilly and welcome your pretty friend,' Sir Freddie twinkled. 'Come and wrap your hands round a hot toddy. Simpkins is doing the rounds with a tray.'

Crowds of the local hunting brigade had turned up in force as well as most of the staff and some of the well-heeled villagers. Plummy accents and braying laughs abounded.

'So where is he? Hope he's better looking than the guy on the fire.'

The estate workers had certainly been busy and I thought that, in the overstuffed bundle of old clothes and sacking, there was an uncanny resemblance to Sir Freddie.

Fran squinted through her owl frames and I was starting to wonder if Kate and Ewan had had second thoughts.

'Perhaps they're over by the soup,' I muttered and we went worming our way through the merry throng and cannoned straight into the Veltmans.

'I say, this is jolly isn't it?' remarked Simeon, once he'd mopped the hot toddy from his jacket. I peered dismally at the few dregs that remained, wishing I'd finished it myself. He patted me on the shoulder and grinned.

'Hmm yes, very jolly. Let me introduce my friend Fran. She's just come over from Marbeck.'

'Oh yes? Marbeck? That's one of our other parishes you know.' He pumped her hand enthusiastically, while Alison stood by silently. It was too dark to catch her expression, but she wasn't exactly bubbling over with excitement. In fact, I thought I heard a muttered sigh, with the word 'drycleaners' just discernible to anyone with sharp hearing. It was time to make myself scarce.

We quickly disentangled ourselves from the pair and headed towards the terrace, where flares were blazing merrily and Simpkins and a couple of others were busy barbequing, slicing, plating up and handing out all manner of tasty treats.

'Is this really a lamb cutlet?' asked Fran, obviously impressed by Sir Freddie's extravagance. 'It doesn't seem right to lash out on all this while you don't even have a phone line in your cottage. I'm sure he wouldn't notice the slightest dimple in his bank balance. Can't you ask him Gilly?' It was indeed an increasingly sore point, but finding time to corner Sir Freddie was difficult. He hardly ever seemed to be around to take calls.

'Next week, I'll ask him next week,' I assured her.

'Well, mind you do. You can't be expected to rely on your own mobile in an emergency can you?' Fran was staunchly on my side.

'Phew! At last!' came a weary voice and much heavy breathing behind us.

'Ewan, Kate what kept you?' I asked, turning round to greet two very out of breath Maxteds.

'Ah, hello, gorgeous,' Ewan chuckled, enveloping me in a chummy bear hug. 'And your friend Fran, I believe. Had to fit in an emergency house call,' he explained, as he ploughed on towards the drinks. 'One of the partners was held up by a jam on the A37, so I had to go instead. False alarm with a home delivery, as it turned out.' He reached for a hot toddy and downed it in one.

'Don't you have any midwives on hand?' I asked. I couldn't imagine Ewan ready with forceps and what have you, standing ready at the business end of some poor labouring woman.

'Oh yes, plenty of those, but it's a first-timer, so Simon – the chief partner – thought a belt and braces approach was called for. God, I'm ready for this.'

'I see what you mean about his hair,' whispered Fran, as Kate and Ewan went to fill their plates. There were enough flares and fairy lights for Fran to notice his crowning glory. 'A bit too gingery for my liking, but plenty of presence and *very* eligible. You should definitely hang in there.'

We mingled some more, waiting for someone to light a blue touch paper. First though, we had something else to set our pulses racing.

'Ladies and gentlemen!' announced a rather stiff and starchy voice through a microphone. Clearly no expense had been spared for Freddie's birthday bash. 'The cutting of the cake!'

'Blimey, you'd think it was a wedding!' murmured Ewan, in my ear. 'Look at all this,' he continued, 'and the bloke can't even fork out for your phone line!'

'My sentiments entirely,' put in Fran acidly.

'Eavesdropping again, Miss Quinlan?'

'I've told her myself,' Fran informed Ewan, ignoring my remark, 'and she's promised to tackle his lordship next week.'

'Right,' replied Ewan, nodding.

Someone with a high squawky soprano voice started 'Happy Birthday' and we joined in with gusto, an octave lower, following it with rapturous applause. Sir Freddie plunged a shining blade into the cake, camera flashes recorded the moment and the first rocket zoomed into the sky in a shower of silver sparks.

'Speech, speech!' called out a Hooray Henry voice, but Sir Freddie shook his head dismissively and smiled broadly.

Rockets rocketed, Catherine wheels whirled, sparklers sparkled and the rest looked pretty impressive, while we all oohed and aahed, until that awful noise. I'll always remember it. It was an agonised groan.

First of all, I thought it was someone reacting to a silly joke, so I `didn't pay much attention. But it wasn't *that* sort of groan. Then there was a gasp followed by a shriek. More hot toddy on someone's beloved tweed jacket I thought, but the shriek was followed by a buzz of animated chatter, with more gasping. All the while the fireworks fizzed and crackled, so it was difficult to work out what was happening.

'Quick, someone phone for a doctor,' came a frantic voice. Ewan turned sharply and pushed his way through the crowd, with me following on behind.

'Kate, go and get my bag, quick!' he ordered, a look of grim determination on his face.

'It's Sir Freddie,' someone murmured anxiously, as we squeezed through. 'He's had a funny turn.'

Sir Freddie had crumpled to the ground, his face ghostly pale, in the light of the flickering flares.

'Sir, sir!' gabbled poor Simpkins, cradling his master, as he kneeled on the stone flags. Sir Freddie's mouth gaped and his arms hung limply at his sides.

'I'm a doctor,' Ewan told him, rushing to the old man's side and starting to go through the usual doctor's checklist. The rest of us stood watching in horrified silence, except for the rockets which were going through their set display. I gazed up at the rainbow colours exploding in the air above us, incongruous with what was happening several feet below. 'Excuse me, the doctor needs this.' It was Kate, finding her way blocked by a group of whimpering pensioners.

'Clear the way please,' rang out a voice that sounded like Harry Woodfine.

Stethoscope round his neck, Ewan continued his ministrations, but his patient remained pale and still. At last there was silence. The last rocket had cascaded in a glorious red shower, while most of the party was oblivious, each one holding their breath and caught in suspended animation. After no response from mouth-to-mouth resuscitation, Ewan started pumping Sir Freddie's chest. I'm not much of a one for prayers, but I said a few in those agonising minutes. The Almighty must have been truly amazed to have heard from me again. The last time had been when I was at Tim's bedside. Simpkins knelt, head in hands. The poor chap looked distraught and I remembered what I'd heard about his special relationship with Freddie. After several minutes of pumping then trying more mouth-to-mouth Ewan shook his head and sighed.

'I'm sorry,' he said quietly, 'there's nothing more I can do.' He scrambled off his knees and quickly organised blankets and an ambulance. I was dumbstruck. There was poor Sir Freddie, now dead to the world, with a smear of butter cream from his birthday cake still stuck in the corner of his mouth. Dowagers and doting cousins and sisters dabbed their eyes daintily with lace hankies, retired regimental fellows blew their noses noisily and took medicinal swigs from hip flasks and stiff upper lips struggled to keep up appearances.

'Good chap, old Freddie,' muttered one of the men behind me mournfully, 'even if he *did* bat for the other side.' All around there were sobs and moans as friends and acquaintances drifted away. On that evening, when my dear landlord shuffled off his mortal coil, the course of my life looked set to change. However, for the time being, it was time to concentrate on the needs of the shocked and wilting amongst us. Once the ambulance crew had done their stuff, Ewan joined us, a shivering threesome, as we waited beside the dying embers of the once magnificent bonfire.

'You'd better come back for a hot drink,' I offered, copying Mum's usual default reaction to shock and crises. Kate gazed at her brother with concern and gave his shoulder a squeeze.

'You did what you could,' she murmured gently to him. Ewan shrugged and shook his head.

'But you always hope. No matter what state they're in, it doesn't stop you hoping, even when they're eighty. He might have had another ten years.' We turned and walked back to the cottage, and on the way I slipped my arm through his. 'You were brilliant,' I told him. 'Don't blame yourself.'

We walked the rest of the way in silence, so many thoughts buzzing round my head. With the owner of Frintley Grange gone, where was my security?

Chapter 22

Trouble at St Cuthbert's

In the days that followed, I imagined the estate being sold to an oil magnate who'd bulldoze Bramble Cottage to make room for a golf course or health spa. Ewan must have been reading my thoughts. Later that week he texted me with a surprising offer.

'There's always room for you in the Maxted residence.'

I texted back a polite but neutral reply, then cornered Kate in the staffroom.

'Was this your idea?' I asked, showing her Ewan's message.

'No, Gilly. We were just speculating about your situation. None of us want to see you and Minnie homeless.'

'It won't come to that. I'm sure there are tenant's rights or something like that, and no, I'm not lodging with your family Kate. They're lovely people, but living under the same roof as the amorous Ewan would be asking for trouble. His bedtime clinch still comes back to haunt me and my tonsils are still recovering from the shock.'

Kate grimaced and giggled but said no more. She was realistic enough to imagine it wouldn't take much for Ewan to stop champing at the bit and set off, at a canter, down the oak panelled corridors and stand pawing at the bedroom door of an unchaperoned young filly. Why was it, I wondered, that I kept thinking about Ewan and his set in horse racing terms? I suppose it went with the territory, to use another well-used cliché.

I wasted no time in contacting Gosling, Potts and Sawbridge, being slightly frantic about the roof over my head being guaranteed until Christmas at least.

'We're waiting to hear from the nephew in New Zealand,' one of the partners told me. 'We need his instructions. He's sole heir to the estate.'

A little more strategic questioning revealed that Simon Lanary, son of Sir Freddie's brother Willoughby, had an extensive sheep farm and it sounded unlikely he'd want to trade that in for a rambling estate in Dorset.

'Might he want to appoint a manager?'

'I'm afraid I can't speculate on the Lanary family's plans,' the female on the phone told me archly. 'As a sitting tenant you're quite safe for the time being. We'll be in touch when there's anything you need to know, Miss Bonning.'

Well, that put me in my place. It was all right for them, with their comfortable middle-class des-res with underfloor heating and double glazing … *and* broadband. I wondered how they'd cope living in a spiders' graveyard, with only a mobile phone for security. The timing of Freddie's demise had properly scotched my hopes of a phone line and a few more creature comforts, including a cat flap for Minnie. Although asking the estate to install a cat flap might have been rather cheeky. As the outside temperatures plummeted, closely followed by icy drafts sniping at me through any unplugged gaps, I started to wonder if my refusal of the Maxted offer had been rather too hasty. I thought back longingly to the pretty bedroom with the draped four-poster and had a mental tussle with my cautious side about my decision to eschew the delights of grand living. Minnie had taken to cuddling up on my pillow at night, and her soothing throaty purr was often the last sound I'd hear before drifting asleep. It was sufficient compensation for living at Bramble Cottage. Minnie would have probably been consigned to the barn with her brothers and sisters if I'd been brave enough to move lodgings.

We were in the throes of Christmas preparations by then, and my little orchestra was shaping up quite promisingly. Phoebe and Flavia had been given a little solo apiece, which kept their mum happy. The thought of Mrs McArdell ambushing me every day, haranguing me about her daughters' musical merits in addition to Mrs Pudwell and her fixation with spelling tests was more than I could cope with. Dashing off a couple of instrumental parts for the twins made a lot of sense. After all, it was only a few bars, with exactly the same number of notes for each, just in case they compared parts and decided I was favouring one of them.

'I've written these solos especially for you,' I'd told them when dishing out the music. Their eyes widened eagerly and they giggled in a way that was becoming increasingly irritating. The words 'spoilt brats' floated round in my head once or twice, followed by 'blame the parents'.

At about the same time Simeon's appearance in the staffroom increased noticeably. He usually had some list or other in his hand and kept *craving a minute of your time, my dear*, as he so politely put it. Oh yes, Junior Rev was clearly revelling in his organiser's role for the Carol Service. In fact, his attention to detail started to border on compulsive.

'I'm sure it'll be fine,' I told him patiently, when yet again he tried to persuade me that a visit to the church for the purpose of arranging seating was necessary.

'Actually, not a bad idea,' commented Olive, who'd overheard Simeon's suggestion and my breezy rebuttal. My heart sank. 'Fitting in all your musicians might be tricky,' she ventured. 'I'd take a tape measure if I were you. Those choir pews are a tight fit.'

'But I wasn't thinking about putting the orchestra in the choir pews. The violinists need bowing room for their arms.'

'Ah, I see,' she replied with a chuckle. 'Violin bows up noses or in ears? Hmm, I should definitely take up Simeon's suggestion though.'

'After school today then?' he suggested. 'I'll pick you up if you like.'

'Oh but I could drive. It's not that far, then I could go straight home afterwards.'

'But you'd have to lug all your marking along with you and there's bound to be other stuff you need to do in class afterwards. No, let me pick you up. I have to pass by anyway. Then I can drop you back here afterwards,' he insisted. The man was certainly determined to get me in his car and as Olive was still in earshot I hardly dared protest. It was inevitable that I'd have at least another hour of work to do after the church visit before I could even think of going home. So there I was, cornered, and Simeon knew it, judging by his wide grin.

When I emerged from my classroom a few hours later, Simeon was bouncing around with boyish excitement outside the staffroom door.

'My lady, your carriage awaits,' he announced importantly, with a sweeping bow. I had my trusty metre stick with me. It seemed a better weapon for keeping frisky curates at bay than an old cotton tape measure. 'I see you've come prepared,' he added, eyeing up my equipment.

We settled in his compact VW, the metre stick gripped between my knees and a clipboard tucked into my school bag.

'It's really very thoughtful of you Reverend Veltman,' I said in my best business-like school marm's voice, my eyes locked on the road ahead.

'Anything for you, my dear.' Hmm, that's what I was afraid of, I thought.

A tractor hove into view and Simeon applied the brake suddenly. I shot forward and for a moment lost grip of my dignity and my trusty weapon.

'Sorry about that,' he gasped and I felt a hand land on top of mine. 'Didn't mean to frighten you.' He squeezed my fingers before I could withdraw my hand.

'Reverend Veltman!' I exclaimed.

'Please think of me as Simeon,' he replied smoothly.

I took a deep breath, snatched my hand away and wrapped it round my metre stick, wondering what the penalty for attacking a member of the clergy whilst in control of a motor vehicle might be. He was almost as bad as Desmond Morsby. What had I done to deserve being pursued by middle-aged men? I wondered if I should start reciting the Ten Commandments at him, to rein him in, but my knowledge of that particular part of the bible was shaky, to put it mildly. However, I *did* recall there was something about not coveting 'thy neighbour's wife or maidservant or ox or ass or anything that is thy neighbour's.' The trouble was, I was always coveting the contents of Kate's wardrobe, so I guess I wasn't exactly blameless. But – I thought again, as we eventually pulled up outside St Cuthbert's, which was on the edge of the village, rather than in the heart of it – coveting your friend's leather jacket wasn't quite the same as a married clergyman being over familiar with a young schoolteacher. Being a man of the cloth *and* on the governing body meant he should be setting a good example. I knew I was definitely on firm ground there.

I grabbed the door handle, almost threw myself on the verge and sped up the path, trying to beat Simeon to the door before realising it would be locked and he'd have the key.

'Rats!' I cursed, under my breath, not wanting to be beholden to him, and not wanting to prolong this fact-finding sortie for any longer than absolutely necessary.

Eventually we entered the gloom and Simeon scurried off to flick a few light switches. At once the chancel was bathed in light and Simeon pointed out the possibilities for seating my choir and musicians. Certainly the four choir pews seemed about the right size and I'd calculated the length of each row when the children had squatted on the P.E. benches in the school hall.

'Thirty-five centimetres per child,' I told him, 'and fifty children in the choir.'

'Right-oh, I'll measure the pews.'

He set to work gleefully, while I considered the possible space for the orchestra. I couldn't tuck them up at the altar rail. They'd be partly hidden by the choir and various architectural details and I'd never hear the end of it from the McArdells if their precious pair weren't in prime position.

'Four metres,' Simeon reported. 'Seems about right.' I was aware of him behind my right shoulder as I made notes.

'Yes,' I confirmed. 'That's room for about eleven children per pew or more if they're really skinny.'

'We can always put some extra chairs at the end of each one,' suggested Simeon, and he made a note.

'And I need twenty-two for the orchestra, which will have to be across here,' I indicated, pointing to a wide space by the chancel steps.

'Right-oh, we'll arrange to bring the chairs from school the day before. There's at least two four-by-fours from the governing body that we use on a regular basis. A couple of trips should do it.'

'But I'll need at least *one* practice here. It'll take long enough to get them seated, organised, music stands set up…' I told him, panicking at the thought of seventy or more children going hyper a week before Christmas. Suddenly the prospect of it all didn't sound so jolly. Big mistake. I'd lost my cool, opened up my big mouth, revealed my insecurity and Simeon's pastoral side had heard the call to action just as clearly as if the Angel Gabriel had put a trumpet to his lips and blasted the air with a reveille or two. Oh yes, Junior Rev was at my side in a shot, patting, consoling and assuring me of his support.

'I'll keep the little blighters in order for you, Gilly,' he promised with his best sympathetic pastoral voice replacing the more business-like one. 'Just let me know when and I'll be ready. We can't have you bearing all the strain, your first term too.'

'And the McArdells watching my every move, marking my conducting skills and noting exactly where their girls' chairs have been placed, to give them maximum exposure.'

The floodgates of panic had opened, and out it spilt like juice from an inexpertly snipped carton.

'Oh, those McArdells,' he agreed dismissively, 'typical behaviour, if I might say, but don't quote me.' He winked and nodded and, to my great relief, moved away, giving me back my personal space at long last. We fished out our diaries and made tentative plans for a 'walk through' as Simeon described it.

'Thanks, I'll check with Olive before going any further. Sorry about the emotional fall-out. Things are a bit fraught on the domestic front at present.'

I gathered up my belongings and made a move towards the door.

'Ah yes, I thought that might be a bit tricky for you. There are a lot of people concerned about you, Gilly.'

Naturally, I thought. Anyone who knew about the precarious position of Bramble Cottage, with Freddie's sudden demise, was bound to have speculated about my situation, especially in a close-knit community like Churlbury.

'Well, thank you. I think the strain is starting to affect me,' I admitted, nodding.

'Be firm, Gilly, take charge of your life. Don't let anyone take advantage.' My eyes snapped in his direction. This was quite a surprise. Did he know something about the letting agents that I ought to know as well?

'Oh I won't,' I assured him. 'I've already had my say, but it's not up to me. Someone else has to make a decision, after all.'

He pursed his lips and frowned. 'Well, please bear in mind that there are plenty of spare rooms in the village. I'm sure you'd have oodles of offers if your domestic arrangements turned sour. In fact Alison and I have more than enough rooms for the two of us.'

'Oh well, that's very kind, but I'm sure something will get sorted out, and I have to bear in mind the needs of... well, you know... she's a dear companion,' I sighed, wondering if the Veltmans really would want to accommodate Minnie as well. I doubted it. One of them was bound to have some sort of allergy. In fact, I suspected that Simeon's generous gesture had been a spontaneous unilateral offer and something that Alison wouldn't necessarily welcome.

'She?' Simeon retorted sharply.

'Oh yes, definitely she,' I replied. 'Kate confirmed that before I brought her home.'

'Brought her home?' he asked, clearly confused. 'Your companion's female? But I thought you said it was one of the Maxteds. I know Kate has got a brother...'

'What?' I giggled. 'You thought I had a man hidden away?'

'Well, er... um,' flustered Simeon, 'crossed wires I think.'

'Crossed wires? I should think so!' Then I thought back to the Sunday afternoon when he'd called unexpectedly and our rather odd conversation. Yes, he was definitely slow on the uptake as well as being blind when it came to spotting trays of kitten food.

'Oh dear,' he murmured, shaking his head, 'silly me... so er... who is she? Of course, I've no problem with two ladies living together. It's quite common isn't it and most of us round here are very broad-minded. After all old Freddie well, er... you know... he um...'

'Batted for the other side?' I said smirking.

'Well yes, if you want to put it that way.' I collapsed into giggles. The poor man really did have a gift for getting the wrong end of the stick.

'Minnie's a *cat!* She's black and white and about four months old.'

Simeon gulped and started a lot of rapid blinking. 'A cat? Really? Oh, what a relief!' He started towards the door, head down, a flush of embarrassment on his cheeks. I couldn't help a quiet snigger. No wonder he'd behaved as he did. Lots of people were concerned about me, were they? If Simeon thought I had a man sharing my bed, who might he have told? Purely in a pastoral way, of course. Alison? And who might she have told while stamping their library book or filling in their request card, or while queuing in the post office?

I followed Simeon out of the church and returned to his car while he wrestled the door into submission with its ancient heavy key. As I sat in the passenger seat and rearranged my limbs around the metre stick, I recalled some odd behaviour by some of the waiting mums in the playground. With some alarm I speculated on what lurid fabrications on the state of my private life might have been gossiped around Churlbury. How awful! How embarrassing! Simeon was particularly quiet on the drive back to school until the last minute, when I was extricating myself and trying not to propel myself into the gutter.

'Oh I see the *For Sale* boards are up,' he mentioned casually.

'The what?'

'On the estate.'

'*For Sale* boards?'

'Yes, I thought… well, I assumed you knew.'

If I hadn't felt insecure before, I did then. 'No, I'm sure I'd have noticed if there was a board up when I left home this morning and I've certainly heard nothing from the agents. They promised they'd let me know when there were any developments.'

'Perhaps there'll be a letter waiting for you at home?' Simeon said, giving me one of his encouraging smiles. 'And don't forget my… er… *our*… er, offer.' Hmm, I thought, as I waved goodbye, better run it past Alison first. The thought of sitting down to breakfast with the tight-lipped Mrs Veltman would not be my ideal start to the day.

What do they say about stress levels? The life-changing events that give us most stress, such as moving house, starting a new job, bereavement, illness or divorce and so on? Organising a carol service ought to feature in that list, after the stress I experienced in the run-up to the great day. If the staff thought that coping with Messrs Zebedee and Kale was stressful, they should have a crack at managing the junior prima donnas of Churlbury C. of E. choir and orchestra for a session or two. Then they'd know what stress was, especially with the interference of Mesdames McArdell and Sparks . The latter's daughter, Lavinia, had a sweet voice, but almost permanent drool escaping from her nostrils. Trying to convince Jodie Sparks that noisy sniffs every few notes made it impossible for Lavinia to sing the first verse of 'Once in Royal' made very little impression on the woman.

'But she's got the best voice in the whole school. Her last teacher said so,' whined Jodie yet again when she collected her daughter from one of the after school practices.

'I'm sorry, Mrs Sparks, Merlin Westropp has already been chosen to do the solo. Lavinia's on-going nasal problems need to be sorted. She can hardly manage a line of the carol without sniffing loudly.'

'Merlin Westropp?' Jodie sneered. 'Are you sure he'll turn up? Those Westropps aren't renowned for their time keeping. I've heard he's always losing things and turning up late!'

'Well, this might be the incentive he needs,' I told her firmly, with my fingers crossed behind my back.

All the while, my precarious domestic situation hung over my head like the Sword of Damocles, as rumours flew round the village about various sightings on the Frintley estate.

'I heard there was a pop star nosing around,' remarked Cheryl Clynes, as she scanned my tray of kitten food.

'No, I heard it was an opera singer,' put in Pru, who was struggling with a bag of spuds and two cartons of milk.

'Are you sure?' disputed old Mrs Skilliter. 'Our Russell heard it was going to be a theme park.'

'What? Like Alton Towers?' asked Pru. 'I doubt it. There are bound to be preservation orders on some of those trees, and what about access? The village roads wouldn't cope.'

'And what about Bramble Cottage?' I protested.

Cheryl Clynes pushed my change across the counter and shrugged. 'Rumour and speculation,' she murmured. 'Russell Skilliter probably made that one up just to wind up the old girl. I'm sure the pop star sighting was closer to the truth. My hubby saw a flash limo with blackout windows coming down the drive the other day.'

'Well, I suppose it could have been royalty,' suggested Pru, dumping her shopping on the counter.

'Pru!' I exclaimed, 'you're just as bad as the rest!'

'Well, it would certainly improve my takings,' reflected Cheryl. 'After all, Camilla's sister doesn't live far away and I gather it's done wonders for the village stores.'

'Trouble is, we'd have all them papperonis turning up with their cameras,' grumbled Mrs Skilliter.

'Paparazzi,' I snapped, squeezing past her considerable bulk, and fed up with all the hype.

'And the same to you, dearie,' she sneered, disagreeably.

Yes, there had been obvious activity around the estate. On several occasions I'd had to swerve to the side of the drive, teetering by the ditch, while a much grander vehicle flew past me, spraying gravel in all directions and showing a total disregard for any stray pheasants or other wildlife that might be taking a leisurely constitutional. Then, a few days before the Carol

Service, when my nerves were raw and my energy level was at an all-time low, an official-looking letter plopped through my letter-flap with a Shealton-on-Stour postmark. A minion at Gosling, Potts and Sawbridge had managed to find time to write and tell me what I already knew: that the estate was in the process of being sold. The following day, the additional sign – *'Sold, subject to contract,'* was nailed onto the *'For Sale'* boards. The shock of catching the words in the beam of a passing lorry, as I was waiting to turn into the drive, seemed to constrict my insides and had me gasping. The timing at G. P & S was evidently running several weeks in arrears. Would a letter in February, announcing the completed sale be forthcoming, I wondered cynically? Oh yes, and that would probably be followed the following day with a notice to quit.

With the final rehearsal planned for the following morning, I had to wring some sense out Mr Gosling and Co. who seemed to have conveniently forgotten about little old me. By the time I'd disentangled my legs from Minnie's and spooned out her supper, the plummy tones of the recorded message was all that greeted me.

'How dare they slope off home...' I started to fume, then noticed the time was several minutes after five. Minnie paused briefly from wolfing down her tuna in gravy and eyed me curiously. 'Hmm, Minnie my sweet, we might have to find another home,' I sighed, tickling her ears.

I set the alarm half an hour earlier and was in school on the dot of eight the following morning, but with hasty last minute preparations gobbling up every available second, the chance of making phone calls was as likely as Class 5B not squabbling over whose turn it was to open the next advent calendar door.

'Now remember,' I told the class once they'd settled down somewhat, 'we expect to see you all wearing your school uniform on Sunday afternoon.' There was a groan followed by a forest of arms in the air. Flavia McArdell was waving hers frantically.

'Yes, Flavia?'

'But, Miss, Mum's bought us new dresses to wear.' She screwed up her face in a 'it's not fair expression' and turned to her sister, who aped the same expression and nodded vigorously.

'School uniform is to be worn. You've all had a letter and if you've conveniently forgotten to show it to your parents, then I suggest you do so when you get home. The Carol Service is *not* a fashion show and Mrs Karthew will be very disappointed if anyone dares to turn up in the wrong clothes. In fact, I'd have serious second thoughts about allowing anyone with a solo to perform if not in their proper uniform!' There was an ominous silence. We reached morning break with scowls still plastered over several faces, but I was resolute.

With hardly time to draw breath, let alone gulp down half a mug of coffee, it was time to assemble my fractious musicians and frog march them along to St Cuthbert's. Meanwhile chairs were carted off and various governing body bods put on an impressive display of teamwork.

'All ready for the off then, Gilly?' chuckled Junior Rev, doing his frisky puppy impression, as soon as we had our noses through the door.

'Miss Bonning, to you,' I hissed at him, glaring a warning.

'Right, chaps and chapesses,' he announced, 'let's have you all in these pews – in silence – while we organise the chairs.' There were a few sniggers, but Simeon seemed to be able to command respect, and they all duly filed in and sat wide-eyed and silent. Two teaching assistants busied themselves with music stands and Olive chivvied the nativity cast into the vestry.

'Just ask Reverend Veltman to give us a nod when you're ready to start,' she called, before disappearing.

On turning round I couldn't believe who had just sneaked in, and was trying to hide behind a pillar: Mrs McArdell. Flavia and Phoebe were all a-twitter and their friends were joining in. My previously orderly bunch was starting to fall into disarray. She may have been on the governing body but that didn't give her the right to turn up unannounced.

'Right, choir members come forward in silence and fill up from the far end,' I told them, indicating the choir stalls. 'Now musicians, leave your instrument cases in the pews and take your places, just like you do at school. And no tooting from the recorders. Not a peep until we start!'

I took up my conductor's position and opened up my music folder.

'Right, Mrs Stebbings, we'll start with 'Once in royal'. Merlin… where's Merlin?' I demanded, surveying the choir stalls in panic.

'In the vestry, Miss,' piped up Sorrell Pudwell.

'Give me strength!' I seethed, under my breath, as I marched off to retrieve him.

'Thought I had one extra child,' Olive muttered. 'He seemed to think he was a sheep as well.' She rolled her eyes and propelled him in my direction.

I positioned Merlin in his centre spot, but Mrs McArdell had now squeezed herself into the woodwind section and was having a heated exchange with the twins. The steam that had started to build up in my head was approaching boiling point.

'Mrs McArdell, could you possibly go and give Mrs Karthew a hand if you want to be of help? I assume that's why you're here.'

She gave me a withering glance and reluctantly picked her way through the music stands, managing to topple a couple of them on the way.

'My girls tell me they're not allowed to wear their new frocks. It's most unfair!' she snapped.

'It was all in the letter they were given last week,' I told her calmly. 'School policy. Now if you don't mind, I'd like to get this practice started. Mrs Karthew would be pleased to have your help with the shepherds and so on and you can discuss *her* policy on the wearing of uniforms at school functions,' She turned and sniffed peevishly, and strode out of the church. Keeping my expression neutral, I turned back to the orchestra and gave Pru her signal to start.

Chapter 23

Enter the Oborns

The following morning, after speaking to Henry Gosling, I knew little more of my fate. The estate had been purchased by the Oborn family, but the subject of tenancies was uncertain. After that, I spent most of the day preparing myself for Ewan's Hunt Ball. Apart from the venue, it was much the same as the Lifeboats fundraiser, with champagne flowing and Ewan in sparkling top form. He knew how to make a girl feel special and I was ready for plenty of that, although I still couldn't summon up genuine enthusiasm for his company. That certain something was still missing. Before the last stroke of midnight – in a manner of speaking – I was delivered safely back to Bramble Cottage. A full moon beamed at us from a clear sky.

'Need my beauty sleep,' I told him, with a sigh, as he leaned forward for a goodnight kiss. 'Big day tomorrow.'

'Beauty sleep?' he reached out and traced the curve of my cheek with his thumb. 'You don't need beauty sleep, my sweet,' he said.

'Don't you be so sure. Sunken eyes and great floppy bags don't look so attractive first thing in the morning.'

'Great floppy what?' he spluttered, eyeing the area where my cleavage was snugly wrapped in several layers. 'Wouldn't mind an eyeful of them first thing in the morning!' Ewan's hint at an overnight stay didn't go unnoticed.

'Under the eyes you fool,' I giggled. 'The rest of me hasn't reached the saggy, floppy stage yet, thank God.'

'No nightcap or bedtime story?' he wheedled.

'Definitely not, Mr Doctor Man,' I replied primly.

'You'll come over at Christmas, promise me that,' he said eagerly.

'Christmas?' I murmured, in surprise. 'But that's *family* time. I couldn't be away from Mum and Dad...'

'Boxing Day then? Come and see how the Maxteds celebrate!' It sounded tempting.

'Okay, it's a date.' As I closed the door, I felt guilty. Was I just using him? Was I giving him false hopes? Or should I follow Fran's advice and hope a small spark might ignite between us?

Sunday afternoon arrived, icy cold and still shimmering with a covering of frost despite a pale sun peeping shyly through gloomy clouds. By four thirty, I was hard at work in St Cuthbert's, arranging chairs and unfolding music stands. A huge Christmas tree had been set up next to the pulpit, twinkling with multi-coloured fairy lights and festooned with stars and bells that each class had contributed. At five, Olive and an army of helpers arrived with a collapsible clothes rail, and cases full of costumes. All the while, Chief Rev, Henry Woodfine bustled around with carol sheets while Pru played a selection of Christmas favourites, to keep up our spirits. For a brief moment I entertained a maverick thought that some spirits of the other sort might have helped quell my nerves – namely a couple of gin and tonics. I'd had a weirdly unnerving nightmare the night before. In it, Mrs Sparks ran forward just as Merlin was about to sing the first verse of 'Once in royal'. She put a bag over his head and told the congregation that her daughter had been cruelly robbed of what was hers by right and that she, Lavinia, was going to sing instead. Then Mrs McArdell, dressed as Cruella De Vil, stood up in the middle of 'Star Bright', denouncing me as an impostor, claiming that *she'd* composed it, and that I had merely stolen it from her study. I'd woken up trembling, with my heart pounding, only to find Minnie singing loudly in my ear.

At five thirty, the children started straggling in, and I held my breath and crossed my fingers anxiously, waiting for an appearance of the Westropps, in particular Merlin. 'If he doesn't show up I'll never hear the end of it from Mrs Sparks.'

'He'll show up,' Kate assured me, sotto voce. 'I bribed him with a gold star...'

'Oh yes, very tempting,' I murmured back sarcastically. 'I was hoping that two minutes of fame was enough to do the trick.'

'...and a ride on one of our horses,' she added, with a twinkle.

'What?' I gasped. 'You're shameless, Kate Maxted. How are you hoping to keep *that* secret? If the Sparkses or McArdells get a whiff of your magnanimous offer, there'll be a riot!'

'It was Ewan's idea. I told him about the ear bashing you'd been having and anyway, he knows Roland Westropp. He's a porter at Dorchester Hospital. Roland's been told to keep his mouth shut.'

'Hmm, well that's very kind of the pair of you,' I replied grudgingly, 'but can we trust Mrs Westropp and little Merlin to keep *their* mouths shut?'

'It's done the trick though,' breathed Kate smugly. 'There they are, the whole family!'

Sure enough the whole Westropp clan, complete with grandmas, granddads, aunts and uncles were heading in my direction. Meanwhile Kate sneaked off and went to help with the wise men and shepherds who were having beards and fake tan applied in the vicar's vestry. Merlin was scrubbed and polished to perfection, with about half a tub of gel on his hair, as he took his place at the front end of one of the choir pews.

'It was ever so good of the doctor to... you know,' whispered Mrs Westropp, her eyes sparkling with excitement.

'But mum's the word,' I whispered back. She nodded and grabbed Roland's hand to go and nab a ringside seat.

By the time Pru's mighty organ was thundering out the final verse of 'Hark the herald' and the Mothers' Union ladies were ready to sally forth with mulled wine, squash and mince pies, proud beams glowed on many a parental visage and great sighs of relief might have been heard from the entire staff contingent of Churlbury Primary. 'Star Bright' had been a triumph, even if I say it myself, and Lavinia Sparks had made up for her solo disappointment by being one of the heavenly host, who twirled and skipped around the chancel in layers of polycotton and tinsel. If there was any unsightly drop, dripping from her nose, nobody noticed it. Even the McArdell parents looked suitably chuffed I noticed, as I turned and led the cast and musicians in a final bow. Who cared if one of the wise men had dropped his sequin-covered plastic margarine tub on a sheep's head or that Mary had handed the baby Jesus to Joseph feet first.

'Well done, Gilly!' squealed a familiar voice in my ear, as I was folding music stands and struggling with piles of music.

'Fran! Fancy seeing you here!'

'Well, after all those desperate texts, I thought I'd come and see if your parents from hell were as bad as ours,' she whispered.

'Shush,' I hissed back, checking for eavesdropping parents, 'watch out for flapping ears!'

'What a crowd,' she gasped. 'Whoa, those mince pies look yummy. Just spotted one with my name on it.' Off she dashed to waylay one of the perm and pearls contingent and then catch up with Kate.

When the clearing up was done and I'd fielded compliments and comments with increasingly glowing cheeks – although that might have been linked with at least three paper cups of mulled wine – I spotted Ewan chortling with a group over by the font - some of his patients, I assumed. They looked much too old to be parents of anyone of primary school age.

'Well done, Miss Bonning! What team work!' crowed Simeon appearing beside me, with Alison in tow.

'And what a turn out!' I remarked. 'All down to your wonderful website, no doubt!'

'Ah well, probably not, although the world and his wife seem to have turned out,' he replied modestly. 'Probably that piece in the local rag helped. We had to put out extra seating all along every aisle. Wish we had this sort of turn out on a Sunday. Might help the fabric fund.' He glanced down at his wife who was staring fixedly across the pews, her brow furrowed. It struck me as odd that she wasn't involved with the mulled wine and mince pies team until I wondered if, having lost a baby, Alison found it too painful to belong to an organisation where one of the chief topics of conversation might be family life, and in particular children and grandchildren.

'Lost in thought, eh Alison?' he asked casually, tentatively putting an arm round her shoulders.

'No... that woman with the camel coat and black furry hat... there's something familiar about her.'

'Probably from one of the other churches,' put in Simeon, half turning to locate the woman in question. It was one of the group that Ewan had been with, but they'd stopped chatting by then, and he was on his way over, looking pleased with himself. 'Er no, don't recognise her,' continued Simeon. 'Not even part of the Christmas and Easter brigade.' Alison, however, was transfixed. As the group moved towards the door, she followed their progress, her eyes narrowed in concentration.

'Perhaps Ewan can shed some light on them,' I suggested brightly.

'Ah yes, the good Dr Maxted,' commented Simeon, 'Welcome doctor, seems an age since poor Freddie's party.' They nodded at each other companionably.

'Well, well,' Ewan chuckled, once he'd given me one of his bear hugs and had pumped Veltman hands enthusiastically. 'Just met the new owners of the Frintley Estate.'

'Ah, the Oborns. Yes, Henry Gosling told me about the new owners yesterday.'

'Yep, your new landlords, Gilly,' he announced, rubbing his hands gleefully. 'Put a good word in for you, too. Said you were the model tenant.' I shot him a warning look. Really, there was no need to put pressure on them. Ewan was rarely very subtle or discreet.

'But who was she before she was married?' muttered Alison, her eyes like flints, cold and sharp. 'That's what I'd like to know.' It seemed an odd sort of remark. Simeon gave a helpless shrug, while Ewan and I exchanged a raised eyebrow or two. There'd been a sinister edge to Alison's voice that promptly killed any sense of euphoria. How dare she spoil my evening, I thought angrily, hoping I could maintain a neutral expression.

'What was her name?' Alison demanded of Ewan. 'You looked as if you were getting on surprisingly well. Do you know them?'

'Er, no… er… well Mr Oborn is… um, Edward, I think. No, Edmund, that's right. Then there's two sweet daughters too, er Poppy and Nina,' he told us grinning.

'But what was *her* name?' Alison demanded of Ewan, who was evidently more interested in the younger element of the Oborn family. I'd never seen Alison so animated, although 'worked up' would have been closer to the truth.

'Well, that's just the trouble,' replied Ewan apologetically, 'Edmund was doing the introductions and then someone coughed very loudly just behind me and I didn't quite catch the name. Could have been Lillian?'

'Lillian?' retorted Alison. 'Not Miriam then?'

Simeon sighed heavily and squeezed her shoulder tighter. 'Oh no, not *that* again.' He shook his head despairingly, giving a clue to something he'd obviously prefer to forget.

'Well… it could have been Miriam I suppose,' admitted Ewan helplessly. 'As I said, someone coughed and I thought, well I'd find out sooner or later. I mean you're bound to hear,' he continued, addressing the last part of his remark to me.

'Hmm, Miriam Fifield… robbed me of my inheritance she did,' Alison snapped, staring at the Oborns as they filed through the porch..

'Ali, please,' begged Simeon in despair. 'She did *not* rob you of anything, and anyway that's all past history. And Mrs Oborn is not necessarily Miriam Fifield.'

Ewan and I felt like a couple of spare parts. Well, *I* did, and if we hadn't been in a public place and Alison hadn't been the curate's wife, I'd have been tempted to smack her round the face. For a few glorious moments I imagined doing it; imagined the sound of my hand across her cheek and the shocked expression in her eyes, but... well I valued my job too much. Of course I'd *never* do anything like... er... well perhaps Lena Tuffin would be the only candidate. There I'd been, a few minutes earlier, glowing with a sense of achievement before this woman started airing her dirty washing in public and spoiling the air of celebration. Inside I was fuming. Ewan and I exchanged surprised glances. I guess we both felt sorry for Simeon too. No wonder he suffered from wandering hands and wandering eyes, if that's what he had to put up with at home.

'Think I'd better take her home,' muttered Simeon, surreptitiously in our direction. One or two people must have picked up the atmosphere in our corner of the church, as there was a brief awkward pause in conversations and quizzical glances. 'I hope I can rely on your discretion, you know...' We nodded.

He steered Alison towards the door, her mouth glued shut in a hard line and her eyes screwed up like a cat's bottom.

'And pour a double brandy or two down her throat,' I murmured, when they were well out of earshot.

'Or give her a good seeing to. That'll give her something else to think about,' chuckled Ewan, with mischievous grin.

'Robbed her of her inheritance? What was all *that* about?' I mused. 'Do you think the name *was* Miriam?'

'Honestly, Gilly, I don't know.'

He glanced around until he spotted our Chief Rev, deep in conversation with Pru and husband Alan.

'But your vicar might. When I was chatting to the Oborns he was hovering, I noticed. Probably lying in wait, hoping to sign them up or whatever vicars do when new parishioners turn up. He'll probably have all the info.'

'How did you know he was the vicar?' I demanded.

'Ah, well the collar was a giveaway!' he sniggered.

I didn't like to put him in his place, but I knew for a fact that we had the area bishop and at least one rural dean in the assembled company. We made our way across to where Harry, Pru and Alan were now chuckling. There were tears rolling down Pru's cheeks.

'I almost fell off my organ seat when William Jerram dropped that plastic pot on Kayley Jones' head!' she spluttered. 'And as for Posy Wilkins and Darren Brinkly! They seemed to be playing pass the parcel with baby Jesus most of the evening. Then, when Posy turned to one of the shepherds and piped up that baby Jesus didn't have a willy, I thought I was going to wet myself! It was all I could do to stop myself giggling. Had to stuff a hanky in my mouth.'

Goodness, I thought, glad I missed that little comedy moment. It had to have been when the angels were flapping their wings and dropping tinsel all over the chancel.

Eventually we were able to join in on the conversation and discover more about the new owners of the Frintley Estate from Harry. 'Yes, it was good to meet Sir Freddie's replacement, as it were,' he confirmed eagerly. 'Mr Oborn is head of a prestigious architect's firm. Correction, I think he owns it and has several offices around the country. It's such a relief to know he won't be likely to destroy the Grange and all its wonderful character.'

'Did you get as far as first name terms?' I asked innocently. 'It would be useful to know, seeing as I'll be living on their doorstep for a while… er… even if I don't know what their plans are for Bramble Cottage.'

Harry's look of concern was touching. 'Ah, poor Gilly. Of course this must be very unsettling for you, and here I am chuntering on. Yes, now I noted the names in my diary. I have a shocking memory these days… have to write everything down,' he muttered, ferreting around under his surplice and checking all his pockets for his aide-memoire. 'Yes, here we are… Edmund and Miriam, and their daughters Poppy and Nina!' he looked up and beamed.

'Lovely, thank you, Harry.' We said our goodbyes, wished him an early 'Merry Christmas' and wandered towards the door.

'Miriam Oborn,' I breathed forlornly, wondering if we'd witnessed the opening of a Pandora's Box of horrors.

Chapter 24

Learning to forget

I was wrong about Tim, Lena and their jeweller's shop tryst. Not surprisingly, Lena wanted me to jump to the wrong conclusion – that Tim was about to splash out on one of those sparklers he'd been gawping at in the window. It hadn't been anything like that; probably a birthday present – hers not his – a watch or some little trifle. You see just a couple of weeks into the New Year I heard the news – via Mum – that they were engaged. It happened on New Year's Eve and there was an announcement in the *Growdon Gazette* the following week. When she told me, I was surprised rather than shocked. I'd already assumed that it had happened, no matter what Mum had said at the time. Poor Mum, I felt sorry for her ringing me up.

'Gilly?' At least ten seconds ticked by while part of me – the part ruled by my heart – was overcome with disappointment, that Tim hadn't had some sort of Damascus road experience that some people speak of: that blinding flash of light, when truth comes flooding in and all the clouds of doubt and delusion are swept away. And the other part of me? Well, to be completely honest, *that* part – the head part, the bit with feet planted firmly on the ground – was relieved. Ever since Lena Tuffin had breezed into Tim's life, I'd seen him in a different light. He was nice, yes, but there is such a thing as being *too* nice, *too* accommodating, and *too* willing to please. He had become easy prey for predatory females like Lena Tuffin. He'd rolled over, paws in the air, and given in. And did I really want a nice guy like that? *'Yes darling, of course darling, anything you say darling,'* for the next however many years a marriage might last? With a passive, over-accommodating nice guy like that, it might not last very long. I could almost imagine myself dying of boredom.

So, I mused, that's what Tim and Lena were up to on New Year's Eve. Mine hadn't even had a whisper of romance, unless you count being

243

propositioned by the village idiot. Before the end of term Pru had given me an invitation to their regular New Year's Eve bash and had even persuaded me to help with the last minute catering. In truth, it wasn't as formal as that sounds. It was more like: *'If you're not doing anything on New Year's Eve, you could always come round to ours.'* I meant to invite Ewan when I'd seen him over Christmas, but had clean forgotten. Ironically, by the time he phoned to invite me to a friend's yacht in Weymouth – an impromptu get-together that all the Maxteds were attending – regretfully I felt I had to refuse. I knew Pru was relying on my promised help. By then we'd had the odd cup of coffee together, planning, making lists and thinking up silly party games. It was fine as parties go, but I couldn't help regretting my own and Ewan's badly timed phone calls. Pru and Alan's son Phil was down from Manchester. He was quite good looking as a matter of fact, but was a hardened Man.U. supporter who could bore for England on the subject of his beloved team.

'Gilly?' Mum's voice on the other end of the phone, had taken on an agitated quality. Did she think I was reaching for the gin and a couple of packs of paracetemol ready to sink into oblivion?

'Don't worry, Mum,' I sighed. 'Kind of expected it. I thought it had happened three months ago. Don't know why it took them so long.'

There was a heavy sigh. 'Well, I'm relieved you're taking it so calmly Gilly. Dad and I have been worried about you, especially after that time you saw them outside the jewellers. And you didn't say much at Christmas.'

'Oh, the day I scared a few innocent motorists and pedestrians,' I joked, remembering that Saturday in lurid Technicolor. 'She can have him. I thought he'd remembered, he seemed to have remembered a lot more when we were talking, but I'm obviously no match for Miss Tuffin. Ah well, there's plenty more…'

'Fish in the sea?' ventured Mum hopefully.

'Or doctors on country estates?' I added casually.

There was definitely a squeal from Mum's end. 'Really, Gilly? Do you think this Ewan is the *one?*' Did I think so? Could I, hand on heart, be honest about my feelings for him?

'Not sure, Mum. He's okay, he's good company…'

'And he bought you that phone thingy.'

'It wasn't just him, Mum. The whole family chipped in, and it's what you call a smartphone.'

Yes, the Maxteds had truly surprised me with their generosity on Boxing Day. We'd just polished off the last mouthful of a truly fabulous dessert and drained the third bottle of champagne, when Ewan produced a package, all gift-wrapped in pretty block printed paper and a raffia bow.

'For you, Miss Bonning,' he announced importantly, passing it across the white damask, narrowly avoiding a cluster of cream church candles. I imagined a small box of chocs inside, but the way the four of them were exchanging glances, I had second thoughts. 'From *all* of us,' he added. 'We hope this will keep you well connected.'

'Well connected?' I echoed with a giggle. 'That sounds intriguing.'

Oh dear, I thought, taking the present and turning it round in my hands, not chocolate then. No, but something much, much better and much more difficult to accept: an all-singing, all-dancing smartphone with all the features I'd dreamed of and lusted over, but hadn't quite got around to buying for myself. Bramble Cottage, my car and Minnie's necessary vet's visits seemed to have gobbled up most of my money. I *could* have settled for a cheaper version with a modest monthly contract, but not me. My sights were set much higher.

'Oh… my… you're too generous…' I faltered, feeling guilty about the box of biscuits I'd brought with me as a gift to the family. It was from the most exclusive of Shealton-on-Stour's independent retailers, but even so, it didn't quite compare with the Maxted family generosity. 'It's too much… really you shouldn't have…' Had I been whingeing too much about the phone line business and bending Kate's ear for the umpteenth time in the staffroom so that they'd all decided to chip in together and put me out of my misery? I was aware that my cheeks seemed to have become very hot. '… and all my moaning and … and…'

'Not at all,' Kate assured me gently. 'We *wanted* to give you this.'

They all nodded and made positive agreeing noises.

'Thank you.' I hugged Kate, who was sat next to me, then turned and squeezed Jeremy's hand. It was awkward as far as Ewan and I were concerned. I hadn't really thought of him as a boyfriend. We weren't exactly going out regularly. It was more of an 'ad hoc' basis, so I suppose it was more of a casual friendship, although I'd sensed that Ewan was keen to progress it somewhat. Nevertheless, I hadn't thought our casual friendship warranted splashing out on a special Christmas present. Receiving a gift from the family was altogether more comfortable, and on reflection, I was grateful for that. At school, Olive had organised a £5 Secret Santa amongst the staff team, so Kate's gift was taken care of in the general lucky dip. The fact that she'd drawn out the address book and pen that I'd donated was quite co-incidental.

'So you'll be on the internet all the time, I suppose.' Mum's voice cut through my daydreaming.

'What? Oh well, not *all* the time. There's still the little matter of broadband connection but I can use it at school or in the library.'

'Well, it'll take your mind off other things, which can't be bad.'

'Mum, I've a set of books sitting here waiting to be marked, a few lesson plans to knock into shape, plus a cottage to clean and Minnie's litter tray to scrub and disinfect. That'll keep me suitably employed.'

'That's good.' There was a false brightness about her voice. I recognised it, having perfected that same art, all linked with the Gilly Bonning self-preservation strategy.

'You realise it'll be Liz next.'

'Next for what?'

'Announcements... in the paper.'

'Really? You think so? Don't sound so apologetic Mum. If Professor Lenz whatever-he's-called pops the question, I shall be the first to rush off to snap up a Monsoon bargain for the big day.' I was already preparing my congratulations for Fran and Tony when theirs happened. It was only a matter of time.

It's amazing what your mind dwells upon while you're scrubbing off blobs of cat poo from the lip of a litter tray. I'd run out of those ludicrously expensive litter tray liners and Minnie sometimes left it too late to reach the optimum squatting position. So, I was busy cleaning up the evidence and my chain of thoughts went from Simeon to Alison to that puzzling business about Miriam Oborn. I felt I needed to warn her that there was a potential mad woman cunningly disguised as a curate's wife, who might try to pin her against a pillar in a dark side-aisle of St Cuthbert's and grill her about the mysterious inheritance matter. If *I* were Miriam Oborn and knew what was rumbling in the troubled breast of Mrs Veltman, I'd swiftly convert to Islam or join the Sally Army; anything to avoid dagger eyes across the coffee cups after Matins, or worse.

By mid-January, however, the local grapevine seemed to confirm that the Oborns were nowhere near moving in. I'd seen for myself a convoy of vans trundling down the drive with Sir Freddie's furniture and effects en route to some local auction house, followed by a prestigious painting and decorating firm arriving a few days later. The Murlesses were still around in their staff quarters, but Simpkins was said to be off on one of those European river cruises that you see advertised every ten minutes or so on the TV commercial breaks most evenings.

'I bin told we could stay on, like,' Stan explained when I went to find out what he knew. 'For the time being,' he added. 'They'll be wanting their own staff but I'm lending a hand for a while. Then we'll be put out to pasture when our council flat's ready.'

'Bout time too,' wheezed Lily, rolling out pastry in her neat little kitchen. 'I'm ready for my nice council flat after two weeks in Lanzarote.' She put aside her rolling pin and reached for the kettle. 'You'll stay for a cuppa I hope, Gilly?' she asked. I nodded. It was my only way of extracting more information. Gosling, Potts and Sawbridge's lips were so tight they could have been superglued together.

'You've heard nothing then, my dear? 'Bout staying on in the cottage?' Lily asked, pushing a plate of penguins and custard creams across the table. 'Tuck in, you look like you could do with fattening up. We've got some Christmas cake left, if you fancy a slice.'

'No this is fine thanks, but as for the cottage, every time I call the agents they fob me off with the same line: *'Oh, so-an-so's busy with a client,'* or *'We'll write to you when we've heard from the Oborns.'* Stan and Lily nodded in unison and dunked their penguins thoughtfully.

'Tis a rum do, Gilly,' agreed Stan, scratching his ear. Lily nodded again. 'Still, you'll hear soon, likely as not. They *did* say summat about a party, and that we were all invited.'

'All?'

'Rest of the tenants an' workers anyway,' confirmed Stan. A trickle of melted chocolate had collected in the hollow beneath his bottom lip.

Oh yes, I wasn't the only tenant; the others were estate workers, the ones who tended livestock, mowed the meadows and cleared fallen branches in the woods and thickets. In my early days at Bramble Cottage I'd taken a stroll one Sunday afternoon and wandered past character cottages with gleaming paintwork, well-manicured front lawns and fertile vegetable patches, on the far side of the Frintley acres.

'Chance to give the glad rags an airing!' wheezed Lily, between gulps of builder's brew. 'If I can still get into 'em!'

'So, any idea when that'll be?' I asked. More head shakes, this time dislodging the chocolate pool under Stan's lip. 'And any idea when you'll have to move out?'

'When the council nobs write and tell us our flat's ready,' Stan reminded me. 'We be stayin' put till then.'

Ten days later two letters lay on the mat as I heaved my bags of marking and mud-spattered games kit over the threshold. After the dark tunnel of doubt, despair and disappointment I'd been trudging through, two pieces of good news were definitely due. Ewan's *good word* or the Oborns' own decision on the subject of tenants had kept my foreseeable future on the Frintley estate secure. The chance to air our glad rags and feast our eyes on the new décor at the manor was set around the middle of February – other halves and partners were included.

'Try keeping me away,' chuckled Ewan, when I phoned to invite him. I'd never discovered who had been his lucky partner at the yacht shindig and Kate had the good sense to keep quiet on the subject. What Ewan did when I wasn't with him was not my business and I was determined to stay cool and detached about that. Still, I sensed the chuckles down the end of the phone were more to do with feasting his eyes on the shapely curves of young Poppy and Nina Oborn, than which shades of Farrow and Ball paint were gracing the walls of their new home.

'Hopefully there won't be any Veltman fury fallout,' ventured Ewan, when we were synchronising watches over the phone the day before.

'Oh I shouldn't think there's any danger of that. Sounds as if it's an estate do. The invitation said 'At Home' rather than 'Party.' I think it's a *getting to know you* sort of affair.

'That's a relief. I wouldn't want to administer sedation to Mrs V to stop her lobbing bread rolls or threatening her hostess with a carving knife.'

'Relax, you fool,' I giggled. 'It'll be a quiet evening eavesdropping on lambing season anecdotes and the price of hay, you mark my words.'

A seemingly endless hum of car engines purring past my front gate the following evening alerted me to a certain underestimation on my part. I'd squeezed myself into the puffball skirt and bolero, twisted my hair – now grown to a decent length – into a topknot and secured it with a rose clip and experimented with a new blusher and eye shadow. It might be only an 'At Home', but I couldn't imagine the Miss Oborns passing up a chance to glam up for the occasion, so why shouldn't I, especially as Lily was doing the same.

'Hey, Miss Schoolmarm, you've scrubbed up particularly well this evening,' remarked Ewan, looking pretty tasty himself, although he'd stopped short of wearing his DJ. There was an attractive twinkle in his eyes. Had it been there before, and I'd not noticed it or *chosen* not to notice it?

The wide sweep of gravel that fronted Frintley Grange was bristling with Fords and four-by-fours and everything in between by the time we arrived.

'Just a small gathering, eh?' Ewan paused to drool over a shiny maroon Mercedes. 'Hmm, think you might have misread this one.'

Dicky-bowed flunkeys welcomed us into the vaulted hall – painted the softest of sage greens – where guests were served champagne cocktails from silver trays. Stan and Lily hovered by the entrance to an elegant drawing room, Stan's vintage suit jacket straining across his ample frame. They nodded and smiled proudly in our direction. A short distance away, Miriam and Edmund stood greeting guests as they shuffled past, drinks in hand.

We joined the queue, which gave me a chance to study my new landlords, especially Miriam: mid height and build with dark, short hair, a welcoming smile and understated jewellery. I warmed to her at once. Her dove grey, linen trouser suit and black patent loafers hit the right note of casual elegance. Poppy and Nina giggled together behind their mother's shoulder, both blonde and wavy haired, having inherited their father's genes.

'We'll never remember all the names,' I heard Miriam chuckle, as we edged ever closer. It felt like a receiving line at a wedding with the bride and groom missing.

'What chance the Veltmans are on the guest list?' I hissed in Ewan's ear. So far I'd spotted a sprinkling of dog collars, but none from the home team.

'Well, if they are, she's either drugged or on a tight lead, judging by the absence of bread rolls flying around or dangerous cutlery being wielded in our hostess's direction.' We couldn't help sniggering like a pair of naughty school kids.

'Ah, Ian is it? We met before Christmas,' said Edmund, shaking Ewan's hand.

'*Ewan* Maxted,' my escort corrected, 'and let me introduce you to your tenant, Gilly Bonning, who masterminded all the music at that splendid Carol Service.'

I felt a blush spread across my cheeks as Miriam and Edmund beamed and exchanged pleasantries. Much as I'd been tempted, it wasn't the time to give Miriam a health warning about a certain local librarian, although I could always advise her of the best time to pick up her bedtime reading matter. There was already quite a bottleneck gathering behind us. Strains of modern jazz numbers wafted through the drawing room from another grand salon at the rear. We accepted a morsel or two from another silver tray, wandered through and started to mingle with other guests, some of whom made up the school's governing body.

'Should have trained as an architect, if I could have advanced past the matchstick men phase,' Ewan commented ruefully, appraising an impressive display of paintings and a few choice pieces of marble and porcelain. 'Plenty of money here.'

'Could be from the Oborn forebears, passed down through the generations, rather than gambled away on the stock market. And anyway, don't know why you're complaining, your parents aren't short of a penny themselves.' Clearly, I felt I knew him well enough to tease him about his family's obvious affluence. By this time, we were a whisker away from a portrait in oils.

'Hmm, but no pieces like this one. Note the artist's signature here.' He pointed to a corner and I blinked in surprise to see the name of a world renowned master.

'See what you mean,' I gulped. 'My little sis Liz would be green with envy if she knew I lived a mere five minutes from this.'

Flunkeys appeared with trays of delectable nibbles and fresh glasses of champagne cocktails. With spirits lifted and cheeks flushed with the overflowing beneficence, we wandered further to sit and enjoy the music. Ewan took my hand and squeezed it. 'I've missed seeing you,' he murmured. 'Shame about New Year's Eve.'

'But that's just one evening,' I shrugged. 'People get carried away with it, but it's just the end of yet another year.'

The reminder of Tim's proposal on that particular evening was something I preferred to forget.

'Overrated you mean? Oh, Gilly, you disappoint me. Where's your sense of romance?' Ground into the gutter along with flakes of paint from Bill Kerridge's bike frame, I thought gloomily. Then I reminded myself that I'd seen the light about Tim's *real* character. I shook my head.

'Sorry Ewan, just a few bad memories, and ones I'm determined to try and banish from my mind.'

'That's my girl!' He leaned forward and kissed me lightly on the cheek.

The trouble was, with Valentine's Day a matter of hours away, my mind was going through its usual preparation for coping with disappointment. It had happened every year since the accident. I seemed to be turning into a real sourpuss. Just then I spotted our hosts wandering through, chatting with Olive and her husband Mike. Poppy and Nina were following on, in the grip of an elderly stranger – stranger to me anyway – with white bristling moustache and military bearing.

'Look, Ewan, I just want to see if I can have a quick word with Miriam. Why don't you go and rescue the girls,' I suggested, nodding in their direction.

'Alison Veltman?' mused Miriam, after I'd casually mentioned that a local resident had claimed to know her. I knew that wasn't strictly true, but my conscience wasn't unduly troubled. 'Ah yes, the Veltmans *were* invited, but wrote back to say they had a prior engagement.'

'But you seem to have made up for it,' I joked, pure relief flooding through me. A puzzled glance flashed across Miriam's face.

'Clerical gentlemen, I mean.'

'Oh yes, Father Dominic and Father Paddy could make it, such dear friends,' gushed Miriam.

'Father?' I bleated.

'Yes, they're Roman Catholic priests, from our last parish. I'm Roman Catholic, although Ed's strictly C. of E.,' she explained. Edmund gave her a companionable squeeze.

'Roman Catholic? Oh that's a... that's wonderful!' I replied, rather too enthusiastically for such everyday information. Any eavesdropper might have concluded that I'd just learned they were second cousins to royalty or had scooped a fortune on a Euromillions jackpot. I was elated and relieved at the same time. The chances of dangerous Sunday morning encounters for our new residents seemed to diminish by the second and my guess was that Simeon had personally vetoed the party invitation. There were a few more puzzled glances and raised eyebrows.

'Oh, you're Catholic as well, are you, Gilly?'

'Er… no,' I flustered, realising I'd soon need a set of ropes and grappling irons to climb out of the hole I was digging for myself. 'But, er… some of my relations are,' I improvised. 'But, er Alison said she knew you, although it was by your maiden name… Fifield?' I continued, determined to unearth a few crucial facts. Miriam and Edmund nodded.

'That's right,' Miriam confirmed. 'Of course I will have known Mrs Veltman by another name if it was a long time ago.

'Oh I think it *was* a long time ago,' I blustered, hoping to find out more.

'Well, I knew an Alison Braysmore years ago. My godmother was her Aunt Verity.'

'Was?' I was guiltily aware that my questions were bordering on downright nosy.

'My godmother died when I was… well before I was married.'

'Oh yes, before my time,' agreed Edmund.

'She died at a relatively young age. Early fifties is quite young isn't it?' Miriam commented, frowning.

'Oh no age at all,' I prattled on awkwardly. The death of a godmother and Alison's mention of an inheritance, however, stared to make a little sense. It meant that Miriam and Alison's families had been linked in the past.

'Ah, look there's Walter Flemington,' I gasped with relief. 'I expect you've been told about his famous music festivals.' Whether they were famous I cared not, but a change of subject was now overdue. Meanwhile Ewan, looked in his element with the young Oborns draped on both arms and hanging on every word of his witty repartee. Given the right company, namely young, female and attractive, he could turn on the charm as easily as flicking a light switch.

'Walter!' I called. The champagne cocktails had already bolstered my confidence, loosened my tongue and dispelled any stray shrinking violet qualities – not that there *were* many of those. Walter ambled over, looking more pensive than I'd have expected in such an impressive setting, with food and drink flowing. Perhaps he wasn't a jazz enthusiast, I surmised.

'Oh yes, we've been told about the celebrated festivals,' confirmed Edmund, turning to welcome Walter into the conversation. 'That was one of the good reasons to meet.'

'I've been telling our hosts about your wonderful festival,' I giggled, hoping that Walter would ditch the pensive look and jolly up a bit. In fact his expression was bordering on one you'd associate with Eeyore of Winnie the Pooh fame.

'Not *my* festival,' he corrected kindly. 'I have a wonderful committee who do most of the legwork, and Felicity McArdell is a godsend.'

Not the words that would have readily sprung to my lips, I thought, but at least I was now forewarned for the summer.

'And I was hoping you'd be in my little orchestra, Gilly. A little bird tells me you play the clarinet.'

Three pairs of eyes locked onto my flushed face, and to make matters worse, the sound of Ewan's chuckles and the Oborn girls' titters were much closer.

'Oh, um yes, that sounds great. Er, I'd love to play Walter, as long as there aren't too many sharps. Four is about my limit.' Whoever the 'little bird' was, deserved to meet Minnie when she was in hunting mode.

'As it happens Walter,' put in Edmund eagerly, 'our Poppy's a half-decent viola player if you're interested.' Walter immediately became very interested.

'Is that so? I thought Jane Venables would be playing, but she's told me there's a grandchild due around that time, which might curtail her involvement. First grandchild, I gather. So I'll need another viola.'

'Poppy's more than half-decent,' added Miriam. 'Don't listen to my husband.' She chuckled and gave him a playful shove. 'It was a toss-up with Poppy whether she'd go for art or music after her 'A' levels. Art won, but she likes to keep up her music in her spare time.'

'Excellent, I'll put her on my list, as long as she's happy for her parents to volunteer her services.'

'Don't worry, Walter, we'll let her decide.'

Walter nodded and smiled briefly. The pensive reappeared almost at once, and Edmund turned to with a concerned glance. By now Ewan and the girls had joined the circle.

'I say, old chap, are you all right? Are you feeling unwell?' murmured Edmund.

'Oh no, not unwell,' sighed Walter. 'Just heard some sad news. Heard it from er…' he turned to stare round the room, then shook his head sadly. 'It'll affect my brother Johnny of course. He had a horse running at Lingfield next week.'

Walter was starting to ramble. Now six pairs of bemused eyes were on him, waiting for the nub of his sad news. Perhaps the horse had broken a leg and had been put down. That would be sad indeed.

'Just heard the trainer's been killed in a helicopter crash.' There was a collective murmur of 'how awful', how tragic', 'ghastly' and the rest.

'Yes tragic,' agreed Walter nodding. 'Joe Rescorla was a top trainer.'

'Joe Rescorla?' I gasped, feeling the hot flush on my cheeks dissipate rapidly. 'He trained Bazooka Billy.'

'Didn't know you were a racing fan Gilly,' remarked Ewan, with interest. Walter just nodded glumly.

'I'm not,' I replied quickly, 'but I was in digs with a couple who were. Eric and Doreen were always watching the gee-gees, as they liked to call them. And I saw the trainer a couple of times too, on the TV, I mean.'

I stuttered to a halt and stood studying my shoes, turning over the tragic news in my mind and wondering how Eric and Doreen would react when they heard it. Eric would be very upset, I was sure. I imagined it featuring on the late news, maybe not as the main headline, but probably not far behind, with a reporter at the scene and footage of famous Rescorla victories.

'And his nephew went to my college,' I added as an afterthought.

'Really?' chorused two voices – Edmund and Walter in unison.

'Yes, he was a music student as well and… er…'

'A fellow musician?' mused Walter wistfully.

'In a manner of speaking. I didn't really know him that well.' Not unless you count being roughly snogged in a dark corner of the *Rat and Rabbit*, I reflected. However I couldn't help feeling sorry for the Rescorla family, even if one of them was an arrogant beast.

'Sad business,' murmured Walter, gazing forlornly into his empty glass.

'Looks like a brandy might be called for,' suggested Edmund, taking

Walter by the arm. 'I've got a rather special bottle I'd been saving ' They strolled off towards the drawing room, heads together and Edmund taking on the role of sympathetic host.

'Looks like you're ready for a refill too, Gilly.' It was Miriam this time. There was a tight smile on her face. Poor woman, I thought. First of all I coerce her into telling me about the death of her godmother, cruelly snatched away in the prime of her life, and then we have Walter adding his gloomy news and spoiling the party atmosphere. My fault too. If I hadn't called him over we'd never have known. Miriam turned to go.

'Um, Miriam I was going to tell you about the library.'

'Another time, hmm?' she murmured, 'There are a few guests to catch up with.' She swept away purposefully, leaving the four of us struggling for a cheerful line in conversation.

'It was all my fault,' I mumbled guiltily, then told my companions of the unfortunate death theme that seemed to have dominated the previous few minutes of conversation.

'No, no,' Poppy and Nina chorused kindly, putting comforting arms around me. I was by then feeling distinctly wobbly. Much later, my usual stiff resolve weakened. Ewan didn't return to the Maxted homestead until much, much later and for once, Valentine's Day greeted me with a kiss.

Chapter 25

More than a little awkwardness

A few hours later, I started berating myself about my weakness. But I was in shock, my wimpish side answered back. The way that name Rescorla popped up out of nowhere was to blame; that and my unfortunate and accidental knack of bringing up cheerful subjects of untimely death at my kind landlords' house-warming party. Maybe too many champagne cocktails and at least one brandy didn't help, come to think of it. By the time I'd reached the door of Bramble Cottage, my defences were down and there was I, a damsel in distress. Sir Ewan, The Opportunist had spotted the portcullis rise, the drawbridge lower conveniently into position and he had strode forward to capture his prize.

'Good morning, my sweet,' he growled sleepily in my ear. 'What a wonderful way to spend Valentine's Day.' He sighed contentedly. My eyes blinked open in shock. Had it happened? I gulped and rewound the memory file in my befuddled brain. Yes, it had! Oh no, I groaned silently. An arm reached across and tried to tuck itself around my waist, but I was wide awake by then and rolled away niftily.

'Need the loo!' I'd gasped, scurrying out of the room while trying to secure my flapping dressing gown to cover my confusion and a few other things. Once in the kitchen, Minnie eyed me hopefully from her basket, chirruped a cheery greeting, yawned and then leapt out to entwine herself round my legs. Loo, kettle, Minnie's breakfast... and what else? Breakfast would help. I'd hardly eaten anything at the party and my stomach was starting to rumble in a most outrageous manner. Next, I searched the fridge, wondering what edible delights I could lay before Ewan, to keep his mind off the female flesh variety. Scrambled egg on toast would have to do. A few minutes later there was the sound of footsteps above. Strange, I thought, how well prepared Ewan had been; how promptly a wash bag had appeared from the back seat of his car, with everything a chap might need. And, I mean EVERYTHING.

Oh yes, I'd been carried away by the cuddles on the sofa, the tender kisses that grew greedier by the second, the sweet nothings in the ear and the soothing rhythmic massaging of my back and shoulders. After that, everything seemed a blur, until I woke. One thing I had to admit was that I'd been compliant. Ewan might be keen, very keen in fact, but he was also a gentleman. I tried to shine a metaphorical torch into the deep dark recesses of my foggy memory for details of the encounter – after all, I'd been single for a very long time. Details were few, but I remembered what had happened hadn't exactly been lacking in pleasure. The trouble was, I hadn't been planning anything like that, well not with Ewan anyway. As I scrambled eggs and dunked teabags I'd asked myself if I'd wished it was someone else who'd been doing the cuddling, kissing, whispering, massaging and the rest.

Unsurprisingly, Ewan wanted to stay after we'd sipped our mugs of tea and polished off the scrambled eggs. In fact, I think he'd been hoping the sipping and munching had been carried out upstairs, but I was insistent that downstairs was cosier. The thought of rolling round in bed, getting toast crumbs where no toast crumbs ought to be, horrified me, especially in my sober state.

'Brisk walk? It's a beautiful morning.'

'Mmm,' Ewan had agreed, gazing at me with moon eyes, a gentle smile lifting the corners of his mouth. 'So's the sight in front of me.' It was after that, that he fished out an envelope from somewhere and pushed it across the table. Yes, at last I had a Valentine's card to display on my mantelpiece. It had been ages since… well, not *so* long, I reminded myself, if I counted the anonymous one, which I'd kept, for some strange reason.

However, I managed to persuade him that a bracing stroll around the Frintley Estate was too good an opportunity to miss, especially when it was putting on its spring garb of delicate pale green, decorated with a sprinkling of yellow daffodils. While we strolled I'd reminded him that it was half-term and that I'd promised Mum I'd go over and help her with her spring cleaning. His face fell at my news, but gentleman as ever, had nodded in an understanding way.

'The model daughter,' he said and I'd pushed aside my guilty feelings for the deliberate lie. Mum would be delighted to see me, but the thought of swatting cobwebs in her conservatory wouldn't be one of her top priorities.

'So what did you find out about young Nina and Poppy? You seemed to be making good headway with them last night?'

'Oh yes,' Ewan chuckled. 'Both art students with plans to open their own studio.'

'With the help of the bank of Mum and Dad no doubt.'

'Hmm, they were wondering about Shaftesbury or thereabouts. They're hoping to have somewhere fixed up in time for the Dorset Art Weeks.'

This was something new to me.

'It's at the end of May,' he explained, noting my puzzlement, 'going into June. You can drive or wander around the county, dropping in on artists, potters and what have you and drain your bank balance at the same time. It's brilliant! Some people do the art trails just as an excuse to nose about in someone else's garden. Actually we're right in the middle – geographically speaking – of a bunch of very prolific arty-crafty types. Nina's promised to text me when their plans have taken more shape.' It was no surprise to learn that Ewan was now on texting terms with the young Oborns. By then we'd arrived back at the cottage.

'Tell you what, Gilly,' he said, checking his watch, 'I'll treat you to a pub lunch, a plate of roast beef or whatever you'd like.' Although we'd walked around the whole estate there was no sign of the Oborns, although a number of impressive motors were lined up on the gravel. I'd nodded enthusiastically at Ewan's suggestion, but insisted we found a hostelry away from my patch. I saw enough of Churlbury during the week, after all.

'And what other interesting family details did you uncover last night,' I probed, as we tackled huge slices of meat and crisp Yorkshire puddings swimming in gravy.

'Well, Mrs O has plans to start her own business too. I gather she's not the type to swan around the place giving out orders without lifting a finger herself, unless it's part of her teatime etiquette. Oh no, the girls were keen to tell me that their mum was about to sign a lease for a shop in Shealton.'

'These Oborns seem to have a good work ethic,' I commented. 'Did they divulge the nature of the business?'

'Oh yes, it's to be a bookshop.'

'Oh wow!' I gasped, rather too loudly, causing several diners to turn and stare, their eating irons frozen in suspended animation. 'Sorry,' I whispered, cowering close to my plate. 'If Miriam has a bookshop, she'll hardly have a reason to visit the library.'

'So?'

'Well Alison Veltman works part-time in the library,' I explained. 'Phew, what a relief. First she's a Catholic and now she's about to open a bookshop. It couldn't be better. The chances of the two of them bumping into each other grows less likely by the day.'

Ewan nodded. We'd already discussed our concern about the Alison/Miriam situation, several times.

'Of course you must come over, Gilly. We'll have a day out at the West Quay Shopping Centre in Southampton,' said Mum, when I phoned her after Ewan had finally left. I manhandled Minnie into her basket, bagged up her other accoutrements and loaded everything I'd need for a few days away.

Good old Mum, that was just what I needed, I thought, as I drove to Growdon. My other regret over the weekend had been failing to warn Miriam about the rumbling Alison Veltman time bomb. Because, despite their different church preferences and their chosen careers, in a community the size of Churlbury, they were bound to bump into each other sooner or later. I just hoped I'd not be within fall-out distance when it happened. My *other* regret, you note. The main one being Sir Ewan the Opportunist's overnight stay.

Had I given Ewan too much encouragement about our relationship? Would he assume we were now *an item?* As far as *I* was concerned we weren't, although I'd never been a girl who'd jump into a chap's bed or let one jump in mine just for the hell of it. I bemoaned my weakness. Had I thought, for some crazy reason, that I'd reached The Last Chance Saloon? Ridiculous! I was nowhere near thirty yet. I shook my head in exasperation. In one evening I'd managed to flash the green light at someone who'd settle for amber if he could get away with it, and ruined the Oborns' jolly celebration. I recalled Miriam's frown and regretted spoiling what might have been a pleasant friendship. However, I mused, I might be able to improve the chances if I was able to warn her about Alison.

'No, Gilly,' Mum advised, when later on we were exchanging our own edited highlights of recent days over tea and cake. 'Best to leave well alone.'

'But you should have seen her expression.'

'Who? The new lady of the manor?'

'No, the curate's wife. You could almost see the daggers shooting out from her eyeballs! Mum, I told you before. It happened just before Christmas.'

Mum shook her head. 'Did you? My mind was chock-full of *where did I put that Delia recipe for sticky toffee pudding, oh no, not another empty reel of Sellotape and will the tree lights work this year?*'

'There's obviously history between them.'

'Hmm, well you mentioned the name, so that's all you can do. I don't know why you're so worried. Just leave people to sort out their own differences. Believe me love, I've tried to sort out people's problems myself in the past and ended up being told I was interfering.'

In the end, I had to agree with her, although I promised myself that if an opportunity dropped in my lap, I'd seize it. I'd seen enough of Alison Veltman by then to persuade myself that *anyone* in a head-to-head with her would wish they'd stayed at home and had spent the time re-grouting the bathroom tiles or degreasing the oven. In my imagination there was a *DANGER – DO NOT APPROACH* tape in fluorescent yellow around her. My edited highlights to Mum neatly side-stepped the subject of my overnight guest. One lecture from her was enough. On the subject of co-habiting or anything else of that ilk, she had decidedly old-fashioned views. If Liz announced that she was moving in with her bloke she'd be sure to get a frosty diatribe down the phone, for certain. Come to think of it, Liz has more sense than that. She'd do it and say nothing. Fortunately Minnie's presence proved a welcome diversion. She'd captured family hearts over Christmas, despite her frequent attempts to scale the Christmas tree and dangle precariously by one paw, as if it had been installed as her own feline baby gym.

'Nasty helicopter crash yesterday,' commented Dad. He'd spent the afternoon snoring in his chair and was ready to catch up with the TV news.

'I heard.' A cold wave swirled around my stomach and then made its way to my shoulders, making me shiver.

'Happened over Bath way.' By then it had been displaced as the piece of breaking news and was along with the also-rans, if you were to use racing parlance.

'Tragedy struck the celebrated and popular racehorse trainer Joe Rescorla yesterday evening, as he was on his way home after two of his horses scooped first place at the Newbury meeting,' announced the outside broadcast reporter. 'Both Joe and the pilot died when a suspected mechanical failure caused the helicopter to fall and hit a power cable and explode. The fireball could be seen many miles away as it fell to earth in open countryside. Accident investigators are still on the scene and a spokesman at the Rescorla stables has said that horses entered in next week's meetings have been withdrawn.'

'How awful,' I'd gasped as the reporter described the harrowing details. Then I started to remind Mum and Dad about dear old Eric and Doreen and the happy times Fran and I had had in their sitting room cheering on Bazooka Billy. After a few moments, I realised there were tears streaming down my cheeks and my voice began to peter out, ending in a choking sob. I was remembering a handsome man, in his morning suit and topper, patting Bazooka Billy in the unsaddling enclosure after he had won that handicap, with the crowd cheering, the press snapping away and proud beams on the family's faces.

'Ghastly,' agreed Mum. By the time the weather girl was trilling on about strong winds and blustery showers in the south of England, I had regained my composure. News stories affected me that way, especially when I was at a low ebb or feeling particularly fragile. It was one of those times.

After two days of cold blustery weather, which had us battening down the hatches and turning up the central heating a notch or two, spring decided to put in another appearance. Mum and I had braved the weather for a shopping trip to Southampton, where howling winds from a very grey and gloomy Solent had whipped along the boulevards of West Quay. The rest of the time we'd spent watching daytime TV in the conservatory. Mum's part-time working arrangements could be flexible at times and she'd been able to tweak them to her advantage while I was around. Arriving back at Churlbury later in the week, I was greeted by a pile of post, an empty fridge and several piles of marking. Having three days away didn't seem such a good idea. The spiders appeared to have been having a Dorset convention, with a competition for the largest web in the most challenging and out of reach location. The few slices of bread in my smart spotty bread bin had taken on a sinister green hue and a half empty bag of old salad greens was now a brown and sticky mess. A trip to the village shop for food shopping was urgent – something I dared not include on my journey back from Growdon, knowing Minnie's bladder control wasn't quite as finely tuned as mine. I scrawled a quick list, grabbed a couple of sturdy bags, managed to remember the library book that was due back and drove off to the general stores, leaving Minnie to practise curtain climbing to her heart's content.

Down in the village, the place was awash with children skateboarding around the war memorial and generally endangering life and limb – and not necessarily theirs. Food shopping done, I locked it away in the boot and strode off to the library, hoping it was Imogen's shift. As I approached the double swing doors my heart sank. There were marginally more children inside than their skateboarding contemporaries out in the street. However, the majority were sat in an orderly group on the carpet at the far end, listening to Imogen, who had them enthralled – most likely in some gory tale of blood and guts; *Horrible Histories* being one of her particular favourites. As I pushed open the door a horrified gasp could be heard, followed by a few sniggers. I shifted my attention to the counter, where Alison Veltman sat with ill-disguised disapproval at the noise level her colleague had whipped up at half-term story time. How Alison would have coped with her own moody teenage daughter was beyond me.

'Your friend still hasn't found her ticket I see,' murmured Alison acidly, as she took and swiped my book. It was clear from her expression that she suspected my story was merely a charade.

'Oh yes,' I told her earnestly, 'and she's been bed-ridden for so long. It's difficult for her. She relies on me, you know.'

'Really? Bed-ridden?' retorted Alison. 'You didn't mention that last time.'

Probably because it hadn't occurred to me then, I thought wickedly.

'Oh yes,' I replied, assuming a serious expression. 'So I'll just see if there are any more by the same author – to keep up her spirits you understand. She's not in the mood for serious, high-brow stuff.'

'Stuff?' echoed Alison, abruptly. 'This library does not stock *stuff*, unless you're referring to some of the magazines and novels that clearly appeal to the lowest common denominator. If I had my way, they'd not have been allowed.' She was on her high horse, suited and booted with riding crop in hand.

'I know what you mean,' I agreed, nodding sadly. 'There's a lot of dross out there.' I was thinking particularly of my favourite *OK* and *Hello* mags as I said it. 'Still, if it lures people into libraries, I suppose it's worth it.'

Alison was nodding in begrudging agreement when she stiffened and stared at the space behind my left shoulder. I imagined a stray Zebedee had accidentally found its way within the hallowed walls, but in the absence of noisy snorting, snuffling or muffled iPod pop racket, I guessed it couldn't be. The Zebedees tended to come with plenty of sound effects.

'Right, I'll just go and have a browse,' I whispered. I moved across hastily to the romantic fiction section, leaving Alison working on a range of facial expressions whilst I tried to decide on a name for my fictitious invalid friend. A title by my favourite author, Fantasia Crump, jumped out at me, but before I could bury my head in a copy of *Girl in a Whirl – Love and Longing at the Fairground,* which sounded just the ticket, I heard a greeting behind me that chilled me to my subcutaneous layers, if not to the bone.

'Mrs Oborn, I presume.'

I turned in dread. What was Miriam doing here in a library? Didn't she have her own books to sort, price and display? And the library at Frintley, which I'd caught a glimpse of at the 'At home', certainly boasted enough reading matter to keep a bookworm busy for a lifetime. Did she have some kind of death wish? Well, perhaps not a death wish, but clearly enough time on her hands to mingle with the hoi polloi of Churlbury. To my amazement – and relief – Miriam had a pleasant, bemused expression playing around her lips. Perhaps she hadn't recognised the harridan seated at the desk? Perhaps the young Alison Braysmore had been a fetchingly attractive young thing, who'd withered rapidly in the intervening years? Miriam obviously hadn't, or else Alison wouldn't have recognised her so quickly.

'I'm sorry...' Miriam faltered. No, she obviously hadn't recognised her.

Seeing a pile of *Churlbury Village News* on a table nearby, I snatched one and rushed across to try some damage limitation, disregarding Mum's words of warning.

'Oh Miriam,' I blurted, thrusting a magazine under her nose. 'I meant to bring one up and pop it through your letter box.'

She took it from me, her eyes swivelling between Alison and me.

'Er... thank you, that's exactly what I was after.' Oh good, I thought, perfect timing, Gilly. Perhaps I could grab her by the arm and steer her out and suggest a coffee? Then I came to my senses. What was I thinking? We weren't in Shealton, Dorchester or Blandford where coffee shops abounded and the chains such as Starbucks and Costa had made inroads into the local community.

'Don't recognise me, do you Miriam? Of course, it's a long time isn't it? Over twenty years?' said Alison sounding extremely smug.

It was embarrassing standing there, but my natural curiosity refused to let me move away and catch up with *Girl in a Whirl*. This was much more riveting, and anyway, I felt Miriam needed some moral support. However Miriam was holding her own very well. Although she had been thrown by Alison's remarks, she hadn't lost her poise.

'At Aunt Verity's funeral,' Alison added, her eyes trained on Miriam.

'Alison? Alison Braysmore?' gasped Miriam, a tad flustered. 'Really? Goodness... er... well I never!'

'Indeed,' grunted Alison, more to herself. 'Such a sad occasion it was; shocking in fact.'

'Oh yes,' agreed Miriam, 'none of us knew she was dying.'

'Except the Sisters of Mercy perhaps?'

'Well yes, I suppose she might have told them. It wasn't a silent order. But we were all desperately upset to lose her.'

'A bitter pill?' ventured Alison enigmatically. 'But sweetened for you, of course.'

Ah, I thought, the inheritance.

'Well, it was what she wished. That's why people make wills.'

'Hmm, strange that she left it all to her goddaughter.'

'But that's not exactly true,' Miriam retorted, looking round anxiously to check for eavesdroppers.

'Oh?'

'No, didn't you know, the Sisters of Mercy had a legacy as well, for the convent.'

Alison's mouth tightened into a hard line, then she sighed heavily.

'Ah yes,' she sneered, 'the *dear* Sisters of Mercy. A very deserving cause I'm sure, but not a penny left to her own flesh and blood, not a penny piece!'

'There's no need to be so upset. It all happened a long time ago.' She leaned forward to pat her hand, but Alison flinched as if she'd been scalded, then turned and snatched up her date-stamping gadget.

'Next?' she snapped, looking beyond Miriam. Indeed there were two bemused looking women standing in line, books in hand.

'I'd have thought you'd have got over your disappointment by now Alison. Life is full of hard knocks you know,' Miriam murmured, sotto voce.

'Hard knocks? What do *you* know about hard knocks? Last thing I heard, you had swanned off to some expensive finishing school in Switzerland, frittering away your poor godmother's money, while the rest of us had to make do with the local polytechnic.'

Miriam blanched and blinked in shocked surprise. 'That's none of our business.'

She turned and strode towards the door, leaving at least three people gaping and at least two of them piecing together their version of events for the Churlbury grapevine. Fortunately, Imogen's story time was finishing, and the bustle and chatter from the far end of the building managed to dispel the tension and cover the embarrassment of dirty washing being aired in public, again. What would Simeon think of his wife's waspish behaviour? I went to retrieve the book I'd so hastily abandoned. He'd be mortified.

'Ah, Miss Bonning, I hear you're going to be our third clarinet!' I knew that voice quite well but must have been head down in, 'woman on a mission', mode as I left the library.

'Mrs McArdell? How nice to see you... oh yes, Walter's twisted my arm,' I chuckled self-consciously. 'Third clarinet sounds about my mark... bit rusty you know... haven't played since last summer.'

'Committee meeting coming up this week. Once we've agreed the pieces and rehearsal schedule, I'll drop a copy through your door. I have to go up to Frintley Cottage as it happens, now that Poppy Oborn's agreed to play as well.' We both seemed to be speaking in staccato phrases, and, was I imagining it, or was there a glimmer of chumminess radiating from the woman? Perhaps the knowledge that I was a mere rusty third clarinet made her feel even more superior? Well so be it. I had already proved I was up to the task of composing special solos for her precious daughters and organising a concert. She could think what she liked.

Yes, I was a woman on a mission. Simeon had to know what his wife was doing while his back was turned. She may have thought she was whispering her vicious side-swipes at Miriam Oborn, imagining that the story time group was noisy enough to provide a cover. But no, Imogen's little group were held in suspense, with bated breath just as Alison was pushing her point home about the penury of mere flesh and blood. The timing couldn't have been worse. I wasn't sure when Alison finished her shift at the library, but this was a rare chance to speak to Simeon alone. Despite his past form, I had to tell him, warn him even. As I pulled up outside the house, I saw his car in the drive. So far, so good.

'Ah, Gilly, what a delightful surprise,' he said on opening the door and beckoning me inside eagerly. 'You'll stay for a cup of tea I hope. Alison will be home soon.'

'How soon?' I asked anxiously, then realised that my question might have been misconstrued. Would he think I was there to see him secretly? 'You see, I can't be long, and Alison's the reason I'm here. I think I'll pass on the tea if you don't mind.' He frowned and ushered me through to his study, which was at the front of the house, with a view of the lane. I positioned myself to keep an eye open for the returning Mrs V. How I'd explain my presence there, I wasn't sure. Perhaps the Midsummer Music and Arts Festival or Simeon's assembly themes would sound feasible.

'Wouldn't it be better to wait until she's here?' he asked. 'If there's a little problem or something you want to discuss, it's always much healthier to speak to the person it concerns. There can be so many misunderstandings when people don't communicate.' It sounded to me as if he was spouting a line or two from one of his sermons.

'No, I couldn't possibly do that,' I told him, aghast at the possibility.

'I see, well I can't promise not to tell her anything that I think she ought to know.'

'I'll let you be the judge of that, but I was hoping we could keep this quiet for the moment.' I then went on to tell him exactly what I'd witnessed and saw the pain on his face.

'Oh dear, I dreaded this happening,' he sighed, 'ever since the family turned up in church. In fact I was shocked at her reaction that evening. Naturally she'd told me all about her godmother's will shortly after I first met her. It wasn't a subject that came up much, but when it did, it was clear it had wounded her deeply. Alison and her parents had rather assumed they'd be the main beneficiaries. Although Verity was a nun, she had inherited a fortune from her own godfather many years before. Miriam's family weren't terribly well off and Verity must have decided that passing on her estate to her own godchild was rather like her own experience. The Fifields and the Braysmores drifted apart after that, not that they'd been very close in the first place.'

I tried to put myself in Alison's shoes. How would I have felt if another girl had landed a fortune from one of my relatives dripping in cash? As I didn't have any of those, it was stretching my imagination somewhat. Most of my relatives were in very good health and ranging from hard up to *managing OK but a bit more cash would help.* None of my godparents was noticeably wealthy either. Yes, perhaps I'd feel cheated, *but still after twenty years?* I hoped not.

'The worst part was that there were witnesses!' I told Simeon. 'There were a couple of woman in the queue who must have heard every word. You could almost see them drooling.'

'Who? What were their names? Tell me and I'll have a quiet word with them.'

'I've no idea Simeon. Just have a word with Alison. Please don't tell her I've been here though. Ask her what sort of day she's had, although if I was a betting woman, I'd say she's likely to come back spitting nails. I could almost see steam coming from her nostrils.' Simeon grimaced. 'It's not fair on the Oborns. They should be able to go around the village without being accosted about things that happened ages ago. They're probably even regretting ever buying the estate.'

'I'll do my best,' he agreed. 'And thank you for coming, Gilly. I appreciate your friendship.'

I glanced at my watch. It was almost half past four and I had a hunch that it might be closing time at the library. I imagined Alison ejecting recalcitrant toddlers and their mums, jangling a bunch of keys and asking if they had homes to go to. All was clear in the lane, but my guilty conscience propelled me speedily out of the chair, giving my apologies that I needed to be back to feed Minnie and catch up with a hundred and one other things. By the time I reached the door I remembered the photo and Simeon's last word on the subject.

'Any news on the Rogues' Gallery?' I asked brightly,

'Rogues' gallery?'

'Yes, you took a photo.' He patted the breast pocket of his jacket.

'Ah yes... we're waiting for a faculty.'

'Faculty?' The man was making no sense.

'Permission to erect a board... from the powers that be... can't move a chair without official written permission.' That sounded rather unlikely, but what did I know about what you were allowed to do in churches? 'When we've got our faculty, then we can put up our board. But until then I'm keeping it safe.' He gave a wink and patted his breast pocket again.

I whipped the door open and sprinted down the path before he could start pawing me or do anything that might instigate an interrogation by an irate Mrs V on my next library visit. I was in the car and starting the engine when another one rounded the corner, coming towards me. I gasped in terror and quickly donned the sunglasses that I always kept in the side pocket and then scrunched into first gear, just in time too. As I sped off and flicked a brief glance at the approaching driver I fancied I could see a plume of smoke issuing from behind the wheel. If there really was a God up there, he was certainly on my side that day.

Chapter 26

Something lurking in the wood

In the days that followed, spring made a determined effort to send winter away for another six months at least and I felt positive enough to pull on my wellies and sally forth onto my plot to try and tame the unruly mass of vegetation. Once term had restarted there wasn't much time for digging, hacking and raking, but Minnie and I could manage the odd half hour after school and even more at weekends. On one occasion, even Ewan was persuaded to add his muscle.

'There's a cottage coming free on our estate soon,' he told me one day. There was a hopeful twinkle in his eyes so I had to summon every ounce of tact and diplomacy. Did I really want to be living on his doorstep? Even as a hard working GP, I had learned about Ewan's capacity for packing in an impressive amount of hours on leisure pursuits. He was so focussed he sometimes took my breath away. In fact he reminded me of dear sis Liz at times. But why was he still living at home? It didn't seem to make any sense.

'Thanks for the offer, but I don't think that would be a good idea,' I told him, pausing in the filling of yet another garden waste sack.

'Oh but I disagree. I think it would be an excellent idea. Super-fast broadband, a neat little garden, logs by the barrow load and little ol' me ready at your beck and call m'lady,' proposed Ewan, tugging at a russet lock and bowing in mock humility.

'Hmm, well I'm a bit suspicious about chaps still living at home,' I teased. 'Doesn't the NHS pay you enough to fix up your own pad?'

'Ah well, it's a matter of timing, you see. But if you're suggesting we find a place *together*...?' There was much waggling of eyebrows and a lascivious grin. 'Then say the word and...' He sprinted across a heap of thistles and clamped his grubby hands on my cheeks.

'I wasn't suggesting anything of the sort!' I protested, trying to shake him off.

'God, you're sexy when you're riled,' he breathed softly and gave my lips a thorough pummelling before I could wriggle free. Ewan was determined and persuasive as well as being focussed. I was regretting, not for the first time, that I'd let him into my bed and wished that he'd give my weed patch as much attention as my lips, when a piercing sound rang in my ears.

'Blast!' he cursed, once he'd unpeeled his lips and fished out his mobile, 'forgot I was on call.'

Not long after that incident, I became aware of unusual activity in the thicket beyond my garden fence. Before Freddie's death I'd heard the whine of chain saws from time to time, but with the arrival of the Oborns, there had been a lull in all that. It was well into March by then and Stan came knocking on my door one evening to tell me that he and Lily were moving out the following day.

'Young Mr Oborn will be gettin' in 'is own fella to take charge,' he told me, nodding.

'Will you be sad to leave?'

'No, Gilly, Lily and me cain't wait!' he told me gleefully. 'Now play yer cards right an' you might get the new fella to lend a hand 'ere. I seen a strapping young buck striding roun' the place yesterday.'

As Stan creaked away on his rusty old bike I wondered exactly how young the 'strapping young buck' might be, if he considered Edmund Oborn to merit a similar description. Fifty perhaps?

Around the same time Walter Flemington's orchestra rehearsals were encroaching upon my free time. About thirty of us met in the village hall once a week and the session sometimes took up a whole evening. We puffed and scraped our way through Mozart, Schubert and Haydn and were feeling quite chipper about our efforts until Walter decided to add some Offenbach and Bizet into the mix.

'Just when I thought I'd cracked it,' I sighed to the second clarinet on my right, a balding bespectacled solicitor who smelt of cigars and pickled onions.

'Oh, I shouldn't worry, Gilly. If the part's too tricky, why don't you dig out a garter and some frilly undies and dance instead.' He rolled his eyes suggestively and pointed to the title – *Orpheus in the Underworld*.

'Don't think I'm quite up to the can-can,' I giggled, while the trombones behind us made a few lewd suggestions of their own.

Walter tapped his baton impatiently to restore order.

'Right, boys and girls, let's make a start,' he announced. 'And just in case some of you are wondering, no I *won't* be asking the ladies of the Churlbury Mothers' Union to don their stockings and suspenders for this number. I don't think the festival patrons are ready for that.'

'Nor are the Churlbury Mothers' Union,' quipped a French horn in the corner. We fell about laughing and the chap on timps crashed the cymbal to add to the hilarity. Yes, working with Walter was almost unadulterated pleasure. Admittedly, he worked us pretty hard, but he was charming, encouraging and had a wicked sense of humour, in contrast to some conductors who think they're God's gift to the music world. The timing of the orchestra rehearsals must have been just what he needed too, after the upsetting news about Joe Rescorla a few weeks before.

As far as Ewan and I were concerned, things had quietened down somewhat. He and a couple of old university friends were off skiing somewhere wildly expensive, with a lot of off-piste boozing, I suspected. With my unruly plot still refusing to behave and the weeds ganging up and putting on a show of strength, I decided that a determined assault was my only chance to tame it into submission, if I were to have any chance of growing at least a handful of carrots or lettuces.

'What you need is a compost heap,' Pru had advised, when I was bewailing my lack of gardening skills over coffee one morning. 'Then, when it's rotted down, you can dig it back into the soil. You can put all your teabags and veggie peelings into it too.'

I sighed at the thought of all that heaping and digging until Kate butted in and reminded me that I'd refused Ewan's generous offer.

'Just think, Gilly,' she said, 'you could have been mistress of a beautifully tended vegetable patch, but it's too late now that the Seabrights have moved in.' I didn't waste my breath telling Kate that it wasn't as simple as that. Moving onto the Maxted estate would have had other less manageable connotations.

So, on one bright afternoon in March, I set to work to knock the back garden into shape. At the far end of the property there was a dilapidated fence and a gate barely hanging by its hinges. On occasions, Minnie and I had taken a stroll – correction; a hike – into the thicket to look for primroses and celandines, and my young furry friend had grown very proficient at scaling trees. While I chopped, dug and lugged armfuls of weeds, she skittered around, with her tail fluffed up like a fox's brush. All that chopping and digging was hard work, but I was in a determined mood. Three hours passed by and at last I sank down against the fence having hauled my last armful of sticky grass and thistles. My hands were sore and my back ached. A towering heap in the corner of the garden was witness to my efforts, but by then I was more like a perspiring blob of jelly.

'Okay, Minnie, time for tea,' I sighed, looking round for my little black and white companion. 'I know you're hiding in there,' I called, dragging my aching body into a vertical position and through the gate. 'Fine, young lady, have it your own way,' I continued, in my best schoolteacher tone, 'if you'd prefer to stay out here, you can catch your own supper.'

There was a rustling up ahead of me where some evergreens and hollies created a shadowy mass of branches. Despite my threats, I feared Minnie wouldn't stand much of a chance if she decided to camp al fresco. A sniff of warm feline flesh was bound to have foxy nostrils twitching. I suspected there were plenty of those in the vicinity.

'Minnie! Minnie!' I called, feeling just a bit more irritated than usual and longing for a reviving cuppa. 'Stop playing games!'

I ploughed through a patch of young bracken and past a huge bramble that pulled at my jeans and then snagged my hair and grazed my cheek. I must have looked like a prisoner on the run by then. Through the evergreens I could see and hear movement, but not the mere brushing of leaves by a cat's lithe body. Someone was lurking there. Some*one* and not some*thing*. I stood frozen in fright. Was it a tramp? Was it a poacher? My heart started pounding rapidly. Could it be a Zebedee come to wreak vengeance? Only the week before I'd given detention to young Saul for writing rude words in his spelling book – all correctly spelt. The oldest Zebedee was a sinister looking brute, with enough ironmongery to give you a nasty black eye and a few broken bones if you had the misfortune to bump into him on a dark night… or in the shade of a dark fir tree with the light fading.

My heart started racing as heavy crunching noises came nearer. Fortunately it wasn't the sound of cat's bones being crunched, but rather like the sound of heavy boots stomping through dead leaves and fallen boughs.

'If you've got my cat, come out at once you coward!' I demanded, trying to sound brave. I could see a patch of blue denim through the branches and a pair of legs and sturdy brown boots crashing through the undergrowth. There was a pitiful mewing.

'Minnie!' I whimpered, imagining the eldest Zebedee doing unmentionable things to my little pet. A tall sturdily built frame ducked down through more branches, then came to an abrupt halt, as if eyeing up the opposition and gathering up energy for a final attack. I grabbed a piece of rotten branch that was lying on the ground and struck what I hoped was a threatening pose. No Zebedee was going to get the better of me.

'Did you hear me?' I snarled. 'I'll report you to PC Wakely! I'll report you to the RSPCA!' I added, speedily running out of threats by then. All was still and silent except for another pitiful mew, the sound of my poor heart hammering away under my jumper and the added percussion effect of my knees knocking together. The branches a few feet away started crashing furiously and then something male and very scruffy came pushing into the clearing carrying Minnie under his arm. It wasn't a Zebedee. It was much, much worse and the shock of what or rather who stood in front of me took my breath away. This was my worst nightmare, come to life.

'Oh no,' I gulped in horror. 'Theo Rescorla!'

'What?' he replied, blinking at me in surprise.

'You heard,' I hissed angrily. 'What are *you* doing here?'

'Sorry?' he answered, with a puzzled expression. 'You've obviously mistaken me for someone else.'

'Someone else?' I snapped. 'I know who you are and you know who I am, so don't pretend otherwise.' I lowered the rotten branch and jabbed it towards his chest. 'Think I've got a short memory do you? Treating me as a half-wit, are you? Having some sort of warped joke at my expense? Hmm, it wouldn't surprise me.'

'I'm Ted,' he said, edging away from my rustic weapon. In truth, there was no surly sneer like those perfected by Theo Rescorla of Boxmouth days. Instead his expression was one of innocent surprise.

'Ted?' I echoed and took a tentative step closer, studying the features identical to the ones that had haunted me. 'Really? Not Theo?'

He nodded. 'I'm not the man you think I am. I'm not making fun of you or anything. Look, you can put that branch down,' he said, 'I'm not

273

going to attack you or your cat. Although there was a huge ginger tom in the undergrowth that looked pretty savage. Probably scared this little thing half to death.' He tickled Minnie under her chin and then gently scratched her ears, something she loved. 'She was caught up on a rather prickly branch. Didn't you hear her?'

'Y… yes, I did,' I murmured, still incredulous at the sight in front of me. 'I thought it was one of the Zebedees torturing her.'

'Hmm, I heard you yelling at the absent Zebedee, whoever he is. You had me shaking my boots, I can tell you. He must be a nasty piece of work.'

I nodded, my silent mouth gaping open for a few moments as I appraised the man. If he came from the same gene pool as The Beast, could I trust him?

He was evidently not shaking in his boots any longer. In fact he was smiling and seemed quite relaxed and wasn't a bit like… well his loathsome relation!

'I can't believe it, you look so like… er… you must be identical! Golly identical twins!' I jabbered on, staring at him. Ted had a shorter hairstyle, but the same shape nose and strong jaw. 'I've got identical twins in my class and it's impossible to know who I'm talking to unless they've got their named bobble hats on,' I burbled in wonder. 'So you're *Ted* Rescorla?'

He nodded. 'And you are?' He came forward and extended a grubby hand.

'Gilly.' I wasn't sure if I was ready to shake hands with him, but it seemed churlish not to, especially as he was being so polite.

'Pleased to meet you, Gilly.' We shook hands like new acquaintances at a cocktail party. 'Is that short for Gillian or the long form of Jill as in one of the pair who went up the hill?'

'Short for Gillian, as a matter of fact, but no one uses that any more. Why do you ask?'

'Oh, just interested. And am I allowed to know your surname?'

'Er yes, it's Bonning, Gilly Bonning. I teach at Churlbury C. of E. and rent this cottage – Bramble Cottage – which is rather aptly named. I think someone must have had quite a sense of humour when they named it.'

'Or perhaps it was a warning to any aspiring tenants,' he remarked, peering towards my fence.

'Yes probably,' I agreed, feeling more relaxed by the minute. 'And I suppose Ted is short for something? Edward, I guess. Usually is, isn't it?' He really wasn't a bit like Theo Rescorla in temperament, although they must have been as identical as the two McArdells. I shook my head in disbelief.

'Usually yeah. Funny how a lot of people want to change the names their parents gave them.'

'If you heard the way my dad used to tell me off as a little girl with '*Gillian, stop that*' then you'd understand why I opt for Gilly, which sounds much more friendly.' I stopped gabbling and stared at him, still struggling with a sense of disbelief.

'I really can't believe it,' I said, more to myself than Ted. 'Do you want a cup of tea? I was about to make one when Minnie decided to go AWOL. It's the least I can do to thank you for rescuing her.'

'Okay,' he said smiling, and followed me as I pushed my way back towards the gate.

'It's not much,' I said, carefully unlatching the gate, 'but it's home. I've been flogging myself to death all afternoon, clearing this lot.'

'Haven't you got anyone to help you?' he asked, surveying my handiwork. 'A husband or boyfriend or...?'

'Oh no, no husband,' I chuckled ruefully, 'and I'm not sure if Ewan counts as a boyfriend. He's probably bedding all the chalet maids he can get his hands on at the moment.' Why was I telling all this to a complete stranger? I don't know. I suppose it was because of his lovely smile and easy-going manner and the way Minnie had taken to him so quickly, all snuggled up inside his jacket with her little face poking out contentedly. Anyone who's a cat lover generally meets with my approval.

'Chalet maids?' He rolled his eyes in surprise.

'At some posh skiing resort... somewhere alpine... I've forgotten the name.'

We were on our way to the back door by then, with me lugging an armful of tools and Ted carrying a few more.

'Oh, so not a holiday camp then?'

'Oh no, that wouldn't be Ewan's style. Not posh enough for him,' I simpered, affecting an upper class tone.

'And a bit of a ladies' man then?'

'Hmm, he thinks he's got a wonderful bedside manner. He's a GP you see, but not really my type.'

'Ah.'

'Look, just shove that lot in there,' I told him, flinging open the door to the old coal hole where the tools languished most of the time.

'Quite a catch then, this Ewan.'

'Thinks he is, but well… goodness, you don't want to hear all about my disastrous love life.' I shook my head and pushed my fingers through my tangled locks, where a few dead leaves had taken up temporary residence. 'Come on in and take a seat Ted… oh and you'd better move that pile of marking. Sorry I wasn't expecting visitors.'

I went to fill the kettle and noticed a scratch on my cheek and a smudge of soil on my forehead as I passed a mirror. Ted leaned back on the cushions, stretching out his legs and gazed down at Minnie who looked surprisingly at home. By the time I was setting down our mugs on the coffee table, that was really just an old assortment of cane sticks, held together with a small amount of string and a lot of hope, Minnie was purring loudly.

'You've obviously got a special gift with animals. She doesn't let everyone do that. Ginger nut?' I offered, thrusting a tin under his nose. He fished one out and dunked it in his mug. I giggled as a large piece fell into his tea with a plop.

'Don't always get the timing right,' he chuckled.

'Nor me,' I agreed, dunking carefully and offering another biscuit, which he chewed instead.

'So how long have you been living here?' he asked after a few sips from his mug.

'Oh, just since August. There's quite a community spirit in the place, although that can be a disadvantage sometimes.'

'You mean everyone knows each other's business?'

'Exactly.' I went on to tell him about some of the local attractions as he seemed interested and was about to ask him about his work on the estate – because he was obviously who Stan meant by a 'young buck' – when I remembered the tragic death of Joe Rescorla.

'I was sorry to hear about Joe's death in that ghastly accident. He must have been your uncle I guess. Eric reckoned Joe didn't have any family.' Ted frowned and nodded. 'It must have been a horrible shock for the whole family,' I added quietly. 'Sorry, I've been prattling on when you must have had a tough time recently.'

He shook his head sadly. 'And yes, it was a horrible shock.'

Minnie chose that moment to squirm out of her nest, so I opened up a pouch of jellied tuna and let her tuck in. While she gobbled it down voraciously, I glanced across at Ted, who was sitting pensively with his head back. I went across and sat beside him, which seemed a natural thing to do. I was also feeling guilty about stirring up his obvious grief when we'd been getting along fine, talking about this and that.

'Sorry, Ted. I shouldn't have said anything, but I saw Joe and some of your family on TV a couple of times, so I know a little…'

'On TV?' He visibly brightened up at that. 'Ah, the racing I suppose.'

'Yes, that's right. I was in digs with a couple who were racing addicts – well the husband was – that's the Eric I mentioned. He'd watch every race going, and knew his stuff, all the background, trainers and well… everything.'

'And where was this?'

'Oh at Boxmouth, where I was at college.'

'Ah, Boxmouth. That's where you met Theo, not at Latterton.'

'No, not Latterton. I wasn't quite up to the calibre of the usual Latterton student, and anyway I wanted to go to teacher training college, not a music academy.'

He nodded thoughtfully.

'Tell me about your racing addict hosts.' So I did and then about how we all went crazy cheering Bazooka Billy and then about seeing the people in the unsaddling enclosure.

'Were you there when he won the Lincoln Handicap? I thought it was your twin obviously, because I had no idea there was anyone else.'

'Oh yes, I was there.'

'Ah, that figures of course, with your brother over in France.'

'You knew about that, did you?' he asked.

'Yes, he certainly made sure we all knew about his interview before he went. And… er… it must have been you we saw when Bazooka Billy ran at Ascot, when he came second… Eric and Doreen invited us over for tea because they knew the horse was running and thought Fran and I would like to watch.'

'Yes, I was at Ascot.'

'And there was a girl… very glam… gorgeous clothes…'

'My cousin Sophie.' He smiled as he told me. 'She's engaged to an Olympic rower now, so she's usually seen running along a towpath rather than floating around a racecourse.'

There was a pregnant pause and I regretted stirring up the sad family business, just as I had at Miriam and Edmund's party.

'So,' began Ted, deciding it was time to change the subject, 'what sort of an impression did Theo make at Boxmouth?'

'You really want to know?'

'Well, judging by the way you greeted me when I fell out of the bushes, there must have been one or two things that stuck in your mind.'

'One or two?' I laughed scathingly. 'Or three or four? No, I couldn't possibly tell you. You really wouldn't want to hear.'

'Wouldn't I? You forget I've lived with Theo Rescorla for a long time. I'm sure there's nothing you could say that would possibly surprise me.'

I stared at his pleasant open face and was sure he meant every word, but even so I was unsure about making personal remarks about someone so close to him.

By then it was well after six and I, for one, was not going to last all evening on a couple of ginger nuts and a cup of tea.

'Would you like to stay for supper?' I asked. 'I haven't got much to offer, but you're welcome to share it with me.'

'Really?' He looked surprisingly keen. I nodded. 'Well…' He checked his watch. '…I don't have to be anywhere until about half eight, so as long as you promise to be honest about how Theo let down the family name, I'll stay.' As he said it, my eyes were met by his steady gaze, curiously, there was something about his eyes that made my insides do a little flip. They seemed to have a magnetic quality that I'd never or rarely noticed in a man before, except maybe in the eyes of the unattainable ones on TV.

'Okay, you're on,' I agreed, grinning.

There really wasn't much in my fridge that weekend, as I was driving over to see Fran and Tony the following day, but some sausages, jacket potatoes and a tin of baked beans made a passable meal. We didn't get round to discussing his disagreeable twin until we were facing each other with a plate of hot food in front of us and half a bottle of wine to share. Ted had offered to fix the hinges on my garden gate after finding some screws and a torch, and then had cleaned out Minnie's tray for me, despite my attempt to persuade him that no supper guest should have to do such a disgusting chore.

'So, Gilly, tell me what upset you most about that disagreeable member of the Rescorla family.' As I chewed a piece of sausage I chose my words carefully.

'Well, he was *extremely* confident to the point of being... um...'

'Arrogant?' supplied Ted cheerfully.

'Er... well, since you mention that word, yes, it was one that was on the tip of my tongue.' He nodded in agreement.

'Hmm, what I expected actually.'

'And he liked to call the shots,' I continued, remembering that dreadful time when he'd messed up my audition with his crass playing.

'You mean he was bossy? Opinionated?'

'Well...' I thought twins stuck up for each other, the McArdells certainly did.

'I suppose you could say that.'

'Oh, he's had a lot to learn,' continued Ted. 'And what about his sense of humour?'

'Sense of humour?' I exclaimed, 'I don't think I saw much of that! He seemed to take himself far too seriously.'

As we tackled our supper, I started to tell him about the evening at the *Rat and Rabbit* when the joke book was being passed around.

'And then when I got up and went to the ladies'... oh well... um...' I petered out, remembering what had happened in a dark corner of the bar.

He stopped eating and stared at me. 'What?'

I shook my head. The experience was too embarrassing to talk about. 'Perhaps I ought not to say. It was... actually it was so disgusting... and my friends and I were only having a laugh with someone's book of jokes. It was harmless amusement...'

Before he could get another word out of me I put a great chunk of potato in my mouth and paid a lot of attention to the baked beans, pushing them into a little pile.

'So what happened next? You can't leave me dangling in mid-air, Gilly. It's not fair.' I took a sip of my wine and fixed him with a guarded expression.

'You may not like it.'

'That bad?'

'Awful. He… he… did something…' He put down his knife and fork and took my spare hand in his and squeezed it gently. My insides did another flip as his dark brown eyes gazed at me with concern.

'Look, whatever it was, let me apologise on behalf of that crass individual for what he did.' I put down my wine glass and he reached for my other hand.

'Well… first he grabbed me very roughly.'

'And?'

'He told me he'd shut my blabbermouth… his mates were egging him on.'

'Hmm, I can imagine the scene. So, he threatened you? Then what?'

'He snogged me… horribly… roughly… like… like a sink plunger.'

Ted's eyes opened wide in shock and then his face started to crumple into a grin and he began to chuckle quietly to himself. 'Sorry Gilly, but it sounded so funny – the sink plunger bit – not the fact that he grabbed you of course.'

'It does rather, doesn't it?' I agreed, managing a little chuckle of my own. 'But trust me, it was awful at the time. He was like a raging beast. As a matter of fact I used to think of him as 'The Beast.'

'Did you?' he gasped. 'Well it sounds as if he deserved it. And that horrible sink plunger snog…'

'Made me feel as if I'd been violated.'

His grin had vanished as quickly as it had come. He squeezed my hands and got up from his seat, lifting me out of mine at the same time.

'Not like this then?' He leaned across and gently touched my lips with his.'

I was transfixed, amazed, thrilled and mesmerised all at the same time. This man was gorgeous; the complete opposite of his twin. I couldn't help sighing as he drew away after a few seconds.

'Not a bit,' I agreed, holding his gaze. He leaned forward again and this time he released my hands and put his around my shoulders.

'And not like this?' The kiss was stronger the second time, and not so brief, but it did wonderful things to my insides that I hadn't felt for a long time, if ever.

'No, nothing like it,' I whispered, burying my head in his shoulder. 'And I can't believe this is happening. We only met, what, three hours ago and it's almost as if I've known you for ages… and…'

'Gilly Bonning, it may only be three hours but already I know you're very special,' he whispered. 'That idiot had no right to treat you as he did. If he'd had eyes in his head he'd have seen that for himself.'

'Oh, I'm not so special, really. I'm very ordinary as a matter of fact and…' I tugged at my messy hair. 'I'm unkempt, covered in too much garden and probably in need of a good scrub.'

'You're just right, from where I'm standing,' he told me, stroking my hair – leaves and all. I wanted that wonderful moment to go on forever, but eventually we gave up on the cold remains of our supper and he had to go. I'd never felt like that about any man before, not Ewan or even Tim. The shock of that secret admission took me by surprise.

'I'll be back,' he promised, as he stood at the door, smiling and giving my shoulders a squeeze. There was a strange tight feeling at the back of my throat as if I was about to burst into tears. Instead I leaned across and planted my lips on his. He pulled me close and kissed me so thoroughly that, for the rest of the evening, I seemed to be floating. There was no doubt about it, I was – quite unexpectedly – hopelessly in love.

Chapter 27

Timing is everything

'It must be a new diet or something,' commented Fran, a few minutes after I'd arrived. Tony had poured us all a glass of wine and we were relaxing on Fran's 'new' second hand suite.

'No, not a diet,' I grinned, shaking my head.

'What do you think Tony?' she asked him casually.

'Not sure. Is it a different hair-do?'

'Hair-do?' I spluttered. 'No, it might be a bit longer and I suppose there *could* be the odd leaf still clinging on after yesterday's gardening effort.' He peered round the back quizzically and shrugged.

'Definitely no stray leaves, but there's certainly something different.'

'Make-up!' chipped in Fran. 'You've splashed out on a new foundation or blusher!'

I felt my cheeks tentatively, wondering if I'd suddenly turned crimson.

'No, still my bog standard collection,' I told her, knowing the floating feeling was down to Ted, who I couldn't stop thinking about.

I'd gone to bed trying to relive every minute of those three or so hours – even the bits when I was ranting at him – and had woken up with his face in my mind's eye. In between, I'd had a wildly erotic dream of lovemaking on a rug in the thicket, with only the sound of birdsong for company. When I woke, I was still breathless and gasping, wishing I could drift back into unconsciousness and let Ted go through his wonderful repertoire of seduction all over again.

'Then it must be a man,' she declared, watching me for any tell-tale signs, whilst I desperately tried to keep a straight face.

'Has Ewan pledged undying love and promised to make an honest woman of you?' she asked, with eyes wide and brows raised.

'No, Ewan's more into lust than love, and I've never thought he was my type.'

'Shame on him,' commented Tony, peering into his half-empty glass.

'Hmm, not Ewan then,' said Fran, frowning and putting on such a show of concentrated thought that you could almost hear the cogs turning.

'Tim!' she gasped, her eyes shining with delight at her next idea. 'He's remembered hasn't he? Oh, Gilly, it *must* be that. I can't imagine anything else affecting you like… well, it's pretty obvious there's something up.'

If I hadn't been blushing before, I'm sure I must have been by then.

'Not Tim,' I told them, and watched their eager expressions fade. 'Tim's marrying Lena, remember? Last I heard they're planning an autumn wedding.'

Wow, I thought, I could say that so easily now and not feel upset about it. I could take it squarely on the chin. Meeting Ted had changed my life, but where Ewan figured in it was a different matter. He was due back from his alpine adventure at any time and naturally would expect to take up where he had left off. Wondering how I could handle that, was a problem I'd conveniently pushed to the back of my mind. Before long – and not very long at that – I'd have to confront it.

'Well who then?' Fran probed. 'Someone at school? Don't say that frisky curate has kicked out his mad wife and had a steamy grapple with you in the stock cupboard.'

'Definitely not!' I chuckled, horrified at the picture Fran described. 'Simeon wouldn't go *that* far. He's devoted to Alison, even though I agree that she's slightly unhinged. He whisked her off to a hotel in Sidmouth after her latest outburst, so you can safely assume that he's not planning to ditch her for a new model. Anyway, he's not my type.' Even though he keeps my photo in his breast pocket, I reminded myself, with a shiver.

'So, Miss Mystery Pants, what's the reason for the glowing pink cheeks and bright sparkling eyes and the deliberate avoidance of giving a straight answer?'

'Can't get anything past you, can I, Fran?' I sighed.

'No.'

'Won the jackpot at the W.I. bingo night?' ventured Tony. 'Dug up some Roman remains in the cabbage patch?'

'God, you're persistent, aren't you!'

'Oh yes,' agreed Fran, chuckling. 'This is a two-pronged attack.'

'Let me top up your glass, Gilly, perhaps that'll help to loosen your tongue.'

'I like your subtle approach, Tony.' Okay, I thought, seeing as they were so determined to winkle it out of me, I'd give them an edited version, with absolutely no Boxmouth College twin brother references.

'Yes, it's a bloke,' I admitted. 'He's called Ted and he came tumbling out of the thicket with Minnie tucked under his arm.'

'He was trying to steal her?' gasped Fran. 'And you attacked him with a handy sapling, wrestled him to the ground, put him in a half nelson and he was putty in your hands and the rest is history?'

'Not quite. He rescued Minnie from a ferocious ginger tom, then mended my broken gate and stayed for supper.'

'Ah-ha, an itinerant handyman looking for a free meal,' speculated Tony, with a twinkle.

'Or a poacher with a new recipe for fricasseed kitten that he was itching to try out?' added Fran, wrinkling her nose in disgust.

'No, I don't think they'd go *that* far,' observed Tony.

I watched the two of them batting their crazy ideas back and forth.

'He works on the Frintley Estate.'

'Ah, wasn't far off, was I?' said Tony grinning.

'Shades of *Lady Chatterley's Lover* here,' put in Fran with a saucy look.

'Are you sure his name's not Oliver?'

'Definitely not, and I'm not Lady Chatterley either. I suspect he's probably slightly short-sighted because I was covered in dirt and leaves…'

'What? You rolled in abandoned passion with him on the ground because he rescued Minnie from the jaws of a vicious ginger tom!'

'No, silly! I'd been gardening and was covered in dirt before he came plunging through the undergrowth.'

'He obviously likes the down-to-earth type.'

'Very droll, Fran. What I meant was, he wasn't put off by my scruffy appearance, which is quite refreshing I think.'

'Lucky you.'

'So, when are you seeing him next? I guess it wasn't a one night stand.'

'There haven't been any *nights*, I'll have you know. We've only known each other since about four o'clock yesterday afternoon and he had to leave four hours later.'

'You can pack a lot into four hours though, can't you Tony?' An affectionate glance passed between them.

'You bet,' he chuckled. Still no engagement ring, I noted. That was always the first thing I looked for when I met Fran. I reckoned she'd never text me news of that importance, but would prefer to tell me face to face.

'So it's all very new then?'

'Hmm, trouble is, Ewan's going to reappear on the scene soon, which might make things a little bit complicated.'

Fran nodded. 'Does Ted know about Ewan?'

'Oh yes, I told him I had a disastrous love life and that Ewan had probably been bedding chalet maids in between skiing and sinking lagers, so I think he kind of got the idea I wasn't in a committed long-term relationship.'

'Well, good luck with Ewan when he comes calling, although if he really *is* playing the field I don't think he could possibly object if you found yourself another love interest.'

'True.'

The same thought had occurred to me while Ted and I had been chewing our jacket potatoes, sipping wine and exchanging interested glances. The trouble was, Ewan was a 'have your cake and eat it' sort of bloke. Fran and Tony agreed when I dared to voice my thoughts much later, when the conversation came full circle.

'But he can't expect to have it all his own way,' protested Fran, 'just because he's dripping with cash.'

'So how about you two?' It was time to turn the tables on them, after the grilling I'd received. They exchanged more meaningful glances.

'Well, we survived half-term break with 24/7 company, so I guess things are set fair at the moment,' hinted Tony.

'Only *at the moment?*' protested Fran.

'You know what I mean,' he replied and flung an arm around her shoulders. We'd been out for a bracing walk and were warming up with tea and crumpets.

'If you really want to know,' Fran said significantly, 'we're looking for a suitable flat or cottage somewhere between our schools. If all goes well...'

'Then I may consider making her an offer she can't refuse,' Tony joked.

'What? To love, honour and darn your socks?'

'Something like that.'

However, I had to admit to myself they made a lovely couple as I drove back home later. On the subject of Ewan and Ted, though, I had a lot more thinking to do, at least I hoped I would. After Ted had disappeared into the night, I realised I had no way of contacting him. At least I knew where he worked, but Frintley Estate was huge and each day he could be anywhere on the hundred or so acres, chopping trees or clearing ditches or whatever else might be in his job description. Back at school, I found my concentration lapsing from time to time, as the odd daydream drifted along and hijacked my brain. At assembly one morning, Olive announced that we'd sing a hymn or song and I started playing a different one, much to everyone's amusement and my embarrassment.

'Oops!' I'd gasped and that wasn't my only 'oops' moment.

'Have you missed my darling brother?' asked Kate one lunchtime, after yet another faux pas – of forgetting my break duty. I gave her a dubious smile, which she interpreted as a lovelorn glance and assured me he was planning on a visit very soon. As long as he didn't turn up when Ted was there, I thought.

Of Ted, though, there hadn't been a sign. Each day I wandered down the garden path, through the gate, which was no longer rickety, and into the thicket, hoping to hear the sound of estate workers lopping, sawing and clearing fallen trees. However, there was only the rustle and twitter of flora, fauna and feathered residents. Perhaps he *had* been an itinerant worker looking for a free supper, who just happened to be related to someone I knew. No, he was too open and honest about himself for that. Then I recalled our rambling chat and realised he'd told me very little about himself. He'd referred to having had several jobs, but not exactly what he'd been doing. He had also told me what he was doing was only temporary and that he hoped for something more permanent in the area. So, apart from his name and a couple of his relations, I knew nothing.

Turning round those thoughts one evening and psyching myself up for an assault on some assessment test marking, I was stopped abruptly by a sharp rap at the door. I realised I'd not heard the sound of tyres scrunching on the gravel, but that may have been because my Verdi album was obliterating any but the loudest noises. My heart started pounding rapidly as the prospect of imminent male presence – either one was bound to present a challenge of some sort. I hastily turned off the CD player

'Ewan!' I exclaimed, trying to sound keen, but knowing I was deeply disappointed.

'Gilly! Hey it's great to see you!' He smothered me in a huge hug and homed in enthusiastically on my mouth. I couldn't help wondering how many other mouths might have received the same treatment just recently.

'You'd better come in,' I said, on the possibility of loitering estate workers. Now that he stood there, I knew there was no contest. The spark that I'd always known was missing was never going to ignite now that I'd met Ted. With *him* I was dealing with a roaring flame.

'Coffee?' I had to show willing. He nodded, then as I organised our drinks he started to tell me what a great holiday he'd had, and how Ben and Will had tried to lead him astray.

'Oh yes?' I chuckled. 'So you've been a good boy have you? Well, that wouldn't be true to the usual Ewan Maxted form.' After handing him his coffee, rather than sit down, I wandered round the room, picking up a stray cup, binning an old shopping list, removing a strand of cobweb and anything I could find to avoid his greedy clutches.

'Ah, you know me, poppet!'

Poppet, I thought in surprise. That was a new title.

Time was moving on and the pile of test papers sat waiting for my attention. I needed to encourage Ewan out of the door if I was going to get to bed before midnight. By then he was relating his prowess on the ski slopes and about the charms of one of the instructors and I was smiling and nodding – hopefully in the right places – when there was another knock, but on the back door this time.

'Popular girl this evening,' remarked Ewan, as I went to answer it, my heart hammering, my mouth dry and my expectation raised. It could be Felicity McArdell on festival business or Harry Woodfine with his new assembly themes, but they'd never use the back door, surely.

'Oh, er, Ted!' I gulped, breaking into a nervous smile. He was the best person I could hope to have on my doorstep, but at the very worst time. We exchanged meaningful smiles, while I tried to convey to him that I had company, by much swivelling of eyeballs, raising of brows and surreptitious pointing.

'Hi, Gilly,' he murmured.

'Bad timing,' I whispered. He nodded.

I heard steps behind me. 'Is your visitor joining us?' said Ewan, his tone verging on irritable, although as a GP he was learning the art of the bland smile. 'Oh hello there,' he said, eyeing Ted's muddy boots and well-worn jacket.

'Just one of the estate workers,' I told him casually.

'With... er... a message for all the tenants,' said Ted, who might have been improvising as he glanced in Ewan's direction. Of course, it could have been absolutely true, although you'd expect anything official to be in writing.

'My friend Ewan.' Ted nodded and flashed a brief smile.

'That's right. I'm not one of the tenants,' added Ewan.

'And the message?' I asked hopefully.

'The annual inspection's tomorrow.'

'Tomorrow? What time?'

'What sort of inspection?' Ewan wanted to know.

'Health and safety,' supplied Ted promptly.

Ewan chuckled. 'Health and safety? Seen the state of the roof slates? Now there's a health hazard! If any of these slipped off as Gilly was nipping out to hang up her washing, she'd be a gonner, unless there was some lucky beggar handy to administer a bit of mouth-to-mouth resuscitation.' I knew which lucky beggar would be top of my list – not that I'd necessarily want to suffer a near death experience for the privilege.

'About half past four? Would that be possible for you Miss Bonning? We think it's best to carry out the inspection with the tenant present.'

'Hmm, very wise,' agreed Ewan.

'Absolutely,' I agreed, grinning. 'Four thirty tomorrow then.'

'Thank you, my man,' said Ewan, forgetting he wasn't a lord of the manor addressing a lowly serf.

Ted turned and strode off down the garden path while I stood there wishing I could gag Ewan somehow. It was *so* embarrassing. What I'd witnessed was rather like a couple of stags coming head-to-head, with Ewan doing most of the warning, and Gilly the doe standing by waiting to see who would come out victorious.

'And make sure they note that piece of rotten door frame,' he instructed me as he was leaving a few minutes later.

'I will,' I promised, affecting a look of concern. 'I'll make sure they're very thorough.' As I said it, I imagined Ted being very thorough, but not with door and window frames.

'Can't have my little girl getting injured!' My heart sank again. It had been bad enough calling Ted 'my man'.

'Course not.'

'I'll give you a call later on tomorrow, shall I? See how the inspection turned out? Maybe we could fix up something? Meal? Film? Theatre?'

'Hmm, maybe.' As I sat and marked the assessment papers I'd never felt so gloriously happy. Less than twenty four hours, I thought, and I can feast my eyes on Ted once more. I sighed contentedly. Life really was very good.

The grin that was plastered on my face when I woke up the next morning refused to go away, even when I had to deal with a cloakroom scuffle, missing homework and a rubber arcing its way over the heads of the children when everyone should have been swotting up for the weekly spelling test. Oh yes, I'd given in to parental pressure – mainly Mrs Pudwell's – and had divided the class into three spelling groups, each with their weekly list and test. A glance in the direction of Messrs Zebedee and Kale, who now sat on opposite sides of the classroom, confirmed my suspicion.

'Rufus Kale, report to the staffroom at break!' I rapped, trying to affect an air of displeasure. It wasn't until lunchtime that I plummeted from cloud nine with a heavy thump.

'Gilly, sorry to be a nuisance, but we need to convene an emergency meeting after school,' said Olive, catching me as I came dashing out of the loo. 'I've just told the rest in the staffroom.'

'Oh but—' I began.

'Ofsted, I'm afraid. We knew it was due before the summer. I had a call about an hour ago. They're coming next Tuesday and Wednesday.'

My shocked expression must have convinced Olive that the mention of the dreaded Ofsted was the cause of my rapid change of demeanour.

'But I've got an appointment, a very *important* appointment after school,' I gasped.

'You're not the only one, Gilly. Morris has had to rearrange a dentist's appointment and Fay's trying to get hold of a neighbour to collect her daughter from a ballet exam. I know it's a pain. Could you call and sort yours? We'll need a couple of hours to cover all contingencies, so I think we'd be hoping to finish around half five, as long as we start promptly after the children are off the premises.'

'Well, I would if I could,' I told her, 'but I don't have a number.'

'I expect it'll be in the directory.'

'It's not *that* sort of appointment,' I wavered, imagining Ted arriving eagerly at four thirty and finding the place deserted. 'It's at the estate and… it's also an inspection. I've been told it's absolutely essential that I'm there.'

'Well, I'm sure the Oborns would be very flexible, and I've got their number in my diary.' She started to rummage in her bag while I hastily considered my options, which weren't exactly plentiful. It was half way through lunchtime by then.

'Don't worry about the number, Olive,' I told her. 'It'll be quicker if I just drove back and stuck a note on my door.'

'Oh all right,' she said smiling. 'It's a bit of a bugger, I know – excuse my French. Thanks for being so understanding.'

I beetled off to collect my coat and a handful of drawing pins from a notice board.

'Heard the news?' asked one of the T.A.s as I rushed through the staffroom.

'Just,' I gasped. 'Need to make emergency arrangements. Could you register my lot if I'm held up?'

She nodded. It was certainly time for co-operation and I was convincing myself that Ted would understand when he read my note. Although he wasn't a teacher, he'd surely have heard enough about the dreaded Ofsted inspections to realise they trumped my social life, even if our meeting was masquerading as a health and safety check. I broke the speed limit through the village. Fortunately there were no pensioners on Zimmer frames or stray sheep blocking the way. I pinned notes on both doors using pages ripped from my diary, adding a kiss at the bottom of my scrawled message.

'Now remember, there's nothing to be worried about,' Olive emphasised, as she started to close the meeting. The hands on the staffroom clock hovered around five twenty-five and I was desperately hoping nobody would start asking questions that needed long and detailed answers. 'Our planning and record keeping is up to date. And thanks to your diligence, all the interim tests are marked and logged.'

It was a relief to learn that my determination in that particular area was worth the shortage of sleep two nights before. Nevertheless, telling us not to worry was akin to telling us not to speculate about the likelihood of rain on sports day. In other words, it was a downright certainty – or 'odds on' as Eric would have said – especially for newcomers. Kate and I exchanged glances, knowing we'd both be relieved when Wednesday evening came and we could stop holding our breath and uncross our fingers.

'And don't stand for any insubordination in the ranks,' Olive added. 'I'll have a word with your two troublemakers, Gilly, so rest assured they won't be stirring up any trouble.' I wished I could be so confident. She gave me a knowing wink, and the rest of the staff gave tight-lipped smiles and sympathetic nods.

'Anything else?' she asked. Naturally there were dozens of unanswered questions whizzing around my head; the part that wasn't dwelling on Ted's likely state of mind at that precise moment.

However, I chose to remain silent There was I, faced with my first Ofsted inspection, and all I could think of was a man who I'd known for barely four hours. Had he bewitched me? I gathered up Olive's hand-outs, dropped them in my bag and scooted out to my car with the excuse that I had a cat to feed. No one was taking much notice, as they all evidently had their own domestic problems to deal with – except Kate and her silver spoon existence. For the second time that day I broke the village speed limit. Even at five thirty Churlbury wasn't exactly jammed with traffic and there was rarely anyone but me turning in at the estate entrance. As the car bumped and rattled over the cattle grid, my pulse and heart rate cranked up into the danger zone. I'd been picturing Ted's face since that brief back door exchange and was virtually salivating with excitement.

As I came within sight of my gravel parking area though, a familiar car was already parked there. How could he? Hadn't he anything better to do with his time? Didn't he have patients to see? Pulses to check? Colleagues to consult? Prescriptions to write? Well, if he *did*, he also apparently had added *'checking up on Gilly's safety'* to his long list. I parked behind the empty car and allowed a few shameful thoughts to pass through my mind. If only I hadn't given way to Ewan's persistence, I thought ruefully. If only I'd had the stamina to withstand the effects of champagne cocktails. If only I'd had the honesty to tell Ewan he was fine as a friend, but I really didn't want our relationship to go any further. If only. It had all seemed such an easy option at the time. The glamour of the Maxteds with their grand manor house and social connections had most definitely swept me up and carried me along on a tidal wave of extravagant fun. If I needed a diversion from the depressing Tim and Lena business, that was it. Well, now that I had put that behind me, I had to face up to the consequences of the past five months. Right, I told myself, as I slammed the car door, no shilly-shallying, but it was easier decided than put into practice.

As I reached the gate, I could see that Ewan had already taken charge of the situation in my absence. As far as thoroughness was concerned, he was excelling. However, throwing his weight around might have been a more accurate description. A long ladder was propped up against the front wall, on which stood Ted, with Ewan below, issuing instructions.

'No, across to the right!' he called. 'I can see it from here!' The chances of Ted and I carrying on where we left off looked very slim indeed.

'Ah, there you are, Gilly.' Ewan left Ted to his inspection and strolled over, smiling broadly. 'Thought I'd get the chap to make a start and save time.'

He grabbed my bulging school bag and kissed me lightly on the cheek.

'But why? I'm not a helpless half-wit, Ewan! I'm perfectly capable of taking care of my own affairs,' I told him firmly. 'And anyway, don't you have patients to deal with?'

I glanced up at Ted, who had paused in the middle of whatever he was doing and was watching us in a bemused sort of way.

'Of course I haven't. I finished surgery at four and thought I might as well drop by and make sure nothing was missed. If you'd taken our spare cottage before the Seabrights snapped it up though, you wouldn't be dealing with *this* now.'

I fumbled with the front door key and saw that my note was no longer there. It hadn't been addressed to anyone in particular, so maybe Ewan thought it was meant to be for him, especially with a kiss at the bottom. If so, he would have assumed that I was expecting him.

'That lock's not very smooth, is it? It could easy become jammed, and that would be a problem,' he commented, then turned and called up to Ted to add it to the list. My fuse was grower shorter by the second, as I went straight into the kitchen and filled the kettle. Minnie was already tumbling down the stairs in her excitement, chirruping loudly for supper. 'So I thought if I could get all this done, I could take you out for a meal somewhere,' Ewan continued, wandering in behind me.

By the time Minnie was licking the last of the gravy from her bowl, Ted had also appeared. The two men eyed each other guardedly and it appeared that Ewan had at last detected a chilling in the atmosphere. In fact, there was a bewildered look on his face. It was the first time I'd ever snapped at him and I think it must have come as a shock. Where was the compliant and grateful Miss Bonning, he was probably wondering. Where was the eager companion who couldn't wait to slip into one of her charity shop bargains and slide her knees under the table of a posh new eatery? His question about supper was still unanswered.

'So, how about it, Gilly?' he asked. 'Supper I mean. There's a rather nice Greek restaurant I know you'd love.'

'Sorry Ewan, I don't think I would.'

'Really? He paused thoughtfully and considered a few more tempting options. 'Or what about Italian?'

I shook my head and reminded myself about the shilly-shallying vow. Disentangling myself from Ewan was going to take a little while longer, I suspected, but I had to start somewhere.

'Or Chinese?' He was very persistent. 'There's a new one in Weymouth I'd like to try, or we could always go to that TV chef's place – you know, Hughie what's-his-name? They're usually booked up months in advance, but I know how to pull a few strings. The head chef is an old pal of mine.'

'Some other time Ewan, if you don't mind. I have an Ofsted inspection looming. Kate will tell you all about it I'm sure, so…'

It was then that I realised Ted was no longer in the room, and a gasp escaped from my mouth. 'He's gone!' I rushed across to the door, silently cursing Ewan's magnanimous offers of foreign cuisine. The ladder was still in place, but of Ted, there was no sign.

'Typical bloody workmen,' observed Ewan. I said nothing. The fact that he was hovering in the doorway was enough for me. Keep going, I prayed.

'So, um, I'll give you a call tomorrow maybe?' he suggested, digging in his pockets for his car keys.

'Hmm, if you like,' I agreed casually, 'and we'll see how things are. I've a mountain of paperwork ahead of me. The school's reputation is at stake.' I hoped I was conveying enough gravitas. Kate, I suspected, wouldn't be stressing out about it. She had a particularly agreeable little class, after all. Yes, Churlbury C. of E.'s Year 4 was smaller in number than mine and there weren't any Zebedee or Kale connections. Kate's silver spoon existence overflowed into her working life.

'Right, I won't hold you up any longer,' said Ewan. He frowned and checked the garden for stray workmen. 'Wasn't sure about that fellow, but if he deigns to come back you just make sure he logs that window frame. He didn't appear to have any clipboard or paperwork.'

'Probably gone to fetch it.'

'Hmm, not very organised. Well, see you soon poppet,' he said and gave my lips and tonsils a pummelling for good measure. Oh dear, I thought, as I watched him leave. Far too much shilly-shallying Gilly; three out of ten, must try harder.

I leaned against the door and eyed the ladder, still propped against the wall. The fact that it was still there had to be a good sign. After a circuit of the cottage, and still no clue to Ted's whereabouts, I thought a few mutinous thoughts about Ewan's misguided interference and went to seek solace in the cup of tea that had been overlooked.

'How about fish and chips?' came a male voice from the direction of the stairs.

The yelp that escaped my tingling lips probably told Ted enough. 'Oh sorry, Gilly, but I thought I'd make myself scarce.'

'Ted! You scared the living daylights out of me!' I shrieked as I nipped up the stairs, heart and pulse galloping at top speed. There he sat, on the top step, with Minnie in his arms. He was fondling her ears and her purr had reached its maximum volume.

'Sorry, Gilly.' Seeing him again still had a strange effect on my befuddled brain, just as it had when he'd first come crashing into my life. I had to tell myself that this wasn't The Beast I was entertaining; this was his gentle brother. This was the gorgeous Ted.

'So how about fish and chips, as I've discovered you're not keen on…' and he ticked off the list Ewan had tried on me.

'No, it wasn't like that at all,' I owned up. 'I needed to get rid of him.'

'That's good,' said Ted, smiling. 'It would be a shame if I couldn't take you for a pizza every so often.' I grinned back, especially as he'd used the words 'every so often.'

'I see you've made a real hit there. She adores you.' Minnie was now on her back, squirming on his lap, with her legs in the air, as if to say, 'it's time to tickle my tummy.'

'Well, the feeling's mutual,' he replied, obligingly stroking her under the chin and then across her bulging little belly. 'So… how about those fish and chips?'

'Sounds wonderful!'

He had to dash off to collect an old van but not before I'd had my very own slice of his attention. Standing on the landing with his arms around me was something I'd been longing for since Saturday evening. It was as if there were magnets drawing us together.

'I've lived for this moment,' I admitted as we finally drew apart and gazed into his eyes.

'Me too,' he murmured. 'It seems such a long time.' He gently traced the curve of my cheek with his hand. 'You should never have had that dreadful treatment.'

'Oh *him*,' I sighed. 'Don't worry about what *he* did. You're here and that's all that matters.' Sitting in Ted's van, eating fish and chips out of paper may not sound romantic, but it beat Ewan's magnanimous dinner offer.

'So what about all that schoolwork, Gilly?' Ted asked, as he drove me home. I had a little chuckle. 'No chance of seeing you until after the school inspection then?'

'Not unless you've got your own inspection to carry out?'

'Most definitely,' he said sternly. 'The estate's reputation is at stake.' We collapsed in giggles.

Chapter 28

The school inspection and other tricky matters

I didn't see Ted the following day, but at least we had exchanged phone numbers and had pencilled in a four o'clock teatime tryst for Sunday afternoon. As far as Ewan was concerned, my natural cowardice stopped me from giving him the heave-ho – or was I keeping the friendship going, just in case? Was it an in-built fear of being let down again and being left with nothing? There was nothing about Ted's behaviour towards me that suggested he wasn't sincere, but it was all so quick. Was it too quick, I asked myself from time to time? Would it be like one of the fireworks at Freddie's farewell birthday bash that fizzed for a while, then spluttered and died? So I texted Ewan and told him I was feeling a bit under the weather – nothing serious though, because I didn't want him rushing over to give me the benefit of his wonderful bedside manner – and in the circumstances, I'd rather stay quietly at home.

To my relief he texted back telling me that he and his dad were going down to their yacht – something about getting it ready for the sailing season – so he'd be down at the coast most of the weekend. Then he wished me luck for my Ofsted preparations. Reading that last part of the message jolted me back to the stark truth that I *did* have a pile of schoolwork to deal with. Indulging in an evening with Ted would be truly wonderful, but I would still have to put in a few hours marking maths books as well as reading Olive's checklist and top tips for coping with inspectors. I also needed to tweak my lesson plans and choose the assembly songs and music. We were going to play to our strengths at Churlbury C. of E. But first, I had to call Fran, naturally, to tell her about the impending inspection. Her school was also bracing itself for one, but not until much later in the year.

'So you'll let me know how it goes?' she asked, after hearing me offload all my angst down the phone.

'Yes, but if I don't call until Thursday, don't assume the worst.'

'What, that you were caught throttling one of the famous Zebedees and had been dismissed on the spot?' she chuckled, although it was no laughing matter in my point of view.

'Anyway, any more news of Ted? I can't imagine you going a week without seeing him, unless he *was* a passing handyman or a poacher.'

I told her about the hastily arranged health and safety inspection and how Ewan had started throwing his weight around, which had her chuckling again.

'So does he live on the estate?' she asked. 'In one of the estate cottages?'

'I'm not sure,' I admitted, realising – not for the first time – that I knew very little about him when it came to hard facts. To be honest, I was still at the feelings stage, and my thirst for facts hadn't quite come into play. 'I think he must. His predecessor lived in a flat in part of the house itself, so I rather think that's where Ted's living.'

'Hmm, well what else can you bear to tell me? You haven't said what he looks like. Is there any chance we can plan a get-together – just the four of us?'

As yet, I hadn't revealed Ted's unfortunate connection, and knew that would have to come out eventually if Ted and I became an established item.

'Or you could send me a picture on your fancy new phone, if you've taken one of him yet.' I took a deep breath and decided to tell her the truth, knowing that she was woman enough to take it.

'Actually, Fran, he's related to someone we knew at college. Well, we didn't exactly *know* him. He wasn't the sort of person we associated with, although...'

'Spit it out, Gilly. I'm losing the thread there.'

'Well, *you* thought he was quite fit, I seem to remember, but *you* didn't have to cope with his nasty vicious tongue and...'

I came to a halt, remembering the incident at the *Rat and Rabbit* – not that there was any tongue connection apart from the bit about stopping my blabbermouth.

'Not *The Beast*? Ted's related to *The Beast*? He's related to the posh horse training *Rescorlas*? I don't believe it!'

'He is,' I told her, dreading the next detail I'd have to reveal. 'He's *very* closely related.'

'Poor you, Gilly. That must have been a shock when you found out.'

'Ted's his brother.'

'No!' she breathed in horror. 'What happens if he wants to introduce you to the rest of the family?'

'Oh, I've told him about the unfortunate business at college.'

'And you told him about the episode at the *Rat and Rabbit*?'

'Oh yes,' I murmured, remembering how Ted had kissed me and made me fall in love with him. 'Yes, and he agreed that his brother behaved despicably and that he's arrogant and opinionated.

'Really? That's a relief for you, I guess.'

'Oh yes. In fact, Ted used those words *himself*. He even apologised on his behalf. He didn't need to but...'

'...knew his brother would never see it as necessary...'

'Exactly!'

'Wow, that's surreal! So has he mentioned what his dear relation is up to these days?'

'No, I think he realises I wouldn't be interested and the least said about *him* the better, as far as I'm concerned. But, Fran – brace yourself for this – they're *identical*, in looks I mean, but not in personality.'

'Blimey!'

'You see, I thought it *was* The Beast as soon as he fell out of the bushes. I started ranting at him until he told me I was mistaken.'

'You didn't mention that the other day though.'

'I was still in shock I suppose.'

'Hmm, and what would you do if The Beast pitched up at the Rescorla home when Ted takes you to meet mum and dad? Or just imagine the looks that old beastie boy might give you when Ted stands up to give his speech at the wedding breakfast...'

'Hold on now, Fran, who says it'll come to that?'

'Er yes, I was getting ahead of myself, wasn't I? Dear bro Theo is bound to scupper the whole thing when the vicar reaches the part about if anyone knows any cause or just impediment. That's when he'll rush down the aisle and tell everyone you're not worthy of the Rescorla name because your clarinet playing's not up to scratch,' she chuckled. I couldn't help joining in too. She had a wicked sense of humour.

'We're just friends, Fran.'

'Oh-ho, heard that before. And so, have you discovered anything else worth reporting?'

'He's got a little butterfly tattoo on the inside of his right wrist.'

'Oh, sweet. So did he go to college? And what is his line of work supposed to be, apart from being good at rescuing misguided moggies stuck in holly trees?'

Ah yes, that was a subject I'd started to touch on when Ted and I were devouring chips in his van, but his answers had been rather vague.

'Yes, I asked him all that and he asked me if I'd heard of Leesmore College.'

'Which you have, of course. That's that agricultural place on the other side of Boxminster isn't it? Didn't the students sometimes come over for dances?'

'Yeah, I think they did, once or twice. It was a bit of a trek though. That's why we hardly ever saw them.'

'Ah, so he was an *agricultural* student. That figures.'

We didn't get any further because it was then that Tony arrived. 'Sorry, Gilly, must dash. Tony and I are off looking at possible flats. I'll be thinking of you next week and keeping my fingers crossed.'

'Ah, so the gravy's passed muster at last, has it?' It was *her* turn to give a short answer.

'I'll keep you posted.'

The weather that day was perfect for anyone preparing their yacht for the summer or just wanting to sit and watch the waves crashing on the shore, but I had a mound of preparation to address and anyway, I had a much better prospect peering over the horizon. Outside, my cleared patch was waiting expectantly for some more attention, but apart from Minnie using it as her toilet, nothing much was happening. However, I had a shrewd suspicion that, below the surface, some of the weeds I'd pulled out half-heartedly were mustering their evil selves for a surly resurgence. But with the Ofsted and Ted taking centre stage in my thoughts, the garden would have to wait until the Easter break that was just around the corner.

The next morning I was in school very early – not my top choice for a Sunday – but most of the staff team had decided that if they wanted to spruce up their classroom displays and allocated corridor boards, Sunday would be one of the few opportunities. It was while I was on a step stool stapling a caption to one of mine that my phone started bleeping and crowing, in its delightful cockerel imitation.

'Was that *your* phone?' asked Kate, who was further along the corridor putting the final additions to one of her class masterpieces.

'Yep.' I dug it out of my pocket and blinked with pleasure at the glowing screen. It was Ted suggesting he came earlier than we'd agreed. He had a surprise for me.

As long as it's a nice surprise, I texted back. *How about 3?*

Xellent, c.u. Ted x

'Looks like good news,' remarked Kate, who had evidently been watching me. 'Was my brother sending you a lovesick message?'

'Um no, just a message from a friend.' I pocketed my phone and lugged the step stool back into my classroom, leaving Kate to think what she liked.

"Morning by Edvard Grieg" I typed in the largest font available. Once printed out, I mounted the notice on the board by the CD player in the hall. Oh yes, I had chosen one of the old favourites for our assembly that week; one that was suitably calming, in case the diminutive savage breasts were hatching nasty sabotage plans. You see I remembered that saying about music having the power to calm the savage breast. I used to think it was about calming "savage beasts", but either would do for the kids I had in mind. When it came to the music for assembly, I plumped for calm and restful every time. Anyone playing *Mars, the Bringer of War* from Holst's *The Planets* or Rossini's *William Tell Overture* would need their head examined. I'd stupidly used both of those on my first teaching practice and almost had a riot. The little perishers had started shuffling their bottoms and waving their arms until the Head turned off the music and threatened to stop their tuck shop. And that was after a few minutes of *William Tell.* What possessed me to try *Mars the Bringer of War* I really don't know, but after a similarly worrying result I stuck to jolly old *Morning, Greensleeves* and Pachebel's *Canon* which almost sent them to sleep. In fact, whenever the savage breasts looked in danger of mounting an uprising or if there were high winds or torrential rain battering the windows, I'd reach for my *Soothing Classics* CD every time.

The sun was still putting on an encouraging display when I arrived back at Bramble Cottage. It was even warm enough to sit outside and have lunch, while Minnie skittered up and down the garden path. There was a worryingly huge space to fill on one side, while the other was still full of waist-high grass that would have made quite a reasonable lawn, if only I had something to hack and trim it into submission. If it hadn't been for the fruit bushes and clumps of rhubarb then I'd have felt like giving up. It was at times like that when the thought of a modern flat with a modest window box to tend was very tempting.

'Ready for your surprise?' I'd been loitering at the bottom of the garden at the agreed time, when Ted had come striding through the thicket. There was something about the masterful way he plunged through the undergrowth, that reminded me of Mr Darcy emerging from the lake in his dripping shirt; a scene that had given me more than a little flutter when I saw the film version of *Pride and Prejudice*. I nodded gleefully, just itching to wrap my arms around his wonderful, manly frame.

'But first...' Yes Ted knew that surprises had to wait their turn.

'Hmm,' I murmured contentedly, as we paused for breath, 'that'll keep me going for a while.'

'Glad you're so easily pleased,' he chuckled, moving his arms up to my shoulders and fixing me with his twinkling brown eyes.

'Oh yes, I'm a girl who enjoys simple pleasures, such as fish and chips, and an afternoon poking around in the garden.' That wasn't strictly true: fish and chips and an afternoon stretched out on the sofa with my head cradled on Ted's shoulder would have been more accurate.

'Ah yes, your garden, which needs some TLC, as well as you, of course.' He dug in his pocket and brought out a fistful of seed packets. 'Voilà!'

'Wow!' It wasn't what I might have expected, but seed packets looked full of promise, especially if Ted was going to let me have the benefit of his expertise.

'That's why I wanted to come earlier,' he explained. 'Thought we'd make a start so you can grow your own salad veg.'

'That's brilliant. Thanks Ted.' Well naturally I had to thank him properly, and his mouth was so perfectly kissable. However, just as I was about to take another breath to prolong the experience, an almighty crashing came from the thicket, and it wasn't just the sound of leaves underfoot or branches snapping. There were the unmistakable sounds of voices whispering and sniggering as well. We were being spied upon.

'Trespassers!' I gasped. It was obvious that no estate workers would be out doing their stuff. Sundays had always been quiet days, with only the occasional car motoring along the drive, if the Oborns were entertaining. In addition, estate workers weren't generally known for their whispering and sniggering. 'Or perishing kids,' I added

'I'll sort them out.'

Ted turned and marched off in the direction of the sniggers, but whoever was out there certainly didn't wait long enough to be spotted.

'Scarpered,' he told me a few minutes later. 'But I saw that ginger tom again.'

'Probably looking for Minnie, poor thing.'

'Have you had her done?'

'Well no. Isn't she too young for that? She's only... er... well, I'm not absolutely sure how old she is.' I turned and spotted her lying in the sun lazily washing her ears.

'Might be a good idea, unless you want kittens.'

'Kittens? Perhaps I ought to think about it. So you think that's what old Tommy had in mind? I thought he might be coming to pick a fight or something.'

We sauntered down the path on our way to the shed where I kept most of the rusty old tools that Stan had left behind and paused to tickle Minnie's tummy.

'So girly,' I murmured, 'you'd better be on the lookout for randy toms.'

I confess the thought of Minnie curled up with a family of kittens was quite appealing, although what *she* might think of motherhood was quite another matter. There would also be the job of finding homes for the kittens, as the thought of feeding multiple feline mouths might put too much of a strain on my bank balance. However, with her sunny disposition I thought she'd make rather a good mum. And what about me? What did *I* think of the prospect of motherhood? I'd dreamed of it enough when Tim and I were together. I'd tried to imagine what our baby would look like. Since those days though, I'd put the prospect of motherhood firmly to one side. However, as Ted and I worked, I considered the idea again. This time I imagined a baby with a mixture of Bonning and Rescorla genes. He or she would have a good chance of inheriting green fingers if Ted's genes had anything to do with it. And yes, Ted would make a wonderful father. He was gentle, caring and kind as well as being direct, clear-headed and determined. Considering the difference between him and his arrogant twin, I felt sorry for any girl stupid enough to become involved with someone so utterly unsuited to fatherhood.

Two hours later, we sank down on the edge of the path and gulped mugs of tea while we surveyed our handiwork. Using the emptied packets, I'd marked each row of seeds with them, speared through by twigs and then pushed into the soil.

'You'll need to keep them watered if this weather continues,' Ted told me.

'And I expect you'll want to come and inspect them and see how they're progressing.'

'Naturally,' he told me, grinning. 'Although I've got a lot on. It's family stuff. There's quite a bit to sort out.'

'What, following your uncle's death?' Ted's face clouded over briefly.

'It's been quite complicated.'

'But he left a will and all that?'

'Oh yes, but even so, it doesn't make it easy to carry out some of his wishes.'

'Oh I see.' Although I didn't. 'I suppose your parents have had to deal with that.'

He nodded. 'But you're still working here? I mean the Oborns will still expect you to put in the hours, although I'm sure they'll be understanding...' By the expression on his face, he didn't need me reminding him of the recent tragedy.

He finished the last of his tea and was gazing across the garden in preoccupation. A cold feeling seemed to lodge in my stomach.

'Well, this is only temporary, Gilly... being here. I told you that before. I've applied for a job over in Bransfield.'

'You mean, that place where there's a posh school for the kids of the rich and famous?'

'Yeah. You've heard of it then?'

'Oh yes. There was a bloke at my interview, when Kate and I met – you know Kate is Ewan's sister?' He nodded. 'Well Jeremy told us that he had an interview at Bransfield for a music post the following week. He was a bit snooty about it too. So is it at the school? Does it have huge grounds?'

'It has amazing grounds,' he told me eagerly. 'There are woods and an arboretum, lakes and a river running through the grounds where the pupils practise rowing. It's huge. The main building is a lovely old house – quite grand and about twice the size of Frintley Grange – and it's surrounded by gardens with fountains and lawns. Can you imagine?'

'You paint a wonderful picture. Have you been there?'

'No, that's just from the Internet.'

'Gosh, and you could be working there, keeping it all shipshape, wow!' I gushed.

I was trying to sound enthusiastic, but truly I'd have preferred it if he'd just told me he'd scooped the position of Frintley Estate Manager.

'Well, I'm still waiting to hear if they're going to interview me,' said Ted.

'They'd be stupid not to,' I told him, 'although you'd be miles away and...'

The thought of Ted not occupying Stan and Lily's little flat was somewhat disappointing, to be perfectly honest. That's where I assumed he'd be lodging, or in one of the estate cottages. He'd never told me as such.

'But that wouldn't stop us seeing each other,' he said, taking my hands and squeezing them. It was then that Fran and Tony's observation came back to haunt me. Just an itinerant handyman passing through, was he? Was that why he was so keen? Was he only trying what Ewan had been about from the beginning? Was he only interested in hustling me upstairs for a spot of hanky-panky? Surely not!

'Of course it wouldn't,' I agreed. 'It's only... what... about ten miles away. I suppose you'll be living on the estate there.'

'Not necessarily. In fact probably not. But enough of that. There's nothing definite. So let's not think about it.' But I did, naturally.

While a pizza was browning in the oven and I was trying to be artistic with a bag of salad and a pack of cherry tomatoes, the thought of Ted hob nobbing with the offspring of peers of the realm, politicians and foreign royalty exercised my mind considerably. Then I reasoned that a senior estate worker or even manager wouldn't be much of a catch for a viscount's daughter or the heir to the throne of some obscure principality. No, the junior female staff would be more of a threat and my fertile imagination went off on another track. Having lost one man who I was crazy about, I now feared it happening all over again. If something happened to take Ted away from me though, it would be ten times worse. The special chemistry between us was altogether different from that which I'd experienced with Tim.

'Now don't let those inspectors upset you,' Ted told me as we were saying goodnight. There was a full moon peeping from behind a cloud, casting its light on his face as we huddled together at the garden gate. It eclipsed that time with Ewan after the carol service.

'I'll try,' I told him, 'but it'll feel as if I'm on teaching practice again.'

'Scary?'

'Just a bit. And it's not a friendly college tutor noting your teaching skills on a clipboard followed by a cosy chat in the staffroom. These are strangers who probably couldn't care tuppence about the feelings of the poor teachers they're intimidating. And then the kids are bound to play up, even if you try and bamboozle them with the threat that the visitor is just watching them. Oh no, most of my lot are too sharp to fall for that one. That's what really worries me.'

'Well you just give them the same treatment as you gave me last week and I'm sure they'll give you no trouble.' He was evidently referring to my rant before he emerged from the bushes.

'Was I *that* awful?' And was it only last week?

'Terrifying!'

'That's the best compliment you could have paid me.'

'What, even better than telling you how perfectly wonderful your kissing is?'

'Is it? I thought yours was rather spectacular.' It was, and there was positively no sink plunger action.

'Well, perhaps I ought to just make sure, and you can give marks out of ten while you're about it Miss Schoolmarm.' Ten minutes later we agreed that ten out of ten was a fair score. Earlier that evening, the sofa had witnessed a certain amount of progress in our relationship, but there was definitely no hanky-panky on the first floor. Ted was biding his time, which was exactly how I wanted it.

'So, any questions?' I'd just put the class through their mental maths paces and had set the main task, after introducing the morning's topic and demonstrating a few examples with lots of class interaction. All was going well and the inspector in the corner was even flashing the occasional smile. The usual forest of hands shot up, asking the predictable questions on the subject of drawing lines after the corrections and the use of pencils over pens. I think some of them deliberately trotted those out to show off in front of the visitor.

'Right, so if there's nothing else…'

Saul Zebedee, po-faced for a change, raised his hand and waved it around for good measure.

'Yes Saul?' I said, putting on a fake bright smile, 'Something you don't understand?'

He was quite bright at maths, despite his other failings. He grimaced as if in deep thought – although 'deep' was not a term I associated with him – and then raised a surly eyebrow at the rest of his table. Two girls covered their faces and nudged each other.

'Miss, can I ask a question?'

'Of course, Saul, that's what I just said.' An unusual hush descended over the room. The inspector looked up and smiled benignly.

'What I'd like to know…' said Saul earnestly, 'is who was that bloke you were snogging on Sunday afternoon?'

The class gasped in unison, then titters broke out while I struggled to keep calm and to keep my hands from clenching young Saul's scrawny neck.

'And I'd like to know where your manners are,' I retorted tartly, fixing him with my most menacing stare. He curled his lip defiantly and shrugged.

'Report to Mrs Karthew's office at break time!' He nudged his neighbour and smirked.

'And there's now less than half an hour to do your work,' I reminded the class. Inside I was fuming. Had that little horror been one of the secret sniggerers in the thicket, or had it been one of his odious brothers? The fact that he'd waited two days to say anything was amazing. I'd never have thought Saul Zebedee would have the self-control to hold back tasty little snippets of gossip for two minutes, let alone two days. Maybe it was Olive's announcement in Monday's assembly about the impending visitors that had made him decide to bide his time for maximum impact. I decided to ignore the inspector and concentrate on keeping the class on task. It had all been going so well too. The music in assembly had cast its magic spell of soothing tranquillity over the school and then they'd sung their little hearts out as if they were on *Britain's Got Talent*. I'd been silently preening myself for such a positive start to the day too. And then this!

'So what's all this about?' demanded Olive, to a suitably cowed Saul. He was slouching against the wall outside her office door. 'And you can stand up straight and take your hands out of your pockets.' She flashed me a sympathetic glance and raised her eyes to heaven. 'Best laid plans and all that,' she murmured. 'Well Saul?' she demanded sternly. 'Speak up!' By then I was inwardly cowering, not relishing the details of my private – and very secret – life being aired any further. The fact that my entire class knew was bad enough. I imagined them racing out to their mums, grans and carers and blabbing it out to much amusement at my expense.

'Miss asked if we 'ad any questions, so I asked 'er one,' he replied in his usual off-hand way..

'About the *maths* lesson,' I added, through gritted teeth.

'It's all right, Miss Bonning,' said Olive levelly. 'I'll deal with Saul. So, young man, what did you ask?'

'I asked 'er who she was snogging on Sunday afternoon,' he said, a brazen as you like, as if he'd merely asked for a new exercise book.

At that precise moment Kate walked past on her way to the staffroom. Our eyes met and I wondered how good her hearing was.

'I see,' continued Olive, 'so why weren't you concentrating on your work?' Saul shrugged.

'And what were you doing trespassing on the Frintley Estate?' I demanded. Olive needed to know the facts.

'I weren't there Miss. It were my brothers. *They* told me.'

'So they should know better!' snapped Olive. 'And should know that trespassers will be prosecuted. That means that they were breaking the law!' Saul's bottom lip trembled, which gave me great satisfaction. 'You can stand here,' she told him, 'and you can apologise to Miss Bonning for deliberately disrupting her lesson. I shall be having a word or two with your mother!' The little blighter should have realised that it wasn't wise to tangle with Olive Karthew.

Grudgingly he mumbled a 'sorry, Miss' and then I rushed off to the staffroom to revive my flagging spirits and self-esteem. Kate was hovering by the kettle when I arrived and it didn't take many guesses to discover how good her hearing was. The glance she gave me was distinctly frosty.

'So what's been going on, Gilly? According to Ewan, you were up to your neck in work over the weekend and didn't want any company. That's why he decided to give dad a hand with the boat.' How was I going to explain that away? My mind was working overtime, but there were no easy answers, apart from half-truths and barefaced lies.

'Well, it's complicated,' I murmured, 'it's... um...' With two inspectors sitting only a few feet away, I was painfully aware that my professional demeanour had to stay unruffled.

'Oh, Gilly,' gasped Kate, the frost starting to melt. 'It wasn't anything to do with that guy you used to know, was it?' My brain was still struggling, but Kate's remark propelled it back to those awful Boxmouth encounters and of Theo Rescorla's vile looks and even viler remarks, although I couldn't remember how much I'd told her about that episode in my life.

'Er... yes... it *was* actually, but I'm not sure how it will work out.'

As soon as the words were out of my mouth I realised that Kate might correctly assume that Sunday afternoon wasn't an isolated incident. I gulped down my coffee, wishing that Olive might suddenly decide to have a convenient fire drill.

'So are you going to tell Ewan?' she hissed fiercely, 'or are you going to string him along? He really was very disappointed about last weekend. He'd been planning something special.'

Hmm, I thought, I imagine what Ewan had foremost on his mind, and it wasn't a cosy meal at one of the local watering holes. He would have been aiming for some action in my bedroom.

'I'm *not* stringing him along, honestly!' I protested 'Things have sort of happened by themselves!' I added, trying to keep my voice down.

Of all the cheek, I thought. What gave Kate Maxted the right to lecture me about my life? I never lectured *her*. I wouldn't dream of it. It's not my business. But wasn't I stringing Ewan along? Wasn't I keeping my options open? That little voice in my head – my pricked conscience – seemed to be growing uncomfortably insistent.

'Oh really? Like the snogging on Sunday afternoon? Takes two to tango,' replied Kate, scowling into her mug.

'But, Kate, Ewan and I are just casual friends.'

'As far as *you're* concerned, maybe. Have you thought how he might see the relationship, especially after... well... especially if this guy has come back for good?'

It sounded suspiciously as if Ewan had been boasting about our drunken, unscheduled coupling on Valentine's Day. Mercifully, the bell rang and the rest of the staff leapt to their feet, dumped their mugs and made a stampede for the door, to show the inspectors how keen they were.

'Leave it me, okay?' I told her. 'Don't say anything… please.' We were on our way back to our rooms, the Ofsted inspection taking centre stage in our lives.

'Okay,' she sighed resignedly. 'I suppose the fact that old lover boy has suddenly regained his memory *was* a bit unexpected.' At once I realised what she'd assumed. She thought Tim had been the mysterious man I'd been snogging, to use Saul's delightful phrase. That was why she mentioned "that guy you used to know." I didn't correct her. It was a convenient misunderstanding.

Chapter 29

Dealing with the truth

'So, what do you think you ought to do?' asked Ted. We'd exchanged texts at lunchtime and at five o'clock we were drinking tea and I was giving him an unexpurgated account of the embarrassing bits of my day, especially the bits that included Kate's huffy remarks about my relationship with her brother.

'I have to tell Ewan straight.'

'So you agree with what Kate said?'

'Well… yes, in a way. But you've seen Ewan in action.'

Ted grimaced. 'Oh yes, he's a chap who knows his own mind.'

'And in his mind he's decided that I'm his property.'

'Hmm, he made that point very clear, especially when it came to stray tiles sliding off the roof and knocking you senseless.'

'And I've subtly tried to cool off a bit, hoping he'd detect that I'd lost interest in him – not that there was much at the best of times – but…'

I shrugged and sighed and hoped that Ted might enlighten me about the male psyche.

'I think subtlety might be lost on him.'

'Yes, it's like trying to reason with a steamroller,' I commented grimly.

'As bad as that?' Ted chuckled, although he knew it was no chuckling matter.

'Oh yes, and the trouble is Ted, one night I let things stray over the border into… er… um… well things got out of hand…' I admitted guiltily. I had to tell him, even though it might not do my reputation any good. On the other hand, I thought, he might be cool about one-night stands – although what happened around Valentine's Day wasn't *exactly* a one-night stand. Ewan and I had become quite good friends by then, and what happened between us was the common experience of many couples. For some of my friends, jumping into someone's bed was only one step removed from moving in and setting up home. However, that wasn't the way I saw life. Perhaps mine was an old-fashioned view, but it was what suited me.

'You mean he coerced you?' prodded Ted.

'Well, the trouble was, I'd been knocking back champagne cocktails at the Oborns 'At Home' do and my defences were down,' I admitted. 'I don't think it would have happened if I'd been sober.'

'But that's tantamount to date rape!' Ted's eyes glittered fiercely, and for a moment, I was reminded of his ghastly twin. 'It sounds as if he forced you against your will.'

'It was probably more like me being putty in his hands, to use an overused cliché, I'm ashamed to admit. And when I woke up the next morning...' It was a head in hands moment while I summoned up the courage to admit about my wimpish behaviour, '... it seemed too late to tell him that I didn't really fancy him and a whole lot of other stuff that was swirling around my brain,' I gulped.

'That's not so, Gilly,' insisted Ted. 'If you're unhappy about the relationship...'

'It's not really a relationship, as far as I'm concerned...'

'Well, whatever it is, you need to make a decision, because until you do, all that stuff will carry on swirling around, making you unhappy.'

'You're right Ted.' It was such a relief to talk about it with Ted just sitting there listening and supporting me and not making any demands on me.

'The trouble is, the Maxteds have been so kind to me, although it all started with an invitation to make up the numbers at a charity bash. Ewan was like a stag in the rutting season from the moment he clapped eyes on me.'

'Don't blame him.' Ted took my hand and gave me one of his smiles that made my insides perform their extraordinary gymnastics.

'And there was I, in shock, still trying to recover from seeing Tim and Lena outside the jewellers, about to become engaged – or so I thought.'

'Ah yes.' I'd already spilled out the sorry Tim/Gilly/Lena saga while we were eating fish and chips a few days earlier.

'And so it sort of carried on from there. The family have taken me under their wing and...'

'You feel beholden to them? And beholden to Ewan?' I nodded.

'But you don't love him?'

'No, my heart's somewhere else Ted,' I said bravely. Just to make the point, without saying the words I wanted to say, I leaned close enough to touch his mouth with mine. My insides went into meltdown.

'I'll tell him. I'll be straightforward with him if he tries to persuade me otherwise,' I told Ted later.

'Perhaps this is *my* chance to tell you something that's upset me, well shaken me – if we're into sharing confidences.' I remembered his wistful look when we were out in the garden, resting from the seed planting. 'I've learnt just recently that I was adopted.'

'Oh my!'

'To put it lightly.'

'A shock?'

'Absolutely. I've been trying to get used to the idea.'

'A shock for Theo too,' I added, trying to imagine how Mr High-and-Mighty might have reacted to a change of parentage.

'Yes, a shock for Theo, of course.'

'And you never suspected?'

'Never. People always remarked on a family resemblance.'

'Probably imagined it.'

'No, they didn't imagine it. *Joe Rescorla* was my father, not my uncle.'

The gasp that escaped my gaping mouth was accompanied by great sadness.

'Your *father?* He nodded and was obviously in need of a hug.

'Oh Ted, how dreadful losing him like that. So have you only known since his death?'

'Yes, when the will was read. That's when it was revealed.'

'So you never knew him as father,' I murmured, trying to imagine how devastating that news must have been.

'Only as uncle. And the parents that brought me up are really my aunt and uncle.'

There was a silence in Bramble cottage, broken only by the quietest mew, as Minnie clambered up to join our group hug.

'But what about your mother?'

'Ah, well she wasn't married to Joe, although he was married at the time, to someone who eventually divorced him.'

'So your mum had you adopted? She gave her twins away,' I murmured, under my breath. There was silence apart from the sound of Minnie, who was now purring contentedly.

'And she didn't know that the truth would ever come out. It's all very complicated,' sighed Ted, 'but I'm coming to terms with it. That's why I have to go away for a while. There's a lot to sort out with the stables... decisions to make.'

'But your mum! You know who she is?'

'Yes, I do now, although it took a while to find her.' Ted didn't volunteer any more information, so I stopped myself from any more prodding and prying on the subject.

'And what about the Bransfield job?'

'Still waiting to hear from them. Probably any day now. So we won't be able to meet for a bit, but, Gilly, I promise I'll keep in touch.'

'And I'll put my mind to tackling Mr Steamroller Maxted.'

My opportunity to do just that popped up very conveniently at the end of the week. Ewan had called me and announced he was treating me to a meal at the TV chef's place, having wangled a booking with his old chum.

'Hope you don't mind, but Kate and Louie will be joining us. You and Kate deserve a treat after the rigours of the inspection.'

My excited anticipation plummeted. Kate and I had been avoiding each other since our spat, but I convinced myself that a meal together might help us return to our former friendly relationship. However, a cosy little foursome wasn't going to give me the chance to tell Ewan how I felt. That would have to wait until the drive home, and I'd need every last drop of tact, patience and diplomacy.

So there we were, just finishing our desserts when Ewan's phone beeped at him from his jacket pocket. It was getting late and the atmosphere hadn't been as highly charged as I'd feared.

'Just a sec,' he said, digging out his mobile and leaving the three of us to our chat. My raised eyebrows had caught Kate's attention. 'He's second on call,' she explained.

'That's the first I've heard about it.'

'He said something came up apparently.' Before Kate could say any more, Ewan returned to the table, looking awkward and less bouncy than before.

'Sorry, folks,' he sighed. 'There's an emergency. It'll probably end up as a hospital case, but I need to go and assess it and all that. Melissa's elsewhere dealing with a breech delivery, so it's down to me.'

'But how will I...' I blurted out, seeing my tête-à-tête opportunity with Ewan – where I'd tell him how it was between us – had now disappeared.

'Oh Kate and Louie will drive you back.' Kate and Louie exchanged glances then summoned weak smiles and nodded.

Ewan leaned down, gave my cheek a cursory peck and whispered, 'that's why we had to be a foursome – just in case I had a call.' But that was the first I'd heard about it, naturally. What if he'd had a call earlier? We could have been tucking into our starters or been about to raise our glasses in a toast when his wretched phone beeped. What then? Oh yes, I thought, that would have been a very jolly evening for me, trying to find safe subjects of conversation and playing gooseberry.

'One of the partners is on holiday and one has just gone down with a sickness bug.' He shrugged apologetically and then pasted on a brave smile for the benefit of Kate and Louie.

'I'll catch up with you all later,' he said as he left. The phrase, "best laid plans" came to mind, and the Easter hols couldn't come soon enough. Then I'd conveniently find lots of friends and relations to visit, which would conveniently take me far enough away from Ewan, if I couldn't or wouldn't give him his marching orders.

'Sorry about last night poppet,' said Ewan, when he phoned the following day. 'I was so looking forward to having a nightcap at Bramble Cottage too!'

He chuckled in a dirty laugh sort of way, which indicated the particular variety of nightcap he had in mind. 'So how about I come over later so we can take up where we left off? Just the two of us and hopefully no workmen hanging around to spoil our fun.' By the sound of it, Ewan wasn't just aiming for a cosy cuddle on the sofa with a cup of coffee and a custard cream. On the other hand, here was my chance to tell him plainly that our friendship had reached its limit, as far as I was concerned. Come on, Gilly, I told myself, no time for shilly-shallying.

'Okay, Ewan.'

He came at four and I still felt ill prepared to say my piece. The words had swirled round my head, ending up in a different order each time as I'd rehearsed my speech and tried to imagine what he'd say. In he bounced, very Tigger-ish and set about crushing me in a bear hug and generally pummelling my feeble lips into submission in his usual subtle way. No, I mused, there wasn't that magic melting feeling inside that Ted managed so effortlessly. Eager old Ewan just didn't do it for me and I didn't want ginger babies. There, I'd admitted it to myself. In fact, I didn't want to make babies with Ewan: ginger, blonde, dark or bald.

'Hmm,' he murmured in my ear, 'I've missed you, Gilly, you gorgeous girl. I've missed you and your wonderful body.' He spread a manly paw over my buttocks, just to add emphasis to the compliment. I needed to act quickly before he scooped me up and leapt the stairs two at a time. Warning lights were already flashing in my brain and I cursed myself for not arranging for Fran or Mum to call or text me so that I could disentangle myself from Ewan's greedy grasp.

'Well thank you, kind sir,' I trilled primly, 'but I'm dying for a cuppa.'

'Oh-ho,' he chortled, 'I'm dying for something less prosaic.' He clamped another manly paw on my waist and started fumbling with the hem of my jumper that I'd tucked into my jeans for more security.

'No, Ewan,' I told him, pushing his hands away. I ducked from his grasp and nipped into the kitchen. 'And here's Minnie waiting for her supper.' Ewan ambled in, hands in his pockets, beaming benignly at me as if indulging the little woman her domestic trivialities, sure in the assumption that he'd soon be enjoying some attention.

'There's something I need to tell you,' I began firmly, once the coffee was made.

'Sounds serious, ominous even.' Ewan, however, was still beaming, probably imagining peeling off my clothes, layer by layer. Then his expression changed.

'You're not pregnant are you?' he gasped. 'I'm sure I remembered the condom. Yes, yes, I'm sure I did unless…' His face suddenly looked ashen.

'No, Ewan, I'm not pregnant.'

'Oh thank God. I'd start to wonder whose it was, because I'm always *very* careful.'

Hmm, I thought, there speaks an experienced Lothario, ready for the opportunist conquest, whenever it might present itself.

'Ewan, I don't think this… er… friendship of ours should go any further.' I was careful to put the emphasis on the word friendship. A range of contrasting reactions seemed to zip through his mind, judging by the facial gymnastics.

'But... er... um... maybe I'm hurrying you on a bit too quickly?' he stammered, looking suitably crestfallen. 'But after that wonderful night together, I thought things were going so well. You seemed so happy.'

'Ewan, I hardly remember anything about that night. I was *drunk*! I wasn't in a fit state to know what was happening and when I woke up to find you in bed the next morning, I was in shock!'

'But you never said, not at the time.'

'Listen, Ewan, I said I was in shock. I never intended that to happen.'

'But, Gilly,' he said, with a hurt expression, 'you always seemed quite keen so why tell me this *now*?'

'I've been thinking about us. I've been thinking about my personal happiness and I don't think it revolves around being *your* girlfriend.'

The words were all tumbling out and I wasn't sure if they were what I'd planned, but at least the expression on Ewan's face and his body language indicated he was getting the message. Then a very convenient loophole presented itself.

'Ah, I see,' he muttered. 'Is this anything to do with that chap who had amnesia?'

My immediate thought was that Kate and Ewan had being having a brotherly/sisterly chat. Come on, Gilly, I thought, here's your chance. Choose your words carefully. You don't need to lie. Just be suitably non-committal and hope he jumps to the wrong conclusion.

'Er, Tim... oh the poor chap,' I agreed, nodding sadly. 'It's been a long haul for him.' Every word I uttered was true and I watched Ewan's reaction, hoping I'd conveyed the right amount of gravitas.

'Well, of course I understand,' blustered Ewan, 'although I thought all that was a lost cause – that he was engaged to someone else – thought you were all over that, and that you were single.'

He said a whole lot more and I have to give him credit for keeping pretty cool about it, considering how he'd been when he'd been pawing me and gearing himself up for a spot of action upstairs.

'Things happen,' I commented vaguely. 'Situations change.'

'Indeed they do,' he agreed acidly, then sighed in a resigned fashion.

'And if they change again, remember I'll always be here for you, Gilly, as a *friend*. Of course, I hoped we could be more than friends. Well, I assumed we were more than friends.'

Keeping a solemn expression I nodded and sighed, although inside I was jumping up and down with glee.

'Thanks, Ewan, I appreciate that.'

That was true too. Having Ewan as mate, as someone to chat to, suited me very well. I was sure he wouldn't be single long. There was bound to be plenty of girls who'd jump at the chance of being a GP's partner – in the non-medical sense. How he'd reached twenty-eight without hustling some biddable female up the aisle was quite a surprise. Perhaps by being too keen? The sigh that I sighed when Ewan left the cottage an hour later was mixed with disbelief. Had I really extricated myself from him? It had all seemed so easy. What might Kate say? Well, it wasn't Kate's business, I reminded myself. What was *very* convenient was that both Maxteds had mistakenly assumed that Tim was back on the scene; that Tim had broken off his engagement to Lena and was gearing himself up to slip something suitably sparkly on my finger. As if!

Within a fortnight, term finished and all I seemed to have done was teach Easter songs and hymns, organise the making of Easter cards for my class to copy and dish out speckled mini eggs. I'd texted Ted to tell him the shilly-shallying was over and he'd replied with a smiley face and row of exclamation marks and kisses. However, I knew he had family business as well as work and *that* had to take priority. Without our texting I would have been a regular moping misery. My day out in Shealton changed all that. Although it wasn't a big town, Shealton boasted an old abbey that the staff had chosen as the perfect place to visit for our R.E. studies. I'd volunteered to visit it and then devise a worksheet. While I was there, I'd treat myself to a spot of retail therapy, or window shopping at least, as well as lunch in one of the cafés. Before I got as far as the abbey or within a sniff of a cappuccino or a ham salad baguette, the day had turned sour. I'd found a little side street that was lined with boutiques and the odd café and was feasting my eyes on the inviting window displays, when I caught sight of a familiar profile further along, where the street curved round to the left. I wasn't expecting to see him because of all that family business, which made his appearance in Shealton all the more unexpected. I'd assumed he was away at his father's stables or at his old home with his parents aka his uncle and aunt. My first reaction was to scoot along the street and yell out a cheery 'Hi Ted, fancy seeing you!' because he could have nipped back to the area in between his other responsibilities, maybe to sort out legal intricacies. But something stopped me.

As I moved a step or two closer it was obvious that he was talking or listening to someone rather than peering in a window. Perhaps it was someone else from the estate; or perhaps he was asking for directions and had managed to pick someone who suffered from verbal diarrhoea. I edged along a few more steps, hoping he'd turn and come my way. I then saw that there was another turning leading from the street that had only come into view when I'd moved the last few steps. I also realised that other person was female, but Ted's position blocked the pertinent part – her face – so I was none the wiser.

'Oh come on, Ted,' I whispered, my heart galloping away excitedly. But Ted and the woman carried on. Then he leaned forward, put his hands on her shoulders – or so I guessed from my vantage point – and kissed her. Whether it was on the mouth or the cheek I couldn't tell, but a horrified shock coursed through my body and I turned and fled.

Tears spurted down my face and my nose joined in, in sympathy. He'd told me he'd be away... busy... too busy to see me, but here he was, not too busy to prevent him from meeting another woman in a nearby back street, with whom he was on very intimate terms. No wonder he'd been so vague. I'd wondered once or twice if he was hiding something and now I knew what it was. There was another woman in his life. Perhaps there was more similarity to the beastly Theo than I'd realised? I reached the end of the street, not daring to look behind me, just in case he was strolling along, feeling perky about life in general, unaware that I'd witnessed his betrayal. I rummaged in my pocket for a tissue to mop up the disgusting drool on my chin and rescue my melting mascara. What were the chances of some of Churlbury's little darlings loitering in the vicinity? Pretty high. Once out into the main thoroughfare I quickly turned back to check the way I'd come. No sign of Ted. He must have carried on down the street or taken that other turning. I breathed a sigh of relief, knowing I'd be a blubbering wreck and in no state to interrogate him or make polite conversation or anything in between.

'Gilly, what a pleasant surprise!' I snapped to attention and there were the Veltmans, arm in arm, one grinning and the other staring warily at me. No prizes for guessing who was doing what.

'Simeon! Alison!' I gasped, grateful that the Almighty, in His wisdom, had sent a couple of his servants along to haul me back out of my pit of deep despair.

'Oh, Gilly, you've been crying. Whatever has happened?' Simeon leapt straight into pastoral mode whereas Alison seemed out of her depth. Obviously no maternal tendencies there, I concluded. 'Mugging? Bag snatcher?' he gasped, reaching out to administer his usual patting.

'No, no,' I gulped. 'Just some bad news, you could say.' Well, it was – in a manner of speaking. Alison made muted grunting sounds and pursed her lips.

'Let's find a cup of tea somewhere,' Simeon suggested. So we did and I told them about Ted, how he'd turned up on the estate and how it all had now gone horribly wrong.

'There was I feeling sorry for him, because he'd lost his father and didn't even know that he was adopted,' I snivelled, probably making little sense to people who had no idea who I was talking about. 'He told me he'd be away, but he wasn't.'

The tears started spurting again and Alison passed me a fresh wad of tissues from her shopping bag.

'What is it with me and men?' I wailed. 'The first one has amnesia, the second one has his brain in his trousers and the third one leads a double life!'

There was a pregnant pause while I dabbed my face and gulped tea. Simeon cleared his throat, most likely from embarrassment.

'There *may* be a perfectly innocent explanation,' he suggested helpfully. 'He may have been taking a bit of grit out of her eye... er... or...'

'Not with both hands clamped onto her shoulders.'

'Oh, I see. And is the one with amnesia, the one you told me about before? I thought you said he'd been suffering from something else... overwork was it?' He wrinkled his brow and I guiltily remembered spouting something vague about Tim to give the impression I was spoken for.

'He's engaged to someone else now,' I moaned, feeling sorry for myself, although in truth, I was well over Tim. 'So there's no point discussing the state of his health or anything, is there?'

'Dear, dear, you *are* having a time of it, aren't you?'

After that I decided to change the subject to stop myself feeling any worse. Hearing about the school R.E. topic, he eagerly suggested we all went to the abbey together. Safety in numbers, I thought, as we left the café. Alison hadn't uttered a single word.

A phone call from Mum a few days later set me on another emotional rollercoaster. I'd deliberately kept myself to myself after the day in Shealton. Minnie's company and spring cleaning seemed safe and undemanding.

'Gilly, there's been two chaps asking after you,' she told me earnestly. 'They're missionaries – Richard and Jim – and they said they met you in Bagnalls two years ago. Ray gave them our number because he didn't know how to get hold of you.'

The missionaries, I thought, remembering the chatty chap – Jim – and his brother, who weren't Russian literature fans.

'Oh yes, I remember them.' Then I told her how they'd been in the shop on the day of the accident.

'I've got their number here,' Mum said. 'They're back from somewhere – Thailand I think – and are desperate to speak to you. Perhaps you've made a hit there!'

'No, Mum, I think that's unlikely.' Why should they suddenly want to get in touch? It was a real puzzler. 'Perhaps I'd better come over to Growdon. I could do with a few days away to be honest Mum. I'll bring Minnie of course.' She gave me the number and I thought back to that day in Bagnalls when I was stocking up on mags before my second teaching practice. Was it really two years ago? The following day I drove over to Growdon.

After letting myself in with the spare key – that was still hidden under the same flower pot – and leaving Minnie to reacquaint herself with her new quarters, I met up with Rich and Jim at one of the town's many tea shops. For some uncanny reason I'd been gripped with an odd nervous apprehension ever since Mum's call. I suppose because of the 'out of the blueness' of it all. I'd tried to remember what they'd said when we stood there chatting that day. Much of it was frustratingly hazy, apart from my glowing recommendation for boiled sweets. I recognised them as soon as I arrived; same ponytail, same crew cut and round rimmed specs, same honest, open smiles and definitely no beards and sandals.

'Catching up with good old English cooking,' chuckled Jim, once they'd bought tea and scones. Yes, Jim was the chatty one of the pair and for a moment or two I thought the invitation to meet might be purely social after all, and that Mum was correct in her assumption.

'It's about the accident we witnessed,' began Rich. 'You remember we told you we were in the newsagent's shop when it happened?'

'How could I forget?' I sighed with feeling. 'But you said there were plenty of other witnesses so that's why you didn't hang around. Lena would have been just as good a witness.'

'It's about Lena, as a matter of fact,' chipped in Jim. His expression and tone were surprisingly sombre. I couldn't imagine why Lena should be the main topic. 'We read about her award on the flight, in the local paper we bought before we left; about her local heroine status. We remembered you mentioning her witnessing the accident, but we didn't realise who she was until we read the news story and saw her picture.'

'I was at the Awards evening,' I told them.

'Because of your connection with the poor bloke?'

'Well partly,' I agreed, 'but mostly because Dad had been nominated for an ethical business award, which he won. And Lena and Tim are now engaged, by the way.'

Rich and Jim exchanged glances that involved much raising of brows'.

'So he's not remembered what happened then?' asked Rich. 'Well obviously.'

There was an awkward silence and an icy shiver started making quick circuits round my stomach. I took a gulp of hot tea to try to dispel it, but the icy feeling was stubborn and refused to give up.

'Better start at the beginning,' suggested Jim. Rich nodded.

'We were by the window choosing postcards to take with us when I noticed the bloke – Tim – walking towards the shop, very purposefully you could say; not out for a gentle stroll. Then I noticed that there was someone running along behind, as if they were trying to catch up with him.'

'You mean as if he'd dropped something and they'd picked it up?'

'Yeah, that sort of thing, but it obviously wasn't anything like that. The girl had a look on her face – almost desperation I thought – that wasn't just about handing back something he'd dropped.'

'Although if he'd dropped his credit card,' I added, hopefully.

'No,' chipped in Jim, 'nothing like that.'

'She started grabbing at his arm as she caught up with him, and that's when I nudged Jim, so we both saw what happened next. She was obviously jabbering away, looking very worked up, but he was having nothing to do with her; almost shaking her off as if she was a dog.'

'In fact he half turned,' put in Jim, 'and said something and then carried on walking.'

I listened in horrified fascination as their tale unfolded. Lena was stalking Tim by the sound of it! 'Typical!' I breathed. 'That girl always struck me as having her sights set on Tim, from the first time she bounced into the hospital ward. 'Do go on.'

'He carried on walking, coming towards us and the girl refused to give up,' said Rich. 'She seemed to be calling out, looking very distressed by then. Then, just as Tim reached the edge of the pavement, the girl lunged out and he shot forward, as if he'd been deliberately pushed. That's when the old gent on the bike appeared and they collided.'

'She pushed him?' I breathed in horror.

'Yeah, and that's what I said to Rich here. She definitely pushed him,' added Jim.

'And that's what Penny saw!' I gasped. 'She must have said "pushed him" when I heard her. It sounded like "Pushkin" to Ray – a bit odd I know. We were all convinced that's what she was saying, although we couldn't understand why.'

'Ah, so that's why the chap at the till asked us if we were into Russian literature.'

'Exactly! So she deliberately pushed him? Are you sure?'

My heart started hammering frantically as I tried to picture the scene. It had to be true. Rich and Jim were strangers after all, with nothing to gain from giving their evidence. They were also missionaries, which meant that they were chaps with a faith. Even being a rather sceptical type myself - in matters of religion – I had no hesitation in believing their account of what happened.

'Yes, she definitely gave him quite a wallop. Her face was all screwed up. She looked furious. And then the way he suddenly shot forward! It was obvious. It wasn't the same as if he'd stumbled over something on the pavement.'

'But Lena claimed she'd tried to pull him out of the way; that she'd been the heroine of the hour!' I gabbled. 'She made quite a thing about it, especially as far as saving the poor old gent from being more badly hurt. *And*,' I stressed, 'she persuaded him to support her nomination!'

'What?' they exclaimed in unison.

'He told me himself. Bill told me that according to Lena, Tim had put her name forward, not that it *was* his idea, as I discovered later. Tim admitted as much.' He had simply fallen in with her suggestion.

'She did *that*? She persuaded the two of them to nominate her?' Jim was incredulous. Rich shook his head in disbelief. I nodded.

'Yep, I thought she was being rather opportunist at the time. But to think she pushed him!' Then it was my turn to shake my head in disbelief. 'And to think she turned up at his bedside and discovered he'd lost his memory.'

'Very convenient I'd say,' remarked Rich, grimly. I told them the rest of the sorry saga.

'So, he's recovered *some* memory,' ventured Jim, 'but not those last few moments before the collision.'

'I really don't know. I'm not in touch with him any longer. He's living a different life now. Perhaps he'll never remember. Perhaps there'll be that little island of nothingness for November 21st that'll remain a closed book. After all, it's been almost four and half years now and he's fallen in love with the girl and they're getting married in the autumn.'

Rich got up and paid for another cup each, while Jim and I speculated on memory loss and I told him what I'd learned about it.

'And even if he *did* remember that Lena was responsible for the accident, she'd have her own version and convince him he was mistaken.'

Later, when I got to Mum and Dad's and was telling my incredulous parents and Sean – who just happened to be passing through – what Rich and Jim had told me, we pieced together the ghastly story as far as we understood it. Lena had been stalking Tim, who had tried to tell her to clear off and stop bothering him. She was so incensed by his rebuttal that she lashed out at him and sent him sprawling into the path of the cyclist, who just happened to reach the top of the lane at the same time. Well, that's how it seemed. Poor Penny had seen the whole thing too and it had left her traumatised.

'Ought we to tell Tim?' I asked Mum, earnestly. 'There were *three* witnesses after all.' Mum and Dad looked at each helplessly.

'Two are strangers,' said Dad.

'And the other's loopy,' snarled Sean dismissively.

'How dare you!' I yelled.

'Well she is,' he snarled again, 'No one would take any notice of her.' He slammed out of the door. How he'd missed out on the good-mannered genes I really don't know.

Mum shook her head and sighed. 'I don't see any point in telling him Gilly. He's made up his mind now and he's hardly going to change it, is he? As you said, it's Lena's word against those chaps. She's a cunning one too; sharp as a razor.'

'And not likely to admit her guilt.' They had to agree with me.

'But just imagine,' speculated Dad, 'there they are at the altar, about to say their vows and Tim suddenly has that last flashback.'

'Oh don't be so melodramatic, Gordon,' scolded Mum.

'That would be quite something,' I agreed. 'The words 'I will', might be a tad tricky in these circumstances.'

'It would be even worse if he had a flashback when he woke up on the morning after their wedding night, with Lena lying beside him with a shiny new ring on her finger,' added Dad, warming to the subject.

'Wow!' I gasped. 'Imagine that!'

Chapter 30

Hanky-panky in the rhubarb patch

The thought of walking around Growdon made me shiver; too many memories and too many chances of meeting Lena, Tim and the rest of the Rosewells. So I only stayed with Mum and Dad for a couple of days. Rich, Jim and I had exchanged numbers, but I didn't expect to see them again. It was another of their flying visits. Mum and I had managed to have a heart-to-heart and I was very selective about which details of my disastrous love life I was prepared to tell her.

'Poor Gilly,' she sighed, when I reached the Shealton side street incident. Then she plumped for Simeon's conclusion; that there might be another explanation, that I may have over-reacted. In my opinion, the chances of that were nil, considering my past record. I seemed to be destined for disappointment. My daydreams were about as likely to come true as any fairy story.

'But he said he'd be away, as in *out of the area, in a different geographical location*, and he clearly wasn't!' I retorted. 'He lied to me!'

'Hmm, I must admit *that* bit is worrying,' she agreed, nodding. And so we chewed it over, but were just as perplexed as when we'd started. 'Shame about that nice doctor,' she reflected.

'You've never met him, Mum,' I reminded her. 'Yes, he's probably quite a good doctor and fine as an occasional dinner companion, but he's not my Mr Right, if you want to use a corny phrase. The chemistry's all wrong!'

Then I was back at Bramble Cottage, desperate to sprinkle water over my rows of seeds, although there *had* been a few obliging April showers to encourage them on the way. All the while Ted had been sending the occasional text, to which I dutifully replied – in my own time – and tried to keep brief and to the point. Then he texted:

'missing u, love Ted x'

How could I reply to that? About the same time, a note was pushed through my letterbox signed by someone called Andy, who needed access to replace a rotted window frame. So Ted had reported it, I thought cynically, squeezing it in amid the demands of family and the unnamed woman.

'I'll be over tomorrow then,' Andy told me when I phoned back. 'Reckon I can fix the loose slates in a day or two.' When I asked if Ted was around, he was either deliberately pretending he didn't know or didn't work with him. 'Ted, you say? Hmm, maybe he's temporary or part-time.'

'Er yes, I expect that's the answer.' Or gone swanning off to Shealton to shack up with his ladylove, I thought mutinously.

Nevertheless, although Ted was becoming a memory, by the time the holiday was almost over, Bramble Cottage was snug and watertight. The garden was starting to show signs of new life and so I managed to rig up some netting over my precious seeds to protect them from greedy beaks. A good number of them had now germinated and had pushed up tiny shoots through the soil. Keeping Minnie away from them had also been a headache, until she started behaving very oddly. First of all, it was the sound of her yowl, as if she was in pain. Then she kept racing off down the path, squeezing through the fence and disappearing into the thicket. I told Pru about her as we were having our lunch break one day.

'Oh-ho, sounds as if she's come into season,' she told me, with a chuckle.

The stable door was wide open and the young filly – or in this case the frisky young queen had bolted. With everything that had happened over the Easter break, organising a trip to the vet was something that had failed to reach my 'to do' list.

'You think so?' I gulped.

'Oh yes, you can't mistake a queen when she's in season. It's a very distinctive call.'

'Perhaps I could shut her in the bedroom.' I speculated. 'How long do these shenanigans last?'

'Oh, about four or five days, I believe.'

It was clear that Minnie's forays into the thicket weren't just for a spot of tree climbing, I thought gloomily. When I got home from school that day and went into the back garden to check on my seeds, Minnie was brazenly entertaining Old Ginger, who sat on the path with a lascivious grin on his fat face. He knew it was just a matter of timing. Meanwhile Minnie, every inch the hussy, raced around flirtatiously, calling to him and then every so often, she would crouch low to the ground and swish her tail. Pru had already told me about this stage in the courtship process, so it was no surprise.

'*You* may like the idea of ginger babies,' I told her, 'but not me.' She cocked an eye briefly in my direction, skittered out of reach as I lunged at her and then carried on her come-hither routine, while Old Ginger yawned and casually washed an ear.

When I went outside after supper, it was too late. Minnie and Old Ginger were doing their bit for the proliferation of the Churlbury cat population in the rhubarb patch. I was agog, having never witnessed anything like this before. Old Ginger had Minnie pinned down and secured by the scruff of the neck. This surely had to be date rape! Mind you, she had been making all the running, and although she was yowling, as if in pain, she wasn't exactly kicking out. Then all at once, Old Ginger sprang back and fled for cover behind the gooseberry bushes, while Minnie rushed at him snarling and spitting and then began some frantic cleaning around her rear quarters. This pattern continued for most of the evening until Minnie wearily returned to the cottage, wolfed down her supper and then curled up on the sofa for a nice long snooze. Sixty-three days, Pru had told me, was the gestation period. Yes, in sixty-three days' time I'd have to have kettles boiling and rubber gloves at the ready – well, maybe not. The trouble was, in sixty-three days' time I'd be rather busy with the Midsummer Festival; the timing couldn't be worse.

Wearily I reached for a bag of English books, which had been forgotten in the excitement of Minnie and Old Ginger's courtship ritual. Although it was almost time for my bedtime hot chocolate, I had to push on with my marking. "See Me," I was writing in Merlin Westropp's book, when there was a sharp rap on the front door. My stomach tightened and then my heart quickened in alarm. It was unusually late for casual callers and I wondered if a surly Zebedee was playing some devious game. I threw aside my pen and crept to the door, holding my breath and listening for any tell-tale sniggering.

'Who's there?' I barked, in my best schoolmarm tone.

'Just me,' came back a confident male voice. Me? It sounded like Ted. But was I ready for Ted? What could I say? A picture of Ted kissing the unknown woman flashed through my mind and I went cold.

'Gilly? It's Ted.' I galvanised myself and opened the door.

'Ted!' I exclaimed, a stupid greeting I know. He was beaming as if he had nothing to hide, but I couldn't return his smile.

'Oh, Gilly, how I've missed you,' he said and opened his arms wide for a hug.

My tongue seemed to have frozen in fright. I gulped and swallowed. 'What's wrong?' he asked. 'Oh, Gilly, did I frighten you? I'm sorry it's late, but I saw your lights were still on and I just had to see you.' He took a step closer and wrapped his arms around me. I still couldn't speak. There was an almighty battle going on inside my head. I *had* to know what had been going on, although part of me was remembering Mum's words. 'Hmm, it's good to be back,' he sighed, stroking my hair and then gently releasing me.

'But you've *not* been away,' I gasped, incredulous at his blatant lies. 'I saw you in Shealton! I saw you with a woman!'

'What? Oh but...' he cut in, looking surprised or was it guilty? Yes, definitely guilty, I decided.

'You seemed to know her *very* well, from where I was standing. You certainly weren't helping her across the road or directing her to the station,' I continued, knowing that now I'd started, I couldn't stop. There was that horrible tightening in my throat that signalled tears were threatening.

'And *where* were you standing?' he asked.

'In a little side street. It was about two weeks ago, when I was under the impression that you were miles away.' We weren't exactly glaring at each other, but the fact that he wasn't exactly owning up to it was making me angry.

Ted sighed heavily and rubbed his brow. 'Can we sit down, Gilly? I need to explain something. It's been a rather highly charged time for me, just recently.'

'What about me?' I squeaked. 'You come here and sweep me off my feet and make me... er... make me... Oh, you must know how I feel about you! And then you tell me you're going away and I have to learn patience – a quality I'm not exactly endowed with – and...' If I'd carried on I might well have started stamping my feet and pummelling his chest with my fists or telling him to clear off, but fortunately something told me to stop. I just stood there feeling so wretched. Ted shook his head wearily and made a move towards the sofa.

'Gilly, come and sit. Please listen.' He spoke so gently that my anger started to subside.

'Shall I put the kettle on?'

'No, just sit.' By then he was cuddled up next to Minnie, who deigned to open an eye briefly before tucking herself even tighter and resuming her nap.

Ted patted the sofa and gave a wistful smile.

'Okay.' Seeing him sat beside Minnie reminded me of that first afternoon, when he came bursting into my life. I had to let him have his say, even though I might not like what he was about to tell me.

'The woman you saw was my mother. It's obvious you didn't catch a glimpse of her face, otherwise you would have realised she wasn't some pretty young thing I was chasing.' Yes, my outburst had clearly shown him that I'd been jealous of a possible rival for his affection.

'She lives in *Shealton*?'

'Well, er she lives in the area. I told you about being adopted, well I've only just recently been reunited with my real mother – not that she ever was my mother in the sense of looking after me.'

'Oh Ted.' The humble pie seemed to be sitting on a plate in front of me, with a spoon, ready for me to tuck in.

'Has Theo met her? How is he taking it?' The thought of bumping into Theo Rescorla in Shealton was not a very pleasing prospect. The general proximity and implications were quite disturbing.

'Theo's finding it very emotional. The whole family is finding it very emotional. It's been a shock for my mother. She had no idea what Joe had written in his will, so she didn't know the family skeletons were going to be revealed.'

'But she must be pleased to be reunited with her sons after so long.'

'She's thrilled. She never thought this would happen, although plenty of adopted babies end up meeting their real parents.' As I listened, I found it really sad that Ted's mother had turned her back on her children, although I know people have many very good reasons for giving up their babies for adoption. Then I remembered what Ted had told me about Joe being married already and imagined what a stink there must have been when he and Ted's mum realised about the pregnancy. Could it have been the cause of Joe's divorce?

'Did she know who adopted you?'

'Apparently not. She went through the labour, but never saw the result of her efforts.'

'Never saw her babies?' I gasped. Ted's head went down. He was evidently finding it difficult.

'And she's in a very sensitive situation now.'

'Is she married, with a family?' He nodded. 'Does her family know about all this?'

'Her husband knows, but no one else,' he replied. 'Well, her parents did, but they're no longer alive.'

'Oh, so you have half-brothers or sisters who don't know you!' I gasped. 'And they live in this area? Ah, so that's why you suddenly turned up. It was to do with finding your mum. I'm sorry I was a stupid idiot, jumping to the wrong conclusion and all that.'

'You weren't to know,' he said and held out his arms. It was time to stop silently berating myself. I snuggled up to him and rested my head on his shoulder. It was wonderful, especially after three weeks of trying to fill the vacuum he'd left. Yes, there had been a tangible vacuum, and all that had filled it was loneliness, a shocking revelation of the greedy, scheming Lena Tuffin and doubts about Ted's sincerity. No girl's heart should have to put up with all that, especially when her cat had been having a fine old courtship and spot of hanky-panky in rhubarb patch.

'I think that cup of tea would be very welcome now,' said Ted, some while later.

'Hmm?' I sighed, opening my eyes and admiring his strong chin. 'Sorry... did I drop off? Cripes! ...Is it *that* late?' I groaned, noting the time and remembering half a pile of abandoned, unmarked maths books. It was around midnight by the time Ted left. I was no closer to learning the identity of his mum but I knew how he felt about me, and that was more important than anything else was. Armed with that knowledge, I felt I could mark exercise books by the dozens and deal with a whole tribe of Zebedees. My wonderful Ted had even landed the Bransfield job. Evidently his thumbs and fingers had been green enough for the discerning personnel bod who'd interviewed him. As far as I was concerned, Ted could prick out my seedlings and hoe my carrots any day!

There still hovered over him, however, an air of mystery, but I put that down to the need to be discreet about his mum's delicate situation.

In the days that followed, plans for the Midsummer Festival came more into focus, and with them the need for a few specifics, such as which pieces would my school orchestra perform. I couldn't believe that, with a whole year's warning, I still hadn't made a firm decision. Walter Flemington, aided and abetted by Felicity McArdell were determined to have every item noted – or possibly every note itemised – in the running order with more than seven weeks to go.

'I'll try and make a decision this week,' I told Mrs McArdell after school one afternoon, when she approached me yet again with her clipboard, bristling with an air of efficiency.

'Perhaps you could compose another little piece?' she suggested.

I winced inside. Little? There was nothing *little* about composing and arranging for my raggle-taggle bunch of aspiring musicians. All *she* was interested in was prime solo slots for her precious daughters.

'I'll let you know,' I promised her.

In the music cupboard, there were folders stuffed with an assortment of orchestral sheet music and recorder parts, but the job of sorting through them was daunting. In the spring term, we'd tackled some nursery rhyme arrangements, but they'd not gone down well. In fact, the twins had sneered at them when I'd dished out the parts, and I hadn't been brave enough to admit that I found them dreary as well.

'All good experience,' I'd told them briskly, with plenty of phoney bluster.

'But, Miss,' whined one of them, 'they're so babyish!' After Mrs M had left me in peace, I knew there was nothing for it but to take the bulging folders home and get myself organised. But first I had to make a library call. I'd discovered from a spot of Internet browsing that my favourite author had had a new book published and I was hopeful that Churlbury might possibly have a copy. After *Girl in a Whirl* I was ready for *Dreamboat Danny on the Dodgems*.

As I pushed the door open, I could see I had managed my usual unfortunate timing, unless it was Imogen's holiday, because it was Alison's gloomy countenance that greeted me. I wondered if she'd regained the power of speech, although judging by the set of her mouth, it didn't look promising. I nodded a brief 'hello' in her direction and went for a quick shufti in the A – C shelves. *Tulisa in the Tunnel of Love* and *Helter Skelter Hunk* were there, but I'd already read those. Naturally my make-believe sick friend was desperate for another Fantasia Crump saga, so I fixed on a bright smile and approached the desk. Alison looked up with a weary expression. 'Yes?'

'Could I have a request slip please?' It seemed the best way to avoid any snide comments. There surely must be a nice anonymous box to post it in, I thought. But no, the staff of Churlbury library appeared to pride themselves on personal attention.

Alison reached inside her drawer and took a slip from her secret stash.

'Author?' she rapped, her pen poised.

'Fantasia Crump. It's for my poor sick friend,' I explained earnestly.

'The bed-ridden one who has lost her card?' she replied, with an innocent air that didn't fool me for a moment. If there was a suspicion of play-acting on Alison's part, I was ready to join her in the little charade. I affected a solemn expression.

'Oh yes, poor Fran,' I sighed. 'The doctors have given her a pessimistic prognosis.' I was congratulating myself on a convincing performance when I remembered, with horror, that Fran and Alison had both been present at the Carol Service. Had they been introduced? I racked my brain, but couldn't recall one way or the other, until I remembered Alison's mutinous mutterings that evening. *She'd* never have remembered if I'd introduced her to the Archbishop of Canterbury, I was certain.

'But Fantasia Crump brightens her day,' I added, affecting a sympathetic manner.

'Title?' Alison was back to single words.

'*Dreamboat Danny on the Dodgems.*' Her lip curled in distaste as she wrote and then filled in the rest of the details.

'And how is your *other* friend; the one with the double life?' she asked. Now here was a first; Alison Veltman actually making an enquiry on the state of my lamentable love life.

'Oh er… well Simeon was right about there being a perfectly innocent explanation.'

'Well, that's very comforting, I'm sure,' she said, with a sniff.

'Oh yes, it is. Ted was meeting his Mum, but of course I didn't see it was an older woman, so I assumed it was some bright young thing. Silly me!'

I gave a little giggle, noticing her look of superiority. You could almost see "Gilly Bonning's over-reacting as usual" written all over her face.

'His Mum had him when she was really quite young – well eighteen I believe. The father arranged for the adoption and it's only just come out,' I told her, lowering my voice. 'But it's all a bit hush-hush,' I whispered, 'because not all her family know about her past. I'm sure I can rely on you and Simeon to be discrete.'

Alison's eyes seemed to glaze over. She probably thought I was being overly melodramatic. Then I remembered her own unfortunate experience of motherhood and felt acute embarrassment.

'Er right, must be off,' I gabbled, and grabbed my things and scooted out of the door. Poor Alison; she'd been robbed of motherhood by a dreadful tragedy and there was I talking about babies given away through adoption. My capacity for foot-in-mouth remarks was popping up with embarrassing regularity.

By mid-May Minnie's appetite began to increase alarmingly. Her bright pink pregnant nipples poked proudly through the soft white fur of her belly and her usual sleek outline was showing some modest bulging. She was embracing pregnancy with hardly a whisker out of place and of Old Ginger, there was no sign. I'd wager he was down on the council estate sowing more wild oats. My seedlings were putting on their own valiant show, although there were a few disappointing gaps where the local wildlife had feasted on my lovingly tended little plants. While Ted hoed and watered one evening, I painstakingly trawled through the disorganised orchestra folder and had chosen Beethoven's *Ode to Joy* and the slow movement from Haydn's *Surprise Symphony*. I was sure the percussion section would love scaring the audience with a spot of enthusiastic banging and clashing. Then I had managed to adapt some parts for my intermediate recorders.

'What do you think of my choice?' I'd asked Ted one evening, earlier in the term. 'Is it a bums-on-seats programme?' He shook his head in a 'search me' sort of way.

'The parents would probably turn up if their kids were playing *Twinkle Twinkle Little Star*,' he commented. I felt a flush on my cheek, but didn't dare tell him we'd been ploughing through nursery rhymes the previous term. Then I reminded myself that Ted wouldn't be as bothered as the high and mighty Theo. *He* would do his famous impression of something nasty under the nose and make sure I knew it.

'You're right,' I'd agreed. After that I went into top gear with my orchestra, arranging extra practices for lunchtimes and after school. Despite my slow start the pieces were coming together very well. *Ode to Joy* had a modest note range that my junior recorders could manage, and so I included them in the ensemble.

'I hope you'll be there on the night to cheer me on,' I said to Ted one day. Remembering my first taste of the Midsummer Festival, I pictured the two of us sipping champagne on the vicarage lawn, surrounded by the perfume of roses and Walter Flemington's fan club. Then I imagined us slipping back to the cottage for some private canoodling away from the beady eyes of the McArdells and their well-heeled chums from the opera group.

We were cleaning up after a session in the garden on a particularly balmy and fragrant evening, when blossoms were bursting and the leaves on the trees in the thicket were at their prettiest shade of green.

'Wouldn't miss it for the world,' he assured me, grinning. 'And I promise I won't yawn too much through the rest of the programme.'

'What, not through the W.I. ladies and their old time favourites?' He shook his head.

'Or the Marbeck Singers, who've persuaded my friend Fran to join, by the way.'

Yes, this was quite a revelation. Fran had sworn that dots on a stave had never meant much to her, but maybe that was a measure of the average member of that choir.

'Gilly Bonning, I'd travel to the ends of the world to watch you conduct your little horrors and watch you playing your clarinet.' He had me by the shoulders and was staring at me in a particularly mouth-watering way that neither Tim nor Ewan had managed.

'Ah-ha, you say that, but you haven't heard me playing. I bet if you asked Theo he'd give you a health warning.'

'Really?' chuckled Ted. 'Will I need earplugs then?'

'Of course not! Mind you, the brass section are a bit... well, they can get carried away, blowing their own trumpets and trombones and the rest!'

'It'll be worth it just to sit and watch you,' he said tenderly and then kissed me long and lingeringly enough to make my stomach tingle with desire. 'Now that I've found you, I don't ever want to lose you,' he whispered.

'Nor do I,' I gasped back, once my lips had recovered enough to form a word or three. We might have only known each other for two months, but everything seemed so right between us. Was there a significant question hovering on *his* lips? If there was, I knew what my answer would be.

Up on cloud nine it was as dreamy as my most wicked fantasy until a loud and very insistent yowl brought me back to earth. It was Minnie demanding her suppertime biscuits. Then I recalled, with a sense of foreboding that her kittens were due to be born when I'd be rather busy with Beethoven, Schubert and other tuneful offerings. Maybe she'd have them the day before. Or the day after? Or maybe, she'd just push them out as easy as shelling peas, just as her mother did in one of the Maxted hay barns? Before Ted left, I remembered that Harry Woodfine had asked for help at the rectory with setting up lights and moving garden furniture in time for the festival party.

'Of course I'll help,' Ted agreed. 'Just point me in the right direction.'

'Excellent! I'll give Harry your number.' Then I wanted to know if Ted might encourage his mum along. I hadn't wanted to hassle him over sensitive family matters, but thought there must have been some progress. Now that Ted had hinted at his intentions for the two of us, it seemed only natural to meet her.

'I'll work on it,' he promised, and slipped out into the night.

The poster that Cheryl was taping in the Post Office window the following day, had my heart and pulse racing. Fantasia Crump was on a book signing tour of the south and west and was to be in Shealton in a matter of days. With a little tweak to the timing of my school orchestra practice, I could meet my favourite author and have my own signed copy! I was vaguely aware of three bookshops in Shealton. However, as I only patronised charity shops for my reading matter, when the library couldn't please me, I wasn't too sure of the whereabouts of the shop that was hosting Fantasia's signing.

'Emily the Bookworm? Which one is that?' I asked Cheryl, once she was back behind her counter.

'The one in the Buttermarket, just along from the Oxfam shop.'

'Ah, so not the one near the abbey.'

'No, that's Abbey Books, and the one down Old Swan Passage is Fact and Fiction.'

When I popped into the library to cancel my book request, Imogen greeted me with a breezy 'no problem'.

'Might go along myself,' she confided. 'Fantasia Crump knows how to put together a cracking page-turner.'

'Not that your colleague would agree,' I giggled.

The following Monday I was virtually quivering with feverish anticipation as I drove into Shealton, just before five, swerving past lumbering tractors and scaring innocent dog walkers. The signing and reading had been scheduled to begin at four thirty according to the posters and an article in the local gazette, so it was no surprise that Emily the Bookworm was packed tight with chortling fans when I eventually arrived. Fantasia, decked out in suitably frivolous fairground hues, was holding court to one side of the shop floor, reading mouth-watering snippets from *Dreamboat Danny of the Dodgems* to a rapt audience that ranged from twittering teens to enthusiastic eighty-pluses.

"'I don't care about your dark past," breathed Lydia, as Danny took her in his strong arms. "Ah, but-" Danny's words were cut short as the tent flap was pushed aside and two police constables burst in. "Danny Floxwaite, I am arresting you on suspicion of embezzlement and impersonating a peer of the realm,' declared one, with a bristling moustache, while his colleague clapped handcuffs over Danny's wrists. Lydia let out a shrill cry of distress and tears spouted from her pretty blue eyes.

"It's a lie!" hollered Danny, as the boys in blue hustled him out to the waiting car. Lydia gaped in horror, her hand instinctively clutching her stomach where her own dark secret lay. "Danny!" she shrieked, but it was no use; she was alone.'

A sigh went up around the room. Fantasia beamed at her audience and closed her book with enough finality to let us know that that was all she was prepared to reveal. Then, a great round of applause erupted and a steady stampede began. I might have missed a few minutes of Fantasia's reading, but the slice I *had* heard had certainly whetted my appetite. Copies were snatched from the piles that covered every available surface. The temperature must have risen several degrees as perspiring bodies jostled and elbowed their way to where Fantasia sat, with pen poised, for one of the local photographers to snap her for the *Shealton Gazette*. Beside her a grinning assistant sat by the till and card reader, ready to relieve Fantasia's fans of their cash. It was promising to be a long wait, but once I had a precious copy in my hand, I didn't care a bit. Through the forest of heads, shoulders and ample bosoms, I caught sight of a tray easing its way through the throng. A few crisps or a handful of peanuts would do nicely, I decided, washed down with a glass of orange. I tried to edge forward, but it was no good. I was stuck fast.

Then I caught a glimpse of a face that was familiar. She was young and vivacious, making animated conversation with someone obscured by two elderly matrons. It was either Nina or Poppy, because although I'd seen one of them at orchestra practice in the village hall, I'd forgotten which was which and I hadn't had the nerve to ask about names, hoping I'd remember eventually. They were very similar in appearance, although not as identical as Ted and his odious twin.

'Gilly!' came a voice in my ear.

'Imogen! You made it then! What a crush eh?' We compared reactions to Fantasia's taster and agreed it was her best yet.

'Perfect holiday reading, don't you think?' I sighed.

'Gilly, Imogen!' came another friendly voice just behind us.

'Pru!' we chorused, and grabbed her arms to pull her through to share our tiny piece of floor.

'Phew, what a scrum-down,' she gasped, fanning her face with a Fantasia Crump flyer. 'Haven't seen so many female bodies crammed together in one place since Lulu's Lingerie had their closing down sale. The entire female population of Shealton must be here.'

'Except the staff of Abbey Books and Fact and Fiction,' I put in. 'They must be green with envy.'

'Surprised that there are men here, though,' added Pru, with a chuckle.

'Probably keeping an eye on their wives' buying habits,' suggested Imogen sarcastically.

'I don't know. The one I saw wasn't escorting a spendaholic wife. Oh, there he is,' she said, nudging me and pointing through a sea of blue rinses, demi-waves and neat bobs.

'It's Ted!' I gasped, with pleasure. 'What's *he* doing here?'

'Ted?' They exchanged meaningful glances and rolled their eyes.

'My boyfriend!' I announced proudly. 'He works up on the Frintley Estate.'

'But I thought it was on again with the one from Growdon. That's what Kate told me.'

Stupid me. I hadn't remembered that. A spot of quick thinking was needed.

'Well,' I hesitated, as ruefully as I could, 'it *was* on for a while, but then we both realised we'd grown apart. It was for the best. Then I met Ted.'

'You're a dark horse, Miss Bonning,' teased Pru. 'Up at the estate, did you say?'

'Well, of course that makes sense, doesn't it?' remarked Imogen casually.

'What does?' Judging by her decisive tone, I was missing an important piece of information.

'Him being here, of course. Miriam Oborn runs this bulging emporium. It's *her* shop.'

'Ah, so she's dragged him away from his hedging and ditching to help with crowd control. Strange that he didn't tell me he was going to be here.'

'Did you tell *him?* probed Pru, bringing some of her refreshing commonsense into the conversation.

'Well no.'

The queue shuffled forward a few steps. 'I thought he'd laugh at me. I shouldn't think Ted would appreciate the merits of Fantasia's novels.'

'A bit high-brow, is he then?' asked Pru.

'I can't tell. He's brilliant in the garden with my rows of carrots and lettuces, but...' I paused to find the right words, 'he seems too educated to be hedging and ditching and chopping down trees. He takes care of his hands too.'

'So do I,' agreed Pru. 'Can't beat a good pair of gardening gloves.'

'Of course,' I agreed.

Nina or Poppy at last made her way through the crowd and we gratefully grabbed glasses of juice.

'Thanks... er... Nina?' I ventured hopefully.

'No probs,' she replied warmly. Then I had to admit to her that I hadn't realised that this was her mum's shop.

'I'm very impressed.' She beamed proudly. 'And where *is* your mum? This crowd is amazing. She must be thrilled.'

Nina stood on tiptoe and scanned the seething masses. 'She was over by the freestanding promotion displays,' she said. 'Oh yes, she was chatting to the mayor, I think, and some of the other town councillors.'

I followed Nina's pointing hand. Although the mayor had her back to me, I saw enough of her conversation partner's outline to give me a sense of déja vu. It was the same outline that I'd seen in the passageway, being kissed by Ted. I gasped aloud.

'Ted's mother! Surely not!' Suddenly several loose ends joined up in my brain.

'What's that?' asked Nina. My mind was working overtime. If Miriam Oborn was Ted's mother, then Nina and Poppy were his half-sisters.

'Ted's, um...' I repeated weakly, wondering too late if Ted's secret was still a secret.

'Mother,' supplied Nina. 'Oh yes,' she continued, 'it was a bit of a shock, but a lovely one.'

But he hadn't told *me*, I thought glumly, not even when I'd asked if his mum might come to the festival. Disappointment flooded through me. Couldn't he share a confidence with me? Then I remembered what he'd said about the back street encounter I'd witnessed. If I'd seen Miriam's face I might have already come to my own conclusion.

'How long have you known?' I asked her.

'Oh not long. Poppy and I told him he should tell you,' she explained awkwardly, 'but I think he was worrying about Mum's feelings.' Yes, fair enough, I thought. Just because Ted was calling on me and keeping my garden in order didn't give me the right to be included in all the Oborn family secrets.

Behind me Pru and Imogen were engrossed in their own conversation. I was just about to ask if Theo had managed to cross the channel for a jolly family reunion when the queue moved on and a few impatient fans shunted us from the rear.

'Oops!' A great wave of juice was propelled from my glass onto the jacket of the woman in front.

'I'll grab a cloth.' Nina scuttled off, but we didn't see her again.

'You'll never guess,' I told Pru and Imogen, my mind still reeling with the Rescorla and Oborn connection, 'but I've just found out that Ted is Miriam's son!'

'Really?' said Pru, with interest. 'From a previous marriage?'

'No... er... from...' I petered out, realising I'd probably already said too much.

'Ah, from the wrong side of the sheets,' concluded Pru, rolling her eyes in mock disapproval.

'Golly!' added Imogen, her eyes like saucers.

'Better not repeat it,' I urged them. 'It's been a bit of a sensitive subject. I know I can count on your discretion.' They nodded sagely, giving me another déja vu experience.

Chapter 31

Remembering the past

'Let me.' A familiar hand covered one of mine that was grasping a credit card as I waited for the wilting assistant to serve me. By then Fantasia was also visibly wilting, although the sparkle in her eyes magically reappeared briefly for each of her eager fans.

'Ted!' I gasped with delight. 'Nina told me,' I added, with a meaningful expression, which acknowledged our shared interest in the subject. Better not go all huffy on him, I'd decided as I'd been waiting in line for my audience with Fantasia.

'Ah yes... about Mum,' he murmured, an anxious frown making a brief appearance. 'She said she'd spoken to you. Sorry I wasn't around earlier. I had to go out and rifle the local supermarket for more crisps and juice.' He handed over a ten-pound note to the waiting assistant, who was gazing at Ted in a particularly smitten way. 'I'm sorry you had to hear it from someone else... about Mum. I was planning to call round and tell you after this was over. But if you could keep quiet about... you know...' he whispered, sotto voce. 'There's something Mum's concerned about. So, for the time being I'm Poppy and Nina's *cousin.*'

I gulped in alarm, quickly trying to disguise it as a cough. Hmm, I thought, Nina could have buttoned her own lips. She didn't have the quietest voice and there had been two of my village friends standing close by.

'Um... right... okay... their cousin.' I nodded, convincing myself that it was only the tiniest white lie, if it was in a good cause. But was Miriam Oborn still ashamed after all those years? Single parents were so common now that no one really cared, did they? And back in the eighties, it surely wasn't such a terrible scandal. Maybe Miriam was very sensitive. After all I hardly knew her, so what business did I have to judge? We moved away, the precious signed copy clutched in my sweaty hands. I was feverishly weighing up the likelihood of Imogen and Pru divulging the new Frintley Estate revelation. No, I'd told them to be discreet, so why should I worry? They were both still chatting with Fantasia, who seemed to have developed the art of the rictus grin.

'I'll have to hang about, I guess. Family duties and all that.'

'That's fine Ted. I've a pile of marking and I need to touch base with Pru and Imogen before I go home.' I smiled brightly, and tingled right down to my toes in delight as he stooped to kiss my cheek.

'Ooh, he's quite a catch!' giggled Pru, once we were outside. 'If he's as good in bed as he is in the garden, you'll be very well satisfied.' She winked. I was seeing a different side of Pru. Perhaps *Dreamboat Danny* was a raunchier read than Fantasia's earlier publications, I wondered. Perhaps Pru had been dipping in already and her imagination was suitably ignited. I blinked in surprise while she and Imogen giggled together.

'Just remember what I said about being discreet.'

'Definitely,' agreed Pru, nodding.

'It's my middle name,' asserted Imogen.

'Really?' chuckled Pru, digging her in the ribs. 'You never told me.'

I left them to it. There was clearly no chance of having a sensible conversation with the two of them while they were in *that* mood.

The subject of Ted's – and therefore his twin's – relationship with Miriam Oborn, exercised my mind greatly in the days that followed. Why had the Oborns decided to lie about Miriam's past? Was it Edmund's idea? Was he trying to help his wife keep up appearances; to parade her before the locals as a respectable lady of the manor? Was he a narrow-minded snob? I hoped not. Much as I loved Ted, I couldn't help wishing he didn't have all that emotional family baggage. Having learned to forget about Tim, with his broken memory and then fend off sex-mad Ewan, all I wanted was a nice, straightforward, uncomplicated relationship. Gilly Bonning, it seemed, was not down for "nice", "straightforward" or "uncomplicated" in the great book of life and love. Thanks a bunch God.

The last balmy days of May were followed by the typical cool and damp days of the English summer. Being a fair weather gardener, I peered gloomily at my burgeoning veg patch from the cottage windows, grateful that the seasonal shift had at least spared me from watering duties. Instead of admiring Ted's bronzed legs in his cut-off jeans, I concentrated on the curl of his eyelashes and the generous proportions of his lips at close quarters. And no, I wasn't about to reveal the generous proportions of anything else. Our canoodling was still strictly confined to the ground floor, much to my surprise. Unlike Ewan, Ted wasn't given to urgent grasping and grabbing at my undergarments. At first, it had been a refreshing change, but as the weeks went by, I wondered what was holding him back. Another matter that bothered me was the absence of any invitation to share a homely meal with the rest of his family. Clearly, Nina and Poppy knew I featured significantly in Ted's life, but as for welcoming me into their family circle… well I was still waiting outside, hoping for a friendly wave. The news that Miriam and Edmund had jetted off to Corsica for a week in the sun, however, reined in my frustration somewhat.

Meanwhile Minnie entered the last two weeks of her pregnancy and had developed a voracious appetite. She sneaked chunks of cake left abandoned on the table and wrestled trays of frozen meat onto the floor, which she attempted to eat while still coated in their icy frosting.

'Minnie, you naughty girl!' I'd admonish sternly. However, Minnie washed her whiskers nonchalantly, unmoved by my scolding.

'I'm eating for six,' she seemed to say. I marked off the days on the calendar, and when her pregnancy approached the final week, a cardboard box, lined with newspaper and old towels was prepared as her birthing area.

'There you are Minnie,' I'd coax, picking her up gently and putting her in the box, which was turned on its side. Minnie sniffed suspiciously and then stalked away, her stomach bulging and wobbling as she went. Sometimes, when she deigned to curl up on my lap, I would lay my hand on her belly and feel little kicks and squirms inside.

At school there were barely enough hours to fit in sports day preparation as well as the festival items. Every minute of every lunchtime was claimed by something or other, and Morris and I clashed on one or two occasions when my best string players were expected to turn up for relay practice when I was expecting them for a last minute orchestra rehearsal. Kate was also suitably engaged in masterminding amazing murals, which would be used to decorate the church. As I wasn't seeing Ewan any more, Kate and I had drifted apart somewhat.

'How's Tim?' she'd ask occasionally, and I'd have to choose my words carefully as well as check if Pru was within earshot. Eventually I knew I'd have to admit that Tim no longer featured in my life, especially as Ted would be helping at the festival and would be a visible presence at my side at the party, at the very least. News that Ewan was dating a girl from the yacht club was exactly what I wanted to hear.

'Vanessa's competing at Cowes,' Kate boasted.

'Hmm, lovely,' I replied. 'Minnie's expecting quads at least.' Kate raised a quizzical eyebrow but evidently wasn't too impressed. The Maxteds seemed to have a coolly detached attitude towards felines.

Felicity McArdell and Simeon appeared in the staffroom clutching clipboards and frazzled expressions with increasing regularity. All I wanted was to slump in a chair and gulp down my coffee and not be pestered about exactly how many minutes and seconds each school item would last. We were down for immediately after the interval on the Saturday afternoon. That would give me exactly twenty minutes to wrestle a dozen music stands, a dozen sets of music and twice that number of children and chairs into place, while the audience were guzzling tea and scoffing cupcakes and homemade biscuits. Fortunately, Pru and Olive had agreed to help me.

'Gags and handcuffs at the ready,' Pru had promised, with her usual good humour.

'Might be a tad tricky,' I giggled, 'even for the highly gifted McArdell twins.'

The Midsummer Festival was due to begin on the Friday evening, with solo and group items, so the last chance to rehearse my orchestra in situ was the morning before. Simeon and Felicity turned up as well, with stopwatches and clipboards in hand.

'Grit your teeth, Miss Bonning,' whispered Pru.

'Oh, so you spotted steam coming from my ears did you?' I hissed back, my teeth obediently gritted.

'Don't mind us, will you,' breezed Mrs M, acting in an irritatingly prima donna-like manner.

'We've come to reserve seats for the local dignitaries as well,' put in Simeon, brandishing a handful of photocopied sheets. Olive meanwhile, was doing a valiant job seating my recorder players and after another ten minutes of fussing and flapping, we were able to launch into Beethoven and Schubert.

'Bravo!' called Simeon, as the final chord echoed from the vaulted ceiling. 'Well done Miss Bonning and well done orchestra!' The children beamed and Olive looked suitably impressed as well. Meanwhile Mrs M was pacing the rear aisle of the church with a phone clamped to her ear, looking far from her usually poised and polished persona. How rude, I thought. The twins looked understandably upset as well. We started to pack up, ready to return to school in time for lunch. By this time, Mrs M had pocketed her phone and was striding up the aisle with a thunderous expression on her face. If she was about to criticise my fledgling musicians, I'd have no hesitation in telling her where she could stuff her precious festival.

'This is *all* we need!' she muttered furiously as she came within earshot. 'Bloody stupid man!'

I paused in dismantling a music stand and gaped open mouthed. 'I'm sorry?' I ventured, wishing I could have had one of Pru's promised gags for the woman.

'It's bally Walter Flemington!' she huffed. 'Only gone horse riding with brother Johnny and fallen off. He's broken his collarbone and has multiple fractures on both arms! At a time like this too! The idiot!' Oh yes, Mrs M was demonstrating her boundless reservoirs of the milk of human kindness.

The ominous repercussions of Walter's riding accident percolated my brain in two seconds flat.

'The orchestra, the choir, the er…!' I gabbled in alarm.

'The festival!' snapped Felicity, raising her eyes to heaven and managing to curb her vocabulary.

'What's that?' gasped Olive, who had picked up Felicity's vibes and possibly one or two of her less prudent utterances.

'Golly Moses!' put in Simeon, once we'd conveyed the unfortunate news. Olive looked suitably aghast and shook her head in despair. 'Poor chap.'

'Percy Crosby-Foulkes is trying to find a replacement,' muttered Felicity crossly. 'He has plenty of contacts. Someone from the opera group might be able to help out.'

'Well, I hope he finds someone,' I commented, wondering if our lead violin might be able to wield a baton in Walter's absence. We had our last practice scheduled for that evening, 'Or perhaps you'd fancy having a stab at it?'. Felicity McArdell gave me a withering look and stalked off.

'I don't think she's in the mood for jokes,' whispered Olive.

By the time I returned to the church for the orchestra's final rehearsal at seven, the news of Walter's accident had become old news. Gerald Mortain, the orchestra leader, shook his head irritably as each of us asked the same boring question.

'No, I *don't* know who Percy's bringing,' he snapped.

I'd wrung a promise from Ted earlier in the week, that he'd creep in and listen from behind a handy pew if he had finished with the fairy lights and bunting in the rectory garden by then. The W.I. ladies and Mothers' Union had been churning out miles of little flags that fluttered around the green and criss-crossed the main street. It all looked very jolly. Kate's school murals were also in place. Just then Poppy rushed into the building with her usual precision timing – often at least five minutes late – and sank onto her chair, flushed and particularly animated. At last I'd managed to remember which of the Oborn girls was our extra viola player. Most of us were ready by then, and an oboe struck up with an 'A' so that we could all check our tuning.

Gerald stood glowering, his violin in place as he adjusted his tuning pegs, when brisk footsteps could be heard on the gravel outside and then on the stone slabs of the porch. I'd just discovered a split in my clarinet's reed and was hastily replacing it with a pristine new one. As I tightened the mouthpiece clip in place, a buzz went up from the assembled company. I glanced up, not surprised that Ted had at last turned up, but that he'd brought someone with him and was possibly deciding to listen from a front pew. I reminded myself of his unofficial relationship to Poppy, in case anyone asked.

'Percy Crosby-Foulkes,' said the stranger, approaching our leader with an outstretched hand. 'You're Gerald, I believe. I've brought Walter's replacement. Sorry we've cut it fine.' He wiped his brow and leaned towards Gerald, muttering something too quiet for the woodwind section to hear. I stared at Ted, trying to make sense of the scene before me. So far he'd not turned to nod or smile in my direction, but was wholly concerned with Percy and Gerald, nodding and adding his own occasional sentence.

'Ladies and gentlemen of the orchestra,' announced Percy grandly, 'at very short notice, we've been fortunate to have the promising young conductor Theo Rescorla come and take Walter's place.'

'Oh my God!' I breathed in horror. My fellow musicians on either side stared at me quizzically. This was my worst nightmare without Ted's presence to give me any comfort. Perhaps he was still stuck up a ladder, grappling with bunting or testing fairy lights or sampling a glass of port with Harry Woodfine? Even so, he *could* have warned me that his odious brother was about to bless us with his presence, I thought peevishly. Theo mounted the rostrum and flicked open the score in front of him.

'We'll start with Offenbach, I think,' he announced, and cast a quick glance around the rows of musicians before him, his eyes not lingering long enough to spot me. I cowered behind my music stand and studied the tiled floor. My heart had already started racing frantically at Percy's announcement and now it seemed to be echoing loudly in my ears. I put my clarinet to my lips and concentrated on the notes in front of me. I'd coped at Boxmouth, I told myself, and I'd cope again.

We plunged into *Orpheus in the Underworld* at a brisk lick, but even the can-can section failed to put a smile on my face. For the second time that day I was mentally and physically gritting my teeth.

'Excellent!' exclaimed the beastly Theo, when we finished, and I marvelled at the similarity between the brothers. Sartorially however, Theo was smarter than Ted. No doubt, that was due to their vastly different wage packets. We ploughed on through the programme, stopping every so often to check on a few trifling details that didn't quite please our exalted conductor. However, he seemed to be curbing his acid tongue, which was a pleasant change from the behaviour of his student days. Perhaps his time in France had had something to do with that, I wondered.

'*Ted, where r u?*' I texted, while we were pausing between pieces. But Ted must have had his phone switched off or was being pressed into even more last minute jobs by Harry and Veronica. After two hours, we were all flagging and plans to sink a few pints in the pub were being hatched in the brass section behind me.

'Thank you everyone,' said our conductor, laying down his baton. 'I'll see you all tomorrow evening.'

Before he'd uttered his final word, I was capping my mouthpiece and pulling apart my instrument to stow it safely away in its case.

'Joining us for a swift cider?' asked the first bassoon on my left.

'Another time, maybe,' I replied, clicking my case shut and sliding my music into its folder. 'Need to catch up with someone.'

I beetled out of the building and round the churchyard, to the rectory

347

garden. Harry Woodfine was standing on the lawn, puffing on his pipe. Around him fluttered great strings of bunting, which looped across the rectory roof and round an ancient pergola. Fairy lights twinkled in the apple trees and over garden arches. It was a breath-taking sight.

'Ah, Gilly,' said Harry, removing his pipe for a moment, 'Jolly cheery music, I must say. Well done! Well done!'

'Is Ted still here?' Silly question, Gilly, Harry was obviously alone.

'He *was* earlier, and made a good job of all this.' Harry waved his spare hand around in a vague circle. 'Haven't seen him since… er… not sure actually. Had a few pastoral visits before supper, so don't know when he finished.'

In the kitchen, Veronica was surrounded by the makings of a veritable feast, which indicated it was the M.U's turn for refreshments the following evening. On the subject of Ted's whereabouts she didn't know either and was just as vague.

By the time I was back at my car, a few of the orchestral players were still ambling down the church path, but I was determined to keep my distance. After all Minnie might have started her contractions. Did cats have Braxton Hicks? Perhaps not. Seeing the beastly Theo again was an unpleasant shock, but I had already spent considerable hours facing the prospect of that happening, if I was serious about Ted. If Ted was just as serious about me, then the occasional family gatherings that I'd learn to cope with would mean yet more gritting of teeth, buttoning of lips and practising the art of the fake smile. Yes, I'd also practise the art of reminding myself that any such gatherings were but brief interludes I'd learn to endure. I was sure Ted would have a few pithy remarks for his arrogant twin about past and future behaviour.

With those troubled thoughts swirling round my brain, I drove home to hold Minnie's paw and convince her that it would all soon be over. Yes, very soon there'd be a few furry bundles latched onto her belly, glugging milk for England. But when? All was quiet on the Frintley Estate as I trundled up the drive and parked outside Bramble Cottage. Wasting no time, I dashed up the path and joined Minnie in the safety of the kitchen at the back of the cottage. Here was my sanctuary of peace, far away from the arrogant gaze of visiting conductors. Minnie lazily opened one eye and assessed the chances of a spot of supper.

'Yes Minnie, some comfort food would do very nicely,' I told her, as she heaved her huge bulk into a standing position and had a good stretch. While we feasted together I dug out my irritatingly silent phone. It was so unlike Ted not to reply to my texts, and I had a shrewd idea what or who was commanding his attention.

'*I need u ted!! You should have warned me about theo* ☹'

Oh yes, I could imagine the jolly family reunion up at Frintley Grange, with sisters and brothers adjusting to each other and Miriam and Edmund working on a new strategy of subterfuge. I was on my way to bed when my phone at last sprang to life and glowed enticingly in my hand.

'*Theo is a man of surprises, c u soon, ted xx* ☺'

It wasn't exactly the answer I'd hoped for, and I could have suggested a few more insightful descriptions of his twin. A man of surprises? A man of bad manners and downright rudeness would be more accurate.

The atmosphere at Churlbury C. of E. Primary was so highly charged the following day, we could have powered up the entire county. Last minute costume tweaks for the Year 2 and 3 dance groups took over the staffroom and even the more experienced of my musicians were bubbling over with jangled nerves.

'Blame the parents,' muttered Pru when she brought me my register. A large box of choccy biscuits at break, supplied by Olive, saved a few of us from making comments we might have regretted.

'Even Ewan's promising to turn up tomorrow,' Kate informed me casually, as we munched on white chocolate covered beauties.

'With Vanessa?'

'Er no, I think she's busy,' breezed Kate. Or ditched him? I wasn't convinced.

'Fran's dragging Tony over. Says he's bringing his earplugs,' I giggled. 'He and Ewan should sit together.'

Then I told her about Theo.

'What, that bloke who bullied you at college? The one who snogged like a sink plunger?'

'The very same.' She evidently hadn't heard from any of Ewan's exes that he had the same unfortunate approach.

'God, that must have been awful!' Then I knew I had to tell her about Ted, choosing my words carefully and keeping the local family connections suitably vague.

'So he's just a casual friend, is he?'

'Um, sort of.' Her expression wasn't easy to read, and I wondered exactly how much she'd be passing on to her dear brother. Then the bell rang and we scuttled off like startled rabbits to breath calm and tranquillity over our little broods. Correction, to keep the lid on our little horrors.

'*Be round @ 6, xx*' Ted texted, as I was gathering up my bags and then closing my classroom door with relief.

'*Can't wait*' I replied. Perhaps he'd already lectured his beastly brother Theo about the importance of good manners, although I'd noticed that he'd managed to refrain from unnecessarily arrogant remarks the evening before. Perhaps there was hope for him yet.

Minnie was sitting with one leg aloft, vigorously grooming her lady's parts when I arrived home. She paused briefly, eyed me hopefully and then returned to her ablutions. Was this a sign of impending activity inside her? I'd been reading about feline gestation and labour from a helpful library book, and Minnie's behaviour certainly fitted in with signs of imminent labour. Her body evidently knew how to count to sixty-three, and, having arrived at day sixty-two, was gearing itself up for the following day. This called for extra rations in her bowl. As she was gulping down her supper, there a sharp rap at the door.

'Dear Gilly!' Yes, my lovely Ted had arrived, comfortably dressed in his old cut-off jeans and slightly scruffy T-shirt. He was *my* man and I didn't care that he'd always be second best in earning potential, compared with his brother – I loved him just as he was. I snuggled into his arms and enjoyed a few moments of sheer bliss.

'Are you okay?' he murmured, his nose buried in my hair.

'I am now,' I sighed, 'now that *you're* here.' I didn't have to harangue him about his near relation; after all, the news of Walter's accident and hasty replacement had all happened so quickly. The rest of the family were likely to be reeling from recent developments as well. How beastly Theo had managed to cross the Channel so soon was quite impressive, but that's modern air travel for you. Paris to Bournemouth was nothing really. Instead, I told Ted about Minnie's imminent delivery and its impact on the weekend ahead. Just then she came trotting through the back door, having attempted to wreak havoc in my vegetable patch in her usual endearing way.

Then, instead of settling herself down for a snooze, she started weaving around my legs and mewing. I bent to stroke her head.

'Poor Minnie,' I soothed, 'you don't know what's about to happen, do you girl?'

'She may,' commented Ted, tickling her ears.

'It's been…' I began awkwardly. The subject of Theo Rescorla was an enormous elephant in the room, and for once, I was tongue-tied. 'It's been difficult for me, these last few hours.' We were cuddled up together on my old sofa by then, with mugs of tea and a packet of sausage rolls.

'I can imagine. It's been difficult for all concerned.' He gave my shoulder a squeeze and pulled me even closer.

'Has it?'

'Oh yes,' he said with feeling, 'mainly because it was so unexpected.'

'It was my worst nightmare, Ted. I didn't know how I was going to get through the rehearsal last night, with *him* standing in front of me.'

'Oh, Gilly.' He sounded so sad, as if he was truly empathising with me. 'But you coped?'

'Yes, I had to. I couldn't let the rest down, could I? I couldn't let down Walter and all those hours of practising in the village hall over the past few months. After all, I'd coped at college… *just!*'

Minnie's mews grew louder, and then she repeated her fastidious cleaning. There appeared to be some mucus that was bothering her, and I remembered what I'd read.

'You may be squeamish, Ted, but I think we've just witnessed the plug of mucus coming away. She won't be long now.'

We watched her for a few moments. I was feeling helpless. 'She should be in her box, just in case.'

Ted put down his mug and gently reached for Minnie, but she lashed out with her claws and gashed the little finger on his right hand. Huge drops of blood oozed from the tear and dripped onto the floor.

'Little spitfire!' he gasped, examining the long gash.

'I could think of a few more words, but we ought to forgive her I suppose. If I was nine months pregnant, I probably wouldn't want anyone manhandling me without any warning.'

'What a thought,' he chuckled. The grubby tissue that he was winding around the finger didn't look very hygienic, so I found a plaster and wrapped it round firmly.

'Nurse Bonning to the rescue,' I announced, examining my handiwork.

By the time we were contemplating another cuddle on the sofa, Minnie had commandeered it and was watching us warily. But by then it was just half an hour before the start of the festival.

'Crikey, I'd almost forgotten!' I yelped. 'The McArdells are performing! If I'm not there, I'll never hear the end of it!'

'And I'm supposed to be back at the house,' said Ted. 'Family pow-wow and all that.'

'But you'll be there tomorrow – at the church I mean,' I said, looking for support from him.

'Yes, I'll be there. Didn't I say I wouldn't miss it for the world?' he chuckled, taking me by the shoulders and giving me one of his stomach-churning, toe-tingling sexy smiles.

'But won't some people think you're someone else? It could be confusing, not that I'm suggesting you shouldn't come.'

'Hmm, that could be tricky,' he agreed, with a grin. 'So I'll come in disguise … sunglasses, old floppy sunhat, tatty old shirt…'

'Oh, and some disgusting old trousers fastened with bailer twine,' I added.

'Ah yes, and I'll have a piece of straw sticking out of the corner of my mouth.'

'Perfect!'

Then his face abruptly clouded over. 'Gilly, I want to tell you something.'

'Yes?' I gulped.

'I love you very much.' Bliss! The very words I'd longed to hear. I shuddered with delight.

'And I want you to know something too,' I replied, never more certain than anything in my life. 'I love you very much Ted.'

There was silence in Bramble Cottage for at least two minutes while the two of us clung together, his mouth gently giving mine plenty of attention. If it wasn't for his family pow-wow and my sense of self-preservation from the wrath of Felicity McArdell, I could have predicted our next move might have been up the rickety-rackety stairs for a nice long session of hanky-panky. But no, on that occasion, our heads ruled.

'And Gilly,' said Ted, as we prepared to perform our separate duties, 'I'm not perfect, I can tell you and I've made plenty of mistakes in my time, but…'

'Nor am I!' I admitted, stopping him short.

'But the past is the past and I want you to know that, although I've held back from telling you things, I'm going to change.' I nodded as he spoke, remembering the secrecy about his mum and how I'd felt. 'There's so much I want to say,' he sighed.

'But no time now, Ted,' I protested, seeing I then had barely enough minutes to scrub up well enough for the festival-going public and find a seat prominent enough to be seen enjoying the musical prowess of the charming twins.

'Tomorrow then,' said Ted, leaning forward and delaying my scrubbing up by at least another thirty seconds.

'Yes, tomorrow,' I sighed, back down from cloud nine and ready for the Churlbury Midsummer Music and Arts Festival.

Chapter 32

Midsummer

A shimmering heat haze over the Frintley acres greeted me as I gazed from my bedroom window the following morning. This was what midsummer was meant to be. The first night of the festival had gone well, but the tightly knotted nerves in my stomach were testament to my own anxiety over the hurdles ahead. Ted's bold declaration, however, buoyed me up. Sprawled out on my bed was Minnie, with her bulging belly and no sign of furry bundles making their way into the world. I suggested she might try a few laps of the vegetable patch after breakfast, just to move things along, but Minnie blinked at me sleepily, paid the briefest of visits to the garden and then heaved her bulk onto the sofa.

'Okay pussycat, if you don't get a move on in the next three hours, you're by yourself.' That might have sounded heartless, but I wasn't going to promise her that, given the nod, I'd be ready to don the Marigolds and start boiling kettles of water. Three hours later, proudly wearing my new pre-loved charity shop sundress and market stall shrug, I applied a careful smear of lip-gloss and pinned up my shoulder length locks. I was ready to greet my audience, although all they'd see was the new hair clip that had cost me all of 50p from AgeUK.

The church was filling nicely when I arrived, with fractious junior musicians and flapping parents doing their best to destroy the calm within the ancient walls.

'Jessica can't find her music,' wittered one desperately.

'Dominic's cut his thumb,' moaned another.

'And my cat's about to go into labour,' I wanted to tell them, but I realised *that* news would hardly stand up against lost music and sore thumbs. Just before Harry Woodfine welcomed the audience and cracked a few unnecessary jokes, I spotted a familiar figure, heavily disguised in shades and old straw hat, slip into a side pew.

Ted had kept his promise. Then the W.I. ladies warbled, handbell ringers clanged and a string quartet scraped and twanged their way through Bartok and Haydn. Then, before the bun and tea interval, Pru and I slid onto the organ seat and she let rip with selections from Handel's *Water Music*.

'We make a great team,' she chuckled, once she'd ploughed through a dozen or so pages – and not one had fluttered onto the keys.

During the interval Pru, Olive and I grouped music stands and seated players.

'And it's a good thing I brought some spare music,' I announced casually, casting a warning glance in Jessica's direction. Then we tuned up and I tightened strings and adjusted woodwind joints to my satisfaction. The hordes returned, brushing crumbs from their hands and dabbing icing from their lips.

'I could murder a cup of tea,' I muttered to Olive.

'I could murder a Bacardi and soda,' she replied.

'Grit your teeth and save yourself for the party,' added Pru. 'I have it on very good authority that the Oborns are supplying the booze.'

Encouraged by that, I assembled my troops and we stunned the audience with our joyful *Ode* and *Big Surprise*. Grannies and toddlers shrieked with delight when Justin and Daisy bashed cymbals with devilish glee.

'Now you all know why it's called the *Surprise Symphony* I told the audience, as a parting shot, after we'd taken our bow.

That would have been the ideal time for tea and cakes, but there was another half an hour of entertainment before that. Next, in the space between the conductor's rostrum and the pews, our Year 2 and 3 dancers twirled and floated, all decked out in yellows and greens, as Beethoven's *Pastoral Symphony* blasted out from the speakers. Churlbury C. of E. had certainly made their mark on the festival, and when the afternoon ended, staff and parents joined in some mutual backslapping.

'That was excellent, Gilly,' said Simeon, as he joined us by the urn. I looked up and spotted sunshades and a straw hat lurking in the background. 'Doesn't seem a year since you came for your interview.'

'Excuse me, would you?' I flashed Simeon an extra bright smile and headed straight for Ted, who was nibbling round the edge of a jam tart.

'Hi handsome stranger,' I giggled. 'How was all that to an untrained ear? Or maybe you were wearing earplugs?' Ted dipped his shades and winked.

'Sounded great to me, and I especially liked the faint outline of shapely legs through your dress.'

'What?' I gasped. 'Surely not!'

'Well, just a little,' he whispered, 'and very lovely they were, as was your conducting. Those little horrors kept perfect time. I'm full of admiration.'

Now I started to wonder if some of the thunderous applause had more to do with my legs and less to do with the Beethoven and Schubert.

'And I couldn't take my eyes off you,' he murmured in my ear.

'Miss Bonning!' I recognised the McArdell tone and wrenched myself away from Ted. By the time, I'd finished being introduced to some of her opera cronies, Ted had slipped away. I was just gathering up my music, ready to dash back to the labour ward, when Alison Veltman popped out from behind a pillar and advanced in a determined fashion. Simeon, meanwhile, was chuckling with a clutch of W.I. ladies and was well out of earshot.

'Ah hello, Miss Bonning,' she said in an ultra-friendly way. 'May I congratulate you on your choice of music.'

'Well thank you, Alison.' I glanced at my watch and noted that I'd have a very quick turn-round before the evening's performance.

'Was that your young man I saw you with? The one with the sunglasses and hat?'

'Yes, that's right.'

'The illegitimate one?' she probed.

'Um... yes,' I admitted.

'Who's up at the estate?'

'That's correct,' I replied brightly.

'And how old would he be?' she asked, her tone more suited to a police interview room than a friendly get-together between concertgoers.

'How old?' I blinked at her in surprise. 'Well, about a year older than me, as it happens. He's twenty-five. Why?'

'Oh nothing really, no reason. Just curious,' she murmured casually, but with a glint in her eyes that puzzled me and had my antennae waggling.

I drove back to Bramble Cottage at top speed and flew through the door with palpitating heart and eager anticipation.

'Minnie?' She wasn't on the sofa, nor in the kitchen. 'Minnie?' I pulled out a packet of her biscuits and rattled them into a dish. There was a loud thump from above and then the sound of heavyweight pattering down the stairs. Minnie was just as rotund as ever and as I stroked her ears she had that look on her face that seemed to say, 'Do me a favour, don't ask me when I'm due.' She plopped down on the floor and inspected her undercarriage, where a thin streak of mucus was expertly removed.

'Look sunshine,' I told her firmly, 'I've warned you already. If you want me to hold your paw, you need to get a move on, or cross your legs until at least eleven o'clock.'

Minnie mewed a brief answer and then tucked into double portions of tuna and pilchards in gravy. By the time I was dressed in my black concert gear, she was dozing in the box in the kitchen, where I'd added another old towel, to upgrade her to four-star accommodation. I'd filled a litter tray and closed the kitchen door. The last thing I wanted was Minnie taking an evening stroll and ending up giving birth in the rhubarb patch or under a prickly gooseberry bush.

The church was heaving when I arrived, with singers, musicians, and a fair sprinkling of the audience who'd turned up in good time to bag the best seats.

'Gilly!' squealed a familiar friendly voice. It was Fran, also smartly dressed in concert gear, with a pink corsage on her left boob. Loitering behind her, with a bemused grin on his face, was Tony.

'Hey, strangers!' I chuckled. 'Long time, no see. How's the new pad?'

'Perfect,' giggled Fran. 'In fact, so perfect that...' She spread the fingers of her left hand and waggled them in my face.

'You're engaged!' I exclaimed, stating the obvious, just like people who tell you you've had your hair cut.

'Looks like it,' she agreed nonchalantly. I grabbed her hand and drooled over the sapphire cluster.

'Wow, Tony, this is gorgeous!' Tony draped an arm round Fran's shoulder and beamed fondly.

'Ah, she's worth it,' he sighed, 'and diamonds can be a bit over-rated.'

'Well, I'd settle for a curtain ring or a hula hoop if it swiftly followed after some gorgeous chap dropping to one knee and asking me to marry him.'

'So, no progress with the mysterious Ted then?' Fran asked.

'Oh plenty of progress, as a matter of fact, but we've only known each other for... what... three months?'

'Well, we can't wait to meet him, can we Tony?'

A stream of players was squeezing past us, struggling with instrument cases and dodging music stands.

'Actually guys, I need to warn you,' I whispered, dragging them to one side. 'We've had to have a stand-in conductor, because of poor Walter's accident.'

'Obviously,' said Fran. 'He conducts us as well.'

'Of course,' I admitted, wondering how I could have forgotten. 'So do you know who's conducting the choir?'

'Oh yes, Hazel our secretary. She used to be a professional opera singer. She's well up to it. So, how about your orchestra?'

'The Beast,' I whispered. Fran's eyes widened in surprise.

'What... Theo Rescorla? Ted's twin?'

'Yes. He turned up on Thursday evening without any warning. It was a horrible shock.' Fran shook her head as she digested the news.

'So what happened?' she asked. 'Did you have a stand-off? Did you bash him over the head with your clarinet?'

'What, and spoil a perfectly good clarinet?' I had to laugh, although the prospect of Theo Rescorla appearing any minute was beginning to have a worrying effect on my stomach.

'No, of course not. Anyway, I must fly... we're first on.'

Most of the woodwind section were in place by the time I was in my chair, fixing my instrument together.

'You were cutting it a bit fine,' said a voice on my right.

'But I'm here now, and anyway there's no sign of our exalted conductor and...' I remarked, checking my watch, 'there's still at least five minutes to go.'

I gazed at the pews, spotting Kate and Ewan as they squeezed past an elderly couple to join Tony. Kate's Louie and Ewan's Vanessa were certainly conspicuously absent.

'Good turn out,' observed the bassoon on my left.

'Hmm,' I agreed, then gasped in disbelief. Eleanor and Frank Rosewell had just emerged from the porch and were flapping programmes in the heat. I remembered their attendance the previous year and I was just composing a suitably dismissive greeting for future use when my disbelief was stretched even further. Behind them, walking hand in hand, came Tim and Lena. How could they? How dare they? Was this 'rubbing Gilly's nose in the dirt' time? Was this 'look at us, we're engaged' time? Well, if it was, I didn't care. I had Ted now, and Ted was a far better prospect. Lena and Tim could sit and gloat; correction: Lena could sit and gloat. Her gain was definitely *not* my loss. After that, the Oborns arrived – just three of them – and were shown to front row seats by Simeon, who was carrying out his usher's role very enthusiastically. So far there was no sign of Ted. Perhaps he was still trying to find a parking space? Maybe he'd squeeze in at the last minute as before?

Gerald stood up and nodded towards our oboe player, signalling a general tuning session. The experienced concertgoers settled into listening mode, whereas the Rosewells passed bags of sweets and chatted away as if they were at a cinema or football match. Then Harry Woodfine strode across to the microphone and performed his M.C. duty.

'And without further ado,' he finally announced, 'I'll hand you over to the Churlbury Festival Orchestra and their guest conductor Theo Rescorla.' There was polite applause as Gerald took his seat and our conductor appeared from the rector's vestry, in DJ and black tie. He gave a brief nod and smile towards the audience and then mounted the podium. I had prepared myself for this; giving him just enough attention to follow the beat and no more. A respectful hush fell and even the sweetie wrappers paused mid-rustle. I hadn't seen Ted slip in at the last minute, but I knew he'd be there somewhere, perhaps behind a pillar.

With my clarinet mouthpiece in position, I took a deep breath while Theo raised his baton to bring us in. Watch for the beat, I reminded myself, but as I watched, I saw something that turned me rigid with shock. There, on the little finger of his right hand was a plaster! I might have been three or four metres away, but I saw it clearly, with a butterfly tattoo on the inside of his wrist! A plaster on the little finger? A butterfly tattoo on his wrist? Ted had a plaster on his little finger and a butterfly tattoo inside his wrist! What did this mean? Our conductor nodded and brought the baton down, signalling the beat, and the piece started, although for the first two or three bars I was gasping so rapidly that I was incapable of making any sound at all.

'Fourth bar,' hissed a voice on my right. 'Get a grip, Gilly!' Anger and confusion raced around my brain as I struggled to play the notes that I'd performed perfectly for weeks on end. Who was this man? What did this mean?

In the two bar rest I glanced up and watched him. He looked just as poised as Theo on Thursday evening, and exactly like the beloved Ted who'd slunk in with shades and an old hat just hours before. Was I hallucinating? Perhaps they both had butterfly tattoos, like copycat twins and maybe Theo had cut his finger on a bread knife. But the same finger, on the same hand? Was it some spooky twin thing? Perhaps it was, because the only other possible answer was... My brain struggled with the ghastly possibility. We eventually reached the final chord and I was aware of sweat dripping from my brow.

'What's up, Gilly? You've gone a strange colour, are you okay?' came a voice on my left.

I nodded mutely and dabbed at my face with a tissue. After a minute or so of applause, we began again, with a few more notes landing in the right place this time. By then my mind was made up. I would ask Miriam exactly what was going on. Was it some elaborate game at my expense?

Next, the Marbeck Singers sang a few madrigals and some Vaughan Williams folksong arrangements, but the music just floated by me, as I sat in shock, with the anger inside me growing by the minute. After a while, I gazed blankly at the sea of faces in front of me, or at least the ones I could see between the heads of the cellos and violas. Lena appeared to be checking her mobile, or maybe grappling with more sweetie wrappers, but Tim was staring straight ahead... in my direction... his eyes unblinking, as if he was in a trance. He could stare all he liked, I thought, I wasn't going to get upset. So I reached for my cleaning mop and gave my clarinet a bit of a swab to remove the spit, while the Marbeck Singers moved onto some Latin American numbers. Poor Minnie, I thought, as I sat miserably, wishing I was back at the cottage. But much as I'd have liked to have ducked out of the rest of the evening, I knew I must meet it head-on and I now knew what question I had to ask.

Pru's turn was next, but for once, I wasn't on page turning duty. Felicity

McArdell had been persuaded instead. As Pru's solo ended, and the interval gave us all a chance to stretch our legs and grab a much-needed drink, I galvanised myself for a quick dash over to the Oborns before anyone else could distract Miriam. Trays of wine and juice started to circulate as I reached the Oborns who were chatting to a family in the row behind.

'Er... Miriam,' I called, over the escalating noise. 'Sorry to interrupt you.'

'Miriam,' I tried again, 'Edmund?' He turned and flashed a smile.

'Sorry,' I quavered, 'could I have a word with Miriam. It's rather important, it's...'

He tapped her on the arm.

'Oh, Gilly! Lovely concert!'

'Yes, it is,' I agreed, my pulse racing and my heart flagging up a danger warning. 'But I need to know something. It may sound an odd question, but please bear with me... how many sons do you have?' My voice was shaking by the time I'd reached the question mark.

'How many sons?' she repeated, and gaped at me incredulously.

'Y... yes... you see, I've been under the impression that Ted... that Ted...' I petered out and sighed, hardly knowing how to explain my utter confusion. Sweat was dribbling down my back by then. Miriam reached and took my hands, smiling gently at me.

'Gilly, I have only ever had *one* son... Theodore, or Ted as he prefers to be called these days.' A lightning bolt shot through me and my world turned upside down.

'One son?' I breathed in horror. 'Just one, not twins?' Vivid flashbacks of the past three months played a high-speed PowerPoint presentation in my mind's eye. Miriam and Edmund exchanged bemused glances.

'No, not twins. What made you think I had twins?'

'Well Ted rather implied it... well I thought he did,' I flustered. It was too awful for words to think that the man who had charmed me and said he loved me, was none other than the beastly Theo, the bane of my first year at Boxmouth and the last man I'd want to welcome to Bramble Cottage. What was even more unlikely and disturbing was that I'd told him I loved him.

Miriam squeezed my hands and something like pity or regret showed in her expression. 'Tell me more.'

'You remember I told you at your party back in February that I knew Joe

Rescorla's nephew at college?' She nodded. 'Although I now know he wasn't *really* his nephew…' A look passed between us, as co-conspirators in a matter of great secrecy.

'Well, he terrorised me at college.'

'Surely not!' she gasped.

'Well, we met under unfortunate circumstances and it went downhill from there. I guess my first reaction to him wasn't helpful either. I might have over-reacted just as much as *he* did. After that, I couldn't stand the sight of him, and I think the feeling was mutual. It wasn't helped by the fact that we were both music students, so of course sometimes we couldn't avoid sharing the same space. But the awful looks he used to give me… oh, I *hated* him! I thought of him as The Beast. It was such a relief when he left. Then three months ago, this look-alike comes crashing out of the thicket at the bottom of my garden, with my cat in his arms. Can you imagine how I felt?'

Judging by the expressions on their faces, they were only just keeping up with me.

'Well naturally I went ballistic, shrieking out his name and asking him what he was doing there. But he acted so innocent and bemused, and told me I'd mistaken him for someone else and that he was called Ted.'

'Which he is, of course,' agreed Miriam.

'Are you sure he said you were mistaken?' asked Edmund, keen to get the facts straight.

'Well, I'm not sure I can remember his exact words, but I think it was… Oh yes, I believe he said something like not being the man I thought he was. He even asked my name and where I was at college! As if we'd never met! We even had a chat about names and I remember suggesting that Ted was short for Edward, and he didn't correct me. He even went as far as checking where I'd met Theo, and clarifying that it wasn't at Latterton. He was playing the part of a stranger to perfection.'

Despite the surrounding noise, I heard them both sigh as they digested Ted's duplicity.

'Ah, I can see that was a bit naughty,' admitted Miriam.

'Naughty?' I exclaimed. 'Then I told him how Theo had been so hateful to me at college and he even suggested words such as bossy, arrogant and opinionated, because, when it came to talking about him, even *I* was embarrassed about describing what had happened.'

'He said those words?' asked Miriam incredulously.

'Oh yes, and Ted seemed very laidback about it and said he'd lived with Theo long enough to know all about him.'

'Which he did, in a manner of speaking,' commented Edmund thoughtfully.

'Hmm, and there was I agreeing with him. I already believed he was Theo's identical twin.'

'But did he mention twins or that he had a brother?' probed Miriam.

'Well no, but the way he was agreeing with me about Theo, was as if he was talking about another person. Don't you see?' They nodded.

'And then... oh God... then when I told him about the attack in the *Rat and Rabbit...*!' I shook my head in embarrassment.

'Attack?' gasped Miriam.

'Er, well... it felt like an attack and I was only sharing a few music jokes with some friends. Theo, or Ted or... well he obviously didn't have a sense of humour when it came to jokes about conductors and he grabbed hold of me on the way back from the loos and then... he... he... threatened me, then he snogged me.'

'What?' chuckled Edmund. I glared at him.

'It was rough and rude and HORRIBLE! He told me it was to stop my blabbermouth. When I told Ted this he looked quite disturbed and... well he was so gentle and tender with me that I found myself falling in love with him and...' Tears started to prickle my eyes and Miriam quickly stood up and wrapped her arms around me. 'And... and... it was *him*, The Beast all the time!'

I sobbed on her shoulder, while around us jolly concertgoers clinked glasses and exchanged banter.

'Here, have this.' Edmund had grabbed a glass of wine from a passing tray and shoved it into my grateful hands. 'It sounds as if he was sorry about the Boxmouth episode and was trying to make up for it,' he continued. 'In fact the only way he could do it was to hoodwink you.'

'And I believed him!' I gasped.

'No wonder he was reluctant to invite you up for a meal. He would have been rumbled!'

'You wanted to invite me?'

'Oh yes, Miriam and I kept suggesting it, but he told us that you were either too busy or there was some other excuse.'

'And he's been playing sneaky games with me all the time and has probably been laughing at me behind my back,' I moaned. 'I asked him where he went to college and do you know what he said? He asked me if I'd heard of Leesmore College, and I said that I had… ah, now I get it! He didn't exactly say he'd been to Leesmore, he just mentioned it and let me put two and two together and make five.'

'He's evidently clever at planting ideas and letting you come to the wrong conclusion, which was the *right* conclusion as far as he was concerned.' My guilty conscience awoke from a doze and reminded me that *I'd* played that particular game

'Oh, Ted,' sighed Miriam. 'Now he's been found out, but I can't imagine how he thought he'd get away with this pretence.' I gulped down the wine and remembered the previous night's conversation.

'As a matter of fact, he started to tell me something last night, but I was in a hurry, so he didn't say whatever it was. He admitted he'd kept things to himself, but that he was going to change… I never imagined it would be anything like this.' I looked up across the sea of heads and chattering lips and caught a glimpse of… well, I wasn't sure how I should refer to him any longer. I wasn't sure if I'd ever want to speak to him again or trust him.

'I need some air,' I told the pair.

'Good idea,' agreed Edmund.

I turned and started for the porch, head down and determined to escape the mêlée, but had hardly managed half a dozen steps when someone advanced and blocked my way.

'Gilly,' came an urgent voice in my ear. 'Gilly, stop, I must speak to you.' My frazzled brain performed a quick about-turn. Tim Rosewell was already closer than old friends should be – especially when one was engaged to someone else. Those were the first words I'd heard from him in nine months and it was clear he wasn't about to pass a comment about the weather or boast about his batting average for the season. The fact that Lena Tuffin wasn't holding onto his arm predatorily meant he must have devised some clever distraction tactics.

'I need some air,' I told him. 'You'd better come outside with me. If I don't have a breather, I'll never be in a fit state for the second half.'

'I've had another flashback,' he gasped, as he followed close behind. 'It happened while you were playing that first piece. Everything came flooding back, seeing you with your clarinet.'

The warm air outside hit me like a heavy blanket, but at least I'd left most of the noise behind. I remembered the odd expression on Tim's face when I'd been swabbing my instrument.

'Gilly, I love you! I want to marry you!' he declared fervently, grabbing my spare hand and pressing it to his lips.

'You what?' A few parents turned and stared with interest. 'Stop it, Tim,' I hissed. 'You're engaged!' I tried to pull my hand away, but he clung on defiantly. If Lena had chosen that moment to appear there would have been a blood bath.

'I was going to propose to you,' he protested. 'We were going to that concert, on your birthday and then have a meal. I'd bought you a ring!'

'A ring?'

'Diamond solitaire in eighteen carat gold.' It sounded gorgeous, but I had a shrewd idea on whose finger it now sparkled.

'I see. But then you had the accident.'

'Yes, and I've had a flashback about that too.'

I'd never seen him so animated, and he was refusing to let go, like a terrier with a bone clamped in its jaws. Then I recalled Rich and Jim's version of what had happened. Tim turned nervously and checked behind him and then he licked his lips and leaned closer.

'Lena was stalking me. She wouldn't leave me alone!' he whispered, wild-eyed and fearful.

'Yes, that's what *I* heard.'

'*You* heard?'

'There were witnesses. It only came out recently.'

'Tim!' came a sharp, ringing tone from the direction of the porch. 'What are you doing with that woman?' Lena was on the prowl, a waspish frown creasing her pretty face. Tim froze and gaped helplessly as she tottered across the grass, sinking every step or two into the turf.

'Oh, it's you,' she remarked, with a sniff. 'Trying to steal him back are you?'

'I'm doing nothing of the sort,' I snapped, 'and you can kindly keep your voice down. This is a church, not a fish market!'

Her eyes blazed as she caught the innuendo in my remark and noted

Tim's proximity.

'How dare you!' she hissed. Tim's head flicked back and forth like a tennis fan at Centre Court.

'You pushed me Lena,' he accused her bravely. 'I just remembered that while the orchestra was playing.'

'I beg your pardon?' she snapped haughtily.

'The accident… it was *your* fault!'

'Rubbish,' retorted Lena. 'I saved you, don't you remember?' Several conversations went into suspended animation as Lena grabbed Tim's arm and pulled it free.

'That's not true. Gilly knows it's not true, don't you Gilly?' A bell sounded inside the church, signalling the end of the interval.

'You?' snapped Lena fiercely. 'Thought as much, you lying slag!'

I edged away, now that Tim had been unfastened. Deranged harpy was a description that came to mind.

'Do you need any help?' came a voice. Ewan hurried over, spotting the quivering lips and trembling knees of a clarinettist in distress. 'I think you'd better keep your voice down madam,' he warned, glaring at Lena, 'or you may be asked to leave the premises.' He flung an arm round my shoulder and hurried me inside before Lena could thump me with her bag, or whatever else she had in mind.

'Who were *they*?' he asked, as he steered me back towards the orchestra.

'Tim and Lena,' I snuffled, feeling exceedingly fragile.

'What, the amnesia case?'

'Yes, and he's just realised he's engaged to the wrong girl,' I sighed, 'so it was becoming rather heated out there.'

'Leave well alone, Gilly,' Ewan whispered, giving me a squeeze. 'Just say the word and we can resume where we left off. In fact, I'd go as far as to say… well, you'd make the perfect doctor's wife!'

That was two proposals in five minutes, which was a bit of a record. I looked up and, to my horror, noticed that the Oborns were watching intently.

'I'm sorry Ewan, but I think I must have misheard that last bit, so can we just forget it?' I told him firmly, and clambered past a few stands just before Theo Rescorla returned to the podium.

Chapter 33

Confessions and disclosures

For weeks afterwards, the ripples from the events at Churlbury's Midsummer Music and Arts Festival were the talking point at every street corner and over many a shared cup of tea. The ripples even extended as far as Growdon, with the news that a diamond solitaire no longer sparkled on the finger of a certain hairdresser and that plans for an autumn wedding had been cancelled. On that evening, however, I didn't wait long enough to witness the startling climax to what happened after the performance, but Fran eagerly provided all the gory details. For the remainder of the concert, my eyes were riveted on the music in front of me and I counted the minutes until I could escape to my darling Minnie, labouring all alone in Bramble Cottage.

Offenbach's *Orpheus in the Underworld* was the final item, and as the audience chuckled and jiggled in their seats, imagining lines of dancing girls flashing their knickers, I glanced up briefly to see a triumphant grin on our conductor's face.

'Thank you, ladies and gentlemen of the audience, for making me so welcome,' he concluded, after taking several bows, 'and I especially want to thank my fellow musicians, who have performed magnificently.'

He turned and beamed at us, lingering a while in my direction. Then he strode off and I was ready for my quickest exit yet; all thoughts of drinks under the fairy lights driven from my mind.

'Gilly!' called Miriam, as she slipped from her pew to grab my attention. 'Do come and join us for drinks at the rectory.' I shook my head.

'Sorry Miriam, but Minnie's about to deliver and I need to be with her... my cat, I mean.'

Her face clouded over. 'Oh, right... I understand.'

'Pity,' reflected Edmund, who'd now joined us.

'Excuse me,' came a strident voice behind me. 'There are a few words I need to say to Mrs Oborn.' I turned to discover Alison Veltman with an odd leer on her face. A sense of déja vu from the library incident I'd witnessed made me shiver, even in the heat of the evening.

'Ah, good evening Alison,' said Miriam, cool and poised.

'Is it good?' probed Alison. 'Is it good for me to discover that you cheated me out of my aunt's inheritance, when you were already pregnant with Joe Rescorla's bastard child?' Judging by Alison's choice of language, it was evident that she was a Thomas Hardy fan. Glancing round, I could see that she had also started to attract an audience.

'How dare you!' retorted Miriam. 'That's none of your business.'

'Oh, isn't it?' jeered Alison. 'The terms of the will stated that the recipient could only qualify if she was a chaste Catholic girl who kept loyal to her faith.'

Miriam seemed to shrink before my eyes, her expression guarded.

'Leave my wife alone,' snapped Edmund. Veronica Woodfine edged forward and goggled at the exchange in horror.

'Chaste,' repeated Alison, her voice rising even more and stopping several more concertgoers in their tracks. 'You had an affair, didn't you?' she taunted. 'Joe Rescorla was married and you were still at school.' There was an audible gasp from the assembled company. 'And then your family spread that rumour that you were at an exclusive Swiss finishing school, when the truth was that you'd gone into hiding.' Alison had evidently been unearthing the Rescorla family history. Perhaps she'd even had an interesting fact-finding excursion to Somerset House?

Miriam blanched and grabbed Edmund's arm for support. The words 'restraining order, handcuffs and tranquilisers' floated through my brain.

'That money should have been *mine*!' declared Alison, thrusting her chin forward and jabbing at the beige viscose of her blouse to press her point home. 'I shall lodge a complaint with the solicitors and suggest they force you to pay back every single penny. You took that money under false pretences, and your parents colluded with you.' A chorus of gasps went up and two of the Mothers' Union stalwarts rushed off gabbling about glasses of water and cups of tea. 'Thought you'd get away with it, didn't you? Thought you could parade your bastard son in front of us!' Her voice was taking on Lena Tuffin qualities by then. In fact, they would have made a great double-act.

'But *you* turned your back on the Catholic Church,' replied Miriam calmly. 'So what claim you think you had, has been rendered null and void!' Alison's face took on a strangely distorted expression, and I imagine I wasn't the only one who was tempted to cheer as Miriam scored points off her opponent.

While this had been going on, there was a fair amount of guilt swirling around my mind, and as I made a speedy exit, I made a mental note never again to trust Imogen with sensitive information. Discretion was certainly *not* her middle name. If there had been a mole in the camp, it was her. By that time, Alison's voice had cranked up an octave and I heard a few worried speculations on the state of her mind from some of the nearest witnesses. Riveting though this was, Minnie's impending motherhood was a more pressing concern. Besides which, Alison might have been about to reveal that Gilly Bonning had helpfully given her crucial information.

'Is there a doctor in the house?' came Olive's voice, as I reached the porch. Hopefully someone would have spotted Ewan, but it wasn't until much later that I heard about the strait jacket – unless that was Fran's idea of a joke.

Back at Bramble Cottage, all was quiet, apart from a whimpering sound coming from the kitchen.

'Minnie, sweetheart!' I cried, rushing in to kneel beside the box where she lay. As far as I could see, there was no sign of tiny furry bundles. She was panting and closing her eyes as powerful contractions gripped her little body.

'Come on, Minnie, keep going,' I urged, stroking her head in a show of female solidarity. The fact that there wasn't a single kitten beside her was more than a little worrying, and I wished that Ewan hadn't had a more pressing duty to perform.

Several more contractions convulsed her body, causing her to mew pitifully, until a sac bearing a kitten emerged and flopped onto the towel. Minnie leaned over and sniffed at it curiously.

'Come on now, Minnie, clean your baby,' I whispered, but she seemed unsure of what to do. The little sac lay still beside her and panic seized me. Even *I* knew a little of what mother cats were supposed to do. Wasn't it instinct? Wasn't Mother Nature supposed to take over? I heard a noise in the sitting room behind me and then the door opened.

'You left the front door wide open.' I turned in alarm, fearful of the state of Minnie's kitten and of what I was going to say to my visitor.

'She won't lick the sac away,' I sobbed. 'The kitten's not moving.' There was another huge contraction and the afterbirth slid out. Minnie sniffed at it appreciatively and made quick work of it, but the kitten lay motionless beside her. Eventually she gave it a few cursory licks, but we both knew it had been stillborn.

'I'll take care of it.' I watched careful fingers gently lift the little dead kitten and wrap it in a tea towel. 'We can bury it the garden.' I rested my head against his knee, considering it akin to 'any port in a storm.' A few minutes later a cup of coffee appeared beside me, as I stroked Minnie's head and spoke endearments to her. Then the contractions started again and within a minute or two, another slimy little bundle slithered into the world, squirming as it came.

'It's moving!' I gasped in delight, having imagined the worst. 'Come on Minnie, wash your baby.' She turned and examined it and then briskly cleared the sac from its body and chivvied it onto its front. Out slipped the afterbirth, which Minnie devoured gratefully. The kitten was black, with four white socks, bib and tummy. It blindly crawled towards Minnie's underbelly, snuffled in her fur for a nipple and latched on hungrily.

'It's feeding,' I gasped, gazing in wonder at the tiny scrap of life.

'Have some coffee,' I was urged. 'Minnie needs you to keep alert!'

In the hour that followed, four more bundles arrived in the box; two were miniature versions of Old Ginger and two looked more like their mum. One by one, they homed in on Minnie's proud pink nipples and guzzled away, their tiny claws pounding at her stomach as they fed. It was almost midnight by then, and my legs had gone to sleep, even if the rest of me was wide-awake. A plate appeared beside me, bearing a toasted cheese sandwich and a slightly stale sausage roll.

'Come on, Gilly, you missed out on the party, have some supper,' he urged, crouching beside me and reaching out a tentative hand to tickle Minnie's ears.

'Why did you lie to me?' I asked, concentrating on my sandwich. I hadn't yet summoned up enough courage to look him in the eye.

'I didn't lie, Gilly, but I knew I wasn't exactly honest.'

'That doesn't make sense,' I retorted. 'You deliberately misled me.'

'I know,' he admitted, 'but you wouldn't have allowed me to set foot in your garden if I'd admitted the truth. I wanted to tell you last night, but...'

'There wasn't the time.'

'Yes, and I didn't know where to start.' The silence of midnight was punctuated by the distant chimes from the church tower.

'Can you ever forgive me, Gilly?' he asked, remorsefully. 'I love you so much. I've loved you so much, for so long.'

His voice became muffled and I turned to see that his head was in his hands.

'So long?' I repeated. 'How long?'

'Since that time in the *Rat and Rabbit*, if you must know.'

'What! You loved me then? But you were horrible to me!'

'I was jealous of those friends of yours. I wished I could have been beside you, laughing and joking together and then walking you back to your lodgings.'

'Since *then?*' I gasped, incredulous at his confession.

'Yes, Gilly, since then. And because I couldn't have you for myself – because of how it all started – I became angrier and...'

'Beastlier?' I supplied, frowning at him.

'When you took me to task about the McDowell piece, I knew I'd met my match.'

'What? Really? But you tried to ignore me...'

'You were magnificent,' admitted Ted. I looked up and met his gaze for the first time since he'd arrived. 'You were the butterfly that stamped – as in the *Just So* stories.'

'You're not making any sense, and anyway, the butterfly in the Kipling story was the husband who wanted to silence his quarrelsome wife.'

'Well, okay I was wrong about that, but that's why I had this tattoo, to remind me of you. So many girls clung to me and simpered and rolled their eyes and thrust their cleavages in my face, but you had spirit.'

'Spirit? Hmm, I could call it something else.' My conscience was reminding me of the somewhat taunting salvos I'd thrust in his direction in the past.

We sat in silence, watching Minnie dozing contentedly, while her five kittens suckled and slept.

'So, will you forgive me, Gilly? Will you give me another chance?'

I turned back to him and studied his handsome features and contrite demeanour. I wasn't sure if I'd come to terms with him as Theo and Ted, all rolled into one. I could cope with the two identities, but they were so different in my mind.

'Yes, Ted, I'll give you another chance, on the understanding that you stick to the truth. No more hoodwinking.'

'Hoodwinking?'

'That's how Edmund described it. You know I spoke to him and your mum, don't you?'

Ted sighed. 'Yep, and I know they weren't too impressed by my… hoodwinking. But, Gilly, I promise you, the hoodwinking has stopped.'

'That's good.'

He moved closer and wrapped an arm round my shoulder.

'Did you get a Christmas card with a French stamp on it?' he asked after another silence.

'I did!' So not from Terry Ridgeway or Desmond Morsby after all. That was a relief.

He nodded. 'There was something else I sent, but I didn't have the courage to sign that either.'

'The Valentine?' He nodded again. Then I told him that when I'd watched him on the TV at the races I wished I'd been there as well.

'I don't believe it, Miss Bonning,' he chuckled, giving me a friendly wink.

'Perhaps I was a little bit in love with you already.' He raised an eyebrow in surprise and then leaned forward and stroked my cheek gently, as I realised the great leap I'd made in admitting to myself that I'd fallen in love with Theo Rescorla. I closed my eyes as his fingers gently moved to my neck and then his mouth touched mine.

'So what are you going to do at Bransfield?' I asked him, when we paused for breath. 'Not chopping down trees or weeding the ornamental borders I guess?'

'Head of lower school music,' he admitted ruefully.

The church clock struck half past midnight and we fell into another embrace, our mouths and bodies pressed together in mutual delight. And yes, dear reader, a little later, when visiting time in Minnie's labour ward came to an end, we mounted the rickety-rackety stairs – but only after Ted had gone down on one knee and asked me to marry him.

'Thought you'd never ask,' I whispered. 'And by the way, the answer's yes.'